A Bride by Christmas
by Joan Elliott Pickart

ᗘ ᏯᏄᏆᏇ ᗯ

Luke chuckled and the sexy sound caused Maggie to shiver.

"Are you cold?" Luke said, pulling her even closer.

Maggie's breasts were crushed to the hard wall of Luke's chest in a sweet pain that made her acutely aware of her femininity in contrast to his blatant maleness.

"No. I'm—I'm definitely not cold."

"You feel so good in my arms, Maggie. Perfect, absolutely perfect."

"Well…" Maggie started, then for the life of her couldn't think of one intelligent thing to say.

And the music played on.

Trust Me
by Caroline Cross

ᓂ ᗢᗝᗡ ᓀ

A daring escape, a leap of faith—

Dominic held out his hand. "Come on. It's time to get out." Hard and calloused, his fingers closed around hers.

Lilah drew in a sharp breath at the contact. Climbing unsteadily to her feet, she followed him across the moonlit cell, only to halt as she saw the man-sized opening that now gaped in the seemingly impregnable wall. "You can't be serious. This is our escape route?"

"That's right."

Unlike the ocean roaring in below, he was suddenly far too close. His breath washed over her temple and every sensitive inch of skin on her body quivered. "But how are we going to get down?"

"Easy. We're going to jump."

She took an involuntary step back. "You've got to be kidding."

"Nope." Before she could retreat, he reached out, wrapped his arms around her and hauled her close. "Trust me, Li. I'll keep you safe."

For a moment, the shock of his embrace was so overwhelming she forgot to be afraid.

Available in December 2006 from Silhouette Desire

A Bride by Christmas
JOAN ELLIOTT PICKART

Trust Me
CAROLINE CROSS

SILHOUETTE®
Desire™

First published in Great Britain 2006
Silhouette Books, Eton House, 18-24 Paradise Road,
Richmond, Surrey TW9 1SR

The publisher acknowledges the copyright holders of the
individual works as follows:

A Bride by Christmas © Joan Elliott Pickart 2005
Trust Me © Jen M. Heaton 2005

ISBN-13: 978 0 373 60333 6
ISBN-10: 0 373 60333 9

51-1206

Printed and bound in Spain
by Litografia Rosés S.A., Barcelona

A BRIDE BY CHRISTMAS

by
Joan Elliott Pickart

JOAN ELLIOTT PICKART

is the author of over one hundred books. When she isn't writing, Joan enjoys reading, needlework, gardening and attending craft shows on the town square. She has all-grown-up daughters as well as a young daughter, Autumn, who is in primary school. Joan, Autumn, and a three-pound poodle named Willow live in a charming small town in the high pine country of Arizona.

For all the lovely ladies at Willow Wind

One

Luke St. John walked slowly up the wide steps leading to the porch, and the carved wooden doors of the large Episcopal church. He stopped at the doors, marveling at their intricate craftsmanship.

It really was a majestic structure, he thought, and he could understand why his brother and Ginger had chosen to be married here tomorrow. The event had been many months in the planning, and Robert had confided that Ginger had changed her mind about colors and endless other details so many times the wedding coordinator must be ready to strangle his bride-to-be.

Luke smiled as he opened one of the doors and entered the vestibule.

Ginger Barrington, he mused, was an endearing yet

rather ditzy young woman who had been given a blank check by her father to have the wedding of her dreams. The last he'd heard, Ginger had chosen seven brides-maids for the don't-worry-about-the-cost event.

Whatever. The people in the Barrington-St. John social circle were accustomed to these kinds of extravaganzas. What was important was that Ginger and Robert were deeply in love—and they were, they really were.

Strange, Luke thought. He'd actually felt a twinge of envy on more than one occasion as he'd watched the relationship between Robert and Ginger develop. He'd been startled each time he'd registered that green-around-the-edges feeling. He dated independent career women and that suited him just fine. But then again...

Luke shook his head to halt his jumbled thoughts and glanced at his watch.

He was early for the rehearsal, he knew, but a business meeting on this side of town had ended sooner than expected. There wasn't time to go home, nor any point in returning to the office, so he'd come here with the idea of sitting in the quiet church and relaxing until the others arrived.

Luke crossed the vestibule, entered the large sanctuary, then walked down the aisle past about a dozen pews to finally settle onto one. He swept his gaze over the high ceiling and exquisite stained-glass windows, nodding again in approval.

His attention was caught by a side door opening close to the altar. A woman entered carrying a cardboard box. His gaze was riveted on her as she crossed to the center aisle and placed the box on the first pew, immediately removing a large yellow satin bow.

Luke felt a sudden pain in his chest and drew a sharp breath as he realized he hadn't breathed since the woman had appeared. He leaned forward, resting his arms on the rail in front of him, and drank in the sight of her, missing no detail.

She was so beautiful, Luke thought rather hazily. No, that wasn't the word he wanted. Beautiful was what the career women he dated strove for, which resulted in cookie-cutter perfection in clothes, hair and makeup that varied little from one to the next.

No, this woman, who was now attaching the satin bow to the side of the first pew was…pretty. Yes, that was the word. Pretty in a wholesome, breath-of-fresh-air way that was knocking him for a loop. She was sunshine on a cloudy day, real, what-you-see-is-what-you-get real, and he'd bet ten bucks she wasn't wearing any makeup at all.

Her strawberry-blond hair tumbled to her shoulders in what he was convinced were natural curls, and even from this distance he could see that her eyes were big and brown. Fawn eyes. Pretty, pretty eyes. She was wearing a simple pale pink sundress that suited her to perfection.

Whew, Luke thought. He'd felt it, a funny little hitch in the much-needed breath he'd taken and the increased tempo of his heart. Nothing like this had ever happened to him before. Nothing. This woman had definitely made a strange and totally unfamiliar impact on him.

Luke continued to watch as the woman attached a mint-green bow to the second pew, then matching ones on the other side of the aisle, making it subtly clear that those four rows were reserved for the families of the bride and groom.

She might, he guessed, be the wedding coordinator whom Ginger had driven to the brink of insanity. She appeared very young for such a lofty title, was maybe twenty-four or twenty-five. So, okay, at thirty-two he wasn't too old for her. Good. That was good.

But…a wedding coordinator? Why did a person decide to become one of those? Because their own wedding had been so wonderful they wanted to share the bliss of an error-free event with others? No. No way. She was not married. That was not acceptable. She was a wedding coordinator because she was a romantic, old-fashioned woman who adored weddings and was very good at taking care of a zillion details at the same time. Yes. That was much better.

He had to meet this woman, Luke thought with a sense of urgency. He had to hear her voice, look deep into those incredible brown eyes of hers. He had to connect with her before she disappeared from his life as quickly as she'd appeared. He had to… Man, he had to get a grip. He didn't know what was happening to him, but it was a tad scary, that was for sure.

The sound of voices on the porch reached Luke and he got to his feet and stepped into the aisle just as the woman turned toward him. She gasped in shock that he was standing there and took a step backward.

"I'm sorry," he said, walking forward. "I didn't mean to startle you. I arrived early and I was just sitting here quietly and..." He stopped in front of her, gazed into her eyes and totally forgot what he was going to say.

"I..." the woman said, still looking directly into his eyes. "I'm..." Whoever I am. Heavens, those eyes, those eyes were dark, fathomless pools that a woman could just drown in and not even struggle to escape. And that voice. So masculine and rumbly and yet...it seemed to stroke her like soft, sensuous velvet, causing her skin to tingle and...

He was tall, had wide shoulders, long legs, rough-hewn features and thick, glorious black hair. He looked like someone straight out of central casting.

"You're...who?" Luke said, leaning slightly toward her.

"Who what?" she said, then blinked. "Oh! Yes, of course. I'm Maggie Jenkins, the wedding coordinator. I own Roses and Wishes, which is gaining a fine reputation for coordinating weddings, because that's what I do. I...coordinate...weddings. I'm also babbling, so forget all that. I'm a tad exhausted at the moment, you see. And you are?"

Enchanted, Luke thought, smiling. Maggie Jenkins. Maggie. He liked her name. It suited her, it really did. Oh, yes, hello, Maggie Jenkins, who was not wearing a wedding ring, thank goodness.

"Luke St. John," he said. "The brother of the nervous groom and the best man for this gala event."

"Pleased to meet you," Maggie said, tearing her gaze

from Luke's. "I believe the others have arrived. I'd better go greet everyone and get this rehearsal going so we stay on schedule, because dinner's booked at the restaurant afterward. Excuse me."

Luke turned to watch her hurry down the aisle as the large group of people appeared. He didn't move to join the others. Not yet. He just stood there drinking in the sight of Maggie.

Maggie stifled a yawn of fatigue as she plastered a plastic smile on her tired face and stopped in front of the chattering wedding party.

Was that heat she felt on her back? she thought suddenly. Was Luke St. John staring at her with those…those eyes? Maggie, stop it. She had made a complete idiot of herself with Luke, had overreacted to his masculine magnetism only because she was so tired she couldn't think straight. Once rested, she would view Luke St. John as a very handsome man but big macho deal.

"Hello, everyone," Maggie said brightly.

"Oh, Maggie," Ginger said, beaming, "isn't this exciting? Tomorrow is the big day. I can hardly believe it's finally here."

You're not the only one, Maggie thought, smiling and nodding at the petite blonde who boasted a golden tan and was wearing a royal-blue raw silk jumpsuit.

"Did I check with you to see if you'd found someone to supply only pale yellow and mint-green yogurt-covered almonds for the nut cups at the reception?" Ginger said, frowning.

"Yes, you did," Maggie said. "And, yes, I did. Well,

sort of. I had to order extra nuts, then pick out the two colors we needed." Which took until after two o'clock this morning. "I was going to ask you what you wanted me to do with the almonds we didn't use."

"Whatever," Ginger said, waving one hand in the air. "Where's my sweetie? Oh, Robert, there you are, honey. Do you realize we'll soon be winging our way to Greece? We'll have a whole month to—What's wrong? You don't look like a happy groom."

The handsome young man in his midtwenties, who was wearing slacks and a dress shirt open at the neck, slid one arm across Ginger's shoulders.

"My brother isn't here yet," he said. "We can't have a rehearsal without the best man."

"I'm right here," Luke said, striding toward the group.

"I'm going to go tell Reverend Mason we're ready to begin the rehearsal," Maggie said quickly. "He's in his office and told me to come get him when we were all set."

"Maggie, hon, wait a sec," an attractive young woman said. "I've lost two pounds since the final fitting of my bridesmaid dress. Do you think it could be nipped in a bit before the ceremony tomorrow night?"

Over my dead body, Maggie thought. Don't even think about it…*hon*.

"That won't be necessary…Tiffy, isn't it?" Maggie said, her voice dripping with sweetness. "That's the beauty of that style of gown. There's room for a fluctuation of a few pounds here and there. I promise that you have nothing to worry about."

Nicely done, Luke thought, swallowing a burst of laughter. Maggie had handled the spoiled and pampered Tiffy like a pro. She was really something, this Maggie Jenkins.

"Look on the bright side, Tiffy," one of the other bridesmaids said. "You can eat your little heart out at the wedding reception—and at the rehearsal dinner tonight, for that matter. You know Ginger and Mrs. Barrington picked goodies to die for. Eat and enjoy."

"Well, there is that, Melissa Ann," Tiffy said thoughtfully, then wandered away.

Bless you, Melissa Ann, Maggie thought wearily.

"And don't forget all those delicious green and yellow yogurt-covered almonds," Luke said, finally indulging in a chuckle. He paused. "Maggie, did you really have to sort through tons of those things to get the two colors?"

"No detail is too small for Roses and Wishes," Maggie said, not looking in Luke's direction.

As Maggie rushed away to get the priest, Luke turned to watch her go, a smile tugging at the corners of his mouth.

"Luke?" Robert said.

"Hmm?" he said, still staring after Maggie.

"What's the matter with you?" Robert said. "You're standing here with your back to everyone. Could you be a little more sociable, for Pete's sake?"

Luke snapped his head around to look at his brother. "Yes, certainly. Sorry." He paused. "I must say, Robert, that I'm impressed with the job Maggie Jenkins has done for you and Ginger. Maggie is quite young to have her own business. It's interesting, too, that she's a wedding coordinator who isn't married." Didn't hurt to double-check on that. "Don't you think? You know, someone who didn't have a fabulous wedding of their own?"

Robert shrugged.

"I asked Maggie about that," Ginger said, joining the brothers and slipping her arm through Robert's. "She pointed out that not all pediatricians have children. Maggie loves the challenge of planning a perfect wedding down to the smallest detail. She just doesn't want one of her own. She told me that. She never intends to get married."

Luke frowned. "Why not?"

"Well, gracious, Luke," Ginger said, wrinkling her nose, "it wouldn't have been polite to ask that. I swear, men should be required to take the same social-graces classes that all of us women do." She shifted her attention to Robert. "Sweetie, what if people don't like yogurt-covered almonds? Do you think I should ask Maggie to change what's in the nut cups before tomorrow night?"

"No," Luke said quickly. "Did you notice the shadows under Maggie's eyes, Ginger? She's obviously exhausted, and I'm sure you learned in your social-graces classes that you should be aware of the needs of those around you.

"Besides, I've attended more gala events than you due to the simple fact that I'm older than you are. I assure you that my vast experience has shown me that most people are very fond of yogurt-covered almonds."

"Really?" Ginger said, beaming.

"Guaranteed," Luke said. "So don't even entertain the idea of asking Maggie to stay up all night redoing the nut cups."

"Well, if you say so, Luke," Ginger said. "I won't… Oh, there's Maggie with Reverend Mason. I'd best go say hi."

Ginger hustled up the aisle and Robert stared at his older brother.

"You're suddenly an expert on the popularity of almonds?" Robert said incredulously. "Where did that come from? And you're aware that Maggie is exhausted? What did she do? Say, 'Hi, I'm Maggie and I'm wiped out'?"

"I'm an attorney, Robert," Luke said. "A good lawyer learns to observe people for subtle little nuances that can be extremely important in the outcome of a given case."

"That is such a bunch of crock," Robert said with a hoot of laughter.

"Yeah, well…" Luke frowned. "Forget it."

"You sure sound—what word do I want?—protective. Yes, that's it, protective of Ms. Maggie, big brother. What gives?"

"Nothing 'gives.' Look, just concentrate on marrying Ginger." Luke paused. "You know, Robert, I'm rather…envious of what you and Ginger have together. I've watched you two over the past months, seen you fall deeply in love, make plans for a future together. It's good and I'm really happy for you both. Yep, I admit I'm a little bit jealous."

"You? Envious of me?" Robert said, splaying one hand on his chest. "I find that a tad hard to believe. You have women beating down your door. You've always gone for the type who just wants to have fun but not settle down. There are seven bridesmaids over there who fit that bill. Just take your pick."

Luke watched Maggie approach with the priest and Ginger.

"Things change," he said quietly.

Reverend Mason greeted everyone and explained that they would walk through the basics of the wedding ceremony so everything would go smoothly the next evening.

"Right," he said finally. "Ginger, if you'll stand at the back of the church with your father and be ready to come down the aisle after your bridesmaids and…"

"Oh, no," Ginger said, shaking her head. "No, no, no, I can't do that."

"Why not?" Robert said frantically. "You're not changing your mind about marrying me, are you?"

"Don't be silly, sweetie," Ginger said, kissing him on the cheek. "But you know how it's bad luck for the groom to see the bride on their wedding day before the ceremony? Well, it's also bad luck for the bride and groom to act out those roles at the rehearsal. Didn't you know that?"

"Can't say that I did," Robert said, drawing a deep breath of relief. "So now what?"

"You and I will sit and watch very carefully," Ginger continued, "so we'll know what we're to do tomorrow night."

"Watch who?" Robert said. "We're the bride and groom, remember?"

"We use stand-ins for the rehearsal, silly," Ginger said. "Let's see. Okay. Your father will be the best man and pretend he has the ring, and Luke will be the groom. And…" She glanced around. "Yes, of course. Maggie, you'll be the bride."

"Got it," Luke said.

"I don't think that's a great idea," Maggie said, feeling the color drain from her face. "No. Bad plan. Bad, bad. I need to… Yes, I need to stay at the back of the church and control the spacing of the bridesmaids starting down the aisle."

"What is the spacing?" Luke said pleasantly.

"Three pews apart, but…"

"Have you got that, ladies?" Luke said, looking at Ginger's girlfriends.

Seven heads bobbed up and down.

"Done," Luke said. "That leaves you free to be way behind them with Ginger's dad ready to be…the bride, Maggie. And I'll be the groom."

"Excellent," Reverend Mason said. "Let's take our places, please. The groomsmen need to be up front with our stand-in best man and groom. Mothers, take your places, please. Ginger and Robert, sit where you can observe and hear me clearly."

"But—" Maggie pointed one finger in the air.

"See you soon, future wife," Luke said, smiling at Maggie.

"But—"

"Come along…Ginger," Mr. Barrington said, chuckling as he tucked Maggie's hand in the crook of his arm. "This reminds me of a baseball game. Instead of a designated hitter, you're the designated bride."

She didn't want to be a bride, Maggie thought miserably as Ginger's father led her to the back of the church. Well, she did, but it would never happen. She wouldn't allow it to happen because… No, she was not a bride. Not a real one or a pretend one or a designated one. Not a bride. Not now, not ever.

And to make matters even worse, the stand-in groom was Luke St. John, a man who had made her forget her own name. Good grief, she wanted to go home. Right now.

Everyone except Maggie was chattering and laughing as they took their places, then silence fell as Reverend Mason raised one hand for quiet. He stood at the front of the church with Luke next to him, then the other men in a straight row alongside.

"The organ music you picked for the procession has now begun," the priest said, smiling. "Pretend you hear it. We're ready for the bridesmaids to come forward. What was it? Oh, yes, three pews apart, my dears."

As Tiffy started off, Ginger's father bent down to whisper to Maggie.

"I hope Ginger looks happier tomorrow night than you do at the moment," he said. "I think this is rather fun, don't you, Maggie?"

"That's not quite the word I would pick, sir," she said, attempting and failing to produce a smile.

"But your groom is Luke St. John," Mr. Barrington

said. "He's considered quite a catch in this town. You have to get into your role and realize you're the envy of a multitude of women in Phoenix. Will that thought make you smile?"

"Not really," Maggie said gloomily.

"Well, fake it. My daughter is so superstitious about all this nonsense that she'll probably pitch a fit if you look like you're about to have a root canal. You can be Ginger marrying Robert or Maggie marrying Luke. Take your pick, but remember this is a wedding, not a funeral. *Smile.*"

Maggie nodded jerkily and plastered such a wide smile on her face that her cheeks hurt.

"Now you look like someone just stepped on your foot," Mr. Barrington said.

"Don't get picky," Maggie said, glaring at him while keeping her plastic smile in place. "This is the best I can do."

"For a wedding coordinator," Mr. Barrington said, "you have a strange attitude about being a bride. Fascinating."

No, try terrifying, Maggie thought. Try never going to happen. Try…*she wanted to go home.*

"Now the actual wedding march begins," Reverend Mason said in the distance. "Give the congregation time to rise and turn in your direction and…now…here comes the lovely bride."

Two

He could hear the wedding march, Luke thought. *He could.* A part of him knew that was impossible, yet it was there quite clearly, the wondrous music filling the church to overflowing.

And in the distance, walking in measured steps on the arm of Ginger's father, was Maggie, his bride. *His.* She was lovely, just exquisite. His heart was thundering at the mere sight of her as she came closer and closer and…

Maggie and Mr. Barrington stopped in front of the priest.

"I will ask at this point," Reverend Mason said, "who gives this woman in marriage. And you, Mr. Barrington, will reply 'Her mother and I,' then you'll take your daughter's hand and place it in Robert's."

"Her mother and I," Mr. Barrington boomed, then grasped Maggie's hand.

Without realizing he had moved, Luke stepped forward and extended his hand to receive Maggie's. As Mr. Barrington placed Maggie's hand in Luke's, their eyes met and time stopped.

Dear heaven, Maggie thought, unable to tear her gaze from the mesmerizing depths of Luke's eyes. Luke's hand was so strong yet so gentle as it wrapped around hers. And the heat. Good grief, the heat from his hand was traveling up her arm, across her breasts, then swirling and churning throughout her, causing a flush she could feel staining her cheeks.

She had to get her hand back. And she would. In a minute.

And she had to quit, just stop, looking into Luke's eyes. And she would. In a minute.

"We are gathered here," Reverend Mason said, "to unite this man and this woman in holy matrimony."

Yes, Luke thought, that was exactly why they were there. This man, him, and this woman, Maggie, were about to be united in holy matrimony, become husband and wife until death parted them.

He had never in his entire life felt like this. He was consumed with a soothing warmth of peace that was somehow combined with the coiling heat of desire. The chill within him that he now knew had been loneliness was gone, pushed into oblivion, never to return because Maggie was here. He'd waited an eternity for this, for her, to find his soul mate, and she was here at long last. Maggie.

Oh, man, this was nuts, he thought, unable to stop a smile from forming on his lips. He was an attorney who dealt in facts, absolutes, things being either black or white, proven data, and... Yet he had suddenly been flung—there was no other word for it—flung helter-skelter into a strange new world that embraced the romantic notion of love at first sight.

Oh, yeah, this was crazy. And wonderful. And hard to believe, but he did believe it with his entire being—heart, mind, body and soul.

Maggie Jenkins had come, she had seen, she had conquered. By doing nothing more than being, she had stolen his heart for all time, and he didn't want it back. Not ever. He loved her. It was as simple and as complicated as that. It was exciting and terrifying at the same time. It couldn't, shouldn't, be true, but yet it was.

He was in forever love with Maggie.

"After you have lit the single candle from the ones that will be burning next to it," Reverend Mason was saying, "blow out the others and place them back in the holders. The single burning candle will represent your union, becoming one entity."

Yes, Luke thought firmly.

Yes, Maggie thought dreamily. Wasn't that just the sweetest thing?

Reverend Mason's word became a buzz, like a multitude of bees in the background, as Maggie and Luke continued to look directly into each other's eyes. Then suddenly what the priest said was loud and clear.

"You may kiss the bride."

Luke framed Maggie's face in his hands, looked at her intently for a long, heart-stopping moment, then slowly, so slowly, lowered his head and captured her lips in a kiss that was so tender, so reverent, so…theirs, that tears filled Maggie's eyes. She savored the taste, the feel, the very essence of Luke, yearning for the kiss to never end.

Reverend Mason cleared his throat. "Yes, well, that's fine. Thank you, Luke, Maggie, for playing out your roles so convincingly."

Luke raised his head and both he and Maggie stared at the priest as though they had never seen him before in their lives.

"I, um…" Reverend Mason continued, "I will then introduce Mr. and Mrs. Robert St. John to the congregation, the organ music will burst forth and the recessional will take place. Any questions?"

Ginger jumped to her feet. "No, no questions. It's going to be so beautiful. I can hardly wait until tomorrow night. Thank you so much, Reverend Mason. We're off to the restaurant now for the rehearsal dinner. I do hope you and your wife will join us as planned."

"We'd be delighted," he said, sliding one more glance at Luke and Maggie, who were still staring at him with rather stunned expressions on their faces.

Maggie shook her head slightly to escape from the eerie spell that seemed to have transported her to a faraway place. She stepped back from Luke, averting her eyes, then spun around and forced another big smile onto her lips. Lips that still held the taste of Luke, the feel of Luke, tingled from the kiss shared with Luke.

"Ginger," Maggie said, "I'll come to the restaurant to make certain that everything is as it should be, then I'm going to scoot on home."

"But you're supposed to have dinner with us, Maggie," Ginger said, pouting prettily.

"I had a late lunch," Maggie said. "I couldn't eat a bite. Really."

"Don't be silly, my dear," Mr. Barrington said. "We all know how hard you've worked all these months to make this event perfect for our Ginger. I insist that you join us for dinner, even if you don't eat much. Good. That's settled. Me? I'm starving. Let's get going."

"But—" Maggie said.

"Come along, Mrs. St. John," Luke said, encircling her shoulders with his arm.

"What?" Maggie said, staring up at him with wide eyes. "Who?"

"Oh, sorry," Luke said, smiling. "I'm still in my role, I guess. You and I did get married a few minutes ago, you know. Maggie St. John. It has a nice ring to it, don't you think?"

"*Ginger* St. John has a nice ring to it," she said. "That's who I was pretending to be, remember? I'm Maggie *Jenkins* and that's who I intend to remain."

"Ah," Luke said, nodding.

"And what does 'ah' mean?" she said.

"Only that none of us have crystal balls to see into the future, Maggie *Jenkins,*" he said. "Who knows what might happen? Shall we go?"

Without speaking further, Maggie grabbed the box

that had held the satin bows, then marched down the aisle, snatching her purse from the last pew as she went.

Outside the summer sky was a black velvet canopy sprinkled with twinkling diamondlike stars and a silvery moon, all of which went unnoticed by Maggie as she stomped to her ten-year-old van and slid behind the wheel.

As she took her place in the line of vehicles headed to the restaurant she drew a deep, shuddering breath.

Don't think, she ordered herself. Don't dwell on what took place in that church. Don't relive that kiss, or see again the smoldering passion in Luke's eyes or feel the tenderness of his hands on her flushed face or acknowledge the desire that had swept through her. Do not do that, Maggie Jenkins. Okay. Fine. She wouldn't. *She would not.*

But, darn it, what had happened back there? She had never in her life experienced anything so…so…whatever that had been. It was as though everyone had disappeared, leaving only her and Luke in a wondrous place that was theirs alone. The bride. The groom. The kiss. The undefinable something that in its intensity took desire beyond description. Luke.

Maggie sighed. It was a dreamy, wistful, womanly sigh that caused a soft smile to form on her lips. In the next instant she smacked the steering wheel with the palm of her hand.

"Cut it out, Maggie Jenkins," she yelled. "Just stop it right now. You are acting so ridiculous, it's a crime."

It was amazing, she mentally rushed on, how asinine a person could behave, think, feel, when they were totally exhausted. That, of course, was the explanation for what had happened. Overreaction due to overfatigue. It was all so simple now that she calmed down and thought about it like a rational human being.

At least no one had been aware of how silly she'd behaved while performing in her role of the bride. Well, Reverend Mason had given her and Luke a rather inquisitive look, but everyone else had been oblivious to the nonsense between them.

Well, that was probably not even accurate. Luke had been doing a stand-in thing for his brother, nothing more. She was the one who had gotten all wiggy and weird, not him. Luke had just been pretending to be Robert and seeing her as Ginger. End of story.

Maggie flicked on her blinker and followed the cars into the parking lot of the restaurant.

She'd nibble a bit of dinner, she thought, then be on her way home to bed as quickly as was socially acceptable. Everything was fine. Just fine. She was erasing what had happened from her beleaguered mind. So there.

As the chattering group entered the restaurant, Robert pulled Luke to one side and spoke to his older brother in a quiet voice.

"Luke, my man," Robert said, "care to explain what was going on between you and Maggie during that rehearsal?"

"What do you mean?" Luke said. "We were just playing out the roles Ginger assigned us, that's all."

"Yeah, right," Robert said with a snort. "From where I was sitting, it didn't look like 'let's pretend.' No way.

You've been acting very strange ever since you met Maggie, Luke."

"Robert, Robert, Robert," Luke said, shaking his head. "You've got a typical case of prewedding jitters, not thinking clearly, seeing things that aren't there, the whole nine yards. You'd better get it together or you're liable to pass out at the altar tomorrow night. Trust me. I've been in a great many wedding parties over the years and I've seen your symptoms time and again."

"Really?" Robert said, pressing a fingertip on his chest. "Now that you mention it, my heart is beating really fast."

"That's one of the signs," Luke said, nodding. "I'm telling you, little brother, you've got to calm down. Ginger will never forgive you if you spoil this shindig by falling flat on your face before you can say 'I do.'"

"You're right," Robert said. "Okay. Deep breath. In. Out. I'm cool. I'm fine."

"Robert," Ginger said, coming back to where the brothers were standing. "They're waiting to seat us. Is something wrong?"

"Robert was just very emotionally moved by the rehearsal at the church," Luke said. "But all is well now. You're marrying a very romantic man here, Ginger."

"Ohhh, you are so sweet," Ginger said, giving Robert a quick kiss on the lips. "I love you so much."

"I love you, too, sugar," Robert said.

And unbelievable as it was, Luke thought, he loved Maggie Jenkins. This was definitely a fantastic life-changing night.

The restaurant where the dinner was being held was a five-star establishment, and Maggie had reserved a private dining room for the wedding party.

"Oh," she said softly when she entered the room.

Everything looked wonderful. The staff had really gone all out, per her instructions. The chandeliers were dimmed to create a rosy hue over the room. The crystal glasses gleamed and the sterling silverware sparkled. Wafer-thin china finger bowls sat by each place setting, and yellow rose petals were scattered whimsically down the center of the table that was covered in a pristine white cloth with lace edging.

Nodding in approval at the lovely and oh-so-romantic atmosphere, Maggie hung back with the intention of claiming a seat close to the door so she could make her early exit without creating a fuss. Just as she was about to sit down, Luke took her arm.

"Whoa," he said. "The pretend bride and groom are supposed to sit close to the real bride and groom at this dinner. It's part of the superstition."

"It is not," Maggie said, frowning.

"It certainly is," Luke said indignantly. "You wouldn't want to upset Ginger, would you? I mean, hey, anyone who spends hours sorting through yogurt-covered almonds to get the proper colors for the nut cups certainly wouldn't do anything to blow it in the home stretch."

"Well, Roses and Wishes does aim to please."

"My point exactly," Luke said, propelling Maggie toward the middle of the table. "Which is why you and I

are going to sit close to the bride and groom before
Ginger flips out."

"But I don't intend to stay long and I—"

"Here we are," Luke said, pulling out a chair. "Right
across from the happy couple."

"Mmm," Maggie said, shooting a glare in Luke's direction, then plunking down in the chair.

Waitresses appeared, wineglasses were filled. Soups,
then salads came and went. Then huge plates of roast
beef, baked potatoes and artfully arranged asparagus
were set in front of the diners.

Maggie stifled yet another yawn and stared down at
the meal.

"Eat," Luke whispered in her ear.

"I'm too tired to eat."

"If you don't eat, Ginger will think something has
gone wrong with the wedding plans and you're upset,"
Luke said, "which will cause her to—" he shuddered
"—I don't even want to think about it."

Maggie sighed and picked up her fork.

The conversations around the table were lively with
laughter erupting from one end of the table, then later
the other. Everyone was having a wonderful time.

And Maggie was falling asleep.

The four sips of wine she'd consumed were her final
undoing, and she was suddenly unable to keep her eyes
open. Just as she began to slide off the front of her chair,
Luke flung his arm around her and hauled her back up.
Maggie blinked and shook her head slightly.

"That was a great story, Maggie," Luke said, his arm

still holding her upright. "Really funny. Ah, here comes the waitress with some coffee. Would you care for some? Yes, you would."

"Yes, I would," Maggie mumbled.

"I want to hear the funny story," Ginger said. "Share with us, Maggie."

"Um…" Maggie said, a blank expression on her face.

"Right," Luke said. "Well, you see, Maggie coordinated a wedding where the bride and groom wanted to be married on horseback. That included the minister sitting on a huge stallion, you understand. The stallion was a horny beast, and just as the minister was to pronounce the couple officially wed, the stallion caught the scent of a mare in an adjoining pasture and took off—bam!—just whisked that minister away in a trail of dust."

Everyone erupted in appropriate laughter, then continued on with their own conversations.

"That was the dumbest thing I've ever heard," Maggie said to Luke under her breath.

"I thought it was pretty good considering I was winging it," Luke said, smiling at her.

"Would you please remove your arm from my person before someone wonders why it is there?"

"Just as soon as you get a few jolts of caffeine in you, my bride," Luke said.

"I am not your bride," Maggie said through clenched teeth. "Your arm is disturbing me."

"Oh?"

"What I mean is," she said, "it's heavy. Your arm. And warm. Much too warm. The air-conditioning is on, but there are a great many people in this room and…much too warm. Hot."

"You're hot?" Luke said, an expression of pure innocence on his face. "Because I have my arm around you? Because I'm very close to you and you're very close to me? Isn't that interesting?"

The waitress filled Maggie's coffee cup, then Luke's, then moved on down the table. Maggie leaned forward to grasp her cup, aware that Luke's arm seemed to be permanently attached to her body. She took a sip of coffee, blew on the remainder to cool it, then drained the cup.

"All better," she said. "I'm wide awake, ready to rock and roll. You may have your arm back now, Luke." That strong, masculine and oh-so-hot arm. "Thank you for your assistance."

"Glad to help," Luke said slowly, very slowly removing his arm. He paused. "So tell me, Maggie, why is it that someone whose focus is on producing picture-perfect weddings doesn't want a wedding of her own? Someone mentioned that you don't intend to marry. I'm curious as to why."

"It's a long story," Maggie said, running one fingertip around the rim of her coffee cup.

"I'm listening."

"I'd rather not discuss it." Maggie pushed her chair back and got to her feet. "Thank you for a lovely dinner," she said to Ginger and Robert. "I'll see everyone at the church tomorrow night. 'Bye for now."

"Hey, wait a minute," Luke said, getting quickly to

his feet. "I think it would be best if I drove you home. You might fall asleep at the wheel."

"Oh, no, I'm perfectly fine now that I've had that coffee. Ta ta."

As Maggie hurried from the room with a chorus of goodbyes following her out the door, Luke slouched back in his chair, a frown knitting his brows.

"Damn coffee," he said, looking at Maggie's empty cup.

"What's wrong with the coffee?" Ginger said, peering into her own cup.

"It's fine, honey," Robert said, then slid a grin at Luke. "It perks up sleepy people that other people wish hadn't gotten perked."

"Pardon me?" Ginger said.

"Nothing," Robert said, chuckling. "It's a guy thing between me and Luke. You know Luke, Ginger. He was the groom tonight and Maggie was the bride. Don't you think they made a smashing couple?"

"We're going to discuss smashing in regard to your nose if you don't shut up," Luke said.

Robert burst into laughter. Ginger looked totally confused. Mrs. St. John told her sons to behave themselves, and Luke got to his feet and said he was leaving.

"Great meal," he said. "In fact, the entire evening was very special. Definitely memorable."

"Do tell," Robert said, still beaming.

Luke made an imaginary gun out of his thumb and forefinger and shot his brother, who laughed so hard he got the hiccups.

* * *

Roses and Wishes took up the first floor of an older Victorian house that Maggie rented in an area of Phoenix that had been rezoned for businesses. Maggie lived upstairs, having furnished one of the bedrooms as a small living room.

The kitchen was on the main floor, as well as a powder room. The original living room was the reception area where albums with pictures of weddings were displayed and comfortable chairs grouped for discussing forthcoming ceremonies. The dining room was Maggie's office.

Maggie's favorite feature of the entire place was the enormous old-fashioned claw-foot bathtub in the upstairs bathroom that allowed her to indulge in long, leisurely soaks with soothing warm water up to her chin.

An hour after leaving the restaurant, having battled the traffic to get home, Maggie sank gratefully into the beckoning bubbles in the tub, rested her head on a spongy pillow on the rim and closed her eyes.

Good grief, she thought, what a night this had been. It had been awful, just awful. Luke St. John was a menace. Yes, that was a great word. A menace. A very dangerous, sensuous member of the male species who was a…a menace to her state of mind and did funny little weird things to her body. Her libido or some such thing. Her womanliness in general. He had nudged awake desire within her that she had worked very hard to put to sleep, to tuck away and ignore. Definitely a menace.

No wonder he had women crawling out of the woodwork trying to get his attention. He had an unexplaina-ble something that pushed sexual buttons in women that they didn't even know they possessed.

Well, she was wise to him now. Granted, part of her overreaction to Luke St. John was due to her exhaustion, but she had a sneaky feeling that even well-rested she might be susceptible to his whatever-it-was.

So. Tomorrow night at the wedding and the reception following she was going to make very certain that she kept her distance from Mr. St. John.

There would be no more gazing into his incredi-ble eyes. No more strong, *hot* arms encircling her. And heaven forbid, no more kisses shared that caused her to have naughty images of tearing his clothes off and ravishing his body right there in front of Rev-erend Mason.

There. It was settled. She had her plan. She'd stay away from Luke tomorrow night, the wedding would take place without a hitch and she'd never see him again.

Maggie opened her eyes and frowned.

Never see Luke again? Never? Ever? No, of course she wouldn't. He was a member of the jet-set money crowd, and she was among those who hoped they could make next month's rent. There was simply no way that their paths would cross again.

Why was that depressing?

"Oh, stop it," she said aloud, then closed her eyes again.

That was a thought from the tired part of her brain that the coffee hadn't reached. She was now blanking her mind, relaxing in her wonderful bathtub, preparing to sleep away the hours of the night and awake rejuvenated and back to normal with no lingering images or wanton thoughts of Luke St. John.

"Mmm," Maggie said, feeling the misty fog of sleep begin to dim her senses. "Mmm."

Maggie began to slide slowly lower in the tub. Then lower and lower…until she disappeared beneath the frothy bubbles.

She shot upward, sputtering as she swallowed a mouthful of suds, the wild motions causing water to splash out of the tub and onto the floor.

Her hair was covered in bubbles, which made her look like a frosted cake and, she knew, would result in a sticky mess that would have to be properly shampooed. The floor would have to be mopped, her towel that she'd placed next to the tub was soaked and…

And Maggie burst into tears.

She cried because she'd scared herself to death by sinking under the water and because the bubbles tasted terrible and now her stomach was upset. She cried because she was too tired to shampoo her hair and mop the floor and deal with a soggy towel and…

She cried because no matter how hard she tried she couldn't forget what it had been like to be kissed by Luke St. John and she didn't know how to deal with all the new and foreign feelings she'd experienced.

She cried because after tomorrow night she'd never see Luke again, which *she knew,* she knew, was for the best, but sometimes the best was really stinky and just so sad.

She cried because…because, darn it anyway, she felt like it.

So Maggie cried until she had no more tears to shed and the water in the tub was cold and her hair had dried and was a gummy disaster sticking up in weird spiky things and her sinuses were clogged, causing a roaring headache.

Maggie sniffled as she got out of the tub, picked up the soggy towel and threw it in the water. She marched into her bedroom and crawled beneath the sheets.

And during the night spent on damp linens and a gooey pillow, she dreamed of Luke St. John.

Three

Unable to sleep after the events of the unsettling evening, Luke gave up and left his bed, pulling on a lightweight robe. He wandered through his penthouse apartment, finally stopping by a wall of windows to look out over the city lights that shone into infinity.

Thoughts tumbled through his mind one after another, and he pressed the heels of his hands to his throbbing temples for a moment in a futile attempt to halt the onslaught.

Maggie, he thought, crossing his arms over his chest. She was all and everything he had ever hoped to find in a woman. He had only known her for a handful of hours, yet he knew she was the one, his life's partner.

Half of him wanted to shout the fantastic news from

the rooftops, tell the world that he was in love, had found the woman of his heart.

Another section of his being was terrified that Maggie would never come to feel the same way about him, that she would slip away from him like sand falling from the palm of his hand.

Maggie, for reasons she refused to share so far, never intended to marry. That was not good, not good at all. The mystifying question was why. Had she been terribly hurt by a man in the past? Oh, he'd take the guy apart. He'd…Whoa, he would just waste mental energy going off in that direction.

Maybe Maggie was so focused on her career she saw no room for a man in her life. No, that didn't work for him. He'd dated a multitude of women with that mindset and they were all popped out of the same mold. Maggie wasn't like them, not even close. She didn't have the brittle edginess, that step-over-the-bodies-to-get-to-the-top mentality he was so tired of dealing with.

Maggie was so down to earth, so…real. She'd started a business that made dreams come true for brides, made their weddings a special, memory-making event in their lives.

Ginger and Robert's day was going to be perfect because Maggie had seen to every detail, including sorting through a mountain of yogurt-covered almonds to select Ginger's choice of colors.

Yes, Maggie knew how to make dreams come true, yet she didn't want any of those spectacular weddings to be hers, didn't want to be the bride who would see her groom waiting eagerly for her at the altar as she made her way down the aisle.

Why?

It was as though Maggie had built tall, strong walls around her heart, and his greatest fear was that he wouldn't be able to break through them, get a chance to capture her heart as she had his.

The flicker of hope he had, Luke mused as he continued to stare out the window, was that he'd felt Maggie respond to his kiss during the rehearsal, had seen the desire in her big brown eyes directed toward him. *Him.*

That kiss had been the beginning of the chipping away of that barrier surrounding Maggie. It was a start, a positive one, but he had a long, long way to go.

His first impulse was to ask Maggie out, wine and dine and court her, but a cold knot in his gut told him she'd turn him down flat if he invited her to join him for a night on the town. She'd been upset, really flustered by her reaction to the kiss they'd shared and had beat a hasty retreat from the rehearsal dinner as quickly as she could.

No, the traditional program of flowers, candy and romantic dinners wasn't going to work because he just somehow knew he wasn't going to get a chance to put those things in motion.

He needed a new and innovative plan, Luke thought, narrowing his eyes. And he'd better come up with it very quickly. He'd see Maggie at the wedding and reception, but beyond that he envisioned her being set on automatic "no" if he attempted to get her to go out with him.

Ah, Maggie, why? he thought dismally. What secret

something held her in an iron fist that made her determined to never fall in love, never marry, never be the bride in one of her meticulously planned weddings?

He didn't know the answer to that tormenting question. Nor did he know the answer to how he was going to see Maggie again after Robert and Ginger's wedding. And he didn't know the answer to how he would face a cold and empty future without her.

Well, the first order of business, he thought, heading back toward his bedroom, was to get some sleep. He was about to begin the greatest battle of his life and he intended to win. Somehow. He would be the victor. Somehow. He would crumble Maggie's walls into dust and share her sunshine world with her for all time. Somehow.

Late the next morning Maggie entered the small house where her mother lived and presented her with a lumpy plastic bag.

"What's this, sweetheart?" Martha Jenkins said, holding the bag at eye level.

"Almonds," Maggie said, sitting down at the kitchen table. "Yogurt-covered almonds in every shade of the rainbow except yellow and mint-green."

Martha laughed as she sat opposite Maggie and opened the bag. Martha was a rather attractive woman, although not one that would turn heads when she walked into a room. Her brown hair was streaked with gray, which she felt no need to hide, and she had given up long ago trying to lose the twenty pounds that had crept up on her over the years.

"Just what my pudgy person doesn't need," she said. "But, what the heck, I'll eat every one of them. Are these left over from something you did for the big wedding tonight?" She popped two of the nuts into her mouth.

Maggie nodded. "Nut cups. Nut cups, you understand, that only boast yellow and mint-green yogurt-covered almonds, to please my picky bride." She paused. "No, that's not fair. Ginger is very sweet. She just had trouble making up her mind about things for a stretch of time there. But when you think about it, she has every right to have things perfect for her special event."

"That's true," Martha said, then sighed. "But that doesn't guarantee a happy marriage, does it? The bubble bursts and that's that, as evidenced by the fact that I divorced your father when you were ten. Off he went, never to be seen or heard from again." She ate four more almonds. "These are yummy."

"I think Ginger and Robert are going to be a forever couple, Mom," Maggie said. "If you could see them together... Oh, never mind."

"Maggie, honey, I worry so about you," Martha said. "Why on earth did you become a wedding coordinator when there are so many other things you could have done? Why torture yourself creating those beautiful events for other people when—"

"When I know I can never get married myself?" Maggie finished for her.

"Yes," Martha said, patting her daughter's hand. "Exactly."

A sudden and vivid image of Luke flashed through Maggie's mind and a shiver coursed through her.

"Maybe you're right," she said quietly. "Maybe launching Roses and Wishes was a terrible mistake. I've been fine for the past year with all the preparations being for other people, but…" She stopped and shook her head.

"Is there something different about this wedding that's upsetting you?" Martha said, frowning.

"No, not really," Maggie said quickly, forcing a smile to appear on her lips. "It's just the largest wedding I've done, and after so many months I think I'm just registering a sense of loss, sort of hating to say goodbye to all those people.

"I'm hoping, of course, that my reputation will soar because of Ginger and Robert's event and I'll get to do some ritzier weddings. I guess that's what I want. Oh, ignore me. I'm in a strange mood. Eat another almond, Mom. Yogurt is good for a person."

"Nuts are fattening," Martha said, laughing.

"How are things at the store?"

"Same old, same old," Martha said with a shrug. "I manage the children's clothing department by rote now, I've been doing it for so long. I don't love it, I don't hate it, I just do it. Keeps this roof over my head. I really can't complain, sweetheart. I made my way up the ladder from a salesclerk to the manager and I'm proud of that."

"You should be," Maggie said, nodding. "I'm proud of you, too."

"I'll just keep plugging along until I retire. Since I

just turned fifty, I have a ways to go, though." Martha paused. "Do you feel that type of settled in with Roses and Wishes? Do you see yourself running your business for many years to come?"

"I'm not sure," Maggie said, then popped an almond in her mouth. "As I said, I'm having sort of a letdown after working on this big wedding so long. I'll have a better idea how I really feel after tonight and I get some more sleep, sleep, sleep. I'm exhausted and now isn't the time to analyze how I feel about Roses and Wishes."

"True." Martha nodded, then sighed. "Oh, Maggie, I wish things were different. I'd like to think you'd be planning one of those beautiful weddings for yourself someday, but… Hardly seems fair, does it? I know, I know, no one said that life is fair."

"No," Maggie said quietly, "no one said that."

Mother and daughter chatted for a while longer, Martha bringing Maggie up to date on the gossip in the neighborhood, including the news that another of Maggie's childhood friends was getting married, which did nothing to improve Maggie's rather gloomy mood.

Another bride, she thought as she hugged her mother, then left the house. Another bride that wasn't her. Her mom had said she'd reminded the bride-to-be about Roses and Wishes but, due to a very limited budget, the newly engaged couple planned to exchange vows at the courthouse.

No, she thought as she drove away, she wasn't getting more depressed by the minute because her friend hadn't chosen Roses and Wishes to plan her wedding. It was because her friend was *having* a wedding, had found her special someone and would live happily ever after.

Happily ever after, Maggie mused, then sighed. Every bride and groom believed that was their destiny, that they would be together until death parted them, and for some that was gloriously true. But for others?

"Don't go there, Maggie," she ordered herself aloud. "Go home and eat a ton of yogurt-covered almonds and quit thinking." She drew a wobbly breath. "And whatever you do, do *not* dwell on Luke St. John."

Months ago Maggie had splurged on what she referred to in her mind as The Dress. It was sea-green chiffon with a camisole top and a skirt that swirled in changing hues of color just below her knees. Her shoes were strappy evening sandals with three-inch heels. If the event was during the Phoenix winter, she added a lacy off-white shawl that had belonged to her grandmother.

The fact that she wore the same dress to each wedding was immaterial, she knew, because she went unnoticed, was just a busy figure in the background who bustled around making certain everything went as planned.

Wearing The Dress, Maggie arrived at the church an hour before the ceremony was to begin and checked to see that the flowers were delivered and in place. Two of the candles in front of the altar were yellow, and the single one that represented Ginger and Robert united was mint-green.

Maggie stood in the silent church in front of the candles, remembering how Reverend Mason had explained their meaning while she and Luke were playing out the roles of bride and groom.

Knowing she was acting ridiculous, Maggie slid one of the yellow tapers free, then glanced to the right, envisioning Luke holding the other one. In her mind's eye she saw them moving at the same time, igniting the one larger candle in the center. She blew out the imaginary flame that declared her to be a single entity and saw—oh, yes, she really saw—the dancing light from the larger candle in the middle.

Maggie, stop it, she ordered herself as she replaced the yellow taper. Enough of this foolishness.

She turned and her breath caught as she saw Luke standing at the back of the church, watching her as he held a garment bag over his shoulder with one finger.

Squaring her shoulders and lifting her chin, she walked up the aisle to where Luke stood.

"Hello, Luke," she said, looking at an empty space just above his head. "I was just making certain the candles weren't stuck in the holders or anything. Details, details, details. You just wouldn't believe how many little things there are to keep track of for an event like this. And that's my job, by golly, checking all those details and…"

"You look beautiful." Luke's voice was rich, deep and so very male and sensuous that a shiver coursed through Maggie. "Pretty as a bride."

"Oh, well, thank you," Maggie said, still not meeting his gaze. "This is The Dress. What I mean is—Never mind. It's not important. I assume that's your tux you're holding. Ginger changed her mind three times on the color of the tuxedos before settling on pale gray. I hope you don't mind wearing a ruffled shirt, because she didn't budge on ruffled shirts. So. Well. I'd best go into the bride's dressing room and…"

"Maggie, look at me," Luke said quietly.

"Gosh, I just don't have time to do that, Luke."

"Look…at…me."

Maggie slowly shifted her eyes to Luke's and immediately felt light-headed, as though she might float off into oblivion.

"Yes?" she said softly.

"Will you save me a dance at the reception?"

"No, I can't because I don't actually take part, per se, in the reception activities. I hover around in the background checking those pesky little details I told you about. So, nope, no dance. Sorry 'bout that. Gotta go. 'Bye."

"Maggie, do I make you nervous?" Luke said, frowning.

"Nervous? Me?" she said, waving one hand in the air. "Don't be silly. It's not you, it's the whole evening ahead. The reputation of Roses and Wishes is at stake here. Everything has to be perfect."

"Ah," he said, nodding. "That includes keeping all members of the wedding party happy. Right?"

"Well, yes, I suppose so."

"Then promise you'll dance with me. Just one dance, Maggie. That's not too much to ask, is it? You wouldn't want to make the best man grumpy, would you? Heaven forbid."

Maggie narrowed her eyes. "Do you always get what you want, Luke?"

"When it's very important to me, I do," he said, still looking directly into her eyes. "Is it a deal? One dance?"

"Jeez Louise, all right," Maggie said. "But if some detail goes wrong while I'm dancing that dance, it will be your fault, Luke St. John."

"Fair enough," he said, smiling. "I'll see you later then."

"Fine," she said, then scooted around him and hurried away.

Luke stood statue-still for a long moment, staring at the candles that symbolized two becoming one. He nodded, then turned and walked slowly toward the room where the men in the wedding party were to change into their pale gray tuxedos.

Maggie had prepared herself to deal with a totally jangled and nervous-to-the max prewedding Ginger. To Maggie's amazement and heartfelt delight, Ginger had a quiet serenity about her when she arrived in the dressing room at the church.

"Are you really okay?" Maggie said, peering at the bride.

"I'm about to marry the man I love with my whole heart, Maggie," Ginger said softly. "That's all I can think about, focus on. It's strange, isn't it? I made such a fuss about having the right colored almonds in the nut cups, and suddenly none of that is important."

"I think that's wonderful," Maggie said, smiling.

"And you're absolutely beautiful in your dress, Ginger. I hope you and Robert will be very, very happy together."

"Oh, we will be," Ginger said, nodding. "We will be."

Forever? Maggie thought. Until death parted them and even beyond? What were the chances of that?

"Mother," Ginger said, bringing Maggie back to the moment at hand, "you've got to stop crying or you'll be all blotchy in the photographs."

"I know, I know," Mrs. Barrington said, dabbing at her nose with yet another tissue. "But you're my baby girl and… Ohhh, I'm a wreck."

"It's time," Maggie said, looking at her watch. "Mothers, please go and have the ushers seat you now. Bridesmaids, head for the vestibule. You're all simply gorgeous."

"I look like one of those yogurt-covered almonds," Tiffy said, frowning at her reflection in the mirror. "I don't want to do this."

Maggie stepped in front of Tiffy to block her view of herself in the mirror.

"If you want to live to see another day," Maggie said so only Tiffy could hear, "you'll go get in line, Tiffy."

"You can't talk to me like that."

"I just did," Maggie said.

"Oh. Right. Okay. I'm going," Tiffy said, giving Maggie a wary look, then hurrying from the room.

Maggie threw up her hands. "Well, if Tiffy ever gets married, Roses and Wishes sure isn't going to get the chance to coordinate *her* wedding."

* * *

Over three hundred guests witnessed the wedding of Ginger Barrington and Robert St. John. From her usual place in the last pew in the church, Maggie Jenkins indulged herself by watching Luke St. John during the entire picture-perfect ceremony.

What Luke did for a pale gray tuxedo, she thought dreamily, was sinful. The color accentuated his dark hair and tanned skin. The custom-tailored tux made his shoulders look a block wide. And those strong but gentle hands produced the ring right on cue.

The smile that broke across Luke's face when Robert kissed his wife sent shivers coursing down Maggie's spine.

Reverend Mason introduced Mr. and Mrs. Robert St. John to the congregation, then the organ music swelled and the recessional took place, the smiling bride and groom leading the way back down the aisle. When Luke and the maid of honor went by where Maggie stood, he met her gaze for a brief moment and a frisson of heat swirled throughout her.

How on earth, Maggie thought, very aware of her racing heart, was she going to survive her dance with Luke? A promise was a promise, but… If she was just so busy tending to those details, details, details and managed to keep some distance between her and Luke, the dance might never take place. It would take some fancy footwork on her part and she'd have to stay on red alert as to where Luke was at all times, but she could pull this off.

"Good plan," she said under her breath. "Maggie, you're brilliant."

* * *

The reception was being held at one of the exclusive country clubs in Phoenix. A dinner buffet greeted the guests and the huge ballroom was filled with a multitude of round tables each topped with a mint-green or yellow tablecloth and contrasting color candle burning in a glass cylinder in the center. A ten-piece band would play quietly during the meal, then change to Ginger's choice of dance music after the champagne toasts had been made and the four-tier cake had been cut and served by the army of waiters.

As everything continued to go like clockwork, Maggie began to relax and a wave of utter fatigue swept over her. She sat on a folding chair in a dim corner of the room, nibbling on a small plate of food, and nodded in approval at the final outcome of her months of labor.

She'd done it, she thought. Roses and Wishes had hopefully now wiggled its way into the high-society scene of Phoenix. She'd seen the business cards she'd propped next to the candleholder on each table being slipped into purses and given to men to place in their pockets. Fantastic.

Maggie frowned as she recalled the conversation with her mother regarding whether Maggie truly wanted to continue to plan weddings for bride after bride while knowing she herself would never have that title. Well, she wasn't going to dwell on that now, for heaven's sake. She intended to bask in her glory tonight of a job well done for Ginger and Robert St. John.

Maggie placed her plate on the tray of a passing

waiter, then smiled as Ginger and Robert took the floor for the first dance.

How lovely, she thought. They looked so happy, had eyes only for each other as they moved around the gleaming expanse. They danced so well together and—

Maggie suddenly sat bolt upright in her chair.

Dancing, she thought frantically. Other couples were now joining the bride and groom to enjoy the terrific music and so many people were dancing, for heaven's sake. Where was Luke? She had to keep careful track of Luke.

There he was dancing with Ginger. Now he'd shifted to his mother. Fine. My, my, he was poetry in motion, so graceful for a man of his size. Oops. He'd bowed slightly and given his mother's hand to his father and— no, no, no—he was headed toward her secret little corner, was working his way through the crowd on the dance floor. She was out of there.

Maggie jumped to her feet and hurried to the head table, where she gave instructions for the top layer of the cake to be boxed up so it could be frozen and brought out again on Ginger and Robert's first anniversary celebration.

"Give it to the mother of the bride," Maggie told a waiter. "She agreed to take care of it tonight."

"You told us that at the meeting we had last week," the waiter said, frowning. "I've got it covered, Maggie."

"Of course you do," Maggie said, patting him on the arm. "I'm sorry for nagging." She looked quickly into the distance and saw Luke advancing. "How's the supply of champagne holding up?"

"Fine," the waiter said, rolling his eyes. "Trust me. Everything is going great. Isn't there something else you should be doing?"

"Right." Maggie pointed one finger in the air. "I do believe I'll visit the powder room."

"Good idea," the man said drily. "Don't feel you have to check back here."

"Keep up the great work," Maggie said, then rushed away.

When Maggie entered the powder room, she absently registered the fact that it was bigger than her entire living space at home. There was a huge sitting area with love seats, easy chairs and coffee tables holding attractive baskets of artificial flowers.

Beyond all of that were the stalls, a long mirror surrounded by makeup bulbs and a vanity with eight or ten sinks. The noise level was high as women stood two deep in front of the mirror, touching up their postdinner lipstick, one row peering over the shoulders of the other as they chatted and laughed, a good time obviously being had by all.

There was no point in staying in here with this crowd, Maggie thought, shaking her head. The noise was enough to give her a headache and, besides, her purse was locked in a cabinet in the kitchen, so she had nothing to repair her lipstick with.

Well, there was no problem really about leaving the powder room, because even if Luke had figured out where she had been headed, he wouldn't do anything as crass as to plant himself outside the door of the women's restroom. People with money were very big on proper social decorum, and that maneuver definitely wouldn't go down well here.

Nodding in satisfaction that she was so far doing a dandy job of keeping a safe distance between herself and Luke, Maggie opened the door and walked out into the hallway beyond.

And walked smack-dab into the solid, unmoving body of Luke St. John.

Four

Maggie gasped and staggered slightly, causing Luke to grip her upper arms to steady her.

"Well," he said, not releasing his hold on her, "fancy meeting you here, Maggie."

"Luke," she said, looking quickly to each side, "you can't hang around outside the women's restroom. It's not…couth, not nice at all. Your mother would be mortified."

"My mother isn't here," he said, frowning. "You are. Ever since the music began you've been bouncing around the room out there like a Ping-Pong ball. I have the distinct impression that you don't intend to keep your promise to dance with me. Talk about mortifying a mother. How would yours feel if she knew her daughter hadn't kept her word?"

Maggie opened her mouth to say something in her defense, only to realize she was guilty as charged.

"How about," she said, narrowing her eyes in concentration, "I had details, details, details to check on?"

"Nope," Luke said. "Everything is going like a fine-tuned machine. I'm betting that there's nothing left to check on."

"Oh." Maggie paused. "Well, then, try this. I needed to freshen my lipstick, like all the others in the powder room are doing."

"I might buy that," Luke said, nodding, "except where is your tube of lipstick? No purse, no lipstick."

"Oh."

"Maggie," Luke said, his voice gentling, "don't you want to dance with me?"

"Yes, I do. It's just that I—"

"Good. That's settled then." Luke released her arms and grasped one of her hands with one of his. "Let's go."

"But…"

The door to the powder room opened and three young women emerged, stopping before they bumped into Luke and Maggie.

"Well, Luke St. John," one of the women said, smiling coyly, "what on earth are you doing skulking around outside our private little place? Are you lost, gorgeous man?"

"Not at all," Luke said, tightening his hold on Maggie's hand as she tried to pull free. "I just came to collect my partner for the next waltz. I thought it would be extremely polite on my part to escort her to the dance floor."

"Well, isn't that just the sweetest thing?" one of the other women said.

"That's the way I see it," Luke said. "Come along, Maggie."

"You're a lucky girl, Maggie," the third woman said with a wistful sigh. "I've been trying to get Luke to *collect* me for all kinds of things for years and nothing has worked. What do you know that I don't?"

"I have no idea," Maggie said wearily.

"Enjoy your evening, ladies," Luke said, starting down the hallway with Maggie in tow.

Just as Maggie and Luke reentered the main room, a song ended and the band paused, then began to play a slow, dreamy waltz.

"Perfect," Luke said, smiling as he led Maggie onto the crowded, gleaming floor.

And then Maggie was in Luke's embrace, swaying to the music as though they had spent a lifetime dancing together. He nestled her close to his body and she totally ignored the naggy little voice in her mind that was telling her she was in a danger zone, should move backward, keep space between them.

"Mmm," Luke said, "you smell so nice. What kind of perfume is that?"

"Soap," Maggie said.

Luke chuckled and the sexy sound caused Maggie to shiver.

"Are you cold?" Luke said, pulling her even closer.

Maggie's breasts were crushed to the hard wall of Luke's chest in a sweet pain that made her acutely aware of her femininity in contrast to his blatant maleness. Heat swirled within her, finally pulsing low in her body.

"No. I'm…I'm definitely not cold."

"You feel so good in my arms, Maggie. Perfect, absolutely perfect."

"Well…" Maggie started, then for the life of her couldn't think of one intelligent thing to say.

And the music played on.

The crowd surrounding them disappeared, along with the buzz of conversation from those on the sidelines who weren't dancing. The room itself no longer existed. It was just the two of them and the music, encased in a sensual mist.

Ah, Maggie, Luke thought. He wanted this dance to last forever. Holding Maggie in his arms was heaven in its purest form. She fit against him as though she'd been custom-made. Well, that was actually true. Yes, custom-made just for him because she was his other half, and he loved her with an intensity that was beyond description.

They were dancing like Cinderella and the prince at the ball, Luke mentally rambled on. But in that fairy tale it all fell apart at the stroke of midnight. That poor slob of a prince was left with empty arms and an aching heart, wondering if he'd ever see his newfound love again.

Well, that wasn't going to happen to Luke St. John, damn it. No way. Because he was going to come up with a rock-solid plan that would enable him to see Maggie on a regular basis without running the risk of her turning him down.

But how in hell was he going to do that?

Where was this genius-level plan going to come from? He'd searched his brain for it until he was exhausted, and it wasn't there, he'd come up empty.

Think, St. John. His entire future happiness depended on that unknown plan.

The song ended.

No, Luke thought frantically. Not yet.

"Luke?" Maggie looked up at him as they stopped moving, realizing that he had not relinquished his hold on her one iota.

"Yes?"

"Could we dance to just one more song?"

"Yes," he said. They would dance to a lifetime of songs played just for them. "It will be my pleasure."

Another waltz began and they swayed to the lilting music.

What on earth had possessed her to ask Luke to dance with her again? Maggie thought, feeling a flush of embarrassment warm her cheeks. How brazen was that, for Pete's sake? Not only brazen but dumb, really dumb. She was supposed to be putting distance between them, not practically begging to be kept nestled close, so enticingly close, to his body.

But he felt so good and smelled so good and he danced so smoothly she was transformed into Ginger Rogers. Oh, what harm could one more dance do? She'd never see Luke again after tonight, so why not have the memory of two fantasy-filled dances instead of just one? Sure, why not?

It was sort of like the story of Cinderella, only this handsome prince wasn't going to run all over the kingdom of Phoenix trying on a shoe to find her. No this was it, all there would be, and the very thought of that was so depressing it was enough to make her weep buckets.

Soon—much, much too soon—the song ended. Maggie drew a steadying breath, then stepped back out of Luke's arms.

"Thank you," she said, smiling slightly. "That was lovely. I... Well, I have things to check on regarding the cleanup crew and what have you so... It was nice meeting you, Luke. Goodbye."

"Good night, Maggie," he said quietly.

Maggie made her way through the crowd on the dance floor, and Luke watched her go before weaving through the guests to return to the head table. He sat down next to his father, a distinguished-looking man with a trim build and salt-and-pepper hair.

"Everything went very well this evening, don't you think?" Mason St. John said. "Your brother and Ginger must be pleased."

"Mmm." Luke rocked his chair back on two legs and folded his arms over his chest.

"Your mother is still out there dancing," his father continued. "She's having a marvelous time."

"Mmm."

"The wedding cake was the best I've ever tasted,"

Mason said. "Some I've had over the years have been like sawdust with a plastic bride and groom on top."

"Mmm."

"I do believe you've met your match in Maggie Jenkins, son," Mason said. "You have all the signs of a man who has had the pins knocked out from under him."

"Mmm," Luke said, then blinked and thudded the chair back onto four legs. "What?"

Mason chuckled. "I thought that might get your attention. I've been watching you, Luke. You're a goner. I was beginning to believe there wasn't a woman in Phoenix who could stake a claim on you, but Maggie Jenkins obviously has. What I don't understand is why you look so gloomy."

"It's very simple, Dad," Luke said. "Maggie may plan fantastic weddings but she doesn't want one for herself. She has no intention of marrying. I don't know if you believe in love at first sight, but it has happened to me big-time. I am irrevocably in love with a woman who wants no part of 'until death do us part.'"

"Well, for the record," Mason said, "I certainly do believe in love at first sight. I fell in love with your mother when we were in the seventh grade and one of the rubber bands from her braces flew off and smacked me right in the eye. As for your Maggie? It doesn't take a genius to figure out that you need a plan."

"Oh, man," Luke said, squeezing the bridge of his nose, "don't say that word. I've worn out my brain already trying to come up with exactly that—a plan. And I'm running on empty.

"Maggie isn't going to go for the wine-and-dine routine. No way. She'd head for the hills before she got tangled up in anything that even hinted of courtship, a serious relationship. I can literally see, feel, the walls she's built around herself."

"So chip away at them. That's where the plan comes in," Mason said. "Come on, Luke. You're a St. John. We go for the gusto, we're winners, we don't even entertain the word *defeat*."

"In the courtroom," Luke said. "Dealing with women is a whole different arena, Dad. It calls for understanding the female mind, and I'm not sure there's a man on this planet who can do that."

"Good point. I certainly don't know what makes those wonderful creatures tick, even after all these years," Mason said, stroking his chin. "Well, now, this is going to be quite a challenge for you, isn't it?"

"The most important fight of my life," Luke said. "I really, *really* need an idea."

"Yep," Mason said, nodding. "Keep me posted on this, son."

"Yeah, okay. In the meantime, pass that champagne bottle down here, will you? Maybe there's a magic answer waiting for me in the bubbly."

Mason laughed as he handed his son the bottle. "All that is in there is a hangover waiting to happen."

"Whatever," Luke said, then filled his glass to the brim.

Late the next morning Luke rolled onto his back in bed, opened his eyes and groaned. He closed his eyes again, pressed his hand to his throbbing forehead, then dropped his arms to the bed with a thud.

He was a dying man, he thought, eyes still tightly closed. Some idiot was playing a bongo drum in this brain, every tooth in his mouth ached and even his hair hurt. To even hope to survive he'd have to cut off his head and grow a new one.

"Ohhh, I hate champagne," he said aloud, with another groan thrown in for good measure. "I'm never drinking that junk again. This is somehow all Maggie Jenkins's fault, damn it."

Luke opened his eyes slowly, then eased upward and moved his feet cautiously to the floor. He propped his elbows on his knees and cradled his throbbing head in his hands.

He couldn't believe he'd done this, he thought miserably. He hadn't gotten smashed since his freshman year in college many years ago. But there he'd sat, filling his glass with expensive champagne, chugging it down, filling it again and again and again.

He vaguely remembered his father watching him and chuckling with maddening regularity, then finally extending his hand and asking for Luke's car keys.

So how had he gotten home? Oh, yeah, his dad had driven him with his mother following in their vehicle. Well, at least his SUV must be parked in the garage beneath the building. His mother had seemed to get a kick out of her oldest son's condition, too, now that he thought about it. What rotten parents.

At least Robert didn't know what his big brother had

done. Robert and Ginger had changed into their traveling clothes and with all the proper fuss had left the reception to catch the plane to their honeymoon in Greece.

Their honeymoon. Because they had just gotten married. Mr. and Mrs. Robert St. John. Robert and Ginger were so happy it was nauseating. No, that wasn't fair. He was sincerely pleased that Robert had found his happiness in ditzy Ginger. By this time next year they would no doubt have produced the first St. John grandchild. How crummy was that?

"Knock it off," Luke said, the sound of his own voice increasing the pain in his head.

He was so jealous of Robert and Ginger, it was a crime. And envious of his parents and every other dewy-eyed in-love couple on the face of the earth.

Well, watch out world, because Luke St. John was in love, too, and…and had gotten as drunk as a skunk because the woman of his heart wasn't remotely close to being in love with him. What a bummer.

Luke staggered to his feet, steadied, then shuffled into the bathroom, where he stood under a very hot shower for a very long time. He dressed in jeans and a T-shirt, consumed four cups of coffee with four matching aspirins and decided he might, just might, live.

He wandered into the living room and slouched onto the large sofa, resting his head on the top and staring at the ceiling.

How many people, he wondered, would decide to take the big step and get married after witnessing the faultless Barrington-St. John wedding Maggie had produced the night before? Would her phone be ringing off the hook Monday morning with newly engaged brides-to-be? That was sure what *he* would like to be doing come the first of the week—helping to plan the wedding of all weddings and…

Luke sat bolt upward, then smacked one hand against his forehead as the sudden motion caused a lightning bolt to shoot through his head.

There it is, he thought, his hear racing. Even through the last lingering fog of his hangover it was taking shape, coming together, clicking into place.

The Plan.

"Yes," he said, punching one fist high in the air.

Maggie spent Sunday catching up on Roses and Wishes paperwork, tackling a mound of laundry and cleaning her neglected apartment on the upper floor of the old house.

That done, she shopped for groceries for her Mother Hubbard cupboards. She prepared a nice dinner for herself of baked chicken, mashed potatoes and gravy and a fruit salad, with the smug knowledge that the effort would provide enough leftovers for several days.

What she did *not* do was think.

Upon waking that morning she'd made a firm vow that she would not dwell on the subject of Luke St. John. Not relive the kiss at the altar during the rehearsal or the dances they'd shared.

No remembrances would be allowed of the heated sensations that had consumed her when Luke's lips had captured hers and while she had been held so tightly in his arms during the dreamy waltzes.

She'd shoo away any images that threatened to creep into her mental vision of Luke's deep brown eyes, his thick beckoning-to-her-fingers hair, his wide shoulders and those incredible strong but gentle hands of his.

Through the entire day she concentrated on her chores and kept busy, busy, busy, becoming extremely proud of herself for her restraint and self-control.

Luke and the success of the Barrington-St. John wedding were now old news, done, finished, kaput, and her thoughts were directed toward the start of the fresh week at Roses and Wishes. She focused on the hope that new business from all those cards she'd seen tucked away at the reception would cause the phone to ring off the hook.

She mentally patted herself on the back for doing such a stellar job of keeping her vow. The day had gone exactly as she'd planned.

But then she ran out of things to do.

She had spit-shined the kitchen after dinner, taken a leisurely bubble bath in her super-duper tub, then settled onto the sofa in an old-fashioned, pale pink, soft cotton granny nightgown that was perfect for the warm summer night.

Glancing at the little clock on the end table, she frowned when she saw that it was only a few minutes after eight o'clock. She was tired from her nonstop day but not sleepy enough to go to bed.

"Television," she said, snatching up the remote.

She channel surfed three times, sighed, then turned off the TV realizing there was just nothing on that she wanted to watch.

"Read a book," she said, grabbing a paperback novel on the coffee table.

After reading the same page four times and having no idea what it said, she plunked the book back onto the table and glared at it.

She wiggled into a more comfortable position on the rather lumpy sofa, crossed her arms over her breasts and stared into space.

And thought of Luke St. John.

"This is dumb, dumb, dumb," she said with a cluck of self-disgust.

Well, she thought, maybe not. Perhaps she was approaching this all wrong. Granted, she'd kept Luke at bay during the hours of the day, but she couldn't continue such a frenzied schedule or she'd collapse into an exhausted heap on the floor.

So. New idea. She *would* indulge in dwelling on all that had transpired between her and Luke, *would* allow images of his masculine magnificence to consume her mind, *would* invite the womanly sensual sensations to once again swirl and churn and burn within her. Then she'd wrap all those things up like a precious treasure and tuck them away in a secret chamber of her heart and be done with them for all time. The end.

"Very good," she said with a decisive nod. "Go for it, Maggie."

And she did.

And spent a long night tossing and turning in her bed, alternating between hot waves of overpowering desire and the chill of loneliness.

Late the next morning Maggie sat in the office of Roses and Wishes and stared gloomily at the telephone, which had not rung once since she'd come downstairs.

Well, that was fine, she rationalized. It didn't mean she wasn't going to garner any new business from the success of the Barrington-St. John wedding. She was being much too impatient, that's all. Brides-to-be had to come back to earth from cloud nine and start thinking about what kind of wedding they wished to have. They'd mentally sift and sort, mull it over, then eventually call Roses and Wishes to set things in motion. Sure.

Maggie left the office and went into the reception area, where she straightened albums that didn't need straightening, dusted what wasn't dusty. She switched two easy chairs to opposite sides of the love seat, then put them back where they'd been.

With a sigh she trudged back into the office, sank onto the chair behind the desk and, for lack of anything better to do, doodled on a legal pad and munched on yogurt-covered almonds.

She was tired, she mused, and that was Luke St. John's fault. She'd given him several hours of her evening last night, but she'd certainly not invited him into her bed and the dreams she'd had when she'd finally managed to doze off. Pushy, rude man. He'd refused to stay beyond her bedroom door as ordered, darn it.

The bell over the front door jingled, indicating some-one had entered the house, and Maggie jumped to her feet, nearly tipping over the chair in the process.

She told herself to get a professional grip, for heaven's sake, took a steadying breath as she smoothed her pale blue top over the waistband of her white slacks and actually managed to walk to the main area in a fairly slow, ladylike manner.

Then stopped dead and forgot to breathe.

"Hello, Maggie," Luke St. John said from where he stood just inside the door.

This was absurd, Maggie thought, taking a gulp of much-needed air. Luke wasn't really standing there look-ing incredibly gorgeous in jeans and an open-necked gray dress shirt. She'd conjured up his image from the wanton section of her brain that insisted on reliving all the sensationally sensuous… This was ridiculous.

"Maggie?" Luke closed the distance between them and frowned. "Hello?"

"You're not here," she said, flapping one hand in the air. "Poof. You're gone." She paused, waited, then ten-tatively pressed one fingertip to Luke's imaginary chest, which was definitely hard as a rock. Her eyes widened as she stared up at him. "Oh, my gosh, you really are here. Why are you here?"

Luke folded his arms across his chest and stared down at the floor, his shoulders shaking with muffled laughter.

Oh, man, he thought, how he loved this woman. She was obviously jangled by his unexpected arrival at

Roses and Wishes, and that was good news. Great news. If he hadn't had an impact on Maggie, she wouldn't give a damn if he suddenly popped into her place of business.

She was flustered and didn't know how to hide it, and that was so endearing. Maggie was genuine and honest. He wanted to take her into his arms and...

"Mr. St. John?" Maggie said, planting her hands on her hips. "May I help you?"

"I'm beyond help," he said, meeting her gaze with merriment dancing in his brown eyes.

"Pardon me?"

"Never mind." Luke forced a serious expression onto his face. "Yes, you may assist me, Ms. Jenkins. I am in desperate need of your expertise."

This was it, he thought, feeling a sudden trickle of sweat run down his chest. He was putting The Plan into motion. And it would work. It *had* to work.

"My expertise?" Maggie said, cocking her head slightly to one side. "About what?"

"Weddings. I am responsible for planning a wedding, every detail, beginning to end. No expense spared."

Dear heaven, no, Maggie thought, feeling the color drain from her face. Luke St. John was getting married. How could he do such a thing? He hadn't even brought a date to his brother's wedding, for crying out loud. And crying out loud was what she was about to do, because she could feel the tears stinging at the back of her eyes and...

"Are you all right?" Luke said, frowning. "You're very pale all of a sudden. Why don't we sit down on this nice love seat you have?"

"*I'll* sit on the love seat," she said, shooting him a dark look, "and *you* sit on that easy chair."

Luke raised both hands palms out. "No problem. Whatever makes you comfortable."

Once seated, Maggie directed her attention to an invisible piece of lint on one of her knees.

"I must say, Luke," she said, wishing her voice sounded steadier than the quivering little noise she was hearing, "that I'm surprised by your announcement. I mean, you didn't have a…a companion with you at Ginger and Robert's wedding or…

"What did you do? Put all your women's names in a hat, pull one out and decide to marry her because your brother is obviously so happy, so what the heck, why not?" She paused. "Sorry. That was rude. Very rude." She cleared her throat. "So. You wish to hire me—Roses and Wishes—to coordinate your wedding. I appreciate your confidence. It is a bit unusual that you're tending to this and not your bride-to-be, as it's traditional that the woman… Forget that. To each his own. How many people are you going to invite?"

Luke propped one ankle on his other knee and smiled pleasantly. "A lot."

"Could you be a tad more specific?"

"Not at the moment. Just go with a lot for now."

"And when do you plan to have this life-changing event?" Maggie said, looking over at him.

"The sooner the better," he said. "But I'm not exactly sure at this point in time."

"I see." Maggie frowned. "No, I don't. Call me stupid, but this isn't making one bit of sense. You want me to coordinate a wedding for a lot, number unknown, of guests, and it's to be held the sooner the better, but you don't have a clue as to when."

Luke nodded. "That's it in a nutshell."

A rather hysterical giggle escaped from Maggie's lips. "Do you know anything for certain? Like, for example, who the bride is?"

"Oh, yes, ma'am," he said. "That is etched in stone."

"How nice," she said miserably. "What I mean is… I'm not sure what I mean. This is very confusing."

"It is?" Luke said, an expression of pure innocence on his face. "I need a wedding planned, you're a wedding planner—coordinator, whatever." He shrugged. "Seems to me I've come to the right place, especially after seeing what a dynamite job you did for Ginger and Robert."

"But Ginger knew what she wanted and when she wanted it," Maggie said, throwing up her hands. "Well, sort of. She did change her mind about a ton of things, but generally speaking, she knew. You know—three hundred, give or take, guests, a summer wedding, seven bridesmaids, yogurt-covered almonds in the nut cups, details like that."

"Oh," Luke said, nodding. "Well, I don't know any of that stuff. Except forget the almonds. I don't like almonds, yogurt-covered or otherwise."

"Oh, well, with that data I'm ready to roll," Maggie said, throwing up her hands again. "No almonds in the nut cups." She shook her head. "This is insane."

"Tell me this, Maggie," Luke said, leaning toward her. "How long does it take to put on a production like Ginger and Robert's shindig?"

"At least six months," she said, "and that's going full speed ahead."

"Really? That long? Grim, very grim. Well, if that's the best you can do... Okay, let's aim for a Christmas wedding. How's that?"

Sure, Maggie thought, feeling the threat of tears again. Merry Christmas to Maggie Jenkins. She could watch Luke St. John get married. Hooray.

Darn it, what difference did it make? Why was she falling apart because Luke suddenly realized he was in love with one of the high-society women he dated and wanted to get married and live happily ever after? It had nothing to do with her beyond being a real coup for Roses and Wishes.

So why did she feel so sad?

Why did she want to crawl into bed and cry for a week?

Forget it, just forget it. She wasn't talking to herself about this anymore because she was being absolutely, positively ridiculous.

"Maggie?" Luke said. "Does that work for you? A Christmas wedding?"

"Yes," she said softly as she looked at a spot in space a couple of inches above Luke's head. "A Christmas wedding will be just fine, very beautiful and...special. Definitely a Christmas to remember forever."

Five

Luke nodded and rubbed his hands together. "Actually this schedule will work out perfectly. A holiday wedding. That's really romantic, don't you think?"

"What? Uh, yes, very romantic," Maggie said with a rather wistful sigh as she shifted her gaze to the opposite wall. "It's a magical time of year as it is. And to be getting married then, too? Goodness, that's over the top or however you want to put it."

"Yep." Luke paused and looked at Maggie intently. "I'll tell…*them*…the good news."

Maggie snapped her head around to stare at Luke. "Them? Them who?" She paused. "You mean the families?"

"Nooo," Luke said slowly. "I was referring to the bride and groom."

"Pardon me?" she said, obviously confused.

"Oh," Luke said, snapping his fingers, "I didn't make myself clear on this at all, did I? I do apologize, Maggie. The wedding we're discussing is for my cousin and his fiancée."

"What?" Maggie blinked. "You mean *you're* not… What?"

"Let me start at the top," Luke said, lacing his fingers on his chest. "My cousin…Clyde…"

Jeez, what a name, he thought, inwardly groaning. He should have given thought to the identity of these people before he got here. The bride, the bride. What was the bride's name?

He looked frantically around the room, his gaze falling on the cover of a thick photograph album imprinted with the words *Precious Memories* in gold.

"…and the love of his life…Precious," he went on, "are in London working for the State Department."

"Clyde and Precious?" Maggie said, raising her eyebrows.

"Yep, good ol' cousin Clyde. Anyway, they decided they'd best get married here in Phoenix to keep the families from murdering them. However, they agreed to stay on in their positions as long as possible to train their replacements before returning to the States.

"They did stipulate to their boss, though, that they definitely wanted to be back home for the holidays. So, you see, a wedding at that time of year keeps everybody happy. Are you happy, Maggie?"

"I'm ecstatic," she said, smiling. Because Luke wasn't getting married. He wasn't. Thank goodness, because… Because why? She didn't know, but there was no denying that the dark cloud that had settled over her was gone, poof, just disappeared, because Luke wasn't talking about *his* wedding. "Ecstatic because… Yes, because this is wonderful news for…for Roses and Wishes."

"Of course," Luke said, nodding. "Now let me make something very clear. Precious is a rather unusual young woman. She'd much prefer to just go to City Hall in her jeans and marry her beloved Clyde, but the mothers would freak and Clyde and Precious would never hear the end of it.

"So when I spoke with them on the phone yesterday I suggested that they hire you to arrange the whole she-bang and all they have to do is show up. They're thrilled. Precious said she'd go along with any decisions you make. Clyde? Hey, guys don't care about this kind of stuff. It's a woman thing."

"You mean I get to plan the whole wedding, make it the way I want it to be and… What about the mothers? The mothers will never let me do that. They'll want to step in and put this production together."

"No way," Luke said. "They're as different as day and night, those mothers. My aunt and Precious's mom together are a war waiting to happen. They're not going to know a thing about it.

"They'll get an invitation in the mail, just like every-one else who is invited. They'll pout for a while, I sup-pose, but then they'll jump right into fast-forward and start thinking about becoming grandmothers, and all will be well."

"This is crazy," Maggie said, shaking her head.

"No, this is exactly the way it should be done." Luke leaned forward, only inches from Maggie as he looked directly into her eyes. "You pretend this is *your* dream wedding, Maggie. Make the decisions based on what *you* would want if *you* were getting married."

"Oh…my…gracious," Maggie whispered.

"The thing is, Clyde and Precious feel they'd better be kept up to date on what's what, you know what I mean? Just in case the moms quiz them later on why they decided on something. For example, if you have them get married in a hot-air balloon, they want to be prepared with a solid story about how they have this thing for hot-air balloons. Get it?"

"I…"

"Therefore, I'll be sticking pretty close to you through this whole endeavor so I have all the details straight to pass along to them as we go. My father will take up the slack for me at the office to free up some of my time because Clyde is his favorite nephew. My dad is semiretired, but for this occasion he's willing to put in extra hours.

"So I'd say that about covers it. Remember, no ex-pense spared. Oh, and Precious is about your size, so there shouldn't be any problem about your picking out her wedding dress—if you want a traditional wedding dress. That's up to you. Any questions?"

"I-I'm stunned," Maggie said, shaking her head. "I'm having difficulty comprehending all this because it's so… I can't even think of a word to describe it."

Try *brilliant,* Luke thought smugly. The Plan was nothing short of brilliant. Maggie would produce the wedding of *her* dreams. He had set it up perfectly to be able to stick close to her through the whole thing and he'd be chipping away at those walls of hers little by little, brick by emotional brick.

She would come to love him, just as he loved her. God, she just had to fall in love with him, want to marry him and spend the rest of her life by his side. *Ah, please, Maggie.*

"Will you do it?" Luke said. "I mean, take on this project?"

"Well, yes, of course I will. Yes."

"Great. That's even more than great. Thank you, Maggie, from the bottom of my heart. I'm really grateful. That is, Clyde and Precious will be very grateful to you for doing this." Luke paused. "I realize that you don't wish to ever marry, but that doesn't mean you haven't thought about the kind of wedding you'd like to have if you intended to marry, even though you don't…intend to marry. Right? Did that make sense?"

"I think so," Maggie said, frowning slightly. "Yes, I understand what you said. And I suppose I do wonder about how I would do things each time I coordinate a wedding. It's human nature, you know what I mean?

"For example, when Ginger finally settled on pale yellow as one of her colors, I couldn't help feeling that with so many blond bridesmaids a deeper shade would have been more striking. Of course, I didn't say that to Ginger, but I *was* thinking it."

"There you go," Luke said, nodding. "That's exactly what I was referring to. Have you ever put together a holiday wedding before?"

"No."

"Then you won't be influenced by a previous bride's choices. The decisions will be exclusively yours." Luke beamed. "Won't that be fun?"

"I…"

"You're not scheduled to do another wedding right away, are you?" Luke said. "You're free to concentrate totally on Clyde and Precious's do?"

"Their wedding will have Roses and Wishes' undivided attention," Maggie said, smiling.

"Great." Luke frowned. "Mmm. The church. Which one would you pick?"

"Me? Well, I happen to be Episcopalian, but—"

"Terrific. You can book the same church that Ginger and Robert had. That will suit Clyde and Precious just fine."

"Well, sure. Okay. Goodness, my head is spinning. This is rather overwhelming because it's so…strange. What about bridesmaids? The dresses have to be custom-fitted, you know."

Oops, Luke thought. Quick, St. John, come up with a solution to that.

"Well," he said slowly. "Who would you choose as your attendants?"

"Me? My sister and my best friend."

"That's all? Just two?"

Maggie laughed. "Not everyone has seven bridesmaids like Ginger, Luke."

"True," he said. "Two. I'll pass that on to Precious. Why don't you find out what size dresses your two choices wear, and the seamstress or whatever you call her can adjust to the size of Precious's bridesmaids."

"Well, it's not perfect, but it might work if there's time enough to nip and tuck before the actual wedding—provided, of course, that everyone is at least close to matching in size. My sister Janet wears a twelve. My best friend Patty is a ten."

"And you?"

"Me? I wear a size eight."

"Got it. I'll double-check all three of those numbers with Precious." Luke paused. "There. Problem solved. We're a good team, Maggie Jenkins." Luke looked directly into Maggie's big brown eyes. "A very good team. You. Me. Together."

"Together," Maggie whispered as she stared into Luke's mesmerizing eyes.

She was about to start planning her fantasy wedding, Maggie mused dreamily. The one she would never have but had thought about so very much. And Luke St. John would be beside her every step of the way, as though he was the groom and she was the bride and... This was totally bizarre.

And very, very dangerous.

She had to keep herself grounded in reality through the months ahead, not get emotionally caught up in what she and Luke were doing. It was an unusual project assigned to Roses and Wishes, that's all.

The bride was Precious, the groom was Clyde. She must remember that at all times. And keeping her head and heart straight would be a lot easier if she quit gazing into those compelling eyes of Luke's.

"Well," Maggie said much too loudly and causing Luke to jerk at her sudden outburst, "this has certainly been an interesting meeting." She got to her feet. "As the owner of Roses and Wishes, I'd like to sincerely thank you for your confidence in me to coordinate the perfect wedding for Precious and Clyde."

"You're welcome," Luke said, rising. "Just out of curiosity, what will you do first?"

"Select the colors. There are so many things—details, details, details—that have to tie into them that it's important they are chosen early on." Maggie laughed. "The way Ginger kept changing her mind about her colors was nerve-racking, to say the least."

"You won't have to worry about that type of thing this time, will you?" Luke said, smiling. "You're planning *your* wedding—so to speak."

"Well, yes, so to speak. But not really. Well, sort of, because whatever I decide is how it will be. But then again… Never mind. It's going to take a while to adjust to such a once-in-a-lifetime endeavor."

"That's what weddings should be, don't you think?"

Luke said quietly. "A once-in-a-lifetime, forever-and-ever event for the bride and groom?"

"Of course." Maggie sighed. "But in today's society the forever-and-ever part doesn't mean much to some couples."

"There hasn't been a divorce in our family," Luke said, "for as far back as anyone can remember."

Maggie's eyes widened. "You're kidding. That's amazing."

"Not really," Luke said, shaking his head. "I believe that St. Johns are just very good at listening to their hearts, knowing what is right and real and falling in love with someone who is on the same wavelength. My dad fell in love with my mother when they were in the seventh grade. I kid you not, it's true."

"Awesome," Maggie said. "That's a rather dopey word to use, but it fits. Seventh grade? And there hasn't been even one divorce in your family history? Totally awesome. Almost unbelievable. You don't suppose some of those couples stayed together even though they were miserable because they didn't want to be the first to break that magical spell, do you?"

"Nope," Luke said. "No way. A stranger seeing any of my family with their partners would be able to tell that they're deeply in love. Ginger and Robert will grow old together and be just as happy as they were at their wedding. So will…Precious and Clyde. Yeah, so will Precious and Clyde."

"That's so beautiful," Maggie said wistfully.

"What about *your* family, Maggie?"

She frowned. "We're…" She mumbled something that wasn't quite clear.

"Pardon me?" Luke said, frowning.

"Never mind," she said quickly. "Well, I have my work cut out for me, don't I? And the first order of business is choosing colors for a Christmas wedding."

"I'll leave you to get started on the plans," Luke said, "but I'll be in touch very soon. Goodbye for now, Maggie, and thank you."

"Oh, I thank you, Luke. Goodbye."

As Luke closed the door behind him, Maggie sank onto the love seat and drew a steadying breath as she continued to digest all that had just happened. Then she shifted her gaze to the center of the table that held the albums.

It had been her plan when she'd opened Roses and Wishes, she thought, to always have a vase of roses, her very favorite flower, right there in that spot. She soon realized, however, that the budget would not allow for such an extravagance.

Roses. She would carry… No, no, *Precious* would carry a bouquet of red roses with baby's breath and Christmas greenery all tied together with one red and one white satin ribbon.

She'd named her fledgling business Roses and Wishes because it held a secret meaning for her. Her wishes were simple but not hers to have. A husband, children, a home. Life with a man who loved her as much as she loved him.

Roses. She'd be a bride who carried roses down the

aisle and later grew them in the garden behind the home she shared with her family.

Roses and Wishes. She'd wanted that name where she could see it, her attempt to find fulfillment in helping brides make their wishes come true. Well, this time she got to go one step further. She had chosen roses for the bridal bouquet. Gorgeous, fragrant red roses.

Maggie smiled and leaned her head back on the back of the love seat.

The colors must be chosen for this Christmas wedding, she mused. Well, it really wasn't that difficult. Red roses. And the attendants would wear rich forest-green satin dresses with shoes to match. They would carry bouquets of red and white baby carnations.

The taper candles that would be used to light the one signifying a single entity would be white and the center candle would be red.

And her dress? It would be white as freshly fallen snow, simple but elegant, with a train and a frothy veil—a veil that Luke would lift at the proper moment to kiss his bride and…

"No," Maggie said, jumping to her feet. "Stop it right now. Back up and get it right, Maggie Jenkins."

Precious's dress. Precious's veil. Clyde's kiss for his new wife. This was Precious and Clyde's wedding she was coordinating.

"Thank you," she said, dropping back down on the love seat. "That's better. Don't make that mistake again, Ms. Jenkins. Not once in the months ahead while you tend to the details, details, details."

* * *

As Luke maneuvered his SUV through the heavy Phoenix traffic, he made no attempt to curb the wide smile on his face.

He'd done it, he thought, tapping his fingertip on the steering wheel. He'd set his brilliant plan in motion and it had worked, it had actually worked. Maggie was now committed to coordinating a fantastic wedding for his imaginary cousin Clyde and the ever-famous Precious. Man, he really should have given thought to names for the bride and groom before he'd gone to Roses and Wishes. Oh, well.

Back to The Plan. Maggie would create the wedding of her dreams. *Her* dreams. And if everything went as he hoped and prayed, that wedding would actually take place. Maggie Jenkins would marry Luke St. John at some point during the Christmas holidays.

Of course, there was a long way to go before that ceremony happened. Maggie had to fall in love with him, just as he had with her. She was attracted to him, unsettled by him, was feeling something for him already, he was sure of that.

She had to fall in love with him and trust him enough to be willing to allow him to crumble into dust those protective walls she'd constructed around herself, so he could reach out and take her into his arms…forever.

Yeah, he had his tasks cut out for him, but Maggie was worth fighting for and he intended to win. He *had* to win.

Luke frowned as he suddenly recalled Maggie's

strange response when the conversation had centered on all the happy marriages in his family. He'd asked about her family and—what had she said? She'd sort of mumbled a word and he just wasn't sure what it had been. When he'd pressed, she'd quickly changed the subject.

"Damn," Luke said, smacking the steering wheel with the heel of one hand.

Maybe it was an important clue about Maggie's aversion to getting married, to being determined to plan weddings for other people but never for herself.

He'd said…then she'd said… Oh, hell, what had Maggie said?

Six

That evening Maggie and her best friend Patty sat on the floor in Maggie's minuscule living room eating take-out pizza, sipping sodas and going through a tower of bride magazines page by page.

The two had been friends since elementary school and now, at twenty-five years old, neither could imagine dealing with the ups and downs of life without the other's support.

Patty taught first grade at the same school she and Maggie had attended. Patty's parents had been killed in an automobile accident five years before, so now every spare cent she had went toward putting her younger brother through college.

"Look at this," Patty said, tapping one fingertip on a

page of the magazine in front of her. "Tiny Christmas balls nestled in the bridesmaids' bouquets. Do you like that idea?"

Maggie wrinkled her nose. "It's a bit much, I think. I don't want to overdo the Christmas theme." She laughed. "After all, this is a wedding, hon, not an office party."

"True," Patty said, turning the page. "Forget the icky ornaments." She took another bite of pizza and looked at Maggie. "It's so strange to be sitting here doing this, Maggie. I get so caught up in it, I have to keep reminding myself that we're not really planning *your* wedding."

"I know," Maggie said, sighing, "but this is the closest we'll ever get to actually doing that, so enjoy."

"Don't get me started on that subject," Patty said, shaking her head. "The fact that you won't even consider the possibility of falling in love and getting married because—"

"Patty."

"Okay, okay, I'll shut up." Patty paused. "This whole project is weird. Who ever heard of a bride who didn't give a damn about the plans for her own wedding? Are you sure this Precious person is playing with a full deck?"

Maggie shrugged. "Luke said Precious would just as soon get married wearing jeans at a courthouse. This production is to satisfy the mothers. Mothers I don't have to deal with, which is a blessing. This will be the wedding of…well, *my* dreams. Roses and wishes and…

Anyway, I intend to thoroughly go for it because nothing like this will ever happen again. The only person I have to report to is Luke."

"Luke St. John," Patty said wistfully. "I've seen his picture in the newspaper. He is so gorgeous, he's hot! To think that you actually danced with him at his brother's wedding reception." She stared into space. "To be held in the arms of Luke St. John must have been heaven on earth."

"Close, very close," Maggie said, nodding. "He's a marvelous dancer, made me feel like I was floating on a cloud and…" Sudden heat stained her cheeks a pretty pink. "Forget that. Do you think having the bridesmaids wearing green is corny? Maybe I should start over in my mind and not address the Christmas thing at all."

"Oh, no, don't do that," Patty said. "People will expect a festive touch. Besides, it's what you want. Right?"

"Well, yes."

"Then it's settled. Stay with the Christmas theme, but don't go over the top. What did your sister say about all this?"

"Janet said it was nuts," Maggie said, smiling, "but that she'd be delighted to be fitted for a beautiful dress even if she doesn't get to actually wear it anywhere. As a single mom with three kids, she said they don't provide fittings—la-di-da—in the thrift shops where she buys her clothes."

"How funny." Patty laughed, then frowned. "What

was your mom's reaction? She must think Precious has a screw loose."

"She didn't dwell on Precious's mind-set," Maggie said. "Eat that last piece of pizza. I'm stuffed."

"No problem," she said, reaching for the slice. "So what *did* your mom focus on about this crazy situation?"

"She's worried about me, Patty," Maggie said quietly. "She's afraid that I'll spend all these weeks planning my dream wedding and then fall apart when I have to face the reality of it being for someone else."

She sighed. "In fact, she's concerned about me being a wedding coordinator in the first place. She thinks it was a stupid business for me to start considering I'll never have a wedding of my own. She's afraid I'll spend my life being so sad because I'll be constantly reminded that... Oh, you know."

"What I know," Patty said, shaking her head, "is you won't budge on the subject of your not getting married, and your mom and Janet—and even your brother, for all I know—are on the same wavelength about it. I'm totally outnumbered when it comes to convincing you otherwise."

"So don't try. Heavens, look at this picture in this magazine. The bridal bouquet has green and red candles in it and they're lit, for heaven's sake."

"It boggles the mind," Patty said, laughing. "Talk about being hot. Which brings me back to the subject of Luke St. John. You said he's really nice, not snooty even though he's as rich as Midas?"

"Yes." Maggie nodded. "He's very, very nice."

"And he has a sense of humor and a good relation-ship with his family and dances like a dream and looks as good in jeans as he does in a tux and… Maggie, you'd better be very careful during the weeks ahead. You're going to be seeing a lot of Luke because of this wedding. Luke sounds like he's capable of smashing hearts to smithereens. I don't want one of those hearts to be yours."

"Believe me, I don't either," Maggie said. "I'm very aware of Luke's…attributes, shall we say. But fear not, because I'm on red alert, the walls are up, the door is barred. There's not a chance on earth that I'll fall head over heels in love with Mr. Luke St. John. Nope. That isn't going to happen."

"And now," Luke said, "I have to make certain that Maggie falls head over heels in love with me."

Mason St. John chuckled. "That's definitely top of the list considering you want to marry Maggie Jenkins, have a slew of little St. Johns, then grow old and creaky together."

"Right," Luke said, then cut a chunk out of the enor-mous steak on the plate in front of him.

Father and son were dining at Mason's club, which he had yet to convince Luke to join. Luke had made it clear several years before that he'd consider a member-ship once the private establishment got with the program and allowed women to join.

"I must say, Luke," Mason said after consuming sev-eral forkfuls of succulent roast beef, "that I'm impressed with this plan you've come up with. It's brilliant. And I'm more than happy to cover things for you at the office as this scheme unfolds."

"I appreciate that, Dad. Remember, not a word of this to Mom. She couldn't keep a secret if her life depended on it, plus she'd be calling me constantly with advice about how to win Maggie's heart."

"That she would, bless her," Mason said, smiling. "I just wish you'd… Oh, Lord." His shoulders started shaking with laughter as he pressed his napkin to his lips.

Luke frowned. "Don't go there. I thought you were going to get us kicked out of here earlier because you were laughing so loud. Just don't think about it."

"I'm trying not to, but…Clyde and Precious?"

"I forgot to think of names for my fictitious bride and groom before I went to see Maggie. I was under pressure. I realize they're grim but…" Luke shrugged.

"What's Clyde's last name?" Mason said. "Is he a St. John? Clyde St. John." He started laughing again. "I can't handle that."

"Okay, okay. Knock it off. All right, let's see. Clyde's mother is your sister and she married… Who did she marry?"

"John Smith."

"That's really original," Luke said, rolling his eyes heavenward. "All right. Whatever. Clyde Smith is going to marry Precious, um…Peterson."

"Precious Peterson?" Mason said with a hoot of merriment that drew several frowns from other diners. "Sorry. So this extravaganza is the Peterson-Smith wedding. Got it. Having it during the Christmas holidays is a nice touch. Very romantic." He took a sip of wine. "What happens next?"

"I wait for Maggie to make some decisions and contact me so I can pass on the data to Precious and Clyde. Well, Precious at least. Clyde will go along with things just like any other groom would. Your favorite nephew is a laid-back, go-with-the-flow guy."

"Ah," Mason said, nodding.

"I have to concentrate on Maggie, chip away at those barriers of hers, get her to allow herself to fall in love with me."

"Ah."

"There's a special…something…already happening between Maggie and me, Dad, I know there is. It's rare, important, real. You should have seen her face when she thought I wanted her to plan my wedding to some other woman. She tried to hide it, but she was upset, I know she was. When I finally told her that it was cousin Clyde's wedding, she just lit up. She feels something for me, she cares. I have to nurture that, make it grow, get her to trust me, come to love me as I love her, then agree to be my wife for all time."

"Ah."

Luke glared at his father. "Can't you say anything else besides 'ah'? A little advice would be helpful here, you know."

Mason set his fork and knife on the edge of his plate, folded his arms over his chest and looked at his son.

"Love is very complicated," Mason said quietly. "But

at the same time it's very simple." He shook his head. "It's hard to explain. You construct a sturdy foundation together and build on that as the years go by. One of the bricks in that foundation, Luke, is honesty. Your plan to win Maggie's heart is based on duplicity."

"But—"

"I know, I know," Mason said, raising one hand. "You're convinced that if you try to court Maggie, she'll refuse to see you, won't run the risk of finding herself in a serious relationship. I understand the need for this plan you've come up with. The thing is, will Maggie understand when she knows the truth? Women don't like to be duped. This whole thing could backfire on you."

"You're thoroughly depressing me," Luke said, leaning back in his chair.

"Well, in all fairness, I don't see where you have any choice but to do it this way," Mason continued. "The usual wine-and-dine scenario is not going to work with your young lady, so you've been forced to come up with an alternative approach. A very clever one, I might add."

He chuckled. "Except for the names! I want you to be happy, Luke. I hope your dream for a life with Maggie becomes your reality, I really do."

"Thanks, Dad. This plan will work. It has to. A future without Maggie is not something I'm willing to accept. I'm going to win the heart, the love, of Maggie Jenkins."

At one o'clock the next afternoon Maggie entered a popular downtown restaurant and immediately scooted into the ladies' room. She stood in front of the long mirror above the half dozen sinks and glared at her reflection.

She was nervous, she thought, and furious at herself because she was. Luke had called her early that morning and asked if it would be too much trouble for her to meet him for lunch.

He was waiting for a scheduled long-distance call regarding a case he was about to wrap up and couldn't leave the office to come to Roses and Wishes. The afternoon was jam-packed with bringing his father up to date on Luke's ongoing cases.

He'd spoken with Clyde and Precious, Luke had told her, and wanted to pass on the information he had and blah, blah, blah.

"Oh, sure," Maggie said, still glowering at her image. "Lunch? *Do* lunch? No problem."

Right, she thought dismally. No problem, except for the fact that she was a nervous wreck. That was so dumb. Dumber than dumb. Luke was a client of hers, of Roses and Wishes, nothing more. They were working together to coordinate the wedding of his cousin Clyde and the bride-to-be Precious. The end.

The really humiliating part was that she knew why she was shaky about seeing Luke. Last night she'd had the most sensuous dream imaginable about the two of them. Goodness. She'd wakened in the night all…all hot and bothered, and try as she may she couldn't erase the pictures in her mind of a naked Luke reaching for a naked her, taking her into his naked arms and…

"Stop it." Maggie spun around and stomped out of the ladies' room. "You are just so ridiculous."

She gave her name to the hostess and was immediately shown to a table at the far end of the large room. Luke stood as he saw her coming.

Thank the Lord, Maggie thought giddily, he has his clothes on. Nice suit. Very lawyer-looking suit. Did she look frumpy in white slacks and a flowered blouse? She should have worn a skirt or dress but hadn't wanted to arrive there with naked legs and… Oh, God, she was totally losing it.

"Hello, Maggie," Luke said, smiling, when she reached the table. "It's nice to see you."

Maggie's eyes widened. "See me?" She shook her head slightly and slid onto her chair. "Yes, of course, nice to see me. It's nice to…see you, too, Luke. I really like that suit you're wearing. Excellent suit. I'm *so* glad you're wearing that suit."

Luke frowned. "Are you all right?"

"What? Oh, yes, of course, I am." Maggie busied herself spreading the linen napkin on her lap. "I just didn't sleep very well last night and—" she looked at Luke again "—I'm hungry."

"Well, we can fix that easily enough." Luke signaled to the waitress. "Order whatever you'd like."

The waitress appeared at the table. Maggie ordered the first thing she saw on the menu and told herself to get a grip. Luke asked for a steak sandwich and home fries.

"I really appreciate your coming all the way downtown," Luke said as the waitress hurried off.

"Not a problem," Maggie said. "Did you receive the call you were waiting for?"

"Call? Oh. Yes. Right on schedule." Luke took a sip of water.

Man, I'm crummy at this cloak-and-dagger stuff, he thought. He'd nearly forgotten about his imaginary "appointment" with the telephone. He'd decided to push his luck and attempt to meet with Maggie somewhere other than at Roses and Wishes. The long-distance call had been a great idea, but he'd blow it big-time if he didn't remember what he'd told her.

"What was it you wanted to discuss with me about your conversation with Precious and Clyde?" Maggie said.

"Why don't we enjoy our lunch first, then get into all that after we eat," he said, smiling.

"But you said you have a very busy afternoon," Maggie said.

"Yes, so I do," Luke said, frowning. *Really* crummy at this. "All right. Precious and Clyde will be arriving in Phoenix in the middle of December, so the holiday wedding is great. Right on the money."

Maggie smiled. "Good. I've chosen the flowers and the color of the bridesmaids' dresses with a Christmas theme in mind. Did you ask Precious about her dress size and those of her friends?"

"They're exactly the same as yours, your sister's and your best friend's."

"Isn't that something?" Maggie said. "Then it will just be a matter of nip and tuck."

"Indeed."

Their lunch arrived and Maggie was amazed to find that she'd ordered grilled salmon and steamed vegetables, which weren't exactly her favorite foods but would do in a pinch.

"Now then," Luke said after they'd taken the edge off their appetites. "Clyde and Precious said that they will have just made that long flight from London a couple of weeks before the wedding. They'd prefer to not have to pack their suitcases again and go winging off on a honeymoon right away, which makes sense."

Maggie cocked her head slightly to one side. "They don't want a honeymoon?"

Get this right, fumble-brain, Luke ordered himself. He wanted to plan that oh-so-important honeymoon trip with Maggie when she was engaged to marry him. It was something that they should do together for real, not as part of this charade.

"They'll have a trip later on," he said, narrowing his eyes in concentration. "So what they want is a honeymoon suite here in Phoenix for a few days following the wedding."

Maggie nodded slowly. "I understand. Well, I really don't know what's available because my couples have always left town after the reception. I'll visit some honeymoon suites in the posh hotels and report back to you."

"I thought I'd do that investigating with you," Luke said. "I'll have the time once I bring my father up to speed on my cases at the office, and as the old saying goes, two heads are better than one. You don't mind if I tag along, do you?"

A teenage boy appeared at the table at that moment to refill their water glasses, and Maggie fought the urge to jump up and hug him for giving her a moment to gather her racing thoughts before answering Luke's question.

Visit honeymoon suites with Luke St. John? she mentally repeated. *Honeymoon* suites, where people did what she and Luke had been about to do in her wanton dream? That was not a good idea at all. No, it was a bad plan. Bad, bad. And dumb and dangerous and—

"Maggie?"

But what reasonable excuse could she dish out to Luke as to why he shouldn't come along on the honeymoon-suite tour? she asked herself frantically. Sorry, Mr. You Melt My Bones, but there's a very good chance I might tear your clothes off in one of those romantic suites and get you naked as a jaybird, just like in my dream? Yeah, right, she'd just lay that on him. Not.

"Maggie, are you with me here?" Luke said, leaning slightly toward her.

"What?" she said. "Oh, yes, sure thing, Luke. You can come along to look at the accommodations if you like. But doesn't that sound just a tad boring to you?"

"Nooo," Luke said slowly, then smiled. "Not at all. Not even close."

Maggie narrowed her eyes. "Why not?"

Because he'd be envisioning the two of them in each of those suites, newly married, husband and wife, about to begin their honeymoon here in Phoenix before leaving on their dream trip. No, that didn't sound the least bit boring.

"Why not?" he said. Quick, St. John. Come up with something reasonable. "Because, like you, I've never seen a honeymoon suite in any of the ritzy hotels in town. It will be informative, interesting. Anytime a person has an opportunity to experience something new they should jump at the chance. It's good for the gray matter." He tapped his temple with a fingertip. "Know what I mean?"

"Not really," Maggie said, frowning, "but I'll take your word for it." She paused. "I think it would be best if I made actual appointments for our inspections. I'll get back to you on that."

"Fine. And you said you'd decided on the flowers for the wedding. What did you choose? No, wait, let me guess." Luke drummed the fingers of one hand on the table. "Hmm. You named your business Roses and Wishes. I'm betting that the bridal bouquet is roses, red for the holiday theme with some kind of Christmassy greens and those fluffy things that look sort of like snow."

"Baby's breath," Maggie said hardly above a whisper as she stared at Luke.

"Yeah, that's what it's called. How close did I come to being right?"

"That's exactly what I chose, but…but how did you know?"

Luke reached across the table and covered one of Maggie's hands with one of his. He gazed directly into her big brown eyes and when he spoke again his voice was slightly raspy and very, very…male. Maggie shivered.

"I knew because you're Maggie," he said. My Maggie. Forever.

"Oh," she said. Get your hand back, Maggie Jenkins. The heat—the heat from Luke's hand was traveling up her arm and across her breasts that were suddenly achy and… Get your dumb hand back. Sometime within the next hour. "Huh? You knew what flowers I'd pick right down to the baby's breath because I'm Maggie? I don't think that makes sense."

"It does to me," he said, tightening his grip slightly on her hand. "Yes, ma'am, it certainly does."

"Would you care for some dessert today?"

Maggie snatched her hand from beneath Luke's and looked up at the waitress.

"Dessert," she said, hearing the thread of breathlessness in her voice. "Dessert is a good thing. Yes, it certainly is, but I'm much too full to eat another bite of anything so…no, thank you."

Bingo, Luke thought. Maggie was flustered and that was dynamite. The heat that had rocketed throughout his body as he'd held her hand had traveled through her, too, he was certain of it. Her cheeks were flushed a delicate pink and her voice was trembling slightly. Fantastic.

"And you, sir?" the waitress said. "We have a scrumptious Black Forest cake today."

"A man certainly can't pass up Black Forest cake," Luke said. "Why don't you bring me a slice. With two forks, just in case the lady changes her mind and decides to share it with me."

"You bet," the waitress said. "I'll be right back."

A busboy cleared their dishes, and moments later the

waitress set an enormous slice of cake in the center of the table and placed a fork in front of Maggie, then Luke.

"Enjoy," the woman said, then zoomed away.

"Help yourself, Maggie," Luke said. "Look at that creation. Chocolate cake with whipped cream between the layers and all those cherries in sauce dribbling down the sides like a delicious waterfall. How can you resist a treat like this?"

What she wanted to know, Maggie thought miserably, was how could Luke make the description of a slab of cake sound like the most seductive thing she had ever heard in her entire life? The man just didn't quit.

"Well, maybe just one bite," she said, picking up the fork. She filled her fork, making sure it included one of the fat, gooey cherries. "Mmm."

"Oops," Luke said, reaching for a napkin. "You've got a dab of cherry sauce. I'll get it for you."

He leaned across the table and gently, so gently, dabbed at the spot of sauce, then shifted his eyes to look directly into Maggie's.

Her bones were dissolving, Maggie thought, unable to tear her gaze from Luke's. There was nothing sensuous about having her sloppy eating mopped up like a toddler in a high chair, darn it, but… Oh, yes, there was.

There was something so intimate about Luke tenderly stroking that napkin by her lips as though it was the most important thing he had ever done. She was going to slide off that chair and turn into a puddle on the floor.

"All better," he said, his voice husky. "Good cake?"

"Mmm," Maggie said dreamily. "The best cake I've ever…really yummy."

"Well, it's sure calling my name."

Maggie watched with rapt attention as Luke leveled a serving onto his fork, lifted it to his mouth, then closed his lips—those, oh-so-kissable lips—over the treat, then slowly pulled the fork free.

"Mmm," he said, closing his eyes as he savored the taste.

She couldn't handle this, Maggie thought frantically. She was going up in flames, burning inside with a heat like nothing she had ever experienced before.

Luke set the fork on the table and reached over to take both of Maggie's hands in his.

"Ah, Maggie," he said, "what are you doing to me? What is this thing that spins out of control between us?" It's love, Maggie Jenkins. True and forever love. "You feel it, I know you do."

"No, I don't," she said, trying to pull her hands free. Luke tightened his hold. "Well, yes, I do, but it's just physical attraction between two people who are…physically attracted to each other. I would call it lust, but that's kind of a tacky word. It's certainly nothing to be pursued or acted upon or… May I have my hands back now, please, Luke?"

"In a minute. So you admit that you're physically attracted to me?"

"Well…yes."

"You desire me? Do you, Maggie? Lust is a tacky word. Desire is something else entirely."

"Semantics."

"No, Maggie, emotions. Emotions are intertwined with desire. I truly believe that. The tricky part is to know what those emotions are, what they mean, unwrap them layer by layer like a wondrous gift."

"That's very poetic," Maggie said softly.

"I'm not attempting to be poetic. I'm just expressing how I feel. I want to know what that gift holds for us. Don't you?"

Maggie pulled her hands free and shook her head. "No, I can't."

"Why not?"

"Luke, you just don't understand."

"Then explain it to me. Please, Maggie. What are you afraid of? Why are you so determined to never marry, to plan weddings for so many brides but never one for yourself? Why have you built those tall, strong walls around your heart? There's something happening between us that could be very important, but whenever I bring it up you act like you're about to bolt. Talk to me. Please."

Maggie clutched her hands tightly in her lap and stared at them for a long, mind-searching moment. She nodded slowly, then met Luke's gaze again.

"All right," she said, her voice trembling slightly. "Perhaps I *should* tell you the truth about me, why none of the weddings I coordinate will ever be mine, why I'll never be a bride."

Luke's heart thudded so wildly he could hear the echo of it in his ears.

"It goes back as many generations as my family has been able to track, without skipping even one," Maggie continued. "There's no escaping it, no reason to believe it won't continue on and on into infinity." She sighed. "Oh, people try to beat the odds—my mother, sister, my brother—but it's foolish to do that because it's hopeless."

"My God, Maggie," Luke said, feeling the color drain from his face. "Is it a disease that can't be cured?"

"Well, I don't know if I'd call it a disease exactly, but there is definitely no cure for it. It happens over and over and over again. It's harsh and heartbreaking and I don't intend to allow it to happen to me. I will never, ever get married."

"What—" Luke cleared his throat "—what is it? Does it have an official name?"

"Yes, it definitely has a name," she said. "We're all doomed. It would be so foolish to believe I would be spared, because it wouldn't happen, Luke. My mother, sister, brother all thought they could escape from it, but…" She shook her head.

"What is it?" he said, leaning toward her. "You're ripping me up here, Maggie. *What is it?*"

Maggie took a shuddering breath, then blinked against sudden and unwelcome tears.

"It's…" she said, a sob catching in her throat. "It's the Jenkins Jinx."

Seven

It took several mental beats for Luke to really compute what Maggie had just said. He opened his mouth to reply, then shut it again as he replayed the words once more in his head.

The Jenkins Jinx? he thought incredulously. Did he have a clue as to what Maggie was talking about? No, he did not. A jinx of some kind that had a bearing on Maggie's negative attitude to marriage? Did people really believe in jinxes these days? A jinx that did what? Oh, man, this was nuts.

It would certainly clear things up if Maggie would suddenly laugh and tell him she was just kidding, that what she had said was a silly joke, then tell him the real reason she didn't intend to ever be the bride in one of her beautifully coordinated weddings.

But the fact that at the moment Maggie was a study in misery and that tears were shimmering in her big brown eyes told him that she was dead serious about the Jenkins Jinx.

"Maggie," Luke said finally, "we need to talk about this...this Jenkins Jinx thing, but you're obviously upset, so let's get out of here." He signaled to the waitress for the check. "I'll take you home, back to Roses and Wishes, and we'll discuss this there. Okay?"

"You said you had a very busy afternoon at work," Maggie said, then sniffled and dabbed her nose with the napkin.

"That's what cell phones are for," he said. "So bosses can call efficient secretaries and have them reschedule whatever is on the calendar. My father won't mind getting the word that he's free to go golfing."

"But I drove my van here so you can't take me home."

"I'll bring you back later for your van or you can drive yourself if you feel you're up to it," he said. "We're not postponing this discussion, Maggie."

Maggie sighed in defeat. "I had a feeling you'd say that. I'll drive myself. Meet me at Roses and Wishes." She got to her feet and hurried away.

Luke rose, dropped several bills onto the table, then accepted the check from the waitress.

"Is everything all right, sir?" the woman said.

"Ask me later," Luke said absently, "because right now I really don't know."

* * *

Maggie drove blindly to Roses and Wishes, wishing she could turn back the clock to before her momentous announcement about the Jenkins Jinx.

No, she thought with yet another sad-sounding sigh, there was no point in pretending the Jenkins Jinx didn't exist. Luke was pressing her to explore, actually embrace, the strange whatever-it-was that was happening between them, and it wasn't fair to keep the jinx a secret.

She dashed an errant tear from her cheek.

It just would have been nice, she mused wistfully, to have had more time with Luke, enjoy his company, allow herself to feel so feminine and desirable, before revealing the god-awful truth.

Once she explained it all to Luke, it would hover between them like a palpable entity, a living thing that would make him uncomfortable because she was a weird person from a very weird family.

"I'm so sad," Maggie said as she parked in front of Roses and Wishes. "So very, very sad."

She waited in the van until Luke arrived, then they entered the house together. Maggie left the Closed sign on the door.

"Let's go upstairs to the living room," she said, sounding extremely weary.

"Whatever you say," he said quietly.

In the tiny living room Maggie sank onto a rocking chair and Luke settled on the sofa, spreading his arms across the top as he looked at Maggie intently. She rocked back and forth for several minutes, staring into space.

"Maggie," Luke said, "you can't pretend I'm not sitting here waiting for you to talk to me."

She shifted her gaze to meet his.

"I know," she said. "It's just that I hate to... Never mind. You have the right to know what I meant by the Jenkins Jinx." She drew a steadying breath. "I told you that it goes back many generations in our family."

Luke nodded, aware that the lunch he'd consumed now felt like a rock in the pit of his stomach.

"We all have had to face the devastating fact," Maggie continued, "that for unknown reasons it is impossible for any of us to live happily ever after with our chosen mate. It just isn't going to happen, no matter what. And that, Luke, is the Jenkins Jinx."

Luke moved his arms forward to rest his elbows on his knees and make a steeple of his fingers.

"I beg your pardon?" he said, frowning.

"You heard me."

"Okay, I heard you, but I can't fathom that you actually believe that a jinx, a spell, whatever, has been cast over your entire family."

"Like a gloomy dark cloud," Maggie said, nodding.

"Maggie, come on, give me a break. Things like that don't really happen. So, yes, some of the couples in your clan got divorced, but—"

"Everyone got divorced."

"Everyone?" Luke said, raising his eyebrows.

"Everyone. We researched our family tree as far back as we could and, yes, everyone."

"That's rather…strange." Luke sank back against the cushions. "Whew."

"That's the Jenkins Jinx," Maggie said. "No one understands why we're plagued by it, what we did to draw this lousy card, but there's no denying the truth of it. Oh, there are those who feel they'll be the one to break the spell, end it for all time, because they're so in love, so sure when they marry that it's forever. Then—bam!—it all falls apart and yet another gleeful divorce attorney has a bill to send.

"My mother was a starry-eyed bride," she said. "My father left us when I was ten. Poof. Gone. My sister has been divorced twice, my brother once. My grandparents, great-grandparents… Oh, I can go even further back than that, I guarantee you. We all agree we're doomed."

"But—"

"Therefore, Luke, I never intend to fall in love and marry. I'm not going to have my dreams shattered and my heart broken. I'm not. So I create fairy-tale-perfect weddings for others to…to satisfy my romantic soul. But I'm beginning to wonder if Roses and Wishes is a dumb thing to be doing because it just emphasizes over and over what I'll never have."

"But you're planning the wedding of *your* dreams for Precious and Clyde," Luke said.

"Yes, and it's probably foolish, but I'm giving it to myself like a gift to cherish before I make a decision about whether I want to continue as a wedding coordinator."

Luke got to his feet and began to pace—as well as

he could in the limited space. He dragged a restless hand through his hair and narrowed his eyes in deep concentration. He finally stopped in front of Maggie's rocking chair, planted his hands on the arms and leaned down, speaking close to her lips as she stared at him in wide-eyed surprise.

"No," he said.

"No…what?" she said, aware, so very aware, that his lips were mere inches from hers.

"No, I won't accept this," he said. "So, okay, your family seems to have had more than your share of divorces, but there is no such thing as an honest-to-goodness jinx, Maggie."

"That's what my sister's second husband said—at first."

"Maggie, you're an intelligent woman," Luke said, his voice rising. "How can you buy into this malarkey?"

"Facts are facts," she said, matching his volume. "We checked as far back as we possibly could, hoping, praying, we'd find even one couple that stayed together on our family tree. There wasn't one. Not one, Luke. The jinx is real and I won't allow myself to think I could be the one to break it, make it disappear, because it's here to stay. That's the way it is and there's nothing I can do about it."

"It's impossible," he said none too quietly. "A jinx is a superstition, a…a… Damn it, this is the most frustrating conversation I've ever had in my entire life."

"Well, excuse me all the way to Sunday," Maggie yelled, "but the truth is the truth."

'Oh? Well, try this truth on for size, lady," Luke hollered.

He released his white-knuckle hold on the arms of the rocking chair, gripped Maggie's shoulders, hauled her to her feet…and kissed her.

Maggie stiffened in shock, but as Luke's kiss gentled and he dropped his hands from her shoulders to wrap his arms around her and bring her close to his body, she nestled against him. Her arms floated upward to encircle his neck, her fingertips inching into his thick ebony hair.

The kiss was hot. It was desire, not lust, with unnamed emotions intertwining with the want and need. The kiss was powerful enough to push aside for that tick of time the existence of the Jenkins Jinx and allow them to savor the taste, the feel, the very essence of each other. The kiss was theirs.

Luke broke away first to draw a much-needed breath but didn't release his hold on Maggie. She gazed up at him, a dreamy expression on her face, her lips moist and slightly parted, beckoning.

"Ah, Maggie," Luke said, his voice gritty with passion. "I want to make love with you so damn much. From the moment I first saw you I… Do you want me, Maggie? Do you want to make love with me?"

"Yes, I do," she whispered. "But—"

"Forget the jinx thing for now. We'll tackle that later…later…yes. All I can concentrate on now is you, me, what we'll share. But, Maggie, I would never take advantage of you, pressure you, attempt to seduce you into doing something you'll regret." He paused. "I guess what I'm saying is, it's your decision."

Oh, Maggie thought foggily. How could she decide when she couldn't even think clearly? Okay, okay, she was getting a grip now, ignoring the fact that she was still being held in Luke's strong arms, still molded to his aroused body, still…thinking. Yes, she was thinking.

And she wanted him.

She wanted to make love with him because she cared for him so very much and he cared for her, she knew he did.

And because when he realized that the Jenkins Jinx was true, he would chalk her up as being a very weird, creepy woman and keep her at a safe distance from him.

And because she intended to give herself this intimate joining with Luke St. John so she'd have a precious memory to make up for all she would never have because of the Jenkins Jinx.

"Maggie?"

"Make love with me, Luke," she said softly, looking directly into his dark eyes. "I won't be sorry. I'll have no regrets, I promise. We have no future together. None. The jinx is real and I've accepted that. Nothing you can say or do will change my mind about it. But now? Right now? I want—I desire you. So, please, make love with me."

With a groan that rumbled from deep in his chest, Luke captured Maggie's mouth once again in a searing kiss. She returned the kiss in total abandon, holding nothing back, giving as much as she was receiving.

Luke lifted his head, then swung Maggie up into his

arms. She pointed in the direction of her bedroom and he carried her there with long, purposeful strides.

He set her on her feet next to the double bed, absently registering that the room was femininity personified, just like Maggie, with a bedspread patterned with pale pink roses and a matching skirt on a small round table that held a clock and a telephone. The curtains were pink and the dresser was white wicker.

Maggie swept back the spread and blankets to reveal sheets with tiny pink rosebuds, then turned to face Luke again.

"I'm very nervous," she said. "I really don't have the kind of experience that I'm certain you're accustomed to and I—"

"Shh," he said, placing one fingertip gently on her lips. "We're going to be wonderful together, Maggie."

And they were.

With sudden confidence that came from a place she couldn't fathom, Maggie nodded, and as Luke shed his clothes, she removed her own. They stood naked before each other, rejoicing in what they saw, what would be theirs, given willingly.

He lifted her into his arms again, settled her in the center of the bed, then followed her down, his mouth melting over hers.

It was ecstasy. They kissed, caressed, discovered each other's mysteries with awe and wonder. Where hands traveled, lips followed, igniting the heat of their desire into leaping flames that threatened to consume them both.

Luke left her only long enough to roll on protection, then returned to her outstretched arms. When they could bear no more, he moved over her and into her with a thrust that filled her and brought a gasp of pure pleasure from her lips.

The rocking rhythm began, then increased in tempo until it was wild and earthy, wondrous, synchronized to perfection as though they had been lovers forever.

They soared. Higher. Closer. Calling to the other, clinging fast, then bursting upon the place they sought only seconds apart.

"Luke!"

"Oh, Maggie. My Maggie."

They drifted slowly back, then Luke mustered his last ounce of energy to move off her and tuck her close to his side, his lips resting lightly on her moist forehead. She rested one hand on the dark curls on his broad chest, feeling his heart settle into a quieter, steady beat.

"Thank you," Luke said quietly.

"And I thank *you*," Maggie whispered, "for the beautiful memories to keep."

Maggie's lashes drifted down and she slept, content, sated, a soft smile on her lips. Luke held her, sifting his fingers through her silky strawberry-blond curls.

God, how he loved this woman, he thought, feeling a foreign ache tighten his throat. She had given of herself so freely, so honestly, to him. *Him.* She cared deeply for him, he knew that, might even be falling in love with him just as he was already deeply in love with her.

He couldn't lose her. No, the mere thought of it was

more than he could bear. He knew the name of the enemy now—the Jenkins Jinx. That he believed it to be crazy, borderline nuts, meant nothing because Maggie was convinced it was true and planned to never marry to protect her heart from being shattered.

The battle lines were drawn. He was literally fighting for his life, his future happiness, his forever. And he would be the victor, for himself, for Maggie, for what they would have together until death parted them and beyond.

He would win. Somehow. He had to.

"I love you, Maggie Jenkins," he whispered, tightening his hold on her. "You are my life. My wife. Mine."

A little over an hour later Maggie stirred and opened her eyes, only to blink against the bright sunlight streaming through the window.

Luke, she thought, as the mist of sleep lifted.

She turned her head on the pillow to see the empty expanse of bed next to her, then heard the sound of the shower running. She stretched leisurely, then pulled the sheet to beneath her chin, clutching it with both hands.

She'd made love with Luke, she thought, and it had been glorious, beyond her wildest fantasies. Did she regret what she had done? Was she sorry? No. Never.

Her life was not like other women's, with dreams of a husband, babies, hearth and home. To have experienced something as wondrous as she just had with a magnificent man like Luke St. John was more than she'd ever expected to receive, to possess as hers, to tuck away in the treasure chest in her heart.

Was this dangerous? she asked herself. Well, no, not if she stayed alert, kept a tight control over her emotions and the truth of her reality front and center. She could handle this. She would have this time with Luke. And when Precious and Clyde were married, that would be the end of Maggie Jenkins and Luke St. John. She knew that, understood that. Yes, she could handle this.

Luke came into the bedroom fully dressed, his hair damp from the shower. He sat on the edge of the bed and smiled at Maggie.

"Have a nice nap?"

"Lovely, thank you," she said, matching his smile.

"You're very pretty when you're sleeping, very peaceful." He paused. "I'd better get going. You'll let me know when you have some appointments to see honeymoon suites at various hotels?"

"Yes, of course. I'll call you."

"Good." He nodded. "Maggie, you don't have any regrets about what happened here, do you?"

"No, no, Luke, not at all. It was wonderful and I... No regrets. We both understand that this is temporary, what we're sharing, because my life is what it is—jinxed. I know you're not quite believing that yet, but it's true, trust me, and I'll never allow myself to think otherwise. That would be so foolish on my part and it isn't going to happen."

"Mmm." Luke frowned. "And no one in the entire history of your family has figured out a way to break the spell, the jinx?"

"No."

"Mmm." Luke stroked his chin thoughtfully. "Would you categorize the jinx as a superstition of sorts?"

"I... Well, not exactly, because it's true."

"But if you had to group it with something," he said, "a jinx would fall into the arena of superstitions for a lack of a better place to put it. Right?"

"I suppose so. I never thought about it like that." Maggie looked at him questioningly. "Why?"

"I'm just trying to be certain that I fully understand the Jenkins Jinx, what it is."

"It's my reality," Maggie said firmly. "Ask any member of my family and they'll verify what I'm saying. It's sad but true."

"Yeah." Luke leaned over and dropped a quick kiss on Maggie's lips. "I'll be waiting to hear from you about viewing the suites. Eager to hear from you. You'll contact me soon?"

"Yes, sir," she said, smiling at him warmly.

Luke drew one thumb lightly over her lips, which she felt to the very tip of her toes, then he got to his feet and left the room.

"'Bye," Maggie whispered, then sighed in delicious contentment.

After a frustrating stop-and-start drive across town in the surging Phoenix traffic Luke entered the plush offices of St. John and St. John, Attorneys at Law.

"Good afternoon, Mr. St. John," the receptionist said.

"Mmm," Luke said absently as he strode down the hall. The attractive young woman turned in her chair and watched him go, deciding he was definitely a man with something heavy on his mind.

Luke stopped at the desk of his secretary, a plump woman in her fifties, who looked up at him with a rather confused expression.

"I thought you said when you called that you weren't coming in this afternoon," she said.

"I need some data, Betty," he said. "Extensive research."

Betty picked up a pen and slid a steno pad in front of her.

"Okay," she said. "What can I do for you, Luke? What am I researching?"

"Superstitions."

"I beg your pardon? Superstitions? About what? Is this pertaining to a case you have on the docket?"

"Not exactly," he said, shoving his hands into his pockets. "Let's just say it's the most important project I've ever undertaken and let it go at that, shall we? Start with superstitions regarding brides, weddings, things like that, then go further into superstitions in general."

"Brides? You mean, like it's bad luck for the groom to see the bride in her wedding dress before she walks down the aisle?"

"Exactly." He shook his head. "Who comes up with this junk?"

Betty shrugged. "I have no idea, but that business about the dress has been around for as long as I can remember, and I'm borderline ancient." She tapped the pen against the pad of paper. "Okay. I get the drift of what you want about brides and what have you. Then I go to other things like not walking under a ladder or letting a black cat cross your path?"

"Right."

"When do you need this interesting info?"

"Yesterday," he said, then went on into his office.

Late that night Luke was stretched out on the sofa in his living room reading yet again the thick stack of papers that Betty had given him on superstitions.

He frowned in disbelief at some of them and couldn't help but laugh aloud at others. But for the most part he was digesting everything he read with serious intent.

He'd memorize as many of these wacky things as he could, he'd decided, then keep the papers close at hand for ready reference on others.

Luke reached over and set the papers on the coffee table fronting the sofa, then laced his fingers beneath his head where it rested on a puffy throw pillow.

The Plan was in effect, he mused, insofar as Maggie believed she was coordinating a wedding for cousin Clyde and his Precious.

However, now he knew Maggie's secret about the Jenkins Jinx, further genius-level action was definitely called for, an extension of The Plan. Through brilliant lawyer-type persuasion he'd gotten Maggie to agree that the jinx was a superstition. She'd done so rather reluctantly, but he'd take what he could get.

His mission, then, was to cleverly and carefully expose Maggie to superstition after superstition, casually pointing out that, son of a gun, nothing horrible had happened because they'd—they'd what?—walked under a ladder, for example. He'd stack up the evidence piece by piece, inching closer and closer to the Jenkins Jinx and the miraculous fact that Maggie was obviously the one who was going to break its hold on the family because she was immune to the consequences of superstitions.

Man, he was so sharp sometimes, it just blew his mind. This was shining-star thinking, damn it. It wouldn't be easy, that was for sure, would take planning and coordination and... He needed help. It was too big, too important to tackle alone.

Luke sat up and swung his feet to the floor.

His father, he thought. Mason St. John knew about The Plan and understood the need for it, although he did have some reservations about the consequences of duping Maggie. His dad was the perfect person to help with this new addition to the program.

Luke glanced at his watch and swore under his breath as he saw it was too late to call his father.

But first thing in the morning, he thought, he'd corner his dad and they'd map things out. Ah, yeah, this was good, very good. It was the next step in the battle that would eventually win the war.

Luke settled back on the sofa and smiled up at the ceiling.

Yes, there was going to be a Christmas wedding, all right. But Precious and Clyde—who were becoming strangely real to him—would have to make their own arrangements to tie the knot.

The wedding that was being put together at this very moment would unite Maggie Jenkins and Luke St. John in holy matrimony forever, declare them to be wife and husband, soul mates, partners in life and parents of the little miracles that would be the result of their exquisite lovemaking.

His Christmas bride, Luke thought. His Maggie.

Eight

Maggie spent the next two days tackling the stack of paperwork in her office at Roses and Wishes. It was her least favorite part of owning the business, and she often daydreamed about what it would be like to be successful enough to have a secretary.

Not only would the tedious paperwork be taken care of, but Roses and Wishes could remain open while Maggie was off and running to tend to the multitude of details, details, details needed to coordinate the perfect wedding.

But, she mused as she scrutinized another bill for Ginger and Robert's extravaganza, the budget didn't allow for such luxury as a secretary. And besides, she wasn't all that sure she intended to continue with this career choice she'd been so excited about at the onset.

Maggie sighed and read the bill once more, realizing that yet again she hadn't comprehended what was on the invoice. Why? Because her mind kept drifting off and settling on the exquisite lovemaking she'd enjoyed with Luke.

She should have had her desk cleared in one day but, no, not this time. Here it was late in the afternoon of the second day and she was still glued to her chair because her flighty brain wouldn't behave itself.

Maggie flipped the paper in the air, watched it settle on the pile she had yet to even look at, then plunked her elbow on the desktop and rested her chin in her palm.

All right, she thought decisively, this obviously wasn't working well. Sneaky and wonderful images of that afternoon with Luke kept creeping in and disrupting her concentration. So, therefore, she'd indulge in a trip down memory lane, relive every tantalizing, sensuous moment of what they'd shared and finally put it to rest. Then she'd be able to get her chores done like a proper little business owner should.

Maggie stared into space, making no attempt to erase the soft smile that formed on her lips as picture after picture slid into her mind and sensation after sensation swirled within her body.

Heat settled low within her, pulsing and hot, and she shifted slightly on the chair. Her breasts began to ache, yearning for the soothing feeling of Luke's hands, then mouth, on the sensitive flesh. Mercy. Her cheeks, she knew, were flushed and she could hear the increased tempo of her heart echoing in her ears.

Ecstasy in its purest form, she mused dreamily. That's what that joining had been. And at the peak of it, the climax? God, she had no idea it could be like that. It defied description, required words that hadn't even been invented yet.

Imagine what it would be like, she mentally rambled on, to be married to Luke, to be the recipient of all that magnificent masculinity night after night after... It boggled the mind.

Of course, there was more to marriage than just...well, than just that. She and Luke would laugh and talk, eat meals together, shop for groceries, discuss events from the six-o'clock news. They'd choose a house they both knew would be their home, then furnish it room by room, agreeing on choices, compromising where necessary.

And, of course, one of those rooms would be a nursery for the baby they'd create with their wondrous lovemaking. A baby boy? A girl? It wouldn't matter. Then a couple of years later another little miracle would arrive to join the first. Luke would be a fantastic father to all their children, whether they had two or four or...

But each night when tiny heads were nestled on pillows after stories had been read and prayers heard, it would be grown-up time, Maggie-and-Luke time, private time. And in their marriage bed they would reach eagerly for each other, the desire never waning, their heartfelt love growing deeper and stronger with each passing year. Their lips would meet and...

"Maggie?"

Maggie shifted her gaze to focus on the direction the voice had come from. Luke. He was standing right in front of her desk in all his masculine splendor.

He really wasn't there, she told herself, was a figment of her imagination due to the fantasy playing out in her head. No, he really wasn't there, so what the heck….

Maggie got to her feet, leaned forward to grip Luke's tie and pulled him toward her to plant a searing kiss on his lips.

But the very moment that their mouths met, a mortified Maggie realized that Luke really *was* there in living, breathing color. She released her hold on his tie and plunked back down in her chair, wishing she could disappear into thin air, never to be seen again.

"Well," Luke said, smoothing his tie and smiling at her, "that was quite a welcome. Hello to you, too, Maggie."

"'Lo," she mumbled, staring at the middle button on his shirt.

"You certainly make a man feel special, like you're glad to see him, I must say."

"I can explain that," Maggie said, finally meeting his gaze. She sighed and shook her head. "No, forget it. It's too ridiculous." She paused. "I guess you're here because you haven't heard from me regarding honeymoon suites, but I've been buried in paperwork and haven't had a chance to do any investigating yet."

"No, I'm here because I missed you," Luke said, settling onto one of the chairs opposite Maggie's desk. "That's it, pure and simple."

"Really?" A bright smile lit up Maggie's face, then

in the next instant she managed to erase it and adopt an expression of vague interest. "Oh?"

"Yep," Luke said, chuckling. "And since this tie I'm wearing may never be the same, I'd say you missed me, too."

"Well…" Maggie flipped one hand in the air. "Whatever."

"Mmm. My, my, Maggie, I'm surprised to see that you're wearing that shade of blue on a Thursday. You didn't go so far as to take a bath or shower this morning, did you?"

"Huh?" Maggie peered down at the string sweater she wore, then looked at Luke again, obviously confused. "What on earth are you talking about?"

Luke propped his elbows on the arms of the chair and tented his fingers.

"There are certain cultures," he said, "which believe the color blue represents the ocean, the sea. They also think that Thursday is the unluckiest day of the week. Therefore, to tempt fate by wearing that color on a Thursday, you're destined to have an accident in water, maybe even drown."

"That's the silliest thing I've ever heard," Maggie said, rolling her eyes heavenward.

"Not to the people who believe it."

"Which probably number about three. For heaven's sake, Luke, the wrong color on the wrong day and you're deader than a doornail? That's a nonsense-to-the-max superstition."

Luke shrugged with a rather nondescript expression on his face.

"Besides, I took a long bath in my wonderful tub this morning and lived to tell about it," she said, lifting her chin. "So there."

"No kidding? Well, maybe that superstition is garbage after all," he said thoughtfully. "It was so off-the-wall that I was leaning toward believing it. I mean, there must be enough evidence to substantiate it in the first place."

Maggie leaned toward him. "That tie of yours that I just wrinkled is blue, sort of sea-blue. Did you shower this morning?"

"Yes, I did."

"I rest my case. That superstition is nonsense."

Gotcha, Luke thought smugly. Score one for Luke St. John.

"So back to why you're here," Maggie said.

"Well, it's not because I'm bugging you about the honeymoon suites," Luke said. "One of my clients had a bit of an emergency and I had to put on my big-boy-lawyer clothes and meet with him for a long, boring lunch close to here. I just dropped in to say hello and to tell you that I missed you." He attempted once again to smooth his crumpled tie. "And to get my tie killed, I guess."

"I'd offer to replace it, but I don't think I could afford to do that on my budget. How much did it cost?"

"A hundred and fifty dollars."

"For a tie?" she said, nearly shrieking. "That's absurd."

"It's imported silk from Italy."

"Could I interest you in installment payments?"

Luke laughed. "Tell you what. You agree to have dinner with me tonight and we'll call it even."

"Well…"

"I'm in the mood for pizza, if that suits you, so dress very casually. But don't wear blue. Okay?"

"Pizza sounds great but, Luke, you've got to forget about that superstition because it really is nuts."

"I'll try," he said, rising with a dramatic sigh. "I'll pick you up at eight o'clock. I'll let you get back to work now. See you later."

"But…" Maggie said as Luke strode from the room. She smiled as she heard the front door of Roses and Wishes close behind him. "Eight o'clock will be just fine."

She picked up an invoice, then stared into space.

She'd really gotten carried away with her mental fantasy, she mused. Goodness, she'd gone all the way to being Luke's wife and having a slew of his babies. Well, that was all right…except, of course, for the embarrassing tie episode.

It didn't matter how much daydreaming she did because she knew, really knew, that all this was temporary. She could indulge in anything she wanted to with Luke St. John because once Precious and Clyde were married that would be that. No more Luke in her life. In the meantime? She was free to go for it because she had total command over her emotions. Everything was dandy.

That night Luke drove past several well-known pizza restaurants to the far side of Phoenix.

"You must really like the pizza here," Maggie said,

as they settled into a red vinyl booth. "You certainly were willing to drive a long way to reach this place."

"Best pizza in Phoenix," Luke said, glancing at his watch. "I'll go up and place our order. What would you like on yours?"

"Anything and everything except the little fishes," she said, smiling.

"Got it," he said, sliding out of the booth. "Soda?"

"Perfect."

A few minutes later Luke returned to sit across from Maggie and set a slip of paper on the table.

"I'm glad this is Thursday and not Friday," he said. "We have the number thirteen. Thirteen on a Friday is bad news, you know." He looked at his watch again.

"No worse than drowning in the bathtub because you wore the wrong color," Maggie said drily. "Luke, what is with this sudden preoccupation with superstitions?"

"It's not sudden," he said. Oh, man, his nose was going to grow. "I've always been superstitious, but don't talk about it much because people have a tendency to scoff."

"Scoff?"

"Yes, definitely scoff. But, you see, Maggie, I've been doing a great deal of thinking about what you told me about the Jenkins Jinx. My first reaction was to tell you that it was nonsense. I scoffed. And I apologize to you for doing that. Jinxes, superstitions, wives' tales all have merit. I want you to know that I respect your belief in the Jenkins Jinx."

"You do? I mean, you're not going to attempt to talk

me out of it? Tell me it's a bunch of baloney? Try to convince me that I could be a bride, get married, just like anyone else?"

"Nope."

"Oh."

Well, that was good, she thought. Wasn't it? Sure. Then why did she suddenly feel so sad, gloomy and depressed? Luke's acceptance of the Jenkins Jinx meant he was as fully prepared to walk away as she was after Precious and Clyde's wedding. No fuss, no muss. That was…great. But her stomach hurt. And her heart hurt. Her heart actually hurt. Damn it, what was the matter with her?

"Luke, my boy," a deep voice boomed, snapping Maggie back to attention.

"Well, Dad, my, my, what are you doing here?" Luke said, looking up at his father where he stood next to the table.

"Your mother got hungry for pizza so I called in an order and came to pick it up. This place has the best pizza in Phoenix, you know."

"Yes, I certainly know that and you're fortunate to live only a few blocks away," Luke said. "You remember Maggie."

"Certainly," Mason St. John said. "Delightful to see you again, my dear."

"My pleasure," Maggie said.

"Luke, I'm just beside myself," Mason said.

"Oh? Why is that, pray tell?" Luke said.

Pray tell? Maggie thought. For some dumb reason

Luke and his father sounded like they were reading words from a script and not doing a very good job of it. No, that was silly. So what, pray tell, was Mr. St. John beside himself about?

"I lost my acorn," Mason said.

Huh? Maggie thought, frowning slightly.

"Oh, no, anything but that, Father."

"I know, I know," Mason said, resting one hand on his heart. "I didn't tell your mother I was driving over here without my acorn. She'd be worried sick."

"For good reason," Luke said. "But fear not, because I always carry two." He leaned back so he could slide his hand into the front pocket of his jeans. "There you go, sir. One acorn."

Mason curled his fingers around the acorn Luke had placed in his hand, then slid the little nut into his pocket. He clamped one hand on Luke's shoulder.

"Bless you, son. Enjoy your pizza. Good night, Maggie. Farewell, Luke."

As Mason hurried away, the waitress appeared at the table and set a pitcher of soda in the center along with two glasses. Luke thanked the young girl, then filled the glasses. Maggie leaned forward, staring at Luke intently as she waited for an explanation about the bizarre interchange regarding the acorn. Luke glanced around.

"Sure is getting crowded in here, isn't it? That's understandable, though, when you consider that they serve—"

"The best pizza in Phoenix," Maggie finished for him. "Would you care to explain what just happened here?"

"The waitress delivered our soda," Luke said, smiling. "Hey, they just called number eleven. We're getting closer. Man, I'm starved."

"Luke," Maggie said, smacking the table with the palm of her hand. Luke cringed. "What was that whole weird thing with your father about the acorn?"

"Oh, *that*," Luke said. "Did they just call number twelve?"

"Luke," Maggie said, narrowing her eyes and drumming the fingers of one hand on the top of the table. "The acorn. Now."

"You bet," he said, nodding. "Well, it's very simple. It's good luck to carry an acorn on one's person. We St. Johns have toted acorns around for years. Years and years. Never go anywhere without our acorns, by golly. So you can see why my father was so upset about having lost his and not wishing my poor mother to know. But—" he grinned "—I saved his bacon because I always have two. Insurance, you know what I mean?"

Maggie leaned back in the booth and crossed her arms over her chest. "That's stupid," she said.

"It certainly is not," Luke said indignantly. "One could become jinxed, experience endless lousy luck if one didn't carry one's acorn, Maggie. Remind me to find an acorn for you." He paused. "Yo. They just called thirteen. That's us. I'll be back in a flash."

"But…" Maggie said, pointing one finger in the air, then realizing that Luke was long gone.

All the St. Johns were superstition freaks? she thought incredulously. They were intelligent, highly educated people, lawyers and what have you, for heaven's sake, but they flipped out if they lost their acorn? How weird was that?

Luke interrupted Maggie's racing thoughts by setting a huge, fragrant pizza in the center of the table, then sitting down again and rubbing his hands together.

"Now that looks delicious," he said, smiling. "Dig in and enjoy."

"I will, but...Luke, about this acorn thing. Your father didn't say he'd experienced any bad luck or mishaps or whatever while his acorn was missing. Correct?"

Luke nodded as he chewed a big bite of the hot pizza.

"So," Maggie continued, "doesn't that suggest that there is nothing to the superstition surrounding the acorn? That it is just that—a superstition, which is fun and cute but...isn't grounded in reality?"

Luke stared into space. "You've got a point there. When I was a kid I left my acorn in the pocket of my jeans and my mom washed them, turned the acorn into a mushy mess. It was quite a while before I could find another one because it was the wrong time of year. Nothing bad happened to me except that I flunked a spelling test, which was my fault because I didn't study for it."

Maggie picked up a slice of pizza and smiled, obviously pleased with herself. "See?" She took a bite of her dinner.

"I'll give this some serious thought," Luke said. Oh, this was going great, even better than he had hoped for. "Wait a minute here."

"Hmm?" Maggie said, her mouth full of pizza.

"I bet you didn't know that if you say goodbye to a friend on a bridge you'll never see each other again. Well, when I was fifteen I had this buddy. We did everything together, were really close. One summer we were riding our bikes and said goodbye at the end of the day on a bridge. I never saw him again. How do you like that?"

"Why didn't you ever see him again?" Maggie said.

"Because of the bridge thing, Maggie." Luke paused. "Well, not entirely, I guess. His dad was a creep, physically abused his mom and… She took off in the middle of the night with my buddy and disappeared.

"I figured it was because of the parting on the bridge, but now that I really think about it… Well, hell, so much for the bridge belief." He shook his head. "Amazing. All these years I was convinced…mmm."

Maggie smiled sweetly. "This pizza is delicious. Thank you for bringing me here."

"Sure, no problem," Luke said, frowning. "This is rather unsettling. The acorn. The bridge. I don't really have any concrete data to… Just goes to show ya, doesn't it? Things aren't always what they seem to be. Ready for some more soda?"

"No, I'm fine," Maggie said. "Don't be so hard on yourself, Luke. You got caught up in the theories about the acorn and the bridge, have believed them for so long you haven't questioned their validity in years. I think you're being very noble—there's a good word—to accept that the superstitions about them aren't real, aren't true."

"You're right," he said, "and I have you to thank for

showing me how ridiculous I was for buying into those tales." He deserved an Academy Award for this performance, he really did. "Let's just concentrate on the pizza now. This has been a pretty heavy topic for my weary brain. Enough for one night."

"Okay. Do you want to discuss Precious and Clyde's wedding?"

Luke smiled. "Maggie, I'd love to discuss the wedding. You have no idea how much it means to me."

"Well, the church is reserved for December twenty-third," Maggie said, her voice ringing with excitement. "And I got the ballroom at the Majestic Palms Hotel sewn up for the reception."

"The Majestic Palms," Luke said, nodding in approval. "Classy. Very nice."

"I have an appointment next week to meet with the chef to plan the buffet dinner at the reception. I still have oodles to do—you know, decide on the color of the tablecloths, the centerpieces, start shopping around for the exact shade of material I want for the bridesmaids' dresses and, of course, there's the wedding dress itself."

"Yep."

"What about the invitations, Luke? Do you think Precious and Clyde would prefer traditional ones that say the name of the parents or a more modern version where the couple themselves are inviting everyone to share their special event?"

Uh-oh, Luke thought, then took a big bite of pizza to give himself time to consider his answer. The invitations couldn't be ordered with Precious and Clyde's names on them. They didn't even exist. Think, St. John.

"Um…why don't you hold off on the invitations for now," he said finally. "I should run that by Precious and Clyde just in case they have an idea as to what will make the mothers happy."

"Okay. Would you ask them how they feel about tiny holly berries edging the invitations? I thought that would be so festive for a Christmas wedding."

"I'm sure that part will be fine. There certainly are a lot of things to tend to for a picture-perfect wedding, aren't there?"

"It takes months," Maggie said, laughing, "and then—blink—the ceremony is over in about fifteen minutes." She frowned in the next instant. "And in our family the marriage lasts about that long, too."

Change the subject, Luke thought frantically. He didn't want Maggie centering on the Jenkins Jinx, not tonight. Her beautiful eyes sparkled when she talked about the plans for the wedding, and the expression on her face was pure joy.

Not only that, he needed more superstitions for her to dismiss, to attempt to talk him out of believing, if he was to build a solid foundation for his case.

No, the Jenkins Jinx was definitely off-limits this evening.

"You know," he said, "you've never seen my apartment. I was just thinking that I have some mint-chocolate-chip ice cream in my freezer. Would you like to go there for dessert?"

Maggie leaned toward him. "Mint-chocolate-chip?"

"That's the one."

"Two scoops?"

"Three scoops," he said, holding up that many fingers.

"I have no willpower when it comes to mint-chocolate-chip ice cream," Maggie said. "Oh, my, three scoops."

"I thought you might like that flavor," Luke said, appearing extremely pleased with himself. "See how well I'm getting to know you, Maggie? It boggles the mind."

It terrifies the mind, Maggie thought. They were becoming so connected, bonded, on the same wavelength and... Never mind. She wasn't going to get all in a dither about it.

She was about to have three scoops of mint-chocolate-chip ice cream. Ah, yes, life was good.

Nine

"My goodness," Maggie said, taking in Luke's enormous living room. "This is incredible, just beautiful. I've never been in a penthouse apartment before. The view is fabulous. I'd probably lose track of time and just sit for hours gazing out those windows at the city lights. You must look forward to coming home each day after work, Luke."

Not anymore, Luke thought as he stared at the awed expression on Maggie's face. Now it was just a whole lot of empty space waiting for Maggie to fill it to overflowing with her sunshine, laughter and…well, by just being Maggie.

"Ready for that ice cream?" he said.

"Sure. Can I see the kitchen?"

Luke laughed. "Follow me. It's fun to experience this place through fresh eyes."

Maggie gushed on and on about the fantastic kitchen as Luke scooped out the ice cream. As he picked up the bowls to carry them to the table, he dropped one of the spoons.

"Darn," he said.

"I'll get it," Maggie said, retrieving the spoon from the floor and rinsing it under the faucet.

They settled onto chairs opposite each other at the round oak table and Maggie took several mouthfuls of the dessert before she realized that Luke was staring into space.

"What's wrong?" she said.

"I was just wondering what child was going to come visit me and I'm coming up blank."

"I beg your pardon?" Maggie said, obviously confused.

"When you drop a spoon it means a child will visit. A fork brings a woman to your door, and a knife indicates the visitor will be a man."

"Is that a fact," Maggie said drily.

"Yep."

"Mmm," Maggie said, frowning at him.

"It's true," Luke said, leaning toward her. "I dropped a knife last month and—bingo—Robert popped in for no reason other than he was in the neighborhood."

"Robert is your brother. It makes perfect sense that he'd like to see you. It has nothing to do with the knife you dropped, Luke."

"Oh, yeah? Well, another time it was a fork, and

you'd better believe I shoved all the dirty dishes in the dishwasher before the knock came at the door. And there she was, my mother, bringing me some brownies she'd baked." He paused. "I wonder what little kid... Are Girl Scouts selling cookies now or something?"

"Halt," Maggie said, raising one hand. "Has Robert ever come by unannounced before?"

"Well...yes."

"And is your mother in the habit of bringing you homemade baked goods?"

"Yes, but—"

"I rest my case. Your fumble-fingers with the silverware was just a coincidence, nothing more. Another one of those superstitions you should forget about."

"Think so?"

"Know so." Maggie took another spoonful of ice cream. "Mmm. This is delicious. You'd better start on yours before it melts."

"You're really punching holes in my superstitions, you know," Luke said, then started in on his dessert.

"They can control your life if you're not careful," Maggie said.

Luke laughed. "Not all of them. There's one just for women. If she goes out in public and her slip shows, it means her father loves her more than her mother does."

"No, Luke, it means that either her slip is too long or her dress is too short."

"What you're saying makes sense, I guess. Then again...hmm. I'll have to think about this." He paused.

"Enough about superstitions. I'm going to go put some music on. I'll be right back."

A few moments later Maggie stiffened in her chair as the sound of lilting music reached her.

Oh, God, she thought, that was one of the waltzes she and Luke had danced to at Ginger and Robert's wedding. The beautiful song evoked special memories she intended to keep for all time. Did Luke remember why that particular tune was so meaningful or was it just a coincidence that he had put it on? No, men didn't get caught up in things like that. Music was music.

Luke came back into the kitchen and stood next to Maggie's chair.

"Recognize that waltz?" he said quietly. "We danced to it at Robert and Ginger's wedding. I asked the band leader what it was and went out and bought it so I could play it when you came here."

"Really?" Maggie said, a warmth suffusing her and creating a flush on her cheeks. "You did that? Of course I remember it, Luke, but to think that you went to all this trouble to… I don't know what to say."

He extended one hand toward her. "Say you'll dance with me."

From a seemingly faraway dreamy place, Maggie watched her hand float up to grasp Luke's, then she was on her feet and in his embrace. He held her close, moving with the music as he glided them out of the kitchen and into the living room, which was filled with the melody from speakers mounted high on the wall in each corner of the large room.

Maggie nestled her head on Luke's shoulder as they danced, drinking in the feel of him, his aroma, the strength of his body. Around the room they went, so gracefully, so perfectly in step.

It was so romantic that tears burned at the back of Maggie's eyes and desire consumed her, making it impossible to think clearly. She could only feel and savor and wish for the music to never end.

But it did finish, and they stopped in front of the tall windows where the lights of the city spread out in all directions like a fairyland. Another song started, but they didn't move, just held fast to each other. Then Luke shifted enough so he could tilt Maggie's chin up with one gentle fingertip, lowered his head and kissed her.

The kiss was so soft and tender, so exactly right to mark the finish of the memory-filled waltz, that two tears spilled onto Maggie's cheeks. Luke deepened the kiss and she gave herself to him, swept away by the moment and the music and...Luke.

Then he slowly, so slowly, lowered her to the plush carpet. He stretched out next to her, bracing his weight on one forearm as he drew a thumb over her tears.

"You're so beautiful," he said, his voice husky. "I've actually daydreamed about this, about seeing you here in my home, right here in front of these windows with the world spread out before us as though it belongs only to us. Ah, Maggie, I..." *Love you with all that I am, all I will ever be, for eternity.* "I...want to make love to you so much, so very much."

"Yes," she whispered.

He kissed her, then they parted long enough to shed their clothes and reached for each other once again. An urgency engulfed them, a need so great it was indescribable.

With hands never still, they caressed.

With lips seeking more, they kissed.

With passion soaring to unbelievable heights, they waited until they could bear it no longer.

Then they joined, meshed into one entity that made it impossible to decipher where the body soft and feminine and the one so very masculine ended and began.

The music had stopped, but they could hear their special waltz as they rocked in gentle rhythm to the exquisite song that belonged to them alone. The tension built within them, tightening, spiraling, taking them higher, up and away, until they burst into the heavens with the lights of their world beyond the windows showing them the way.

It was ecstasy. It was nearly shattering in its splendor, an explosion of sensations like none before. They drifted, savoring, murmuring the name of the other, until they returned to rest on the lush carpet that cradled them.

Luke moved off Maggie, then shifted her so her back was to his front and they could gaze out at the lights. He buried his face in her fragrant hair for a long moment, then tucked her head beneath his chin.

Maggie drew a shuddering breath, then smothered a sob that threatened to escape from her throat.

Dear God, she thought, she loved him. She was in love with Luke St. John. There was no denying it, nowhere to hide from the truth of it, nowhere to run. She loved him. He was all, everything and more that she'd fantasized about finding in a man, the one who would steal her heart for all time if things were different. If she was a normal woman, not plagued by the Jenkins Jinx. She loved him, but she couldn't have him, and it was just so incredibly sad.

But for now? she thought, blinking back unwelcomed tears. He was hers. Until Precious and Clyde's wedding, Luke was hers. She would cherish every moment she had with him and ignore the ticking of the clock that would signal their goodbye.

"What we just shared was…" Luke said, then stopped speaking for a second. "No, I don't have the words."

"I don't either," Maggie said softly, "but I know that it was… I'll never forget this night, Luke."

"I won't either." He paused, then chuckled. "I think our ice cream has melted."

Maggie smiled. "I think my bones have melted."

Time lost meaning as they lay together in sated, comfortable silence, then Maggie finally sighed.

"I'm about to fall asleep," she said. "I'd better get home, Luke."

"Ah, Maggie, stay. Please," he said. "We'll sleep with our heads on the same pillow in my bed and have breakfast together in the morning."

"I don't think…"

"Please?"

Why not? Maggie thought. In for a penny, in for a pound, or however that saying went. She was hopelessly, irrevocably in love with this man. The damage was done, the heartbreak guaranteed when all of this ended. Why not share everything she could with Luke while it was possible?

"Yes," she said. "Yes, I'll stay."

"Thank you," Luke said, then shifted away from her, rolled to his feet and extended one hand to her. "Come on. I promise my bed is softer than this floor."

Maggie placed her hand in his and allowed him to draw her up into an embrace where his mouth melted over hers in a searing kiss. On legs that weren't quite steady she walked by his side to the large master bedroom that was decorated in gray and burgundy. Luke turned on a lamp on the nightstand, then flipped back the blankets to reveal burgundy sheets.

"Oh, wait," he said. "Make note of which side of the bed you get in on because you have to leave on the same side in the morning or you'll have bad luck."

"Here we go again," Maggie said, rolling her eyes. "Another St. John superstition."

"Well," he said, shrugging, "at least I have a variety to offer. You're zoned in on the Jenkins Jinx and that's it."

Maggie looked up at him and frowned. "Which has generations of proof that validates it."

"That may be true, but you've managed to punch holes in all the superstitions I've presented so far, shown me that there's room for doubt. The same may hold true for your jinx."

"No," Maggie said, taking a step backward. "I'm not going to even entertain the idea that the jinx can be broken. I've seen the heartache suffered by those who thought they could do exactly that. No."

"Okay," Luke said, raising both hands in a gesture of peace. "Forget I said that. I didn't mean to upset you on this incredibly perfect night." He swept one arm in the direction of the bed. "Madam?"

Maggie settled onto the bed with a sigh of pleasure.

"Oh, this is heavenly," she said.

"I'm going to go turn out the lights in the other rooms and dump the soupy ice cream," Luke said. "I'll be back in a few minutes."

"'Kay," she said, then yawned.

Luke chuckled, then strode from the room. When he returned, Maggie was sound asleep. He slipped carefully into the bed next to her, then propped up on one forearm to watch her sleep.

So lovely, he thought. Maggie was here with him, where she belonged. If only there was a golden ring on her finger symbolizing her being his wife, his partner in life.

He was winning little victories each time she made it clear that the newest superstition he'd declared was foolish, should be dismissed as nonsense. Each of those incidents gave him ammunition to demolish the Jenkins Jinx. He was definitely making progress. Wasn't he? Oh, man, he just had to be.

But Maggie was so...so fierce about the jinx, was determined not to fall prey to the belief that she could be the one to prove it untrue, to break the long cycle of disastrous marriages in the Jenkins family. No, she had said. No.

And little victories meant nothing if he didn't win the final battle. He couldn't bear that thought. He'd just keep on as he was, chipping away at that wall of Maggie's. He was going to conquer the demon that held her so tight.

He was going to marry Maggie Jenkins. She loved him, he believed that with every fiber of his being. And heaven knew that he loved her. That love would grow, become stronger, unbeatable, smash the jinx into dust to be blown into oblivion.

Luke nodded decisively, snapped off the lamp, then settled close to Maggie, his head on the same pillow as hers just as he'd promised.

But it was many hours before he finally slept.

Two weeks later Maggie and Luke stood in the honeymoon suite on the top floor of one of Phoenix's exclusive hotels.

"Luke, this is awful," Maggie said with a burst of laughter. "A heart-shaped bed? A color scheme of bright red? Velvet spread, upholstery, even the drapes? A shiny red hot tub? It's so tacky, it's beyond belief."

"Oh, I don't know," Luke said, grinning, "I guess it depends on how you feel about red. This place could sure turn a guy off Valentine's Day. Man, they went nuts in here."

"The manager said it's very popular," Maggie said, shaking her head. "That's a scary thought."

"Yep," Luke said, glancing around. "It's even worse than the one that had forty-two stuffed toy cupids. I counted them, you know, and there were actually forty-two of those chubby little guys ready to shoot arrows. That was a nightmare waiting to happen."

"Well, cross this one off the list of possibilities." Maggie looked at her watch. "I've got to rush. I'm meeting Janet and Patty at the bridal shop for the first fitting of their bridesmaids' dresses."

"Have you…um…looked at wedding dresses yet?" Luke said, sliding a glance at her.

"No, not yet. I'm sure the perfect dress for…for Precious is there because the selection is wonderful. That shop is where Ginger got her gown. They're terribly expensive, though."

"No problem," Luke said. "Don't even think about the money. The sky is the limit…or whatever. In other words, go for it."

"Right. Let's get out of here. All this red is giving me a headache."

"Are you sure you can't come to my place tonight?" Luke said as they started toward the door.

"No, I've got to go see my mother, Luke. You know, have dinner with her, chat, what have you. She's feeling neglected and I don't blame her. I haven't been to her house in far too long. I'll just go straight home from there."

"I'll miss you," he said. "I'm getting very spoiled having you next to me in my bed at night and seeing you when I open my eyes in the morning. It's nice. It's more than nice."

Maggie gripped the doorknob, then hesitated and smiled up at Luke.

"Yes," she said, "I agree. It's very, very nice." She laughed. "By the way, you know that superstition you laid on me last night? I want you to know that I purposely put on my left shoe before my right one this morning and I have not had one bit of unluck, if there is such a word."

Luke braced his hand flat on the door to prevent Maggie from leaving the brilliant-red suite.

"Well, now, aren't you turning into a risk taker?" he said, smiling.

"Not really, Luke. I mean, after all, these are just superstitions that I'm declaring to be untrue. You should be feeling a step-by-step sense of freedom as each one gets checked off your list. I don't think I'm taking any risks by doing that."

"Interesting," he said, frowning thoughtfully. "So you're saying that superstitions, old wives' tales, jinxes are based on a foundation of long-standing foolishness."

"Well, no, not entirely. I was referring to superstitions only. There are certain jinxes that have proven merit."

"So you say," he said thoughtfully. "Or could it be rather a long string of poor judgment? I had this friend in college who was convinced he was jinxed when it came to owning a car. Every used vehicle he purchased turned out to be a lemon. So he quit, gave up, said never again. He rode a bike, took buses and taxis. Man, what a hassle."

"But smart," Maggie said decisively.

"I didn't go with that theory. I convinced him to try one more time, run that risky risk. We went to a used-car lot and he looked at a bunch of vehicles, then settled on the one he would buy if he was going to, which he wasn't. We took it for a test drive and stopped to see another buddy of mine who was a mechanic."

"And he said the car was a clunker. Right?" Maggie said.

"No, he declared it to be prime, good for another hundred thousand miles, so my friend bought it."

Maggie blinked, then frowned. "Really?"

"Really. The last time I saw him he was still driving that thing. He said it gave him cold chills to dwell on the narrow existence he would have had if he hadn't sucked in a deep breath that day and taken that risk, bought the car."

"But—"

"Think about it." Luke dropped a quick kiss on Maggie's lips. "Come on, let's go. You'll be late for the appointment for the dresses."

"The what?" Maggie said absently. "Oh! The dresses. I've got to dash."

They left the suite and as Maggie hurried down the hallway in front of Luke, he punched one fist in the air.

Yes! he thought. He'd scored some points—big-time. The story he'd made up about the guy and car was genius-level thinking, especially since he had done it on the spur of the moment because the opportunity had been so perfect for it.

Maggie had heard every word he'd said, was digesting it in that mighty little mind of hers as evidenced by the fact that she'd momentarily forgotten about the appointment she was almost late for.

He was folding his tent graciously and without complaint each time she declared one of his superstitions, albeit fictitious ones, as nonsense. All he was asking of her was to give up one jinx. One.

The one that would mean the difference between their having a future together or not. The one that would determine their entire lives. The one he had to defeat in the ongoing battle he was conducting to win the war and a forever with Maggie Jenkins.

"I'm just going to tape this hem in place for now," the seamstress said to Maggie, "until the actual bridesmaid is here for the final fitting."

"Oh, I wish it was really me," Janet said wistfully as the seamstress worked on the hem. "This dress is scrumptious. I love this color of green, Maggie. I want to own this dress."

"That's what Patty said before she left," Maggie said, laughing. She was seated on a velvet-covered chair, sipping a cup of tea. "She said this whole business is pure torture because she's had the dress on but it really belongs to someone else."

"She's right," Janet said.

"All set for today," the seamstress said, getting to her feet. "Let me help you take this dress off."

"No, I want to keep it," Janet said, then laughed. "Would it do me any good to throw a tantrum?"

"I'm afraid not," the woman said, smiling.

The dress was removed and the seamstress left the room. Janet began to pull on her own clothes.

"Janet," Maggie said quietly, "may I ask you something?"

"Sure."

"When you married Roger, did you believe that you would be the one to break the Jenkins Jinx, end it for all time?"

"Truthfully?" Janet said, sitting down next to Maggie. "I loved Roger so much, Maggie, that I blatantly ignored things about him that were red-alert signals indicating problems down the line."

Maggie set her teacup on the delicate table next to her and sat up straighter in her chair.

"Really?" she said. "I didn't know that."

"No one did," Janet said, sighing. "I thought I could change him, dum-dum that I was. He gambled far too much, hadn't held a job longer than a year in his entire life, thought money should be spent and enjoyed now with no thought given to the future.

"Even after the babies started coming he didn't get his act together. It was like having another child to raise. When I got divorced, no one asked me why, really. The family just assumed it was the Jenkins Jinx doing its thing."

"And Bill?" Maggie said, her heart racing. "What about your marriage to Bill?"

"Oh, sweetie, that was a joke. I was lonely, broke, scared to death of being a single mother, living paycheck to paycheck, and I latched onto Bill. Six months later I was sick to death of him cheating on me. Ta-da. Divorce number two for Janet the dunce."

"Why…why didn't you ever say that the Jenkins Jinx didn't have anything to do with your divorces?" Maggie said.

"It was easier that way, Maggie. Why tell everyone that I had such lousy judgment, had made such awful mistakes and was paying the price? The whole family felt so sorry for me because I was another victim of the jinx, so I let it stand, kept my mouth shut."

"Don't you believe there really is a Jenkins Jinx?" Maggie said, hardly breathing.

"I honestly don't know," Janet said, frowning. "Is it real? Does this family just have poor judgment in its choice of partners? Or did some of those marriages in our family tree collapse due to the jinx? I don't know the answer to that." She cocked her head slightly and studied Maggie. "Why are you asking me all this? It has been ages since you and I have talked about the jinx."

"I, um. Well, because… Yes, because of Roses and Wishes. I deal with happy brides all the time and…Mom thinks I made a mistake starting a business that only emphasizes what I'll never have because of the jinx. She really believes the jinx is true, you know. Having Roses and Wishes has made me think about it more than I normally would that's all."

Janet narrowed her eyes. "You never could lie worth a damn, Maggie Jenkins. Something is going on with you. Talk to me, little sister."

Maggie got to her feet. "There's nothing to tell you, Janet." She looked at her watch. "My, my, look at the time. I've got to go. I have so much to do. Details, details, details—the list is endless for a wedding."

"*Your* dream wedding," Janet said, rising. "That's what you're tending to."

"Well, it just worked out that way because of this unusual situation with Precious and Clyde," Maggie said. "I explained all that to you. So, yes, this is the wedding I would have if I was going to have a wedding, which I'm not because of the jinx…which you're now suggesting might not be real and…" She slapped one hand onto her forehead. "I'm getting a roaring headache, thank you very much."

"Maggie, there is no way to prove that the jinx is real, no matter what Mom says."

"But we've believed it ever since we were young girls, Janet. We can't pretend it isn't there. We lost count of the divorces in our family tree. There is not one happy Jenkins marriage in our history."

"And there could be an explanation for every one of those divorces just as there is for my two. As for Mom and Dad? The jinx? Come on, Maggie, it was a classic case of the guy who falls for his sexy secretary and thinks he can recapture his youth by dumping his wife and three kids and going off with a bimbo. That's not a jinx, that's a hormone rush or whatever."

"But—"

"I don't know," Janet said, throwing up her hands. "Someday maybe a Jenkins will stay happily married for fifty years and this jinx thing will be old news. Love is powerful when it's right and real. Will that Jenkins be one of my kids? Or will that someone be…you?"

"Me?" Maggie said, her voice a strange-sounding squeak. "Don't be silly. I'm not brave enough to test out the theory that the jinx might not be real. I'm not going to run the risk of having my heart broken to pieces. Nope. Not me."

"Oh?" Janet said, raising her eyebrows. "What happens if you fall head over heels in love?"

I already have, Maggie thought dismally. *And I'm not going to do one thing about it beyond accepting the fact that my time with Luke St. John is measured on the calendar.*

"Let's change the subject," she said. "Want to hear something funny? There's a superstition that when you see an ambulance you'll have bad luck unless you pinch your nose until you see a black or brown dog."

Janet laughed. "That's the silliest thing I've ever heard."

"I know. Try this one. If you have a goldfish in a pond at your home it's good luck, but a goldfish kept inside the house is bad luck."

"Where are you getting this stuff?" Janet said, shaking her head.

"And if the bottom of your feet itch," Maggie rushed on, "you're going to make a trip."

"I'm going to make a trip home right now," Janet said, smiling, "before you lay any more cuckoo stuff on me. Superstitions are nonsense."

"Are jinxes?" Maggie said, suddenly serious. "Is the

Jenkins Jinx as nonsensical as the superstitions I just rattled off?"

Janet sighed. "I don't know. I really don't know. Someone in this family is going to have to fall in love, listen to their heart for the truth, the honest-to-goodness truth of that love and— Good grief, look at the time. I've got to pick up the kids." She gave Maggie a quick hug. "Thanks for letting me play Cinderella in that gorgeous dress. 'Bye."

"'Bye," Maggie said, then sank back down on the pretty chair and stared into space.

Her mind was a mess, she decided. For as long as she could remember she'd believed that the Jenkins Jinx was real. But now? After discussing it with her sister? It was all so confusing, so muddled.

Yes, she was in love with Luke. But, no, she couldn't, just couldn't, run the risk of ignoring the jinx only to discover that it was a genuine curse that hung over her family. But Janet had said that her two failed marriages had nothing to do with a jinx. But then again…

"Excuse me," the seamstress said, coming back into the room.

"Yes?" Maggie said, relieved to be pulled from her jumbled thoughts.

"Time is passing and that wedding you're coordinating will be here before you know it," the woman said. "Are you going to look at our selection of exquisite wedding dresses today?"

"No, not today," Maggie said, an achy sensation gripping her throat as she got to her feet. "I'm suddenly exhausted, so very tired."

"I understand," the seamstress said. "But you will pick the bride's dress soon, won't you?"

"Yes," Maggie said softly. "I'll do it…soon, I promise. I'll have my Cinderella moment, then take the dress off and…and just be me again."

Just Maggie, she thought. Counting down the days until she said goodbye to Luke and was simply Maggie Jenkins. Alone and lonely.

Ten

During the next month Maggie came to feel as though there were two different people existing in her own body.

One was carefree, happy and deeply in love with Luke, enjoying every moment they spent together.

They ate out often, went to the movies, flew a kite in a grassy field, enjoyed a picnic and canoe ride at Encanto Park, shopped at various malls and attended several interesting lectures at Arizona State University. They cooked together—which was a hilarious disaster—tended to details for Precious and Clyde's wedding. And they made sweet, wonderful love.

The other Maggie was consumed by a breath-stopping chill each time she looked at the calendar and saw the time flying by. Summer had turned into fall, school had started again and Phoenix was buzzing with the success of the ASU football team.

They'd celebrated with a special dinner out when they'd finally reserved the honeymoon suite at the very hotel where the reception was to be held. It was perfect, they'd decided. It was decorated in good taste, had a marvelous view of the city lights, a hot tub in the bedroom area and a fireplace in the living room.

Maggie had told Luke that it would be impossible for Precious and Clyde not to like it, while her heart had ached because the honeymoon suite would not welcome Mr. and Mrs. Luke St. John.

Her life, Maggie thought at one point, gave a whole new meaning to the old phrase of laughing on the outside and crying on the inside.

The seamstress at the bridal shop left message after message on Maggie's answering machine, saying she must choose the wedding dress. Maggie created endless excuses why she couldn't get to the shop, as she was terrified she would weep the entire time. The mere thought of selecting that gown, trying it on while knowing it really wasn't hers, was just more than she could bear.

Ginger and Robert returned with glowing reports of their honeymoon in Greece, and the four of them often enjoyed a night on the town. The newlyweds literally shone with happiness, and Maggie had no choice but to sigh and admit to herself that she was green with envy whenever she saw them together.

When Luke announced that it was bad luck to set an empty rocking chair in motion, Maggie dragged him to a furniture store and gave each rocking chair a gentle push to get it going. They dissolved in laughter, apologized to the frowning saleswoman and beat a hasty retreat.

When October marched in and Halloween costumes were featured in every store, Maggie told Luke—again—that the invitations to Precious and Clyde's wedding had to be selected *now* so they could be printed, addressed and mailed.

"Luke," Maggie said one night as they watched a video in her tiny living room, "you keep saying you'll contact Precious and Clyde about the wording on the invitations, but you don't do it."

"I will," he said, his attention on the television.

"When?" she said. She really had no right to nag him because she still hadn't chosen the wedding dress. But, of course, Luke didn't know that. "Those invitations have to be mailed so the RSVP cards can be returned and I can coordinate the amount of food and drink for the reception." She paused. "Are you listening to me?"

"What?" he said, glancing over at her, then back at the screen. "Sure, I hear you. I'll take care of it. I'll call Precious and Clyde tomorrow...or the next day."

"Promise?" Maggie said.

"Hey, would you look at that car. James Bond has the greatest wheels, I swear. No matter how many times I see these movies, I go nuts for the vehicles. Whoa. That baby can really go."

"Mmm," Maggie said, narrowing her eyes.

"If Detroit ever produced one of those, I'd be the first in line to buy it," Luke went on.

"Luke," Maggie said quietly, "I'm beginning to have doubts about the validity of the Jenkins Jinx."

"Yeah, okay. I'd order my car painted in-your-face-red with chrome so shiny that…" Luke stopped speaking, stiffened, then snapped his head around to look at Maggie. "What? What did you say?"

"Nothing," she said, waving one hand in the air. "I didn't mean to speak aloud. It's just on my mind so much that it popped out before I realized that—"

Luke grabbed the remote, turned off the television, then gripped Maggie's shoulders.

"Say it again," he said. "Please, Maggie, say it again. You're having doubts about… Say the words so I can hear them loud and clear. Maggie, you have no idea how much I need to hear you say those words."

"It has become so confusing," she said, meeting his intense gaze. "Whenever I try to think clearly about the jinx, I feel like a hamster running around in one of those wheels and not getting anywhere."

"Go on," he said, not releasing his hold on her.

"My mother told us about the jinx after my father left us," Maggie said, her voice not quite steady. "I grew up believing in it, especially after we researched our family tree and… But I was talking to Janet about her marriages and for the first time in all these years she said she's not totally convinced there is a jinx.

"Maybe, she said, it's just a whole slew of Jenkinses with poor judgment. Or maybe there is a jinx that forces us to make bad choices, or… Oh, I don't know anymore. Janet feels that all it will take to prove there is no such thing as the Jenkins Jinx is for one of us to fall in love—real love, honest, true and for always love—and live happily ever after."

"Yes, yes. She's right. That's good. Great thinking," Luke said in a rush of words. "You have a very smart sister there."

"She said maybe it would be one of her kids that proved the jinx to be nonsense or perhaps it might be…might be…"

"Might be?" Luke prompted.

"Me," Maggie whispered.

"Maggie, yes, it's you," Luke said, his heart soaring. "Maggie Jenkins, I love you so damn much. I am totally, absolutely and forever in love with you. I want to marry you, have babies with you, wake up every morning and have you be the first thing I see. My wife."

"Ohhh," Maggie said, then sniffled as her eyes filled with tears.

"Maggie, do you love me? Do you?"

"Yes. Yes, Luke, I do, so very much. I didn't want to fall in love with you, didn't mean to, but I did. I'm still worried about the jinx because it's been drummed into my head since I was a little girl. One minute I think I don't believe in it anymore, but then I get so frightened and… I'm such a mess.

"But, Luke, do you know what I hang on to like a lifeline to give me courage? It's you. It's you and your superstitions. Your family has believed in those things you've told me for years and years, yet you're so willing to let them go, run the risk of bad things happening because you put your shoes on wrong or forget to carry your acorn or…"

"You're so brave, so strong, so willing to move forward and dismiss those superstitions as nonsense and…"

The color drained from Luke's face and he dropped his hands from Maggie's shoulders.

"If you can have that kind of courage," Maggie said, an errant tear sliding down her cheek, "then I should be brave, too, not hide behind my fears, my belief in the Jenkins Jinx."

"Maggie, listen to me. Okay?" Luke said, his voice raspy. "I have to tell you something. But as you're hearing what I have to say, remember that we love each other. We do. We have a wonderful future together just waiting for us to step up and start living it as husband and wife. Will you do that? Remember that?"

"Yes, all right, but you're suddenly so… What is this thing you have to tell me?"

Luke got to his feet, walked around the small room, then sat back down, taking Maggie's hands in his.

"Maggie, my darling Maggie," he said, looking directly into her eyes, "I never…I never believed in any of those superstitions."

"Pardon…me?"

"I'd never even heard of most of them, had my secretary find them for me on the Internet."

"What? I don't understand."

"I was desperate, don't you see?" he said, giving her hands a little shake. "I didn't know how to get you to demolish that wall protecting you from the Jenkins Jinx.

I thought if you continually witnessed me dumping superstitions that I had supposedly believed in all of my life, you'd come to realize that you could do that with the jinx."

"You didn't believe that having goldfish in the house is bad luck?" Maggie said, her voice rising.

"Ah, Maggie, I had a whole aquarium full of goldfish in my bedroom when I was a kid."

"You—you lied to me? About the superstitions? All this time you've been telling me lie after lie, reciting one superstition after another?"

"They weren't lies, exactly. It was part of a master plan I had to win your love, your heart, to blow the Jenkins Jinx into oblivion so we could be together forever. My father helped me a bit. You know, that night in the pizza place with the acorn and—"

"I don't believe this," Maggie said, yanking her hands free. "What else, Luke? What else did you lie about?"

"I wish you wouldn't use that word," he said, grimacing. "It was a plan. The Plan—in capital letters."

"What else, Luke St. John," she said, her voice ringing with fury.

Luke took a deep breath, then let it out slowly, puffing his cheeks.

"The wedding," he said quietly.

"What wedding?" she said, totally confused.

"Precious and Clyde's."

"What about it? What kind of lies could you possibly tell me about their wedding?"

Luke cringed. "There is no…no Precious and Clyde, Maggie. I made them up. I needed a way to stay close to you after you knocked me over, captured my heart, at Ginger and Robert's wedding. The Plan—I bet you're getting tired of hearing those words—The Plan was for you to coordinate your own dream wedding with me next to you every step of the way.

"Then hopefully you'd fall in love with me, just as I already loved you, and everything would be ready for us to get married just the way you'd always dreamed of."

"That's why you kept hedging about the invitations to Precious and Clyde's wedding," Maggie said, nearly shrieking. "You couldn't ask them about the wording they wanted because they don't exist. And…and…we weren't picking out a honeymoon suite for them it was—"

"For us, don't you see? I wanted our wedding to be perfect for you, exactly what you yearned for. And it will be because you've seen to every detail just the way you want it. I did it for you. Us. You." Luke dragged a restless hand through his hair. "Ah, Maggie, please tell me that you understand that what I did was out of love for you."

"What I understand," she said, getting to her feet and wrapping her hands around her elbows, "is that you are a liar. You are despicable. You made a fool of me. Must have laughed yourself silly when you reported back to your father about the great progress you were making with your ever-famous plan."

"No, it wasn't like that," he said, throwing out his arms. "I had to have something to fight the Jenkins Jinx with because you had it wrapped around you like a fortress. And now you love me. And now you have doubts about there being a jinx on your family and—"

"No, I don't," she said, lifting her chin and ignoring two more tears that slid down her face.

"What?" Luke said hardly above a whisper as he got to his feet.

"I have no doubts whatsoever that the Jenkins Jinx exists, is very, very real, and I am its latest victim," Maggie said, her voice trembling. "I fell in love with a dishonest man, a liar, a schemer, a game player, a damnable *planner*."

"No! You fell in love with a man who loves you so much he was willing to do anything within his power to win your love in return. Because of your belief in that jinx I had to resort to whatever I could do to accomplish that goal. Lies? No, not really. Well, sort of, but—"

"Get…out," Maggie said, tightening the hold on her arms. "Get out of my home and my life."

"Maggie, no," Luke said, "don't do this to us. Don't send me away. We're in love with each other, can have a wonderful life, have babies, grow old together. The superstitions aren't real, don't exist, and neither does the Jenkins Jinx. You're free to love…me."

Luke drew a shuddering breath and extended one hand toward Maggie. "Please, Maggie?" he said, his voice thick with emotion. "Marry me? Please?"

Maggie's trembling legs refused to hold her for another second and she sank onto the sofa, a sob catching in her throat.

This wasn't happening, she told herself frantically.

Oh, please, this wasn't happening. Luke had been playing games with her, with her emotions, her heart, her... There was no Precious and Clyde? How could people who had become so real to her not even exist? And all those dumb superstitions were part of a nasty, devious *plan* to...

How could Luke do this to her? Live a lie day after day, night after night as they made love? He wasn't remotely close to who she had believed him to be. She was a victim of his duplicity.

And she was the latest victim of the Jenkins Jinx.

"Maggie?"

"Leave...me...alone," she said, then covered her face with her hands.

Luke's shoulders slumped and he dropped his chin to his chest for a long moment before raising his head again to stare at the ceiling in an attempt to gain control of his emotions as an achy sensation gripped his throat.

He'd lost the war, he thought miserably. He'd fought the good fight, won some battles, but the ultimate victory was not his to claim. Maggie was sending him away.

She was once again behind the walls, clinging to the jinx, never wanted to see him again. There was nothing more he could do. The only woman he had ever—would ever—love was not his to have and he now understood what a broken heart felt like. This was the greatest pain, the most chilling loss, he had ever experienced.

"I'm sorry," he said quietly, looking at Maggie. "I never meant to make you cry. I never meant to hurt you.

What I did, I did out of love for you so we could be together forever. But I was wrong. I did it all wrong and I'm so damn sorry." He swallowed heavily. "Goodbye, Maggie."

Luke turned and walked slowly from the room, then down the stairs and out the front door of the Victorian house.

Maggie dropped her hands from her face and clutched them tightly in her lap as she gave way to her tears. She rocked back and forth, hardly able to breathe as the tears flowed and the sobs echoed in the silent room.

She finally shifted and curled into a ball of misery on the sofa, crying until there were no more tears to shed. Her head hurt and her heart ached for all that might have been but would never be.

Exhaustion finally claimed her and she slept fitfully, having taunting dreams of acorns, rocking chairs, goldfish and roses. Roses that died, their petals falling and disappearing into oblivion until there was nothing left.

Nothing.

Eleven

After three days and nights of weepy misery Maggie had had enough of her own gloomy company. On Saturday afternoon she called Patty and asked her if she was free to come over. Patty arrived an hour later, took one look at Maggie's pale cheeks and pink, puffy eyes and demanded to know what was going on.

"Tell all," Patty demanded, plunking down on the opposite end of the sofa from Maggie.

And Maggie told all. She sniffled her way through the tale of Luke's deception, of his diabolical *plan,* the endless string of lies he had told. She confessed her love for Luke and announced in no uncertain terms that she was the latest victim of the Jenkins Jinx.

Patty's mouth dropped open at times and she had to

tell herself to shut it as Maggie went on and on with her story.

"I know I have to cancel all the arrangements I've made for the imaginary Precious and Clyde's wedding," Maggie said, dabbing at her nose with a tissue, "but every time I pick up the phone I burst into tears. I'm a wreck. A mess. I may never recover from this disaster. *And I'm just so sad.*"

"That's very obvious," Patty said, nodding. "Whew. This whole thing is… Wow. Maggie, I don't think you're going to like what I'm about to say, but in my opinion this scheme, plan, whatever, of Luke St. John's has got to be the most romantic thing I have heard in my entire life."

"What?" Maggie said, jumping to her feet.

"Sit," Patty said, pointing to the sofa cushion.

Maggie sat. "How can you say that? Romantic? Ha! There is nothing romantic about lies, Patty. Oodles and oodles of lies. Luke doesn't have a superstitious bone in his body, but he made me believe that he… Romantic? Are you crazy?"

"Slow down. Calm down," Patty said, patting the air with the palms of her hands. "Let's back up here. You and Luke were very attracted to each other from the moment you met. Correct?"

"Well, yes, but…"

"If he had suggested at Ginger and Robert's reception that you two date each other, discover just how far that attraction might take you, you would have refused. Correct?"

"Yes, of course," Maggie said. "Something extremely intense happened between us, and I wouldn't have set myself up to have my heart broken by becoming involved with Luke, then falling prey to the jinx. No. No way."

"And Luke," Patty continued, "smart man that he is, realized that at some point and knew he had to come up with an untraditional way to continue to see you. He was determined to be with you, Maggie, no matter what. Think of the time and energy he spent putting his plan into motion and keeping it going."

"Those lies kept things going, all right," Maggie said, glaring at Patty.

"A hunk of stuff like Luke can snap his fingers," Patty said, deciding to snap her fingers, "and have just about any woman he wants. But he wanted you, Maggie Jenkins, and he worked very hard to get you. That, my dear friend, is romantic to the max."

"But—"

"Oh, Maggie, sweetie, the man is so in love with you it just melts my heart. You left him no choice but to be tricky, do anything and everything to be near you, and it was successful because you fell in love with him, too. And what did you do? You threw him out and declared him to be a jerk, or whatever choice description you nailed on him. You need your head examined."

"How can you say that? Whose side are you on?" Maggie said, nearly shrieking. "I thought you were my best friend, not Luke's. I'm talking about lies here, and deception and—"

"And love." Patty sighed wistfully. "Romantic love. Forever love. Will-you-marry-me love. Love in its purest and most beautiful form and—"

"You're getting gushy and mushy," Maggie mumbled. "Really nauseating."

"Well, what would you call it? Maggie, think about it. Really think about all that Luke did to win your heart. It just blows my mind. Good grief, the man was so desperate and determined he even asked his father to help him in his quest to... Oh, wow."

Maggie frowned and stared into space.

"Are you thinking?" Patty said, leaning slightly toward her.

"Yes, but... Well, he did spend a lot of time schlepping around with me to find the perfect honeymoon suite, despite his busy schedule. And he did memorize all those superstitions so he'd be ready to slip them in where he could. And he did keep telling me to plan the wedding of my dreams, all the details, details, details for Precious and Clyde because—"

"Because he was hoping and praying it would really be your wedding because you would be marrying him," Patty said, nodding. "Now you're getting it. Now you've got to admit that this whole thing is unbelievably romantic."

Maggie flattened her hands on her cheeks. "My gosh, Patty, what have I done? All I heard was that he lied to me, was playing a role to carry out his infamous plan and... In the very next second I was convinced that I had fallen prey to the jinx, was in love with the wrong man and… All I could hear was *what* he had done, not *why* he had done it. Then I tossed him out into the snow."

"That's a stretch," Patty said, laughing. "This is Phoenix, remember?"

"You know what I mean. Oh, Patty, I love Luke so much, and he loves me so much, and because of my life-long fears I lost him. I was so horrible to him, so nasty, so…despicable. It's over. Done. Finished. And I have no one to blame but myself. I'm so dumb."

"Yep," Patty said. "You've got that straight."

"Well, thanks a lot," Maggie said, narrowing her eyes.

"Well, for crying out loud, Maggie, you sit there like you're sentenced to weeping buckets for the rest of your days."

"I am!"

"Fine." Patty got to her feet. "One thing is very clear here."

"It is? What?"

"You don't love Luke as much as he loves you."

Maggie's eyes widened. "How can you say that?"

"Easy," Patty said, shrugging. "I opened my mouth and the words popped right out. What else can I think? Luke knocked himself out to win your heart. *The man made a plan.* You? You're just throwing up your hands and feeling sorry for yourself. He fought for you. You're resigned to going through life with a sinus headache from crying. Nope. You don't love him as much as he loves you. No way."

Maggie jumped up again. "I certainly do. I love him with my whole heart and soul and mind and body and…

Forget the body part, because some things are private. But I love him, Patty. I do. You think I can't come up with a *plan* to try to win him back, get him to forgive me? Well, ha! Just watch me. I'm leaping into action. I am woman. Hear me roar."

"Now we're getting somewhere," Patty said, settling back down on the sofa. "Okay, let's brainstorm. Your whole future happiness—and Luke's, too—is at stake here. Let's take it from the top. Think…*plan*."

"Damn that plan," Luke said. "I lost the woman I love because of The Plan, which I thought was so terrific, so brilliant."

"I tried to warn you that women are really touchy about duplicity, son," Mason St. John said, shaking his head.

The pair was having lunch at Mason's club at the same time Maggie was pouring out her heart to Patty. Luke had managed to choke down about half of his meal before giving up, his appetite gone.

"Yes, you did warn me," Luke said dully. "But did I listen? No, not me. I just plowed ahead with The Plan and now I'm paying the price. I am one very miserable man. The thought of never seeing Maggie again, not having a future with her as my wife, the mother of my children is… Hell, what a mess."

"Indeed," Mason said, taking the last bite of his lunch. "Dessert?"

"No, thanks. I'm not hungry. And I can't sleep at night and I'm aging before my very eyes. I'm a complete and total wreck."

"Mmm," Mason said, patting his lips with a linen napkin. "Care for some advice from your old man?"

"You actually have some for me?" Luke said, raising his eyebrows. "After the disaster I made of this situation?"

"Yep. My advice is…time. Give Maggie space and time to really think this through. Luke, women can run circles around men in the wisdom department. They think deeper, more detailed and emotionally than we do, God love 'em. Allow her to sift and sort what happened, what you did and why you did it. Be patient and wait."

"How long?" Luke said, his shoulders slumping. "Until Maggie visits me in a nursing home and tells me she still thinks I'm despicable?"

"Now that," Mason said, chuckling, "was funny."

"There's nothing funny about this, Dad. I've lost the woman I love!"

"So it would appear," Mason said, pointing one finger in the air. "But I'm not convinced of that yet. Time, Luke. Space. Patience. That's your new plan."

"The word *plan* should be banned from the English language," Luke said with a snort of disgust.

"Well, that's my advice, son. Oh, and do me a favor. Don't come back to the office this afternoon even though we decided we needed to work on that project we're facing. I don't think I can take any more of your sunshine mood. Go for a walk, take in a movie, get drunk, do something, but spare me."

"Thanks a bunch," Luke said glumly.

* * *

The following week went by so slowly, and Luke double-checked the date with his secretary so often that she was eyeing him warily and he decided he'd better knock it off.

In the early afternoon of the Friday following lunch with his father, Luke sat in his office staring into space, something he'd done a great deal the past few days.

He should fire himself for lack of productivity, he thought. He couldn't concentrate on anything but Maggie and that god-awful final scene in her living room. Time? Space? Patience? So far it was getting him zip. He hadn't heard one word from Maggie, and the knot in his gut continually reminded him he was terrified that he never would.

The intercom on the corner of his desk buzzed and he stared at it for a long moment, toying with the idea of ignoring it. It buzzed again. With a resigned sigh, Luke pressed the button.

"Yes, Betty?" he said to his secretary.

"There's a woman named Patty on the phone for you, Luke. She says that she's Maggie Jenkins's best friend and that it's imperative that she speak with you. Line one."

"Got it," Luke said, his heart racing as he snatched up the receiver. "Patty? Hello. This is Luke. Why are you calling? Is Maggie all right? Has something happened to her? Talk to me?"

"I would," Patty said, laughing, "if you gave me a chance."

"Oh. Yes. Sure. Sorry."

"Nothing has happened to Maggie, per se," Patty said, "except for the fact that she's terribly upset. Unhappy. Miserable. Sad. You know what I mean?"

"Yeah, I know what you mean," Luke said, squeezing the bridge of his nose. "There's a lot of that going around."

"But that's not why I called," Patty went on. "I'm at the bridal salon where Janet and I were fitted for the dresses that were supposedly for Precious's attendants at her wedding. I'm helping Maggie cancel all the arrangements, the bookings and what have you she made for Precious and Clyde, who don't need them because they aren't really real."

"And?"

"Well, the owner of the shop says these two dresses have to be paid for today, can't be canceled because…well, they're dresses just waiting for final fittings. I don't have enough money to pay for them and I know Maggie doesn't. I don't want to upset her more than she is by telling her I hit a glitch here. Do you think you could come down here and settle the account?"

"Of course," Luke said. "It's the least I can do. Give me the address." He paused. "Patty, I love Maggie, I truly do. Do you believe there's any hope of her forgiving me for what I did?"

"Gosh, Luke, I don't know what to tell you. I've never seen her so distraught, so… It's heartbreaking, just heartbreaking. It just breaks my heart because it's so…heartbreaking."

"Oh," he said, sighing. "That's bad. Very bad. Not good. It sounds like time is not doing the job."

"Pardon me?"

"Never mind," he said with another deep sigh. "Just give me the address of that store and tell the owner I'm on my way."

"Thank you, I'll let her know," Patty said. "I have to leave now because I have another appointment, but I'll assure the owner that you'll be here soon."

"I'll settle up with any of the suppliers that charge a fee for canceling orders. Man, I wish things were different. I wish... Never mind. This is all my fault. Call me if you run into problems."

"Okay. Sure. We may all end up eating a whole bunch of white-chocolate miniature roses that were to be in tiny baskets at each place setting at the reception."

"Roses and wishes," Luke said quietly.

"Yes. Well. 'Bye for now."

"'Bye Patty."

When Luke entered the bridal salon, a copper bell over the door tinkled to announce his arrival. A woman's voice came from somewhere in the distance calling out that she would be there in a minute. He wandered around the main area of the lushly decorated shop, his hands shoved into the pockets of his pants. He stopped in the middle of the room and frowned.

This was where an upper-crust bride-to-be came to select her attendants' dresses and to pick out her own wedding gown, he thought. With his damnable plan he'd forced Maggie to come here, make choices for her dream wedding while believing it was all for Precious and Clyde's extravaganza.

The same held true for the honeymoon suite, the menu for the reception dinner, every little detail, like white-chocolate roses in little baskets, that Maggie had had to deal with.

His plan hadn't been brilliant, it had been cruel. He, Luke St. John, was the scum of the earth and didn't deserve to be forgiven. Maggie must have daydreamed about those white-chocolate roses at some point in her life, had been in the process of making them a reality while thinking she would then watch Precious and Clyde's guests gobble up the sweet, pretty treat.

Yeah, he was definitely despicable. There wasn't a chance in hell that his beloved Maggie would forgive him for what he'd put her through, and he didn't blame her, not one damn bit.

"Sorry to have kept you waiting," an attractive woman in her forties said, hurrying toward Luke. "I'm Selina Simone, the owner of this salon. And you are?"

"Luke St. John."

"Ah, yes, Patty said you were coming. I trust you understand why I must be compensated for the dresses that Maggie selected."

"Of course," Luke said. "I'll write you a check. I'd like Patty and Janet to keep them. Could you see to that?"

"Yes, it will be my pleasure. They're gorgeous gowns. Maggie has such splendid taste and she was so excited when we found that exact shade of green she wanted for her—for the Christmas wedding she was coordinating. Well, I'm sure Janet and Patty will enjoy owning the creations."

"Right," Luke said gloomily. "It will be nice to know that someone smiled in the middle of this mess. Is there anything else I need to take care of here?"

"Well, yes, as a matter of fact there is," Selina said. "There are accessories, you see. The satin ribbons for the bouquets and what have you."

"Whatever." Luke nodded. "Sure."

"Would you mind coming into the back with me, Mr. St. John? That's where my records are, and it will be easier for me to check the order forms."

"That's fine. Lead the way."

"Well, I have something to tend to and will join you in a moment. Just go through that door over there and wait, if you would be so kind."

This was pure torture, Luke thought as he crossed the room. Every second he spent in this place pounded home the truth of how difficult all this had been for Maggie, how painful, how…heartbreaking, to borrow Patty's word. Yeah, well, he deserved to suffer, louse that he was.

He entered a medium-size room that had thick rose-colored carpeting. Cranberry-colored easy chairs were arranged in a semicircle in front of a white wicker arch with artificial greenery and flowers woven through it. A large three-sided mirror was on the opposite wall with additional chairs in front of it. Soft, dreamy music was playing.

Man, Luke thought, look at this place. It just got

worse and worse. Maggie had probably sat in one of those chairs and watched Janet and Patty try on the green dresses. The gowns of her dreams that she'd believed would be worn by Precious's attendants.

And a wedding dress? God, had Maggie been forced to select that already, too? Try it on? The wedding gown she'd wear if she was going to be the bride, knowing that Precious would walk down the aisle in it? He should be strung up by his rotten thumbs for what he'd done to his Maggie.

Luke jerked as the music became slightly louder. It was clearly the traditional wedding march.

Why were they playing that now? he thought, beads of sweat dotting his brow. He couldn't take much more of this. Maggie must have heard it at some point in this disaster and... Where was that lady, that Selina woman? He had to get out of here.

He looked frantically around, hoping that Selina Simone would appear, then a motion beyond the pretty arch caught his attention and he snapped his head back to see what it was.

Then he stopped breathing as he stared through the arch, finally taking a shuddering breath as a sharp pain shot across his chest telling him he was desperately in need of air in his lungs.

"My God," Luke whispered, his heart thundering. "Maggie."

She was walking slowly toward him, her fingers laced loosely at her waist. And she was wearing an incredibly beautiful full-length white wedding dress. It was an old-fashioned Victorian style with a high neck and a multitude of seed pearls on the bodice. It nipped in at her tiny waist, and the skirt swept to the floor in soft, luscious satin folds. The gossamer veil brushed her shoulders and was turned back to reveal her face.

And Maggie was smiling.

"Maggie?" Luke said, hearing the gritty quality of his voice.

She continued to approach with the measured steps of a bride walking down the aisle to meet her groom as the wedding march continued to play. She finally stopped in front of Luke and he swallowed heavily as he looked at her.

"Hello, Luke," she said softly.

"You are…" Luke cleared his throat. "Maggie, you are the most beautiful bride I have ever seen." He shook his head slightly. "But I don't understand what—"

"I'll explain," Maggie interrupted. "Let's sit down."

"Yes. Okay."

Maggie settled onto one of the cranberry-colored chairs, smoothing her skirt out around her. Luke pulled a matching chair in front of her and leaned forward, resting his elbows on his knees and tapping his laced fingers against his lips.

"Luke," Maggie said, looking directly into his dark eyes, "I hope you'll forgive me for the horrible things I said to you when you told me about your plan."

"Forgive *you*?" he said, splaying his hands on his knees. "I'm the one who wants to beg *you* to forgive *me* for being so—" he glanced around, then met her gaze again "—so cruel and heartless and thoughtless and for telling you all those lies and… The fact that I was desperate, so afraid of losing you, is no excuse for what I put you through. I thought I was being so clever, so… Maggie, I'm so sorry."

"Well, we're even as far as plans go," she said, smiling at him warmly. "Patty and Selina were in on *my* plan to get you here today."

"Oh?" he said, surprise registering on his face.

"Luke, I overreacted terribly when you told me about Precious and Clyde not being real people, about how you wanted me to organize *my* dream wedding and… All I could hear was that you lied to me, weren't who you had presented yourself to be. All I could hear was that I had made a horrendous mistake by falling in love with you and had become a victim of the Jenkins Jinx."

"No, I—"

"Please, just listen."

He nodded.

"I was feeling so sorry for myself," Maggie went on, "felt betrayed and… But Patty made me realize that what you had done wasn't despicable, it was romantic, it stemmed from your love for me and from your heartfelt desire to marry me and give me the wedding of my dreams."

"Yes, yes, that's it," Luke said, nodding jerkily. "That's why I did it. But it all blew up and I was convinced I'd lost you forever, that you'd hide behind those walls of yours and I'd never be able to get near you again."

"Luke, the walls are gone forever. After I talked with Patty, I went for a long walk and listened to my heart. I came to know that love, true love, forever love, is stronger than any jinx or superstition. I know that what you and I have together will withstand the good times, the bad, in sickness and in health, until death parts us and perhaps even beyond."

"Ah, Maggie," Luke said, his throat tightening. "I love you so much."

"I love you, too," she said, sudden tears filling her eyes. "I worked out a plan with Patty and Selina to get you here so you would see me in this wedding dress, the one I want to wear when I become your wife. I wanted to prove to you that I don't believe in the jinx or any superstition like the groom not seeing his bride in her dress before the ceremony. I wanted to prove to you that I'm free to live, to love, and that I want to spend the rest of my life with you as your wife…if you'll have me."

Luke stood and with hands that were not quite steady grasped Maggie's and eased her to her feet.

"Maggie Jenkins," he said, giving up any attempt to hide the tears shimmering in his eyes, "would you do me the honor of becoming my wife? Will you marry me, Maggie? Please?"

"Yes," she said, smiling through her own tears of joy. "Oh, yes."

Luke dropped her hands, framed her face, then kissed her so softly, so reverently, to seal the commitment to their future together.

Right on cue the music changed to a waltz—*their*

waltz. Luke drew Maggie into his arms and they danced around the room as though floating on clouds, looking directly into each other's eyes, seeing matching messages of greater understanding and forgiveness, of the love and happiness that would be theirs to share for eternity.

Several hours into the wedding reception of Mr. and Mrs. Luke St. John, the newly married couple had made their escape to the honeymoon suite.

"Oh, my," Patty said wistfully, "it was all so beautiful, wasn't it? Including me in this gorgeous dress. Just perfect. Every detail, detail, detail, as Maggie would say. Right down to those delicious white-chocolate roses. What a wonderful couple Maggie and Luke make. And happy? I think they give a whole new meaning to the word."

"Yes," Maggie's mother, Martha, said, "you're right. Seeing them together… Well, let's just say that there will be no more talk of the Jenkins Jinx in this family. Maggie and Luke have broken that nasty spell, I just know in my heart that they have."

"I agree with you, Mother," Janet said. "And I'd say that my cute brother does, too. He's danced all evening with that pretty girl he met here." She paused. "Didn't you love the wedding gifts Maggie and Luke gave each other? A tiny gold acorn on a delicate chain for Maggie, and she had gold acorn cuff links made for Luke. She told me it was their special way of remembering all that took place before this memorable night. Oh, God, that is so romantic I could weep."

"I already did," Patty said, laughing.

"No more jinx," Martha said, "and no more Roses and Wishes. Maggie has officially closed her business." She smiled. "She said that enterprise made all her wishes come true, so she's thinking of opening a baby boutique to see if that will hurry along the first little St. John bundle of joy."

"My goodness," Patty said, her eyes widening. "Does that sound superstitious to you?" She laughed. "Well, rest up, folks, because here we go again."

* * * * *

TRUST ME
by
Caroline Cross

CAROLINE CROSS

writes romance because life is endlessly challenging and she believes we all need an occasional reminder that good people and true love do exist—if one just looks hard enough and has faith in happy endings.

Winner of numerous awards, including a RITA® Award for Best Short Contemporary, she lives in the Pacific Northwest with her husband of two decades, has two wonderful daughters and depends on her family and friends to keep her grounded.

A devoted romance reader herself, she always hopes that her books can bring others a little of the enjoyment and satisfaction she feels when she reads her own favourite authors.

This is a book about second chances.
I owe mine to two terrific editors, Julie Barrett
and Melissa Jeglinski. Thanks for giving me the
chance to write this book and for always
making me look better.

One

The shriek of the bolt being drawn in the cell block door shattered the sultry afternoon silence.

Lilah jerked her head up. For a second, she remained frozen. Then she scrambled upright, scooted to the far edge of the thin mat that served as her bed and pressed herself back against the rough concrete wall. She braced herself as the door at the end of the corridor crashed open.

Against a dim spill of light, a pair of jail guards staggered into sight. A man hung limply between them. His head lolled. His feet trailed in the dust. As the guards dragged him forward, Lilah stared at tanned, muscular arms, the hard biceps stretching the sleeves of a faded olive T-shirt. At inky hair that gleamed even in the murky illumination. At the trickle of blood beading at the edge of a determined mouth.

With a long-suffering grunt, the jailers hoisted their burden a little higher. The prisoner's head tilted sideways,

allowing her a quick view of a straight blade of a nose and
the strong clean line of a cheekbone.

All of which abruptly seemed familiar.

Her heart leapt even as her mind reeled. *No. It can't be.*
What would the love of her reckless youth, the masculine
yardstick against whom she'd once measured all others,
the man who at times still invaded her sleep and hijacked
her dreams—what would *he* be doing *here*, in the farthest
reaches of the Caribbean, in remote San Timoteo, at one
of El Presidente's private jails?

Her mind must've snapped. It was the only explanation
that made sense, Lilah decided. She'd tried to be brave, to
hold on and be strong, but finally she'd lost it. What's
worse, she was hallucinating.

And yet....

The guards dumped the newcomer onto the adjoining
cell's concrete floor. One of them lingered long enough to
give their newest captive a vicious kick to the ribs, then
exited, slamming first the cell door and then the corridor
door behind him.

Every nerve in Lilah's body screamed for action. Yet the
harsh lessons of the past month had reinforced her innate
sense of caution. Ignoring the pounding of her heart, she
forced herself to stay where she was, to wait for the sounds
of the bolt slamming home and her captors' footsteps receding. Then, unable to remain still another instant, she
launched herself off the bed and across the cell.

She reached the unyielding metal bars, her gaze locked
on her fellow prisoner's face as she slid to her knees. Her
pulse thrummed wildly in her ears as she studied the straight
eyebrows, the strong chin and the killer cheekbones.

This close, there could be no doubt. The years may have added width to his shoulders, heft to his muscles, a few character lines to his handsome face, but it was him.

Dominic Devlin Steele.

Stunned, she tried to think. What on earth could he be doing here? Was it sheer coincidence? An incredible twist of fate?

That hardly seemed probable. Yet the only other explanation was that he was here deliberately, and the only person likely to orchestrate that would be her grandmother. Try as she might, Lilah couldn't imagine a world where Abigail Anson Clarke Cantrell Trayburne Sommers's path would cross Dominic Steele's.

Much less why he'd agree to put himself in harm's way for her.

Then she realized none of it mattered. After a month of fear, loneliness and growing desperation, it was simply wonderful to see a familiar face. Even his.

Especially his.

She reached through the bars. "Dominic? It's me. Lilah. Lilah Cantrell." Fingers trembling, she touched her hand to his cheek.

On some marginal level, she registered that his skin was reassuringly warm. That the faint prickle of his beard against her palm tickled. And that nearly a decade had done nothing to dim the hot little thrill of pleasure that touching him brought her.

But mostly her focus was all on the fact that he was far, far too still. "I can't believe it's really you. That you're here, of all places. The thing is, you need to wake up. Wake up and talk to me. Or at least stop being so still. Please?"

He didn't stir. Biting her bottom lip, she tried to decide what to do now, only to have panic flood her when she realized she didn't have a clue. Her fright gave birth to a lump in her throat and the next thing she knew, she had to press her lips together to muffle a sudden sob.

Her weakness shamed her. So what if seeing someone—anything—familiar emphasized how demoralizing the past month's incarceration had been? So what if she'd begun to lose hope that she'd ever see home again? Or that, as hard as she'd tried to convince herself it didn't matter, she'd started to wonder whether she'd even be missed?

She was a Cantrell. Ever since she could remember she'd been warned against the dangers of self-indulgence, the perils of losing control.

More to the point, you aren't the one lying bruised and unconscious on a dirty floor. She should be focused on how to aid Dominic, not kneeling and wringing her hands like a vapid heroine in a B movie. She could just imagine what Gran would say. "For heaven's sake, child!" the familiar, autocratic voice declared impatiently in her head. "Quit your sniveling and at least try to live up to your family name!"

Like a dash of cold water, imagining her grandmother's disdain steadied her. Swallowing hard, Lilah took a deep breath to force back the tidal wave of emotion that had so nearly swamped her. To her relief, the tightness in her throat eased and her hands quit shaking. Heartened, she wasted no time turning her attention back to Dominic.

First things first, she decided. She'd do her best to see if she could pinpoint where he was injured; then she'd worry about what to do about it.

She set about examining him. Careful to keep her touch as light as a kiss of sunlight, she skimmed her fingertips over those areas of his head and face that she could reach through the bars, checking for knots or blood or anything else that seemed out of place. Next came his neck and throat. Then she cautiously probed the side of him nearest to her, checking each rib, the long valley of his spine, the solid curves of arm and shoulder.

Nothing. Except for the heart-stopping discovery that he was all taut skin and steely muscle, exactly the way she remembered, she remained as clueless as she'd been minutes earlier about his possible injuries.

She fought the return of despair. "Come on, Nicky," she whispered, her old pet name for him inadvertently slipping off her tongue as she rubbed the skin-warmed cotton of his shirt beneath her fingertips. "Quit playing around. I need you. I really, really need you. Wake up. Please please *please* wake up—"

"Jeez, Li. Chill."

"Oh!" Her gaze jerked to Dominic's face and she found herself staring into a pair of familiar grass-green eyes. "You're awake!"

"Yeah." He remained motionless, simply staring at her for several long seconds. Then he gingerly lifted his head an inch off the ground, gave it a slight, tentative shake and winced. "Lucky me." He squeezed his eyes shut again, as if even the cell's shadowy light was more than he could tolerate.

Lilah felt a fresh stab of alarm. What if he had a concussion or a skull fracture? Or—she recalled the boot to the side he'd taken and shuddered—broken ribs or a fractured spleen? Heaven help them both, he could have internal bleeding and not even know it. Her throat dry, she swallowed. "Where does it hurt?"

"Where doesn't it?" he muttered. "Still—" he lifted an admonishing finger "—I've survived worse, so don't go getting your panties in a twist, okay?" With a resigned-sounding sigh, he opened his eyes, raised himself up on his elbow and reached out to lay one large, warm hand over hers where it clutched the bars. "Trust me. I'm all right. I just need a minute."

Trust me. The words washed over her, an echo from their past. How many times had he said just that, after daring her to do something dangerous, forbidden, but oh so tantalizing? How many times had she gazed into those fabulous eyes and lost a battle with temptation?

How many times had his touch made her brain fog while her body had come alive with desire?

Enough to remember him forever.

He released her hand unexpectedly to roll onto his side, breaking her wild thoughts. Grimacing, he flexed his jaw and touched an exploratory fingertip to his cut lip. He scrubbed the blood away with the back of his hand. Then, in one lithe move, he climbed to his feet.

Frozen in place, fighting to appear calm, she watched him take stock. His big muscular body bunched and flexed as he swiveled his head, rolled his shoulders, bounced lightly to test thighs, calves and knees. He rubbed briefly at a spot above his left pectoral and then sent her a pleased look. "Good news, princess. I think I'm gonna live."

Princess. The intimate nickname, uttered in that casual, coolly amused tone of voice, felt like a slap to the face.

Suddenly aware that she was still kneeling at his feet like some obedient harem girl, she scrambled up.

Oblivious to her, he took a slow look around, making a complete revolution as he took note of the solitary barred window set high in the far wall, the worn, wafer-thin woven pads atop the concrete slab ledges that passed for beds, the grate-covered holes that comprised the Third World bathroom facilities.

He gave a soundless whistle. "Man. You really must've pissed off the wrong person. I've seen prisons more cheerful than this." His gaze swung back to her. For a second, something almost dangerous gleamed in his eyes and then his teeth flashed white, destroying that impression. "Wait. My mistake. This *is* a prison."

He was making a joke. A *joke.* Here she'd been terrified out of her wits, afraid he might be irreparably injured, utterly overcome at seeing him again—and he was poking fun at their surroundings.

She stiffened. Humiliation warred with indignation, and indignation won. Not that she intended to let on. No way would she risk what little dignity she still possessed by letting on that he could still get to her.

Besides, she had bigger fish to fry, since his little inventory of his working body parts, coupled with his critique of the accommodations, had given her time to think.

"Your being here isn't a coincidence, is it?" she said, recalling his first words to her and his utter lack of surprise at her presence in a desolate jail cell in an obscure little island country a million miles from home. "As a matter of fact," she went on, ignoring his penetrating eyes to glance pointedly at the bruise starting to darken one strong cheekbone and the lip still oozing blood, "you deliberately did something to get yourself thrown in here because you *knew* this was where I was being held."

Silence. Then his battered mouth quirked. "Score one for the rich girl."

For a second, she had a powerful urge to hit him. Not that she had a hope of reaching him, but still....

Horrified, she took a firm grip on the bars that separated them, reminding herself yet again that she was a Cantrell and as such she would not, could not, lose her temper. Especially not now, when there was so much she burned to know. "How did you find me? How did you even know I was here in the first place? Did my grandmother send you? And why would you come? Why would you put yourself at risk like this?"

Logic insisted his presence simply couldn't be a coincidence, but she still couldn't seem to make sense of it.

After all, even ignoring the astronomical odds against him and her grandmother connecting, it had been ten years since his and *Lilah's* last encounter. Ten years since she'd told him he'd better go and he'd looked at her with the same sort of nonchalant expression that currently graced his face. Ten years since he'd crushed her heart with a careless shrug and the comment that it was "her loss" before stalking out of her life forever.

Even now, the memory hurt. It made the past seem not so very long ago. As did the infuriating way he was currently considering her, so unruffled, so superior, so—so *male*. "Explain what you're doing here. *Now*."

"Tell you what, Li." As cool as a wolf in winter, he padded over, braced his big hands above hers on the bars and leaned forward, his sheer size and proximity making her stomach tumble. "Do us both a favor, sweetheart. Take a deep breath, shut your pretty mouth and I'll tell you everything I know."

Two

Denver, Colorado
Five days earlier

"**H**ey." Dominic ducked his head into his older brother's spacious office at Steele Security headquarters. "You got a minute?"

Gabriel, who was seated at his granite-topped desk, glanced up, then resumed sorting through a stack of paperwork. "Sure. Come on in."

Dom strolled across the flagstone floor. Like all the offices in the ultramodern, low-slung building tucked away in the city's warehouse district, this one boasted a wall of glass that looked out on an interior courtyard. Today, as befitted January in the Rockies, the outside world was a brilliant sea of white, courtesy of the foot of fresh snow that had fallen overnight. "Taggart says we're turning down a case." After Gabe, Taggart was number two in the Steele brothers birth order hierarchy.

"That's right." Gabe's tone was matter-of-fact. "The client's coming in at two. I'm going to recommend she contact Allied."

He stopped, rocking back on the heels of his Italian leather boots. "Why?"

"We don't have the manpower."

"You're kidding."

"Nope." Gabe made a quick notation on a page and set it to one side. "Taggart thinks he may finally have a lead on the elusive Ms. Bowen. Josh is going to be tied up with the Romero trial in Seattle for at least two weeks, and everyone else is either hip deep in the Dallas industrial espionage case or working the economic summit in London. That leaves me, and as much as I wouldn't mind some field work, I'm needed here at the moment."

Dominic studied his brother. To an outsider, Gabe would no doubt appear calm and dispassionate, an image deliberately encouraged by his choice of attire—a starched white shirt, rep tie and severe charcoal suit that just happened to be polar opposites of Dom's own laid-back black slacks and green linen shirt. Only someone who knew him well—like a brother—would be likely to notice the sudden tension lining his mouth and shadowing his eyes.

But then, both Gabe and Taggart were wound pretty tight; Dom had long ago concluded that his two older brothers had spent way too much time in the line of duty— no doubt at the old man's command—and had missed out on hanging loose and living a little.

Not him. Dom had decided early on that life was too

short to spend his time all stressed out worrying about things that might never happen and bracing for every possible disaster. Besides, somebody had to keep Steele One and Steele Two from imploding, and while Taggart was most likely a lost cause, Dom still had hopes for Gabe.

His esteemed older brother just needed an occasional reminder that the world wouldn't end if he enjoyed himself once in a while. Or—he thought as he planted himself in one of the luxe leather chairs facing Gabe's desk—didn't try to stand in the way of somebody *else* enjoying himself.

"Okay, so everybody's busy," Dom said, stretching out his long legs. "What's that make me? The invisible man?"

Gabe frowned down at the paper before him. "You're still recovering. It's only been two months since the shooting. You need more time."

"No, I don't. I feel fine. Hell, I feel more than fine. What with physical therapy, working on my house and all the time I've spent out on the course at Fort Carson, I'm in the best shape of my life. For sure I'm in better shape than some desk-riding cowboys I know."

Gabe stoically ignored the insult. "Forget it."

Dom considered his brother's dismissive tone and reminded himself he was no longer the brash, hell-raising teenager who'd once felt compelled to challenge Gabe's "I'm-four-years-older-than-you" authority.

Okay, so his big brother had founded Steele Security and been the driving force in establishing its reputation as a top-notch organization that could handle anything from high-profile protection to undercover investigations to locating missing persons. But Dom, along with Gabe, Taggart and two more of the nine Steele brothers, had since contributed to the company's growing prestige and were now full partners in the enterprise.

As such, he got a say in things, whether Gabe liked it or not. "I don't think I want to forget about it," he said evenly.

Gabe slowly set down his pen. Raising his head, he met Dom's direct gaze with one of his own. "Let me guess. You're not going to let this go, are you?"

Dom grinned. "Not a chance. So you might as well tell me what's going on and get it over with."

For a very long moment, Gabe continued to stare at him. Then he gave an exaggerated sigh. "Aw, hell. You always have been pigheaded." Reaching over, he snagged a file folder off the top of a stack to his left, speaking even as he thumbed it open. "The client is Abigail Sommers. I did protection work for her when I was first getting started. She was born an Anson, as in the Anson Mining Group, and over the course of eighty-odd years she's single-handedly increased what was already a pretty sizable family fortune. Along the way, she's outlived four husbands and both of her children.

"According to the message she left on my voice mail, her only grandchild is being detained in San Timoteo, an island nation—"

"—in the southern Caribbean. Run for the past dozen years by a corrupt ex-army general, Manolo Condesta, who insists on being called El Presidente." With a chiding look, Dom tipped back his chair and folded his hands behind his head. "I've been living in London the past few years, Gabe, not on the moon. I'm up to speed on all the banana republics. I don't need a lesson in geography or world politics."

Gabe's stern mouth tipped up the faintest fraction. "Got it. Sorry."

Dom shrugged it off. "So what's the grandkid accused of?"

His brother glanced down at the file, even though Dom knew very well all the information was already securely lodged in his encyclopedic memory. "Rioting, assaulting a policeman, resisting arrest."

He gave a nod of understanding. It was an old story—spoiled rich kid takes a trip to a foreign country, gets drunk or stoned and does something obnoxious that pisses off the local officials.

"I'm surprised I haven't heard a word about it in the press. Usually they love this stuff."

Gabe nodded. "True. But Condesta's got an iron grip on info going out of San Timoteo. And due to some bad tabloid press decades ago, Abigail is rabid about protecting her privacy. Everyone who works for her in any capacity signs a nondisclosure contract."

"Okay, but from what I've heard about El Presidente, he'll let people go for the right dollar amount. With all the money Mrs. Sommers has, she must have government contacts who can help?"

"Officially, the U.S. government has no relations with San Tim since it's been added to the terrorist watch list. Unofficially, they've done what they could.

"Problem is, Condesta keeps upping the ante. Abigail said that twice he's set a price, twice she's agreed to pay it. And twice he's changed his mind just hours before the scheduled exchange and demanded more. The asking price is now at one million, with no end in sight, and in the meantime her granddaughter's been held for over four weeks."

"Not good," Dom repeated. While young Miss Sommers most likely was being confined someplace that more closely resembled a country club than Alcatraz, the hard truth was that women were vulnerable in ways men were not. "So what does the client want from us? More negotiations? An extraction?"

"I don't know. All she said in her message was that the situation was untenable and something had to be done."

"She's right about that. And as of now, I'm the guy to do it."

"No." The eldest Steele closed the file as if that settled the matter.

"Yes." His voice for once not the least bit amused, Dom straightened, bringing his chair down with a thump. "I don't need a babysitter, Gabe. What I need is some action. Because if I have to spend another week sitting on my ass doing nothing but counting snowflakes, I'm likely to go tear up some Third World country myself."

"Dammit, Dom—"

"Give it up, big brother. You did a hell of a job taking care of us after Mom died, but we're all big boys now. We can take care of ourselves. Besides—" he forced himself to ease up and summoned an ironic smile "—as has been previously established, you are not, as the kids say these days, the boss of me. I'm going to San Timoteo, and that's all there is to it.

"That being the case," he went on without missing a

beat as he picked up the file and climbed to his feet, "it appears I've got some reading to do, so I'll let you get back to your paperwork. But I'll see you and Mrs. Sommers in the conference room in—" he glanced at his watch "—an hour. Don't be late."

Just for a second, Gabriel's green eyes narrowed dangerously. Then his expression unexpectedly relaxed and he unbent enough to murmur a caustic two-word epithet that started with an *F* and ended with a *U*.

Laughing, Dom headed for the door.

Abigail Anson Sommers didn't look like anyone's dear old grandma, Dom decided, observing her as Gabriel ushered her into the conference room. Tall and slim, she had finely modeled features, thick, upswept white hair, impeccable posture and the aloof expression of an absolute monarch.

He stepped around the large, glossy table to pull out her chair.

"Thank you, young man," she said as she took her seat, her manner pure queen to commoner as he and Gabriel also sat.

"My pleasure," he replied, secretly amused by her not-so-subtle effort to put him in his place.

Foregoing formal introductions, she got straight to the point. "According to your brother, you had something to do with that Grobane incident," she said crisply. "The one that was in all the papers."

"Something," he agreed, settling back. He met her probing gaze with an unflinching one of his own. She could pry all she wanted, but he had no intention of discussing his last protection detail with her. And not just because it would be a breach of client confidentiality, even though that concern might be considered by some to be gone with the wind due to all the media attention the incident had re-ceived.

But because, unlike the press and the public, he didn't consider taking a bullet for a client heroic. Nope, he'd screwed up, failed to follow his gut and was just damn lucky the bad guy had been a lousy shot. He still had nights when he would lie awake in a cold sweat thinking how close Carolina Grobane had come to being injured or killed.

He didn't think he could've lived with that. And he sure as hell didn't intend to rehash it—or court praise for some-thing he considered to be far from his most shining hour, popular opinion be damned.

Evidently mistaking his silence for modesty, something approaching approval registered on Mrs. Sommers' auto-cratic face. "Gabriel also mentioned you served our coun-try as a Navy SEAL. And that you received numerous medals and commendations."

This time, he sent his brother a reproachful look, which was met with a slight, live-with-it shrug. A little ruefully—apparently St. Gabe wasn't above some minor payback—he returned his gaze to the client. "Yes, ma'am, that's true."

She pursed her lips. "He also assures me that if anyone can get my Delilah out of this mess she's in, it's you."

"Possibly."

"*Possibly?*" Her arctic-blue eyes drilled into him. "And what exactly do you mean by that, pray tell?"

"It means I have a general idea of your granddaughter's situation, but I'd be doing us both a disservice if I made any promises until I know more," he said easily.

There was a prolonged silence as once again she considered him, then she abruptly murmured, "Hmmph." Leaning sideways, she reached into her large handbag and pulled out a fat document-sized manila envelope.

"I anticipated this," she said brusquely. "It's all here. Delilah's original itinerary. A list of the people she met with. Transcripts of my conversations with that detestable Condesta's representatives. Photos of and information about the compound in Santa Marita where she's being held. Oh, and a photo of her, of course."

"This should be very helpful." Dom took the proffered envelope and set it down in front of him. "First, however, I think we'd better establish what, exactly, you want me to do. Take over negotiations? Handle the exchange?"

To his immense gratification, she snorted and said briskly, "Certainly not. I have lawyers to do those things. Lawyers and advisers and business managers, whom I allowed, against my better judgment, to convince me that dealing with Delilah's captors was the right thing to do…" She trailed off, then squared her shoulders and ratcheted up her already ramrod posture. "I may be old, Mr. Steele, but I'm not stupid, at least not often, and I don't care for extortion. I want you to go to San Timoteo and bring Delilah home where she belongs."

He did his best to squelch an inner cheer. "Okay. But there are still things we need to discuss."

Her mouth curved in a moue of annoyance. "If this is about your fee—"

"No, ma'am," he assured her. "I'm sure you're good for it." He swallowed a grin at her huff of indignation, then got down to business. "What I want is some insight into your granddaughter. Is she a leader or a follower? Easygoing or high-strung? Quick off the mark or more of a deep thinker?"

"Why on earth do you need to know all that?" she snapped.

"Well, let's see." He lazily drummed his fingertips against the tabletop. "I guess because it would be helpful to know what to expect. Is she likely to scream or faint when I show up? Will she feel compelled to offer her opinion about every move I make, or will she do what she's told? Is she going to get hysterical if we have to make a run for it and she breaks a nail?"

Abigail's icy blue eyes glinted. "You may count on Delilah to behave sensibly, Mr. Steele. I didn't raise her to indulge in histrionics. She's a level-headed, responsible young woman as befits her station, and I can assure you she understands that sometimes duty—or circumstance—requires one to subvert one's emotions and do what needs to be done."

"Okay," he said mildly. "But if she's such a paragon of virtue, then how'd she wind up enjoying Condesta's enforced hospitality?"

"I never claimed my granddaughter was perfect," she said stiffly, raising her already elevated chin another fraction. "For all her many sterling qualities, once in a while, on exceedingly rare occasions, Delilah can be unexpectedly…stubborn.

"This trip was a perfect example. Although it could

easily have been handled by one of the staff, whom we *pay* to do this sort of thing, and despite the fact that she has countless obligations that require her attention at home, she insisted on personally going to San Timoteo to inspect a school that had applied to the Anson Foundation, a non-profit organization my late father started, for funding.

"As I understand it, once her business was completed she decided to attend some sort of local celebration. It got out of hand, the police were called in and when the young man she was with was threatened with arrest—" her lips tightened "—Delilah foolishly objected."

Dominic nodded. The granddaughter might be a few years older and a little less flaky than he'd initially envisioned, but the rest of the story was still pretty much what he'd expected—a classic case of Rich Person Behaving Badly. "So how do you think she's holding up?"

"I'm sure she's managing. The Anson blood runs in her veins," the old lady said coolly, as if that said it all.

And maybe it did, Dom decided. At least it didn't sound as if the granddaughter was likely to wilt like a hothouse flower at her first sight of him. Or complain endlessly about his choices and methods, or because he hadn't brought her champagne and caviar or her own private masseuse.

Not that he'd ever intended not to rescue her if given the opportunity. Even if Mrs. Sommers had revealed that her darling Delilah had all the charm of a polecat on steroids, he'd planned all along to go to San Timoteo to relieve El Presidente of his unwilling guest.

But he wasn't a fool. For all his no-sweat approach to life, he believed in doing things right. And in the security business, that meant careful planning and meticulous preparation, which meant obtaining all the information you could.

Still, it was probably past time to end the suspense and let Queen Abigail know he was willing to save her bacon, so to speak. "All right. I'll do it."

"Excellent!" Mrs. Sommers abruptly appeared years younger, for the first time revealing the genuine concern hidden beneath her crusty exterior. "How soon can you leave?"

"Sometime in the next forty-eight hours. Let me look this over—" he tapped the envelope "—make some calls and I'll get back to you later today with any other questions that crop up and a more definitive timetable."

"Excellent," she repeated. Grasping her purse, she started to stand.

Already formulating a list of things he needed to do, he pushed to his feet. Once again, Dom and his new client shook hands and then Gabe offered his arm to escort her from the room. The two were almost to the door when Dom reached in and drew out the sheaf of papers. Paper-clipped to the top was a five-by-seven color photo. He glanced at it.

A shock like the blast from a stun gun jolted through him.

"*This* is your granddaughter? Lilah Cantrell?" Damned if his voice didn't come out in a croak.

Mrs. Sommers turned, still graceful despite her years. "Delilah, yes. Her father was the product of my union with my second husband, James."

He fought to keep his expression neutral. It took only

a second for him to realize why he hadn't made the connection: when he'd known Lilah, her grandmother's name hadn't been *either* Sommers or Cantrell, and the family mansion had been referred to as—he racked his brain, and suddenly he had it—the Trayburne estate.

But even so… He felt Gabriel's sudden scrutiny like a touch. Yet Gabe being Gabe, his brother didn't let on. "Come along, Abigail," the other man said smoothly. "Margaret has the paperwork you need to sign at the front desk."

The second they'd cleared the threshold, Dom turned his attention back to the glossy studio image clutched in his hand. A fine-boned blonde with china-blue eyes, a tantalizing mouth and an expression both reserved and challenging looked back at him.

Well, hell. Delilah Sommers was actually Lilah Cantrell. And despite her grandmother's claims to the contrary, *Lilah* was every inch a self-centered society princess.

That he knew from personal experience.

Because Lilah Cantrell was the first—and only—woman he'd ever fallen hard for. The one woman he'd never been able to predict. The only woman ever to have shown him the door before he'd been sure he was ready to go.

And definitely the last woman on earth he'd deliberately seek out.

He uttered the first half of Gabe's earlier curse.

"Something wrong?"

He jerked his head up, startled to find his older brother standing in the doorway watching him.

He immediately blanked his face. "No."

And there wasn't, he told himself firmly, shoving the picture back into the envelope. So what if he'd just agreed—no, insisted—on not just seeking Lilah out, but being allowed the privilege of saving her shapely little prima donna butt? He was a pro and he intended to act like it.

After all, the past was just that—the past. And he and Li had been barely more than kids at the time of their clichéd summer fling. What's more, he'd known from the start they had no future. If in the intervening years he'd occasionally thought about her with a pang of regret, it was only because the sex had been incredible. Hell, more than incredible. Maybe the best of his life—

"You sure you're all right?"

Gabe's question yanked him back to reality. He thought about it for all of half a second and then felt a genuine smile form on his lips. "Yeah, I am. Why wouldn't I be? I get to leave this Popsicle weather, go where I can work on my tan and foil some bad guys in the bargain. *Plus* we get paid for it.

"Trust me, bro. I can handle it."

Three

"So you do this for a *living?*" Lilah's eyebrows, shades darker than her pale hair, rose eloquently. "You—your brothers—are mercenaries?"

Apparently he hadn't explained things as well as he'd thought. Just as this particular rescue mission wasn't turning out to be the cakewalk he'd predicted.

That didn't mean he had to stand here and let her get things wrong. "No," Dom said flatly. "Mercenary implies no standards, no ethics, no values, no rules—and we stand for all those things. We don't break U.S. law, we don't work for anybody who isn't one hundred per cent legit. Trust me. We can afford to be choosy."

He refrained from adding that, in his opinion, he and his brothers had a lot in common with the guy whose nickname they shared, the one with the red cape and big *S* on his chest. Like him, they believed in justice and cared enough to risk their lives for it.

What's more, unlike the majority of the populace, they'd all honorably served their country; every one of them was former military Special Operations and had put in their time on numerous tours of duty in Iraq, Afghanistan and even darker corners of the world.

To her credit, Lilah appeared to get the message. She worried her bottom lip for an instant, then seemed to catch herself. Squaring her shoulders, she forced herself to meet his gaze head-on. "I'm sorry. I didn't mean to imply anything…negative. Or—or to suggest I'm not glad you're here. I am. It's just…it's unexpected."

He couldn't argue with that. "Don't worry about it."

God knew, he didn't intend to. After all, it looked as if things were finally going his way. And that was good, since for a while, he had half-seriously started to think of this job as the Extraction from Hell.

First, his flight into San Timoteo had been diverted. Then, when he'd finally gotten wheels down, he'd found his local contact had vanished. Which was why it had taken him a frustrating thirty-odd hours to discover that: (A) Lilah wasn't where she was supposed to be; (B) that once he had located her—here, at what the locals called *Las Rocas,* an isolated, heavily guarded compound sixty-five rugged, sparsely inhabited miles from Santa Marita, the nation's capital and only large city—his best bet of getting her out was to get himself thrown in; and (C) the best way to do *that* involved volunteering to get his ass kicked.

Complicating matters further, his satellite phone had been confiscated by San Timotean customs and the last intel he'd received had warned that a big storm was due in at the end of the week. What's more, thanks to this required detour to the island's remote south coast, he and Lilah had missed their scheduled ride out of the country. So now, in addition to everything else, he was going to have to improvise that part of the rescue plan, too.

But then, he liked to improvise. And he was good at it. Good enough that, so far as he could see, there was now only one problem that might really give him grief.

And she was standing a few feet away.

Hell he'd forgotten just how pretty Lilah was. Damned if she still didn't look just like the Disney version of Cinderella, all gilt hair and big blue eyes and the sort of skin you usually only saw in body lotion commercials.

Unfortunately—at least as far as he was concerned—unlike a proper G-rated fairy-tale heroine, she was also hot. She'd been hot at eighteen and, if his current itchy-fingered reaction to her was any indication, the subsequent years hadn't done a thing to dim her fire.

Not that there was anything blatant about it. Or her. Far from it. She had a way about her, all elegant carriage and air of restraint that made a guy think of garden parties and symphony openings, not mud wrestling and strip joints.

And that was a big part of the problem. Call him perverse, but at age twenty it had been her *look-but-don't-touch* demeanor that had first attracted him. He'd always loved a challenge—still did—and her sorority girl air of being unattainable had been like a red flag snapped in a bull's face. All it had taken to hook him had been one look. After that, the only thing he'd been able to think about was sinking his fingers into her pale silky hair, cradling her close and kissing the primness right off that delectable mouth.

Of course, that'd been then and this was now. He was thirty years old. A man, not a boy. And she hadn't just burned him all those years ago, she'd barbecued him. Which was *not* an experience he had any intention of repeating.

So how to explain the gut-wrenching, skin-tightening, gotta-have-some-of-that desire that had blasted through him the instant she'd laid her hands on him earlier?

"I just want to be sure I understand," Lilah said, mercifully interrupting his thoughts.

Well, yeah. That makes two of us, sweetheart. I'd like to understand how I can be standing here thinking of all the different ways I'd like to have wild, swing-from-the-chandeliers sex with you when I haven't seen you in ten years.

"Gran came to your office and hired you to rescue me?"

"That's right."

"And your brother has worked for her in the past. That's why she went to him and how you came to be here?"

"More or less."

"And after we…knew…each other you left Denver and joined the Navy?"

"Yeah. Now, if you don't mind, we don't have a lot of time before the sun goes down and the guards bring dinner, so let me ask the questions." He'd think about his backstabbing libido later. Say back in Denver. Over a tall cool one at his favorite tavern. In the year 2025. For now, it was time to get down to business.

"How do you know that?" she asked.

"Know what?"

"About dinner."

He reminded himself to be patient, that it was under-standable she'd have questions. "Because I spent yester-day surveilling this place. There's a big tree about five hundred feet from the compound entrance. It's tall enough that I could see them ferrying food from the kitchen. Now I need you to tell me whether they come back after dinner to pick up your plate or wait until morning."

"So far, they've always left it until morning."

"Good. Do you see anybody in between time? Do they do a bed check or come in when the guard changes shifts?"

"No. Why?"

"Because." He felt for the opening in the seam of his pants just below his hip. "If that's the case, then once the food comes we essentially become invisible until dawn. And I plan on us being gone from here way before then."

Disbelief—and a gleam of longing?—flashed in her eyes. Yet she was too well-schooled to expose her emotions longer than that single moment. "Well, yes, that would be nice. But short of dematerializing and squeezing through the bars—" her voice was suddenly cool and uninflected "—I don't see how you're going to accomplish that. And even if you could, you'd still have to get the corridor door unbolted and then get past the guards you're so intent on avoiding. Somehow I don't see any of that happening."

He pulled the thigh-length, razor-thin cutting blade free from its hiding place. "Neither do I. That's why we're not going out that way."

"We're not?" Lilah's lips parted in astonishment.

And just like that, that prickly *wanna-touch* sensation washed over him. Because she really did have the most luscious mouth....

"No, we're not," he said firmly, forcing himself to concentrate on their surroundings, to triple-check that he hadn't overlooked anything, even though the layout was already firmly inscribed on his brain. Located on a windswept headland on San Timoteo's southern tip, the cell block occupied the far end of the walled-off compound that was also home to a commandant's residence and modest barracks.

The jail itself was the shape of a basic rectangle. At the top of the shorter, western wall was a solid iron door that opened from a guard house into a narrow corridor boasting a single small, skinny window. The corridor, roughly five feet by forty, fronted four small, barred cells that were identical in size and shared a common solid back wall. Their only other notable feature was their utter lack of creature comforts.

Deciding the surroundings were stark enough to depress even his overly active libido, Dom returned his gaze to Lilah.

Who'd taken yet another step back from the bars and was now standing in the sole shaft of sunlight, allowing him to see what he'd missed before due to the deep shadows that draped the room like a heavy blanket.

A smudge of bruises circled her right wrist, a larger contusion ran from shoulder to elbow on her opposite arm, and a fading but still telltale smear of yellow-tinged purple marred one side of her jaw.

The sight made him go cold. Suddenly wishing he could turn back time and have a real go at the sons-of-bitches guards instead of pulling his punches the way he had when he'd let them overpower him, he struggled to contain his anger and keep it out of his voice. "Lilah."

His voice may have sounded normal, but clearly something—the rigidness of his stance, the muscle that had twitched to life in his jaw—must have tipped her off to his sudden tension because she went very still. "What?

"Did they hurt you?" he asked softly.

"Hurt me?" Despite her cautious response, the fingers of her right hand reflexively touched her battered wrist, revealing she knew what had prompted the question.

"Were you raped?"

Abruptly, her expression cleared. "No." She shook her head. "No. I'm not positive, but I think El Presidente issued orders that I was off-limits…that way."

"Oh, yeah? Why would he do that?"

"I'm not sure. Maybe because he only wants my money."

"So the bruises are from what?" he persisted.

"This—" she indicated the area above her hand and gave a little shrug "—one of the guards got a little rough. The rest—" inexplicably, a faint flush colored the curve of her elegant cheekbones "—are from when I was being held in Santa Marita. There was a car accident. Well, I suppose accident might not be exactly the correct term—"

"But nobody forced themselves on you?" he interrupted, wanting—needing—to be sure.

"No."

"Okay, then. That's…good." As if his vision had suddenly improved—maybe he'd taken a harder hit to the head than he'd thought—he now saw that in addition to having been roughed up, she was on the brink of being not slender but fragile, the kind of look people got when they'd gone too long without adequate food.

The discovery didn't improve his temper. He wanted her out of here *now*. Even more than he wanted a piece of the guards, and he wanted that pretty damn bad.

The fierceness of his feelings caught him off guard, but he'd think about it later. Over that beer he planned to drink back home. Without a certain blue-eyed, satin-skinned blonde to distract him and make him crave things he didn't need.

"If we're not leaving through the door, how *do* you plan to get us out of here?" Lilah asked.

She was nothing if not persistent. "If I tell you, will you stop with the Twenty Questions?"

"Yes, of course. I—"

"Deal," he said flatly, cutting her off. "To answer your question—we're going out through the hole I'm going to cut through the wall."

Lilah watched in shock as Dominic turned his back on her. Stepping close to the expanse of rough gray concrete that formed the back of the cell block, he began to run his hands over it like a blind man exploring a lover's face.

A score of questions screamed for answers in her head, competing for space with a dozen exclamations. The two common themes seemed to be "how on earth?" and "you're out of your mind."

Yet his silence, combined with his averted back, made it perfectly clear he didn't want to talk.

Well, neither did she, Lilah thought, retreating to her bed. She could use some time to think. And to sift through all the contradictory emotions that were bouncing around inside her like rubber balls in a cement mixer.

She was barely settled, however, and nowhere close to sorting through the jumble of doubt, hope, fear and frustration vying for her attention, when the sound of the bolt being drawn in the outer door splintered the silence.

Her gaze snapped to Dominic. In the fraction of time it took for the door to swing open, her jailmate whirled and slid down the wall to sit in a crumpled heap on the floor, his arms dangling limply, his eyes shut, his head flopped to one side.

If she hadn't known better, she'd have believed he was an injured man just barely holding on to consciousness. Heaven knew, the guard certainly bought it. Flicking the big American a dismissive look, he said something clearly contemptuous in San Timoteo's version of Spanish as he headed for Lilah's cell.

To her surprise, Dom answered back, his voice slurred convincingly.

The guard laughed. The sound was ugly, as was the lecherous look he sent Lilah's way as he stooped down and slid the small tin plate clutched in his meaty hand through the gap at the base of the bars. He stood and spoke again, blew her a noisy kiss, then strolled back out the door.

The second the sound of the bolt sliding into place faded, Dominic straightened. "Bastard," he bit out, his voice low but lethal.

Curiosity overcame Lilah's earlier pique. "What did he say?"

"Nothing you need to hear."

She pursed her lips. It was hardly the response she'd been seeking, but at least he was talking to her again. "I never knew you spoke Spanish."

"I learned as a SEAL." He hitched his muscular shoulders a fraction of an inch in one of his trademark shrugs. "Turns out languages are easy for me."

"Oh."

His gaze flicked to the plate. "You should eat."

She considered the meager portion of beans and flat bread. The food was an unappetizing shade of gray, and she knew from experience it looked far better than it tasted. Even so, the sight of it made her stomach squeeze and her mouth water.

Yet how could she eat when he didn't? "We'll share it."

His reply was immediate and forceful. "No. We won't. You need it a hell of a lot more than I do."

He clearly didn't intend to budge. Since arguing would no doubt be fruitless, Lilah dutifully stood and retrieved the plate. She picked up the crude wooden spoon, unhurriedly ate exactly half of what was there, then walked over and slid the plate under the narrow gap between the floor and the bars.

Without a word, she went back to her bed. When she turned, he was giving her a hard look. She gazed unflinchingly back.

With a curse that made her wince, he reached for the plate, jerked it close, and ate.

"Do you really think you can hack through solid concrete with that flimsy bar?" she asked a moment later as he mopped up the last morsel of beans with the last scrap of bread. "And what about the guards? Won't somebody outside notice what's going on?"

"The wall's aren't made out of concrete. They're made out of concrete *block*," he corrected, climbing to his feet.

"Cemented together with a local mortar, which is made out of straw and mud, and which is what I intend to go after. My flimsy little bar, in contrast, is made of a space-age titanium alloy ten times stronger than tempered steel. And nobody's going to see what's happening because the back wall's built right on the edge of a drop. So yeah. I think my plan will work."

He walked over and chucked the empty plate at the outer door with a fierceness that startled her. Yet when he turned, he appeared calm and in control, and when he spoke it was with an easy confidence she wanted desperately to believe in. "Give me a little credit, okay? I didn't just get myself tossed in here hoping an idea would come to me. I know what I'm doing."

"Yes, of course," she said faintly. He might look like the boy she'd known, but clearly he was all grown-up. What's more, he was right. He was her best, her only, hope of escape and questioning him at every turn wasn't doing either of them any good.

"And now, since our hosts really don't seem inclined to check up on us despite my bad manners—" he slid his blade free of its hiding place and once more headed for the back of his cell "—I might as well start. Why don't you try to get some rest? You're going to need it for later."

She was being dismissed. Again. Yet this time she didn't take offense, simply did as he suggested and laid down. Partly because there was nothing to be gained by arguing, but mostly because between the heat, the lack of nutrition and the internal uproar his presence caused her, she was worn out.

She curled on her side, tucked a hand beneath her cheek

and lowered her lashes, pretending not to watch as he started his assault on the wall, using his handy-dandy blade thingy to hack away at the mortar.

God help her, but she couldn't take her eyes off him. And it wasn't only because of the mesmerizing way his back and shoulder muscles bunched and shifted with his every move.

No, it was also because of her realization that she'd been fooling herself for years, believing the picture she carried of him in her mind was accurate.

It hadn't been. She knew that now; the proof was right in front of her. At some point in the passage of time, she'd clearly forgotten just how vividly alive he was. Just as she'd forgotten that when she was in his presence, the whole world seemed sharper, brighter and infinitely more interesting.

It had been that way from the very first time she'd laid eyes on him, she thought, remembering….

Once again, it was a hot, lazy June day. She lay languidly on a chaise longue by the swimming pool at Cedar Hill, the palatial Denver estate owned by her grandmother's newest husband.

Off in the distance, she heard the distinctive whine of an approaching lawn mower and ridiculously, her pulse skittered. Grateful for the camouflage of her sunglasses, she casually shifted her head to the left toward the emerald swath of the five-acre back lawn. She was rewarded for her effort by the sight of a tall, bronzed young man cutting the grass.

She'd first noticed him the previous week; he wasn't the

regular lawn man, and a casual inquiry of Mr. Tomkins, who looked after the pool, had provided her with the information that he was a vacation fill-in.

Whatever the reason for his presence, with his broad shoulders and confident swagger, he was hard to miss. She knew he'd noticed her, too. Unlike the well-mannered boys she was accustomed to, he'd stared boldly at her, his gaze lingering in a way she'd told herself was totally annoying.

Which hardly explained why she'd been lying here for the past hour, hoping to get another glimpse of him. Or why just looking at him now made her throat feel tight. Nor did she understand the panic that bloomed inside her when, as if he'd sensed her regard, he abruptly brought the lawn mower to a halt, shut off the engine and began to walk toward her, his long legs rapidly eating up the distance between them.

Before she could act on a sudden impulse to flee, he was standing at the wrought iron fence that encircled the pool. "Hey."

For a moment she couldn't move. Then, driven by pride and an abruptly awakened sense of self-preservation that warned he was a threat—although to what she couldn't clearly pinpoint—she slowly sat up. "May I help you?" She used her best drawing room voice in a desperate bid to hide the way her heart was pounding.

"Yeah." He flashed her a smile that made her stomach flip. "Would you mind getting me a glass of water?"

A bead of sweat tracked down the column of his neck, adding to the damp that made his black T-shirt cling to his muscled chest, and an unfamiliar heat twisted through her.

Embarrassed, she reached up and slid her sunglasses off, using the action as an excuse to look away. "Pardon me?"

"I'm thirsty. You don't seem to be doing anything, so if you wouldn't mind, I'd appreciate you getting me a drink."

Her gaze snapped back to him as she tried to decide which was more unsettling: his nerve or her realization that an unfamiliar part of her wanted to do his bidding. "I don't think so." She picked up her book and sat back, waiting for him to take offense and stalk away.

He didn't. Instead, he cocked a hip and leaned closer, muscles flexing as he rested his tanned dusty arms against the top of the fence. "Aw, come on. You're not too good to mix with the hired help, are you?"

Stung that he'd think such a thing, she ratcheted her chin up a notch. "Of course not."

He raised one straight, inky eyebrow. "So what's the problem?"

Their gazes locked. To her fascination, his eyes, which she'd expected to be dark due to his near-black hair and olive complexion were a clear compelling green. And his mouth looked hard and soft all at the same time, the lips full and….

She scrambled to her feet, appalled by the direction of her thoughts. Tossing her long braid over her shoulder, she marched over to the wet bar and filled a tall glass with icy water from the tap, staunchly ignoring the fact that her hands were shaking. Head high, she stalked back to the fence and thrust the tumbler at him. "Here."

He took her offering with lazy grace, purposefully brushing his rough, calloused fingers against hers in the exchange. Raising the glass, he tipped back his head and drank, his strong, smooth-skinned throat rippling. She waited, unable to look away, as he licked the last bead of moisture from his lips once he'd drained the glass. "Thanks." He handed her back the glass.

Her own throat felt dust dry. "You're welcome. Now please go away."

He acted as if he hadn't heard her. "My name's Dominic. Dominic Steele. What's yours?"

"I see no reason for you to know that," she said coolly.

"Ah, but that's where you're wrong. After all—" his gaze dropped from her eyes to her mouth, lingered, then unhurriedly came back up "—how can I ask you out if I don't know your name?"

If she had any sense, she'd walk away. Yet she stood rooted to the spot. Silence stretched between them. Then she heard herself say in a breathy way that was totally unlike her, "It's Lilah...Cantrell."

"Lilah," he repeated. "That's perfect. A pretty name for a pretty girl." The faintest of smiles crinkled the corners of his vivid eyes and her knees instantly went weak. "Come on, Lilah, go out with me. Please?"

She knew she should say no. She could just imagine her grandmother's reaction to her dating someone from the lawn service. Then again, Gran was gone for the rest of the summer on her honeymoon cruise. And except for the staff, Lilah was alone, as usual, the weeks until her sophomore years at Stanford started stretching interminably before her.

Still, except on rare occasions, such as last winter's charity cotillion and her senior high school prom, she didn't really care to date. She'd always found the opposite sex to be either crass or boring, or both.

Dominic Steele was neither. In the past five minutes, he'd managed to turn her ordered world upside down—surprising, annoying, intriguing and charming her all at the same time. Which was no doubt why what was left of her common sense was shrilly insisting that nothing good could come from the pull she felt merely standing close to him.

The prudent thing to do was say no.

Oh, come on, whispered an unfamiliar little voice in her head. *Aren't you just a little tired of always doing the right thing? Of forever being the straight-A student, the dutiful granddaughter? After all, you're not a child any longer. And no matter what Gran says, you're nothing like your mother—*

"You're not afraid of me, are you?"

Her spine stiffened automatically. "Please," she said with a faint sniff.

"So prove it." He looked at her expectantly.

"Oh, very well." She did her best to sound blasé, but it was hard to do with her heart thundering like a drum solo. "I suppose I could rearrange my schedule."

Satisfaction flashed across his face. "Great. I'll pick you up at eight." He turned to walk away, then twisted back around. "Oh, and Lilah?"

"What?"

"Wear pants."

"Why?"

His expression turned enigmatic. "You'll find out tonight." As assured as a prince, he strode away, leaving her to stare after him, already questioning the wisdom of what she'd done.

She got her first inkling of what she was in for when he'd roared up the drive that night on a gleaming black motorcycle.

Grateful again that Gran was away, Lilah had reluctantly allowed Dominic to coax her onto the back of the bike. Once there, she'd found she had no choice but to wrap her arms around his lean hard middle, press her cheek against the warm hollow between his shoulder blades and trust him to keep her safe.

Looking back later, she'd been able to see that their ride that night had been the perfect metaphor for the relationship that followed. It had been wild, scary, exciting and exhilarating, with Dominic taking her places she'd never been before.

Within hours, she'd begun to fall in love with him. Within days they'd become lovers. And after that....

"Li? You awake?"

With a start, she opened her eyes. She blinked, surprised to find that while she'd been strolling down memory lane, night had fallen. The cell block was cloaked in darkness except for a single weak arrow of light streaming in the small barred window. It was just enough illumination to reveal Dominic standing over her. Startled, disoriented, suddenly not sure she wasn't dreaming, she gazed up at him. "But…how did you get in here?"

"Lock pick. In my boot." He held out his hand. "Come on. It's time to get the hell out of Dodge." Hard and calloused, his fingers closed around hers.

She drew in a sharp breath at the contact. Climbing unsteadily to her feet, she struggled to come to grips with the shift from weeks of waiting to sudden action. By the time her head had cleared, he'd led her out of her cell and into his.

She continued to follow him, her gaze locked on the solid outline of his back, when, without warning, he stepped to one side.

She rocked to a halt, a stiff salt breeze slapping her in the face, and stared at the man-sized opening that now gaped in the previously solid, seemingly impregnable wall. Beyond it stretched nothing but a vast black sky littered with glittering silver stars.

"Dear God." With a start, she remembered he'd said something about a drop, but she'd never, ever, imagined *this*.

She took a cautious step forward, craned her neck and looked down. There, so far below it looked to be miles away, the ocean rolled in with an impressive crash as it met the perpendicular cliff face. "You can't be serious. *This* is your escape route?"

"That's right." Unlike the water, Dominic was suddenly far too close. His breath washed over her temple and every sensitive inch of skin on her body had goose bumps.

She tried to ignore her rapidly disintegrating nerves. "It's got to be at least a hundred-foot drop."

"More like fifty."

"But how are we going to get down?"

"Easy." All of a sudden, the lazy humor was back in his voice. "We're going to jump."

For a second, Lilah was sure she hadn't heard correctly; then she was afraid she had. "You're kidding, right?

"Nope."

"But that's crazy! If the fall doesn't kill us, getting

dashed by the tide against the cliff will do the job. That is, if we haven't already hit a submerged rock!"

"No rocks," he said calmly. "The tide's on its way out. And the waves sound a lot worse than they really are. It's a clean shot down, with more than enough depth to be safe. I checked."

He'd checked. The knowledge brought reassurance, which was crazy in itself. If ever there was a man not to trust, he was the one.

Yet it wasn't as if she really had a choice, she realized. Not anymore. She didn't want to think what would happen if they were still here when the guards showed up in the morning and saw Dominic's handiwork.

"Look," he said quietly, his face in shadow, which only served to make his voice even more compelling, "I know you've always had a thing about heights—"

"No. It's all right. If you—if this—" she stopped, swallowed, reached down deep to steady herself "—if this is what we have to do, this is what we have to do."

He moved out of the darkness and into the moonlight, an odd expression on his face that she couldn't identify. "You mean I'm not going to have to tie you up and gag you to get you to jump?"

She shivered at the picture his words conjured. "No," she said quickly.

"Too bad." That crooked, cocky grin that had always made her stomach flip-flop flashed across his handsome face. "Then let's do it."

"*Now?*" She took an involuntary step back.

"Yeah. Now." Before she could retreat farther, he reached out and wrapped his arms around her.

For a moment, the shock of his embrace was so overwhelming she forgot to be afraid.

And then she forgot to be anything else as he lifted her off her feet, took two powerful steps through the crude doorway he'd created and vaulted them out into the wind-whipped void.

Four

The night breeze danced through the palm trees that fringed the small cove, while the moon played hide-and-seek with a flotilla of clouds. Still, the silvery orb provided sufficient light to guide Dominic and Lilah as they waded through the surf toward the shallows and the tiny sliver of beach beyond.

"Easy," Dominic said, as a wave broke early and Lilah stumbled. He reached out to steady her.

"I'm okay," she said instantly. It was one thing to be touched by him when fear was crowding everything else out of her mind. Without that distraction, however, she was suddenly aware of how easy it would be to step a little closer, allow herself to lean against him, give in to the desire to feel his arm around her—

Rattled by her thoughts—*get a grip, Lilah*—she shrugged off his hand. "I'm just a little tired."

"Yeah, well, after the fall and crawl we just did, that's normal."

Normal? For her. But for Dominic? She slanted a sideways look at him. Moving effortlessly through the thigh-high water, his olive T-shirt and fatigue pants molded to his muscular body like a second skin, he looked larger than life, like some matinee-idol action hero come to life. What's more, he was practically vibrating with energy; for all the toll the past half hour had taken on him, he might have just completed a few leisurely laps in a heated pool. But then, as she now knew in a very up close and personal way, he was every bit as good at the rescue business as he'd claimed.

It had been his firm hold and unwavering calm that had gotten her through that terrifying fall that had gone on forever and the plunge down, down, down into the pitch black water that had seemed to go on even longer.

It had been his reassuring voice telling her to breathe that had kept her from breaking down altogether when she'd finally surfaced, her body screaming for air.

And it had been his steadying presence that had given her the fortitude to ignore her trembling muscles and burning lungs to make the endless swim along the curve of the coast to this little niche that the waves had carved out of the cliffs.

Which somehow made it all the more humiliating that now, with the water finally receding to their knees and solid land only yards away, she was shaking so hard she couldn't walk while fighting an inexplicable urge to cry.

"Li?" She sensed Dominic stopping and turning toward her. "What's the matter?"

The unexpected gentleness of his voice nearly did her in. She swallowed. "Nothing. I just need a moment to catch my breath, that's all." To her horror, a sound mid-way between a sob and a chuckle promptly escaped her, revealing her words for the lie they were. "Oh God, I'm sorry," she said, both her voice and her knees suddenly shaking. "I don't know what's wrong with me. All of a sud-den my legs feel weak and I want to laugh and cry and dance and shout all at the same time and—oh God, I haven't even thanked you yet!"

"No need for that," he replied. "I'm only doing my job. And you're having a normal reaction after a huge adren-aline rush."

Adrenaline might explain her crazy emotions. But not why she felt stung by his response. But then maybe she didn't want to be just "a job" to him. Although what she did want, she had no idea. Not that it mattered. Despite his disclaimer, she owed him her freedom, and very possibly her life.

So is this how you intend to repay him? By breaking down? By acting like the self-indulgent debutante he once accused you of being?

No. After what he'd done, he deserved better.

She straightened and forced herself to meet his eyes. "You may not need to hear it, but I need to say it," she said with all the dignity she could muster. "Thank you, Dom-inic. Thank you for coming here and getting me out of that awful place."

To her surprise, instead of the "hey, no big deal" she'd expected, his gaze flickered over her, then he shrugged and abruptly turned to survey the grove of palms. "Don't thank me yet. We've still got a ways to go before we're in the clear."

His dismissal cut even deeper. Ignoring the voice of reason that cautioned her to just let it go, she reached out and touched the solid curve of his shoulder.

He gave a start at the contact and swung around to face her. "What?"

A bead of water rolled down his temple and just like that, the reckless part of her, which she'd been sure had died with their romance, yearned to lick it off with her tongue. She lifted her chin. "No matter what you think or what happens next, I'll still be grateful for what you just did. Nothing can change that."

"Dammit, Lilah—"

Another comber swept in. Pushed by the wind, it was stronger than those that had preceded it had been, and it snatched at the sandy bottom beneath their feet. Caught off guard, Lilah swayed and Dominic immediately reached out to brace her, gently wrapping his fingers around her upper arm.

Which might have been all right if she hadn't lost her balance, taking a step that brought the back of his hand into intimate contact with the yielding curve of her breast.

She heard his breath catch, saw his eyes lock on hers and felt the old wildness that only he had ever been able to tap into surge through her blood, demolishing everything sane and practical in its path.

She didn't care. All she could think was that she might have died tonight. *They* might have died tonight. Somehow, in the face of that, all her inhibitions and concerns didn't seem to matter.

Blanking her mind, she gave in to instinct and closed the distance between them, yielding to the temptation to frame his face with her hands and feel his hair slide like wet silk through her fingers.

He stared down at her, his face shadowed, his eyes washed of color by the moonlight. "Lilah—" he said, the note of warning in his voice unmistakable.

She ignored that, too. Instead, she sketched a path from temple to cheekbone to press her fingertips against the forbidding curve of his lips. "Shh," she whispered, the blood pounding so loudly in her ears it was the only thing she could hear. "Just…kiss me, Dominic."

For one endless second, he didn't move, just continued to stare down at her with that totally unreadable expression. Then with a primitive sound low in his throat, he locked one arm around her thighs and the other around her waist, lifted her up and found her mouth with his own.

The press of his lips was heaven. He'd always been a terrific kisser and that hadn't changed. He seemed to know exactly how much pressure to apply; how long to wait before he changed the slant of his mouth to gently bite her bottom lip; at what point she was desperate to have his tongue slide into her mouth.

Heat poured off his body and she soaked it up, welcoming the hard grip of his hands, the knowing play of his mouth, clinging to him like a vine to a trellis.

And then, as quickly as it had started, it was over as Dominic abruptly dumped her onto her feet, tore her hands from his neck and stepped away. "Enough," he said harshly.

Dazed and dismayed, her blood still running hot, Lilah automatically took a step forward. "What?" she asked uncertainly. "What's wrong?"

"*Don't*," he said sharply, taking a giant step backward as if she carried some infectious disease.

She jerked to a stop, no less shocked than if he'd slapped her face. In a rush, the world around her came into sharp focus: the water lapping at her calves, the palm trees rustling, the moon drenching everything in its soft silver light.

And Dominic, his expression frigid, staring at her as if she were a stranger. One he didn't particularly like.

Dear Lord. What had she done?

"Come on," he said, his voice clipped and devoid of all emotion. "We need to get out of the water and off this beach. Now."

And without another word, he turned and strode away.

Her throat aching, her body suddenly overcome with fatigue, Lilah swallowed the host of questions she longed to shout at his back.

They didn't matter, she told herself. Because she already knew everything she needed to. Although Dominic clearly didn't find her physically repulsive—the heavy thrust of his erection had been ample proof of that—he also clearly didn't want her enough to forget and forgive their past.

Well, fine, she thought. That was his right. No matter how humiliated she felt, how desperately she wished she could erase the past ten minutes, how much she wanted to hide her face and never have to see him again, she would respect his wishes and keep her distance.

It was the least she could do.

Holding firm to that thought, she blinked back the wash of tears blurring her vision, squared her shoulders and set off after him.

"*What the hell?*" Dom stared with a mixture of disbelief and disgust at the Jeep he'd hidden in a dense tangle of vines a good fifty feet off the road.

Or, more correctly, what was left of the Jeep. Which wasn't much. The bare metal frame squatted forlornly on the rusty rims, stripped by some enterprising local not just of its leafy camouflage but of everything that mattered— the engine, the radiator, the gas tank and all four tires. Damned if even the seats weren't gone.

The Extraction from Hell, Part Two, he thought sardonically, the frustration he'd felt ever since he'd been forced to end that mind-blowing embrace with Lilah threatening to explode.

What the hell had he been thinking?

How easy it would be to shift some clothing and bury yourself deep inside her?

His mind's instant and mocking reply had him clenching his jaw against the urge to let loose with a string of profanity.

That's just priceless, pal. What a great way to repay Li for the gutsy way she handled the jump, even though she was clearly scared out of her mind. How professional of you to just blow off procedure and conveniently forget that her safety comes before anything—including you. Besides, she told you right up front what she was feeling—and it was gratitude, not lust.

But did you care? Hell no. You were more than ready to jump her bones right then, right there, out in the open where anybody with two eyes could see you. Anybody who, if they'd happened to be up on the cliffs with a rifle, could've picked you off like ducks in a bathtub. Especially Lilah, whose pale blond hair makes her an easy target.

And now this.

God help him, but it had been his belief that all he had to do was walk half a mile, retrieve the Jeep and drive like hell back to Santa Marita, where he planned to steal the first boat or plane he found that could quickly get them to a friendly harbor, that had given him the strength to pry himself away from Lilah's soft, yielding, made-for-him body.

Instead, barring a miracle—and really, what were the odds of a supercharged Hummer dropping out of the sky in front of him?—they were going to get to spend a considerable amount of time together.

This time he did swear, out loud and with enough vehemence to curl the leaves on the surrounding trees.

Then, knowing he could no longer avoid it, he turned to face Lilah. Not unexpectedly, she was staring fixedly at the carcass of the Jeep, conveniently avoiding his gaze. "I take it this was to be our ride out of here?" she said quietly.

"You got it."

Still not looking at him, she caught her lower lip between her teeth and worried it; his body immediately reacted, remembering her taste. "So what do we do now?"

"What do you think?" He didn't even try to temper the bite in his voice. After all, he'd already proven he couldn't be trusted to stick to business; it was up to her to keep him in line, so the more he offended her the better for both of them. No matter how much he wanted her. "We walk."

"Oh." She released her lip and her chin came up. And still she didn't look at him.

Well, isn't that what you want?

Damn straight. And if that meant behaving with all of
the grace and maturity of some adolescent kid who'd
caught his most prized piece of anatomy in a vise, so be
it. It was for Lilah's own good.

"Stay here," he said curtly. Tearing his gaze from her,
he turned and strode around the Jeep and into the jungle
beyond to the smallest of the surrounding palms, the one
with a distinctive crook halfway up its trunk. Stepping
around the tree, he squatted down and dug through the
thick undergrowth until his hand encountered a familiar
piece of nylon webbing. With a grunt of relief, he dragged
the backpack toward him, hefted it up and slung it over one
shoulder, then returned to the clearing.

His momentary sense of satisfaction vanished.

The good news was that Lilah was standing right where
he'd left her, exactly as ordered. The bad news was that she
was in the process of squeezing the salt water out of her hair,
which meant her arms were raised up and back, stretching
her white cotton blouse across her breasts. And said cotton,
being damp like the bra beneath it, was nearly transparent.

He dumped his pack on the ground, ripped it open with
more force than he'd intended and yanked out his extra
T-shirt. "Here. Put this on," he said, lobbing it at her. "That
white stands out like a neon sign out here."

Displaying excellent reflexes, she snatched the shirt
out of midair. Then, for the first time since the beach, she
looked straight at him, her opinion of him written clearly
on her face—and it wasn't pretty.

He stared stonily back, daring her to comment.

Wisely, she didn't. She drew herself up and began to
unbutton her blouse, her movements slow and deliberate.

Then she slipped the garment off, shook out his shirt and just as unhurriedly pulled it on. She freed her hair, smoothed it back, glanced down at the shirttail hanging clear to her knees and gathered it up, securing it above one slender hip with a knot in the excess fabric. Her gaze came back to his. "All right?" she asked, her voice cool except for the faintest note of challenge.

Well, damn it all to hell anyway. Just what he'd needed to top off the night—a private striptease. Not only was the image of her smooth stomach and gently rounded breasts now permanently seared on his retinas, but somehow she'd managed to make even his old black T-shirt look good.

"Terrific." It was definitely time for some exercise. And while he longed for a real out-of-body, wear-himself-out challenge, like swimming the Bering Sea or bench-pressing Volkswagens, he was going to have to settle for a stroll dialed down to Lilah's current strength level, dammit.

He reclaimed his watch, clipped his knife and a water bottle to his waistband, tossed a second water bottle to Lilah, shrugged into his backpack and settled it in place. "Stay behind me," he told her brusquely. "Once we're on the road, if you hear anything that sounds out of place— a human voice, an approaching vehicle, a dog barking— get out of sight in the underbrush and wait for me to come find you. You understand?"

"Yes."

"Then let's go. The more distance we put between us and El Presidente's henchmen before they realize we're gone, the better." With that, he set off.

Thanks to the jungle's dense growth, it took them a

good five minutes to negotiate the stretch from the Jeep to the road, although road, Dom thought, was a generous term for the narrow dirt track that ran from the compound where Lilah had been held to a five-hut village some twenty-five miles inland.

A village where, on his trip out, he'd managed to render himself invisible by pushing the Jeep past the slumbering villagers in the dead of night. And where he now hoped to acquire some sort of transportation, since by the time he and Lilah arrived there, the search for them should have moved on.

Should have being the operative term. Because the advantage of being an unknown quantity that he'd had previously would be gone. Once the guards did their breakfast check, they'd know he wasn't the crazy lost American hiker desperate for water that he'd pretended to be when he'd stumbled out of the brush and demanded to be let into the "villa" *por favor.*

Come morning, things were probably going to get interesting.

But then, come morning, he planned for Lilah and him to be safely tucked away somewhere they couldn't be found, catching some z's. Although, the chance of him getting much sleep with her close at hand seemed about as likely as the pope announcing he was in favor of polygamy. Or the Rockies ever winning the World Series.

Or Lilah ever again wanting to have sex with him.

With a resigned sigh, he took the mental picture of Lilah lying beneath him—her hair spread out, her head thrown back with pleasure as he thrust himself inside her—and shoved it out of his head.

They trekked along the road for nearly two hours without exchanging a word. Dom could hear Lilah behind him, her breathing growing increasingly harsh and labored. Which, when he stopped to think about it, made sense, since at some point he'd really picked up the pace. And *that* meant she was really having to work to keep up with him.

So? Your first priority is to get her to safety, not to be Mr. Nice Guy.

Except this was a marathon, not a sprint. And it wouldn't do either of them any good if she wore herself out tonight to the point she couldn't walk tomorrow. "You okay?" he asked, shortening his stride.

"Yes."

Despite her declaration, he could hear the exhaustion in her voice. Yet it was pretty clear she was prepared to walk all night rather than admit she was tired. Of course, Lilah had always had a core of steel deep inside her. She might look delicate, but she had enough backbone for ten women. A very nice backbone—

Knock it off. "Well, I'm not okay." How was that for an understatement? "So let's take a break." Matching action to words, he stopped.

She didn't say anything. At first, it was because she was catching her breath. But then, well, hell—why should she want to talk to him?

Then again, she probably had the right idea. Maybe if he acted as if she were invisible, his testosterone level would fall back to something approaching normal. He took a swig of water and a good long look at their surroundings before he finally slid a glance her way.

He was just in time to see her limp over to the nearest palm and brace her hand against it. "What's the matter?"

"Nothing. I just—I think I stepped on a thorn." Cocking one leg at the knee, she leaned over to examine the sole of her foot.

Her pale, slender, *bare* foot.

For a moment Dom couldn't believe it. In the next instant, without a conscious decision, he'd obliterated the distance between them. "Where the *hell*—" he demanded, scooping her into his arms "—are your shoes?"

"In my waistband," she said breathlessly. "I took them off."

He looked around, then stalked toward a fallen log. "Why the hell would you do that?"

"Because they're sandals. Wet sandals with lots of little straps coated in sand that were rubbing my feet raw. There was no way I could wear them and keep up with you." He could hear an uncharacteristic huskiness that he wasn't sure what to make of. "I'm sorry. I just—I didn't want to slow you down."

"Dammit, Lilah, you're not in charge here. *I* am. That means you don't get to 'want' anything—or have any ideas or questions or make a decision—that you don't run past me first. You understand?"

"Okay," she said.

He gave the log a kick to test its density, then set her down, dumped the backpack to the ground, knelt and dug out his penlight and the first aid kit.

Taking a deep breath to steady himself, he picked up her injured foot and examined it. To his relief, other than one long, ugly-looking sticker and the start of a blister on her heel, the damage wasn't as extensive as he'd feared.

Yet as fear receded, awareness made an appearance. He was suddenly acutely conscious of the delicacy of her foot, the softness of her skin against his hand, how easy it would be to lift her ankles to his shoulders and bury his face against her most intimate, feminine place....

"This actually isn't too bad," he said in a desperate attempt to distract himself. "A little disinfectant and some antibiotic, followed by waterproof bandages—" he removed the thorn and did the Florence Nightingale bit, then turned his attention to the other foot, tending to another blister and two small but angry-looking cuts "—and you should be fine. Tomorrow, I'll rig some kind of shoes for you. In the meantime, I think we've done enough for one night. It'll be light in another few hours. We might as well make camp and get some sleep." He painstakingly began to pick up his litter and stowed everything back where it belonged.

"I guess I need to thank you," she said, her voice even huskier. "Again."

And that's when he made his fatal mistake.

He looked at her. And just like that, all the self-protective anger drained out of him like air escaping a punctured tire.

Because this close, there was no way he could miss seeing the faint pulse hammering at the base of her throat, the beckoning bow of her soft pink lips, the flawless finish of her skin—and the gleam of tears in her heavily-lashed eyes.

Tears that he'd put there. After she'd managed to keep it together through weeks of incarceration. After she'd done whatever he'd asked tonight, bravely performing feats he'd seen trained soldiers balk at their first time out.

"Aw hell, princess, don't. Just...don't cry."

"Oh, God." She hurriedly pressed the heels of her hands to her eyes. "I'm sorry." Clearly embarrassed, she lowered her hands and, though the effort was obvious and more than a little shaky, from somewhere she dredged up the strength to smile. "I won't. Promise."

And just like that, he was toast.

With a groan, he gave in to the need that had been riding him for what felt like a lifetime instead of mere hours. Rising up on his knees, he leaned forward, tangled his hands in her hair and kissed her.

Five

As a general rule, Dom considered kissing an art.

There was something incredibly seductive about lazily exploring the curve of a woman's mouth, savoring her taste, discovering what pushed her buttons.

Kissing Lilah, however, belonged in a whole different category. Goodbye art. Hello full contact sport.

It was annoying as hell. And more than a little humbling. But whenever he laid so much as a finger on her, much less his mouth, he seemed to go a little crazy.

It had been that way from the beginning.

Not too surprisingly, since he'd been barely out of his teens at the time, it had been his sincere and fervent desire to nail the pretty little rich girl that had first sent him striding across the million-acre lawn he now knew belonged to Abigail Sommers.

His aspiration had grown a thousandfold after his and Lilah's first face-to-face meeting. Up close, she'd been even more striking than he'd foreseen, a gloriously deli-cate blonde with an aristocratic air he'd expected—and an underlying vulnerability he hadn't.

He'd sure as hell never dreamed she was a virgin. Or that his eventual discovery of that particular truth would unleash in him a protective streak of monster proportions.

It had also never occurred to him that once they did have sex, rather than having his curiosity satisfied, he'd want her even more.

But he had. The fact that he'd been young and arrogant was no excuse for his lack of perception.

Because despite his age, he hadn't been some naive, clueless kid. He'd been an army brat, a gypsy, who'd lived on more than a dozen posts and been exposed to all sorts of people. He'd had a job of some sort since he was ten, a necessity when you were one of nine kids, your mother was dead and your old man made barely enough to put food on the table.

He'd also been sexually experienced, and had thought—with a cockiness that now made him wince—that he knew all he needed to about the opposite sex.

He hadn't.

He's gotten his first inkling of that on their first date.

He'd picked Lilah up that night on his motorcycle, an old Harley his brother Taggart had helped him rebuild. Other than his first SEAL mission, it had been the only time in his life he could remember being nervous. Not that he'd let on. He'd have allowed someone to rip out his fin-gernails one by one before he'd have admitted this wasn't just another date with just another girl.

Yeah, right. That whole delusion had taken a definite

hit as he'd ridden up the long circular drive with its broad flower beds and twinkling lights and walked to the huge front door, which had been flanked by soaring panes of stained glass and protected by a portico as big as the entire living room of his old man's place.

None of which had mattered once Lilah came to the door.

She'd been dressed in slim white slacks and a pale blue sweater-set several shades lighter than her eyes. Her smooth, shining hair had been pulled up in a ponytail high on her head and she'd had demure little pearl studs in her ears. Her perfume had been light, just a hint of vanilla and musk, totally unlike the fragrances of the other girls he knew.

She'd looked and smelled expensive, like something he could work for his whole life and still never be able to afford.

Yet once he'd assured her he wouldn't let anything bad happen to her, she'd trusted him enough to climb onto the back of his bike. And she'd thrown propriety to the winds and held on to him for dear life just as he'd planned when he gunned the engine and opened the throttle to send them hurtling down the drive.

He'd taken her first to Carlin's, a hamburger joint off Miner Street where some of the guys his age who worked for the lawn service liked to hang out. When they'd walked in, her attention had stayed focused solely on him. She'd earned unexpected points by not acknowledging the open-mouthed stares of the other men.

Over the course of the next hour, she'd surprised him further by revealing that some of what came across as haughtiness was actually shyness. And that behind her cool, watchful facade she possessed a wry if understated sense of humor and a sharp intelligence.

She'd only tensed a little when they'd finished eating and he'd slung a proprietary arm around her as they walked out and got back on his bike.

Their next stop had been Diablo Point, an overlook north of Denver that faced the soaring rise of the Rockies to the west. It had been a perfect Colorado summer night; the weather had been mild, the moon full, and the stars had seemed to hang in the vast and endless sky, close enough to reach up and touch.

Taking her hand, Dom had led her under the sheltering branches of an enormous ponderosa pine. Neither of them had spoken, just stood there looking out at the moonlit vista stretched so magnificently before them.

And then he'd kissed her and it was as if somebody had blown off the top of his head. His self-control had vanished, abducting his ability to reason when it went. In a flash he'd gone from man in charge to male in need— urgent, no-holds-barred, not-above-begging need.

Not that he actually *had* begged or anything. No, before it had gotten to that, a miracle had occurred and he'd dimly realized that the one person in worse shape than him was Lilah; although she hadn't made a sound, the way she'd been crowded up against him, her arms twined around his neck, her body trembling as she inexpertly welcomed the suggestive thrust of his tongue, had told him all he needed to know.

She wanted him.

The old adage about knowledge being power had

proven to be dead-on. For whatever reason, the awareness that she'd found him as big a turn-on as he'd found her had given him the strength to slow things down.

He'd managed to hold off making love to her until their fourth date, an entire ten days later.

That had been a life-altering experience, to put it mildly. He hadn't just felt…desire. He'd felt exalted, exhilarated, as if his body were too big for his skin. He'd never wanted it to end.

It had been one hell of a feeling. And it hadn't been until years later, when he'd been based at Coronada as a SEAL, that he'd been able to finally put a label on it.

He and a woman he'd been dating had gone to her place one night after dinner, and before getting caught up in other pursuits she'd switched on her favorite movie video, *Titanic*. Dom hadn't paid much attention at first, but at some point in the process of making the lady very, very happy, he'd glanced up to see Leo DiCaprio on the TV screen, his body spread-eagled into the gusting wind at the bow of the enormous ship, a blissful grin on his face, shouting, "I'm the king of the world."

After years of successfully banishing her from his mind, Dom had thought instantly of Lilah. And that's when it had hit him. What he'd felt when he had been with her had been nothing less than a raging case of king-of-the-world syndrome.

Of course, that wasn't the situation now.

Hell, no. You've got a much bigger problem. Or haven't you noticed—déjà vu all over again—that once more you're on the verge of deep-sixing your rule about not getting intimate with a client?

Not going to happen, he instantly assured himself. Yeah, so maybe he was feeling a little more ardent than usual from just one kiss. But then again, it had ceased being a mere kiss about five seconds after he and Lilah had locked lips, morphing into a blatantly sexual session of making love with their mouths.

And yeah, he supposed his breath was sawing in and out of his lungs. That what he currently wanted most in life was the opportunity to rediscover the contours of her body with his hands, lick every single salt particle left by the ocean off her skin and continue to claim her breath as it left her lips. And that every atom in his body was straining to get closer to her with just one objective in mind.

That didn't mean he was anywhere close to being out of control. Just like earlier on the beach, in the wake of their escape, he was simply a little…overhyped. The craving to have sex, to plant his seed and ensure his genetic survival, was a perfectly normal male reaction to taking risks with his life. He was pretty damn sure he'd read that somewhere.

Besides, Lilah sure as hell wasn't objecting. She was breathing every bit as hard as he was. So what did it matter if she was also holding herself very still, had her eyes firmly shut and her hands tightly clasped?

It took a sec for the ramifications of that last thought to penetrate the hot fog clouding his brain. But when it did, he felt as if he'd been sucker punched and he immediately jerked back. "Lilah? Baby? What's wrong? Do you want to stop?" See? He had control to spare.

"No. *No.* I just don't want—please don't…" She trailed off, pursed her lips and bowed her head, obviously unwilling to go on.

"What?" he prompted. To his irritation, he realized that, having blown the dam of his restraint, he couldn't not touch her. Still, he restricted himself to cupping the delicate curve of her jaw, not running his palms over her nipples the way he really wanted. "Come on. Talk to me. What's going on?" He gently nudged her chin up.

With a sigh so faint he almost missed it, she reluctantly met his gaze. "I'm sorry," she said quietly. "I know I'm acting like a twelve-year-old. And surely it's obvious I like…kissing you. But down on the beach, I did something to annoy you and I don't want to go there again." She stopped and swallowed. "I just don't want to be at odds with you."

Nope, he was definitely not the boy he'd been. Because in the face of her admission, he realized he was about to jettison his pride, something that had been beyond him a decade ago.

And though he wanted to believe he'd do the same for anyone willing to expose their fears the way Lilah just had, he wasn't sure. And that set off a warning. Because while he definitely aspired to have sex with her, that was *all* he wanted.

Right?

"It wasn't you," he said abruptly, telling himself now wasn't the time to go down that particular road. "Until we get off this island, your safety has to be my first priority. No exceptions. Us standing on the beach, out in the open like that, was a really bad idea." Apparently not all of him had received the order to stand down. On a mission all its own, his thumb traced a path down her cheek, then stroked the curve of her bottom lip. "The truth is, I was ticked at myself."

For just a second she looked puzzled and then understanding flashed in her eyes and the tension holding her
rigid eased. "So it was you, not me."

His mouth twisted. "Yeah." He climbed to his feet.
"Now I think I'd better quit screwing around and start
earning some of the money your grandmother's paying
me, huh? Will you be okay here by yourself while I go find
us a place to make camp?"

As unpredictable as ever, she managed another slight,
tired smile. "I think I can handle it."

"Good," he said, suddenly impatient to go. The fact that
his gut had gotten an unfamiliar kink in it the instant she'd
smiled didn't have jack to do with it. He had a job to do
and the more attention he paid it, the sooner they'd be
shaking off the dust of San Timoteo. And that was in both
their best interests.

He gave her one last, reassuring look. "I won't be long,"
he said briskly. And then he melted gracefully into the
darkness.

Lilah awoke cradled in Dominic's arms.

For half a second she thought she was dreaming. But
the tickle of his breath on her temple and the steady beat
of his heart against her back quickly dissuaded her of that.

She wasn't sure how long she lay there, afraid to move,
wondering if she should wake him, before she finally succumbed to temptation and settled a little closer. Allowing
herself a quiet sigh of pleasure, she tried to reconstruct the
previous night.

There'd been the walk, of course. After the first twenty
minutes, when her feet had started to hurt and her lungs

to burn, she'd dubbed it the San Timotean Not-Quite-A-Death March in a desperate attempt to keep things in perspective.

Next they'd stopped, and Dominic had yelled at her and—oh, God—then he'd suddenly been so kind that it had taken all of her strength not to cry.

And then they'd kissed. The memory of *that* was enough to set off a hot little glow inside her even now, hours later. After that, there'd been that brief but wholly unexpected talk, punctuated by Dominic doing a remarkable vanishing act, disappearing into the night as if he were a part of it.

True to his word, he hadn't been gone long. Ignoring her protests, he'd carried her to the spot where he'd already spread a tarp and put together a shelter. Then he'd made her drink some water and eat something remarkably filling called an MRE that he'd produced from what she was starting to think of as The Truly Amazing Bottomless Backpack.

After that, things got very hazy. She had a dim memory of starting to fall asleep while still sitting up, of Dominic laying her down and covering her up. Just as vague, she remembered opening her eyes—it must have been near dawn—and seeing him sitting cross-legged with his back to her, as still as a rock, keeping watch.

She had a much sharper image, however, of the moment when he'd finally stretched out beside her, big, solid, deliciously warm and exquisitely male.

Now, sunlight danced at the edges of the shelter's shaded overhang and birds sang, heralding a new day. The nighttime chill was a mere memory; it was already hot and muggy.

Her cheek was pillowed on the satiny bulge of muscle above the crook of Dominic's elbow, while his other arm was wrapped snugly around her waist. Their legs were tangled together, the smooth fabric of his pants legs tickling the bottoms of her feet.

It was hard to believe that yesterday at this time—had it really been only yesterday?—she'd been alone. Imprisoned. On the verge of losing hope. More than a little afraid.

Not that that last was any great surprise. Over the past weeks, Lilah had come to realize she'd spent most of her life being afraid: of disappointing her grandmother, of disgracing her family name, of turning out to be like the mother she'd never known.

According to Gran, it had been Lilah's beautiful, reckless mother who'd been responsible for Lilah's father's death. Like a siren of old, Melanie Morgan Cantrell had lured Abigail's son James into forgetting his duties and responsibilities with a combination of gaiety, laughter and an utter disregard for his obligations. If he'd been attending to business the way he should have been—the way Gran had expected him to—he'd never have agreed to attend that frivolous house party in Montana, much less gotten on the small plane that had crashed in the Rockies, killing everyone on board, including his young wife.

Although Abigail had never actually said it in so many words, Lilah strongly suspected her grandmother felt Melanie had gotten exactly what she'd deserved.

Gran had been far more open, however, in stating that no matter what it took, she wasn't about to allow her only grandchild to follow in Melanie's careless footsteps. She'd raised Lilah to be everything her mother hadn't been: reserved, deliberate, dutiful, responsible.

And while Lilah's only living relative seemed to be pleased with the results, where had they gotten Lilah? Over the past weeks, the answer to that had become painfully clear.

She was nearly thirty and alone. She was unable to claim anything except might-have-beens as her own. She lacked the memories of a life fully lived to sustain her.

But that could change. *She* could change.

The possibility, which had seemed like so much wishful thinking only days ago, seemed tantalizingly within reach when considered from the shelter of Dominic's arms. As did the question of where to start.

She wanted Dominic. She could try to delude herself into thinking that the overpowering attraction between them the past twenty-four hours was merely a reaction to their being thrown together in a very stressful situation. That if they'd met again on the street or some other benign social situation, they would've exchanged polite hellos and nothing more.

But deep down, she knew better. She knew that there was a part of her that had never quit thinking or caring about him. That from the instant she'd looked up and seen him being dragged into the cell block by those guards, she'd wanted him back in her life—whether it was for a lifetime, a year, a week or an hour. She wanted a chance to find out if they could have a future now that they were both grown-up.

And then what? What if it doesn't work out? Losing him before nearly destroyed you, and this time the stakes will definitely be higher. Are you really willing to take that risk?

Yes. Without a doubt or a hesitation, the answer was yes.

Her mind made up, she took a breath and pressed a lingering kiss to the bend of Dominic's elbow.

She felt the change as he awoke instantly. Like a switch being thrown, his body seemed to hum with an energy that hadn't been there a second before.

She twisted in his arms, shifting so she was looking up at him. His face was creased with sleep, his cropped hair rumpled. But his clear green eyes were totally alert.

He was so beautiful, she thought, not caring that it was a word rarely used to describe a man. More than a little amazed at her audacity, she reached up and smoothed a fingertip across one straight black eyebrow. "Good morning."

"Yeah." Something flickered in his eyes as they played over her and then his gaze hooded over. "You get some rest?"

"Yes." Her heart beat faster as she realized that she— and her wandering fingers, which were now toying with the thick silky hair cropped close to his temple—were responsible for the wariness he couldn't completely disguise.

The realization lit a little fire inside her, giving her the courage to slide her hand to the back of his head and tug him closer.

Inches apart, they regarded each other. Lilah wet her lips, prepared to throw caution to the wind. "Dominic—"

His name was only partly out of her mouth when he tensed, his gaze becoming unfocused as his concentration shifted outward. "Shh. Do you hear that?"

"What?"

"That."

She strained to listen, but still it was an anxious moment before she heard the rumble of trucks and men's shouted exchanges off in the distance. "Do you mean the—"

"Damn, damn, damn!" Without warning he scrambled out of the shelter and onto his feet. "Come on!" he ordered between his teeth. "Move!"

Her heart pounding, she crawled after him, still not entirely certain of the cause of his urgency. "What is it? I don't understand! Surely you expected them to look for us. Didn't you?" She was barely clear of the shelter before he'd rolled up and stowed the tarp and the thin blanket that had been covering them in his backpack.

"Oh, yeah." His face grim, he tossed her now-dry sandals to her, then knocked down the makeshift lean-to of palm and plantain fronds he'd built to conceal them overnight and spread the foliage around. "But I sure as hell didn't think they'd bother to bring in dogs to track us."

"Dogs?" A chill went down her spine as she fumbled into the shoes, which felt tight after their dowsing of the previous night. She struggled to fasten the buckles.

"Yeah." He slipped the backpack on, settled it into place and adjusted the straps. "Can't you hear them?"

Now that he'd pointed it out, she could. She was suddenly able to isolate a distant baying from the rest of the far-off sounds that didn't belong to the jungle's normal hum. "Oh, my God."

He looked up, hesitated a fraction of a moment, then reached out, gripped her by the shoulders and tugged her close. He looked down at her. "Pay attention. I'm not going to let anybody hurt you. I swear."

She parted her lips to assure him she trusted him to keep her safe, but before she could say a word, his mouth came down and claimed hers.

The kiss was quick but potent, the firm press of his lips momentarily displacing her fear, the unhurried heat of his heart against her palms more reassuring than any words.

He set her away from him. "Ready?"

Lips tingling, she nodded.

"Whatever happens, stay close and do exactly what I tell you, do you understand?"

"Yes."

"Good girl."

"Let's go, then." He set off, his long legs quickly eating up ground as he wove a path only he could see through the undergrowth.

Her eyes locked on his broad back, Lilah was hard on his heels.

Six

"They're getting closer, aren't they?" Lilah gasped, as she and Dom scrambled up yet another shallow, bracken-covered rise.

"Maybe a little," he conceded, lengthening his stride as they crested a hill and the ground briefly leveled out. He didn't see any reason to tell her that even though they'd exchanged a brisk jog for a dead run wherever the terrain allowed, experience told him the hounds would catch them sometime within the next half hour. That is, unless he could locate the source of the muted rush he could hear coming from somewhere to his right in the foliage-choked hills ahead of them first.

After all, it wasn't as if he couldn't handle a few hounds, he thought grimly, as he ducked under a thick, trailing vine. If it became necessary he could and would take them out courtesy of the 9mm automatic wrapped in a waterproof pouch at the bottom of his pack, a weapon he'd purchased on a back street in Santa Marita.

But he didn't want it to come to that. Sure, it would buy him and Lilah some time, but it would also give away their position every bit as much as the dogs themselves. Plus the handgun would have to be used at close range to be effective. And though taking such action would keep Lilah physically safe, there was nothing pretty about shooting other living things, threatening or otherwise. It would be damn traumatic for someone who'd led the sheltered life she had, and he'd prefer to spare her the experience if he could.

Not that he thought she'd protest, much less fall apart on him. He was starting to accept that she was a little less spoiled and a lot more intrepid than he remembered. And though he couldn't decide if that was because she'd changed or he simply hadn't been entirely fair to her over the years, he supposed it didn't matter.

What did was that with every hour they spent together, she continued to surprise him. Earlier today, it had been awakening to find them entwined together like two strands of the same rope. He couldn't recall a time since he'd qualified as a SEAL that he'd slept through anyone getting that close to him. Yet somehow she'd managed to slip past his defenses undetected.

Now he was finding himself surprised and impressed by the way she was keeping up with him, even though he was a nearly a foot taller, a good hundred pounds heavier, and hands down better shod than she was. Plus there was the not-so-inconsequential fact that he was *trained* to do this kind of high-speed evasion.

Somehow he doubted it was a skill that appeared on the how-to-be-a-successful-debutante checklist.

Yeah, smartass. They must've left it out to make space for the how-to-tie-a-guy-up-in-knots-just-by-breathing sequence.

God knew, Lilah had that particular ability down cold.

Because just beneath the edge of his fixation on getting them clear of their current situation was his intense, unwavering carnal awareness of her as an attractive, desirable female.

Of course, that was no longer any great surprise, either, he admitted, as he shoved a branch out of his way, held it a second to give her a chance to get clear, then grabbed her hand again to tow her up a short but steep incline. At some point during the night, as he'd sat in the inky darkness listening to her sleep, he'd accepted that the odds of them making it back to civilization without having sex were absolutely nonexistent.

And because he had, he'd subsequently decided it was a waste of energy to resist the inevitable. He wanted her. He was pretty sure she wanted him, too. They were two unmarried adults over the age of consent, and if they could find some pleasure in the midst of danger, why shouldn't they pursue it?

No reason on earth, he assured himself.

Of course, before that could happen, the small but pressing matter of evading their pursuers had to be dealt with first.

"Don't worry," he told her, grabbing her hand and lending her his strength as the vegetation thinned unexpectedly and he picked up their pace even more. "They're not going to catch us. Trust me."

She let loose with a brief, swallowed laugh that made him jerk his head around to look at her. "Dom, I do," she said, wincing as a strand of her hair caught on a thorny branch for an instant before her forward momentum tore it free. "I don't know why, but I do. Although I must confess—" her hand tightened on his as she followed him up and over a fallen log "—I'd love to hear your escape plan."

"Give me a few minutes and I'll show you," he reassured her. Having committed the area's topography to memory, he retrieved his mental map, checked his bearings and shifted their path even farther to the right.

With what felt like agonizing slowness despite their wide-open pace, they worked their way down and across the small valley floor, dodging vines, going under and around tree limbs, doing their best not to trip over the plant roots that twisted over the leaf-littered ground.

Off to the south, a distant clap of thunder rumbled. A quick glance toward the coast showed Dominic that a low ceiling of gray clouds now crowded the horizon. Whether they'd arrive in time to aid him and Lilah with their current problem was debatable, but it was still nice to know that inclement weather was headed this way. A little rain would be the icing on the cake of their escape, insuring that the dogs had not so much as a hint of a trail to follow.

Beside him, Lilah stumbled and he checked his stride to steady her. "You all right?"

"I'm fine," she said instantly.

A quick glance was all it took to reveal her assertion was open to debate. Her pants and shirt were torn, she had an angry-looking welt on one cheek, a long scratch on one forearm and numerous small bloody scratches on her ankles and feet. The injuries made him wince—she had such smooth, tender skin—but since there wasn't a damn thing he could do about them at the moment, he did what he was trained to do.

He shoved his concerns into a dark room in his mind and slammed the door until he had the time to deal with them.

He forced his attention back to cat-footing it through the amazing forest of car-sized boulders suddenly rising out of the verdant ground. Just when he was starting to think that he'd miscalculated their location, the land opened up and his navigating skills were rewarded with the sight of a wide ribbon of silver flashing through the foliage ahead. Skirting piles of deadfall no doubt deposited by flooding during the rainy season, he led Lilah down one last long slope, around a dense thicket of mangrove and out into a narrow clearing.

Stretching before them was a wide creek bed, the crystal clear water rushing swiftly over a bed of rocks. Without breaking stride, Dom plunged into the calf-high water. "Just a little farther," he told Lilah, sliding his hand up to grip her upper arm and steady her against the current, "and you can rest."

Moving as swiftly as he dared given the slick footing, he jogged downstream, staying in the center of the riverbed as it twisted and curved through a series of switchbacks.

Not until half a dozen bends separated them from the spot where they'd entered the water, which was growing steadily deeper, did Dom slow his pace.

Dead ahead, the stream split around an island the size

of a flatbed truck. Judging it perfect for his purposes, he twisted around and scooped Lilah into his arms.

"What are you doing!" Her eyes going wide in her damp, flushed face, she locked her arms around his neck.

"Giving you a boost." Having reached the island, he deposited her atop its fern-choked bank, disengaged her arms and took a half step back. He slipped his pack off, slung it to the ground and retrieved the gun, shoving it in its oilskin wrapper into the back of his waistband. "Take this—" he gestured at the pack "—get out of sight behind that—" he indicated the man-sized boulder that straddled the island's center "—and stay put. I'll be back."

"Back?" She scrambled to her knees, shoving the tangled mane of her hair off her face. "What do you mean? Where are you going?"

"I'm going to go lay a diversionary trail."

"But—"

"Do you understand what I just told you?"

"Yes, but—"

"You trust me, right?"

"Yes, but—"

"Then go," he said sharply. "I won't be long."

He watched as her mouth slammed shut and her chin came up. Reassured that she'd do as he'd asked, he started to turn away, only to have her surprise him one more time.

"*Wait.*" Leaning forward, she wrapped her arms around him and gave him a fierce hug. "Be careful," she murmured, pressing a kiss to his cheek.

Then she let go, sank onto her heels and he turned and set off back the way they'd just come.

* * *

Dominic's backpack weighed a ton.

Stunned at the idea that he'd actually been running beneath its weight, Lilah gritted her teeth and hauled it toward the big rock the way he'd instructed.

Although "instructed" was putting an exceedingly pretty construction on it, she reflected as the pack bumped over the uneven ground. *Ordered* was more like it.

No doubt she'd have found that exceedingly irritating under different circumstances. Yet it was hard to take issue with the man when he was risking his life for hers. Particularly when he continued to prove that, just as he claimed, he was more than qualified to deal with whatever fortune threw their way.

He was also in even more incredible shape than she'd already noted, she mused, as with a final yank she towed his backpack into the little copse behind the boulder and collapsed on her backside beside it. Not only did his body seem to be one long stretch of so-hard-you-could-bounce-a-nickel-off-them muscles, but nothing seemed to tire him out.

Out of nowhere, an image curled through her mind of lying within the circle of his arms, his chest gleaming with sweat as the two of them rocked together, his fingers laced through hers, his mouth latched to her nipple, his hips grinding tirelessly as he filled her. And then they'd move together for satisfaction, and he'd rock deeper and deeper and deeper until she was screaming his name—

With a choked laugh at the ache that suddenly throbbed between her thighs, she flopped onto her back and squeezed her eyes shut. *Oh, that's rich, Lilah. Dominic's off playing hide-and-seek with a bunch of bloodthirsty dogs and their equally bloodthirsty handlers and you're making him the star of your X-rated fantasies.*

Yet even as she told herself she ought to be ashamed, she simply wasn't. It had been a very long time since she'd been with a man. In point of fact, in all the years since Dominic there'd been only two, and both those relationships had been sadly unsatisfying.

So she was entitled to dream a little. After all, it wasn't as if she had something better to do. And heaven help her, even if the opportunity to turn her fantasy to reality should magically transpire, she wasn't sure she could scrape together the energy to pucker up her lips, much less engage in hot, sweaty, world-rocking sex.

The truth was, not only did every muscle in her body hurt, but she ached in places she wasn't sure even *had* muscles. Odd places, like the tops of her feet and the backs of her knees and the inner curves of her sides beneath her arms. Heck, thanks to her hair getting snagged by every kind of the native flora, even her head burned.

She was also certain that she'd never, ever been this dirty before in her life. Opening her eyes, it took only a quick look to confirm that all the exposed parts of her skin were coated with dust that was charmingly stuck to the sheen of perspiration that covered her. Her scalp felt gummy, her hair stiff and a quick sniff was enough to confirm that she smelled worse than a wild goat.

Not that she had a clue how a wild goat smelled. But it had to be better than her....

Wrinkling her nose, she twisted onto her side and stared longingly at the stream flowing by just a few feet away. She supposed it could actually be considered a river since, in just the stretch that she and Dom had traveled, it had doubled in width and gone from a few inches deep to several feet.

Whatever the correct term, it looked deliciously inviting, even if the water wasn't steal-your-breath cold the way it was back home in Colorado. But still…squeezing her eyes shut, she imagined stripping off her clothes and immersing her hot, sweaty self in its clean, cool depths. The thought of rinsing the salt from her hair and the grime from her skin was a temptation almost too appealing to resist.

Except that Dominic had told her to stay put. He hadn't said to bathe or wash her clothes or work on her sidestroke.

He'd told her to get out of sight and wait. So she would.

Rolling onto her back again, she covered her eyes and did her best to relax, telling herself she'd lay there for the rest of her life if that's how long it took for him to return. And put her energy into praying that he was safe, wherever he was.

She wasn't sure how much time passed. At some point—twenty, forty, sixty minutes after Dominic's departure?—she thought she heard the dogs barking and men shouting to each other, but the sounds were faint and quickly faded away.

And then the sun disappeared behind a sluggish smear of clouds and she totally lost track of time. Overcast or not, the day remained hot, humid, oppressive, and she may even have dozed for a little while.

It was the splash of rain on her face that jarred her back to awareness. For a moment, she simply lay still, looking up at the gray sky, wondering if she'd imagined that wonderful dampness. And then a handful more fat, wet drops splattered across her hot skin. Licking her salty lips, she remained prone and was rewarded as a minute later, a sound like dozens of chattering castanets seemed to approach as the wind rattled through the treetops, bringing with it more rain.

Then there was a crack of thunder and the sky opened and it was like being hit with the spray from a garden hose. Scrambling upright, Lilah raised her face to the deluge, welcoming the cool, cleansing torrent.

It only took another moment for her to realize this was an opportunity not to be missed. Reaching over, she began searching through the many pockets sewn into Dom's pack. She hit the jackpot on her fifth try; tucked into a small plastic-lined sleeve was a pristine bar of plain white soap.

Lilah couldn't have been more thrilled if it had been the finest French mill. Newly grateful for the privacy of her hiding place, she had her sandals, slacks and Dom's T-shirt off in a New York minute, draping the clothing over the nearest bush.

She washed her face first. Then, giving in to vanity, she soaped her hair from roots to ends, almost moaning with delight as the rain drummed down, leaving the long strands feeling smooth and silky as she ran her fingers through them, working out the worst of the tangles. She gathered the slippery mass into a thick rope and twisted what water she could out of it, but it was a lost cause since it was still raining as if it would never stop.

Giving up, she concentrated on scrubbing the rest of her body. She did her arms, legs and feet after first soaping her more private places, smiling inwardly as she imagined Millie, her grandmother's very fastidious housekeeper, reacting to the discovery that Lilah had laundered her imported silk underthings while she was still in them. Then she again tipped up her face and simply stood there, letting the rain sluice over her.

"So. Is this a private party?"

At the sound of Dominic's voice, her eyes flew open and she nearly jumped straight out of her freshly washed skin. She spun around, her heart jammed in her throat in the second before she saw it was really him.

"Or…"

Arms crossed, one hip propped against the side of her sheltering rock, he took his time speaking as his gaze slid slowly over her, leaving a trail of goose bumps in its wake.

"…can anybody come?"

She swallowed, trying to defeat the lump still making it hard to breathe as relief warred with awareness.

Thank God he was all right.

And yet, the way he looked… At some point in his excursion, he'd tied a rolled black bandanna around his well-shaped head. With a day's plus beard shadowing his lean cheeks, his wet T-shirt molded to his broad chest and washboard abs, and that very male look on his unsmiling face, he looked like some modern mercenary poster boy.

Lilah swallowed again, asking herself what she was waiting for. He wasn't more than a few feet away. Two steps and they'd be toe-to-toe. One more and she'd be in his arms, and after that….

After that, she could quit imagining. She could experience what it would feel like to peel off her bra and panties, wrap her arms around his neck, her legs around his waist, and lean back against the rough wet warmth of what she was starting to think of as her boulder.

She could feel his mouth on hers, hot and hungry as his hands slid over her wet slippery skin, cupping the weight of her breasts, shaping her nipples, gripping her spread thighs. And then he'd come driving home, making her eyes squeeze shut and her stomach hollow as he thrust himself into her. Her back would bow, her toes would curl and her fingers would clutch the smooth, steely heat of his wide shoulders—

"Water's rising." Dominic's voice, as jagged as a whipsaw, jerked her back to reality. She watched, her pulse still racing, as he straightened, yanked the bandanna down around his neck and raked a hand through his thick black hair. "As much as I hate to say it, you'd better get your clothes on. We've got to go."

"What?" Her throat was now so tight the word was barely more than a whisper.

But he heard her. "Look around." His gaze raked her one more time, then his mouth hardened into a thin line and he bent over and began securing all the flaps she'd undone on his backpack. "The stream's coming up. Another twenty minutes and this will all be underwater. We need to get to higher ground. And we need to do it now."

"Oh." Oh, indeed. Suddenly she was acutely aware she was still just standing there, eating him up with her gaze, while her nipples—along with the rest of her flesh—were clearly visible through her transparent underwear.

She snatched her soggy T-shirt from its leafy resting place and yanked it over her head, then struggled into her wet pants. By the time Dominic straightened, she had her sandals on and buckled and had retrieved the soap from the dirt where it had slipped unnoticed out of her hand.

"Here," she said like a good little soldier, offering him the bar.

His piercing green gaze swept over her. As if he could see straight to her soul and see the sudden uncertainty there, the promise of satisfaction suddenly raged to life in his eyes. "Soon," he said in a gravelly voice, his fingers lingering on hers a second before he took the soap and shoved it out of sight.

And just like that, with that single word of assurance, the chill that had been creeping over her skin vanished.

She waited as he scrubbed his palm against his camo pants, then she stepped close, slipped her hand into his and let him lead her toward the water. She hesitated, however, as she took her first good look at the tame little stream that was now a torrent. "Wow. It's going really fast, isn't it?" Having grown up where she had, she'd heard of flash floods, of course. But she'd never imagined a landscape could change so fast.

"Yeah, but not as fast as it's going to. So hold on to my waistband and don't let go, okay?" Dominic said, slinging the pack over his left shoulder so she'd have access. "And quit looking so worried. We don't have that far to go and as I told you before, I'm not going to let anything happen to you."

"I know."

"Good. But just in case you need an incentive—" one more time his gaze kissed her face, only this time he flashed that killer grin that ought to come with a label warning vulnerable women to guard their hearts "—if you're a good girl I'll give you a real thrill when we get where we're going."

She lifted her chin, doing her best to look cool and confident even though she suddenly could barely breathe. "Oh, really?"

"You can bet on it." And then, in one of those lightning transitions she was starting to expect, he was all business, turning and waiting for her to get a firm grip on him before he struck out into the rising water.

To her surprise, the water still didn't feel very cold. And though she was taken aback to find it swirling from her knees to her waist to just below her breasts as they reached the midway point, it seemed to her they were making good time.

She never saw the chunk of debris that struck her. One second, she was staring fixedly at Dominic's broad back, marveling at his strength as he plowed ahead like a one man Navy destroyer; the next something slammed into her knees, knocking her legs out from beneath her, then bashed into her elbow, striking her hard on her funny bone. Pain shot up her arm and her fingers went slack, sliding out of the belt loop that had kept her anchored to Dominic.

And then everything went gray as she went under, the water closing over her head as she was swept away, tumbling over and over in the teeming current.

Seven

It wasn't going to be bloodhounds or unpredictable weather or El Presidente's men that was going to do him in, Dom thought.

Nope. It was going to be Lilah, pure and simple. Every time he turned around, the woman did something that threatened to give him a heart attack.

With a vicious curse as the drag of her weight vanished from the back of his waistband, Dom flung his pack at the river bank and wheeled around to search for Lilah in the churning water. For what felt like the longest moments of his life, he saw nothing.

Fear, so foreign it took him a moment to identify it, ate at him. Recognizing it as the enemy, he shoved it away and concentrated.

Where the hell are you, princess? Come on. Don't you go and die on me now. We've got some seriously unfinished

business to attend to. So give me something to work with.
Anything. Come on, come on, come—

As if she'd heard his demands, Lilah broke the surface
some fifteen feet away. Relief nearly dropped him to his
knees in the instant it took for her to part her lips and suck
in a lungful of air.

He launched himself in her direction, his SEAL training making him as secure in the water as he was on land.
Not content to simply let the current carry him, he used
the bottom to propel himself forward. Yet he hadn't covered more than a few feet when the water yanked her back
down and she disappeared from sight.

He felt a flicker of panic. *Easy.* Tamping down the excess of emotion flashing through him, he scoured the area
downstream with his gaze, picking up his feet and letting
the water carry him as he waited for her to reappear. When
too much time had ticked past and she hadn't emerged, he
drew a deep breath and plunged beneath the surface, but
it was no use; there was so much dirt and debris clouding
the stream that visibility was zero.

He shot up, dodged a mangled tree as it slowly wind-
milled past his head and scanned the area around him
again, searching, searching—for an arm, a foot, an inch
of black T-shirt, a glimpse of sunny hair. Since failure was
not an option, he took an iron grip on his emotions and
looked again. And again.

And then he caught a glimpse of something out of the
corner of his eye. Whipping his head to the left, he saw
her pop up some eight feet away like a cork escaping a bottle. Her eyes looked huge in her pale face as she coughed
up a rush of water. Clearly panicked, she screamed his

name as the current spun her around and she fought to keep her head above water.

"Hang on!" he shouted back, his own voice barely audible over the rush of the water.

She turned instantly in his direction, and even though her voice was all but drowned out, he clearly saw her lips form his name again and a fresh wave of relief rushed through him. If she could tread water and talk she couldn't be in too bad shape, he tried to assure himself.

And then she lost her battle to stay afloat and went under a third time.

He didn't think but simply reacted, shoving the tree out of his way as he instinctively calculated her most likely trajectory. In the next instant, he was under the water, slicing powerfully through the turbulent depths, thrusting aside anything unfortunate enough to impede him, relying on intuition tempered by years of experience to guide his path since he couldn't see jack.

Fifteen seconds later, his hand hit what he recognized instantly as the soft curve of her hip. One more kick and he had her, hooking her around the waist with his arm and reeling her in. Once he was sure she wasn't going anywhere, Dom didn't waste any time. Driving upward, he propelled them into the life-sustaining air.

The second they surfaced, she clamped her arms around his neck and her legs around his waist, practically strangling him as she buried her face in the crook of his shoulder. She held on to him for dear life, her body shivering as she hungrily sucked in air. "Thank God," she whispered. "Thank God. I was so scared. But I knew you'd come. I knew. I knew."

"Shh. It's okay, baby," he soothed, running his hand up her back and under her drenched hair to rub the nape of her neck. "It's okay. You're all right. I've got you." He tried to give her a second to compose herself, but when a piece of debris punched him in the lower back, it added urgency to his already keen awareness of the danger still facing them. "Look, I need you to do something for me."

"Anything," she said shakily.

"We need to get out of the water. And to do that, you have to let go of me. You need to trust *me* to hold on to *you* so I can get us out of here. Can you do that?"

There was a second's silence. "Yes," she said finally. This time, her voice was steadier. Yet for several heartbeats, the death grip she had on him didn't slacken.

And then, as she'd done so many times in the past twenty-four hours, she seemed to dip down into some hidden cache of composure and pull herself together. Letting out a long, shaky breath, she loosened her hold on him and eased back. He saw her throat work and something twisted a little inside him. "I'm all right." A pale ghost of a smile materialized at the corners of her mouth. "So save me already. Please?"

Yeah. She was definitely going to be the death of him.

Just not right now. Not wasting another second, he got her into the right position for a rescue hold, wrapped his arm around her chest and struck out for the bank. Despite the power of his legs, the surging water and his water-logged boots served to slow him down. Still, it wasn't long before he was able to get his feet underneath him, scoop Lilah into his arms, shift his balance and trudge carefully out of the water. He quickly surveyed their surroundings. Without breaking stride, he headed for higher ground.

Lilah lifted her head, glanced around, then looked at him. "You can put me down," she said softly. "I can walk."

He glanced at her, struck by what a sea of contradictions she was. She looked as fine and fragile as the most delicate piece of crystal, but she possessed a core of steel that continued to amaze him.

With a start of surprise, it occurred to him that there was a hell of a lot he didn't know about her. Sure, he knew all about the rich debutante stuff, and yeah, given that they'd been out of touch for so long, he could hardly expect to know how she'd spent the past decade.

But when he really thought about it, he realized that what they'd mostly talked about the summer they'd spent together—when they *had* talked—was him. His brothers, his bad relationship with his father, what it was like to grow up in a household of guys without a mother, his dream of getting the hell out of Denver.

Back then he'd had no intention of following the family tradition of going into the service. It was all right for the old man to be career army, for Gabe to risk his life being an unsung hero in the Green Berets, or Taggart to put in time in Somalia and Bosnia doing really spooky Ranger stuff he still wouldn't talk about, but Dom had thought he was on a different track.

Then Lilah had dumped him and he'd just wanted to go somewhere, be someone, fast. The navy, and then the SEALs, had turned out to be the best answer to that.

But when it came to Lilah, what did he know? After a moment's reflection, the answer came back—*not much.*

He knew she'd lost her folks when she was still a baby, that she'd been raised by her strict, high-powered grand-mother who'd had the good taste to be out of the country on an extended trip the summer they'd spent together, and that he'd been her first.

That was about it. Scour his memory as he might, he couldn't remember having a single conversation about her hopes, her dreams, what she wanted out of life. Of course, looking back, that was most likely because in his youth-ful arrogance he'd just assumed that what she wanted was *him.*

"I'm serious, Dominic." Expression intent, Lilah touched her hand to his face to get his attention. "You don't need to carry me."

"Yeah." Even as he glanced at her, he didn't slow. "You're probably right. Or you would be if I was inclined to listen to you. Which I'm not."

"But—"

"Shh. I'll be laying you down soon enough, princess. You can count on it."

His choice of words was deliberate. As was the way he held her gaze an instant before he let his own slide to her mouth. Briefly loosening the reins on his restraint, he let his eyes trace the soft fullness of the lower curve, the lit-tle bow that held court dead center in the middle of her upper lip. Slowly, his gaze climbed her face, rising from her mouth, to the delicate curve of her earlobe, brushing the elegant planes of cheek and temple before coming back to meet her eyes.

The hunger riding him must've been clear on his face because a slight flush bloomed at the tops of her cheeks.

"Oh." The single word was just the merest hint of a whisper, the faintest exhalation of breath.

"Yeah." He found the grace to dredge up a smile. "Oh."

He wasn't sure what he'd expected. Maybe a maidenly retreat to go with the blush or a more pointed protest. He sure didn't expect her to settle closer and murmur, "It's about time." Any more than he'd anticipated that she'd let her eyes drift shut and commence stringing a line of kisses along the sensitive flesh where his jaw met his throat.

God. Did she know how to light his fire or what?

He picked up his pace, his long legs devouring ground as he strode across a graveled wash. Spying a narrow trail that gently switchbacked up a long rise, he began to climb. Thanks no doubt to the adrenaline still pumping through him, he felt tireless, as if he could walk forever.

Except that he had a different plan for burning off all this excess energy.

The trail leveled out, dropping down into a modest clearing with a surprising vista to the south. A grove of trees with wide, fan-shaped leaves formed a dense canopy overhead, while an elevated bank sporting a dense padding of moss spread across the most sheltered edge of the small overlook.

Dom recognized on a purely visceral level that this was the place. Another few strides and he was at the bank. Then he was sinking onto his knees, laying Lilah back against the moss, bracing his weight on his hand and following her down.

He felt a shiver go through her. Shifting beneath him, she once again did the unexpected and aligned her hips with his, greeting the heavy thrust of his lower body with a shallow bump and grind that nearly blew off the top of his head. "Ah, Nicky," she murmured, her voice breaking just a little as she rubbed against him like a needy kitten. "I've missed you so much."

Knowing that nothing short of a full-out nuclear attack could stop him now—and even that was doubtful—he bent his head and kissed her.

Lilah parted her lips and drank him in. He tasted the way a man should, she thought, like sex and heat and the sort of steady strength a woman could depend on. His mouth was hard and warm like the rest of his big muscular body, with a leashed power that made her feel both rock-solid safe and deliciously vulnerable all at the same time.

She savored the suggestive thrust of his tongue, meeting it with a softer probing of her own. He made a deep sound in his throat, and she pressed her advantage, shifting the slant of her mouth to bite down on the pad of his lower lip.

He groaned. Deepening the kiss, he pushed up on his palms and rocked his pelvis against the notch of her thighs. The long hard shape of him against her most intimate place sent her arching against him. Tangling her hands in his hair, she tried to tug him closer, wanting to feel his entire body against her, wanting him inside her.

It was like trying to move a rock. Blatantly taking advantage of his superior size, he refused to budge, limiting their contact to the hot joining of their mouths and the steady rock and grind of their clothing-cushioned pelvises.

He was slowly driving her mad, she thought as she

strained beneath him. Her need for him inside her grew stronger and stronger. And yet for all her escalating impatience, a part of her enjoyed the anticipation building within her.

It had been a long, lonely stretch since she'd last felt this way, and it was gratifying to know her escalating hunger was in no way one-sided, which was obvious when Dominic finally came up for air and was panting just as hard as she was.

And that was good, Lilah thought. Because if the past weeks had made her see how much of her life she'd wasted by being afraid to go after what she wanted, the past day had shown her how quickly that very life could be snatched away.

"No more," she said in a breathy voice that she barely recognized, reaching down to tug at his T-shirt and yank the hem out of his waistband. She thrust her hands under the damp cotton, unable to stop the murmured sound of satisfaction that tore from her throat as she ran her palms up the taut flesh of his abdomen. Stretched drum-tight over slabs of muscle, his skin was smooth and hot.

"No more what?" he grated out, dropping his chin as she pushed his T-shirt over his head and slid it along his arms.

"No more waiting." The instant he raised his left hand to free himself of his T-shirt, she took advantage of his position, pushing aside the soft cotton to rub her cheek against his bare chest. "I want you. Now." Shifting her head, she sucked hard on his nipple.

"Holy sh—" He snapped upright, his chest heaving as he stared down at her, a flicker of surprise in his glittering green eyes. "You're not kidding, are you?"

She shook her head. "No."

For an endless second, he continued to regard her. And then something in his face changed just a fraction, making him look a little harder, a little edgier, a little more—as impossible as it seemed—male. "All right then," he murmured.

In a lightning leap, he was suddenly on his feet, standing between her ankles. Taking a step back, he reached down, unlaced and removed his boots, then undid his pants, peeled them down and kicked them away.

Lilah was so stunned by the sheer beauty of his naked body towering before her that she forgot to breathe. The storm had passed as quickly as it had blown in, and the sun had returned. Its rays filtered through the steam-shrouded trees, shadowing his grass-green eyes and dappling his wide shoulders with gold.

He had a soldier's physique; his long legs were roped with muscle, his thighs substantial. Her hands involuntarily fisted as her gaze followed the path she'd just touched, from the strong column of his throat, down the sculpted planes of his chest and across the muscled flatness of his stomach.

She looked in awe and sympathy at the marks of duty: a thin slashing scar that bisected the top of one arm; another, wider one that curled beneath his lowest right rib and disappeared around his side; a newer, still slightly pink, puckered mark high on his left side.

And then her gaze was caught by the thin trail of jet-black hair that started well below the flat indentation of his navel and arrowed down like a one-way road to the heavy thickness jutting up from his thighs.

With an ease that she was certain only existed in the male of the species, he stood his ground and let her take him all in. Finally, however, his voice sliced through her absorption. "Lilah?"

"Hmm?" Feeling more than a little light-headed, she lifted her eyes to his.

"Breathe, baby," he said gently. "Before you pass out."

Suddenly dizzy, she did just that, her heart pounding so hard that it hurt. "Right." She shut her eyes, not realizing she'd pressed her thighs together in an instinctive effort to relieve the building ache until she felt his hand cup her there.

Her eyes jerked open and she found him kneeling beside her. "Easy," he soothed, even as he slowly moved his fingers against her, making the world tilt even more.

Without warning, the delicious pressure vanished. Her eyes jolted open as he slid his arm under her back, propped her up and quickly stripped away her shirt and bra. "Soon," he murmured, repeating what he'd said an hour—a lifetime—ago. His mouth slid like liquid heat along the arch of her throat as he made short work of her sandals, slacks and panties. "Soon," he repeated. "Just. Not. Yet." The words were interspersed with kisses as his head dropped lower until his mouth closed over one nipple.

"*Dominic.*" She wove her fingers through his still damp hair, loving its slippery, satiny texture. He lifted his head just long enough to cup her other breast in his hand and lower his mouth to suck her there, too.

She freed her hands of his hair and gripped his shoulders, her fingers barely denting those steel-sleek curves as she arched beneath him, moaning shamelessly.

Then his hand made its own journey, skating down, raking through her dark blond curls, his knuckles grazing her before his fingers parted her wetness. "Damn, but you feel like silk," he said hoarsely as one long broad fingertip nudged inside her. As if he had X-ray hands, he zeroed in on her most sensitive spot, found it with his thumb and pressed just enough to make her jaw go slack.

"*Dominic.*" With strength born of desperation, she caught his chin in her hand and dragged his head up.

His mouth glistening from the feast he'd made of her breasts, he lifted his heavy-lidded eyes to look at her. "What?" The rasp in his husky voice sent a ripple of anticipation down her spine.

"Just...*this,*" she whispered, her voice trailing off entirely as she leaned close, boldly ran her tongue along the seam of his lips, then tilted her head to one side and followed up with a deep, openmouthed kiss.

She couldn't have made her desires any clearer if she'd sent him an engraved invitation. But when she opened her eyes he was still braced above her, his expression impossible to decipher.

Oh, God, what if she'd just made a total hash of things? What if he was put off by her demands, turned off by her desperation?

After all, she wasn't the girl she'd been. She was ten years older, a woman. One who, for the first time in her life, wasn't afraid to ask for what she wanted.

She wasn't willing to hang back anymore and let someone else take the initiative. She had, after all, sworn just hours earlier that whatever it took, she was done being just a bystander who let life happen to her.

So? What now? Give up? Go back to what you were?

No. She forced herself to meet his gaze without flinching. "I need you inside me. I *want* you inside me. Please, Dominic—don't make me beg." Although she would, she realized a little wildly as she waited for his answer. She'd beg, cajole, bargain—bare her soul if she had to. She'd do whatever it took.

There was a breathless second when nothing happened and then it was as if she'd thrown a torch into summer-dry tinder. A shudder went through him and he caught fire.

"*Damn it, Lilah,*" he said between his teeth in the second before he took her mouth. In the next instant, he was wrapping his arms around her, pushing inside her, filling her and driving into her. Up, up, up.

And Lilah was with him every step of the way, wet, hungry, needy. "Oh, yes. *Yes.* Keep—like that—"

Clutching his broad shoulders, she dug her heels into the back of his thighs and tipped up her pelvis, trying to get closer, wanting him even deeper.

Everything about him excited her—the satiny heat of his skin beneath her fingertips, the curved muscles bulging in his arms and shoulders as he thrust into her, the rock-hard slap of his stomach against hers. It felt right, so right. As did this wild, rough, ferocious ride.

She needed his power, his fierceness, needed to feel his massive body pounding into her. She needed him to want her as much as she wanted him.

He did. "Easy," he said against her lips as he gasped for breath. "Easy, baby, don't—oh *yeah*. Do that. Don't stop. Don't. Stop."

He lowered his head and again caught her upthrust nipple in his mouth. The scrape of his teeth and lash of his tongue sent a fresh tremor of pleasure curling through her. Combined with the change in the angle of his penetration, it jolted her up and over the top.

"Dominic. Oh. *Oh*." She held on to him with every ounce of her strength as satisfaction beckoned, just beyond her reach. Dimly she heard him give a choked roar and felt his big body begin to shudder. And then her own pleasure blasted through her, sweeping her away.

And everything else ceased to matter.

Eight

Dom lay sprawled on the tarp from his pack, which he'd retrieved in the last glimmer of twilight earlier that evening. Nestled in the crook of his arm, her head resting on his shoulder, Lilah slept with the stillness of complete exhaustion.

She was entitled, he thought, absently rubbing his cheek against the silken crown of her head. Even he'd found the day physically challenging, so it was no great surprise she was worn out.

Still, it was hard not to chafe at their slow pace. On his own, he would have hiked all the previous night and day and probably arrived in Santa Marita by now.

But with Lilah, her stamina impaired by weeks of poor food and confinement, it just wasn't possible. He had no choice but to do his best to pace their journey in a way that preserved her limited strength.

Making adjustments to suit the situation was just part

of the job, he reminded himself. Even if it gave him far too much time to think about matters he'd prefer to ignore.

Because if he were sleeping, he wouldn't be thinking.

Like why just the innocent press of Lilah's thigh against his hip, the wash of her breath tickling the crook of his neck, the warm weight of her breast against his chest, was enough to keep him in an unrelenting state of arousal.

Or how there was a reckless, unfamiliar part of him that would like nothing better than to shift her beneath him and satisfy that persistent hunger.

And he sure wouldn't have to think about the moment when he'd looked down at her earlier as he carried her out of the water and felt something inside him shift.

It had taken him a while to figure out what bothered him most, but as the moon rose high in the sky he knew it was that last thing.

Damned if he didn't like her. Not just as somebody to share his body and his bed with, although there was no denying that was a factor. But also as a person, a fellow human being. Granted, if all you did was count up the hours, they hadn't spent a great deal of time together. But when you spent crisis time with someone, when you faced danger together, you quickly got their measure. And Lilah was simply not the pampered, self-absorbed, status-conscious snob he'd painted her to be.

Dom shifted, feeling restless. This wasn't the way things were supposed to go, he thought somberly. Hell, if he were honest about it, he had to admit he'd never even considered liking her as a possibility. He wasn't particularly proud of it, but the hard truth was that he'd expected this little interlude to cure him of his yen for her.

He'd thought—well maybe not *thought,* exactly, since his brain hadn't been the organ doing the bulk of his decision-making at the time—but he'd believed on some level that giving into his desire for her would prove, once and for all, that he'd exaggerated their past pleasures, that he'd been deluding himself into believing that sex with her had been something special. He'd expected that sleeping with her would get her out of his system once and for all and allow him to relegate her to the past where she belonged.

Instead, he wanted in the worst way to roll her onto her back and bury himself deep inside her once again. Far more alarming, a reckless part of him that he barely recognized wanted to hold her close and tell her things—his secrets, his needs, his fears, his hopes.

And he didn't like it. He didn't like it at all. He knew what his old man and his brothers had gone through when they'd lost his mother. He may only have been nine, but he'd seen—and felt—the void her passing had left. And it hadn't taken him long to realize that no one else would ever fill that vast black hole. It had also seemed to him that the best bet to avoid falling into a similar abyss was to steer clear of attachments.

Yet with the reckless optimism of youth, he'd gone ahead all those years later and let himself fall for Lilah. And then she'd dumped him.

It had hurt at the time. Although in truth, he still wasn't sure how much of his pain had sprung from actual love and how much from injured pride.

It really didn't matter, because in the end Lilah had done him a favor. Like a sharp slap to the face, her rejection had brought him to his senses and made him think long and hard about what he really wanted. And what he'd concluded was that it wasn't a good idea to invest himself in someone else so much that losing them could put a permanent hole in his life. Unless it concerned his brothers—and for a while his SEAL teammates—he'd found it was better by far to rely on himself, to keep his own counsel, to guard his own back.

And when it came down to it, nothing had changed. This—whatever *this* was—was just an interlude, a minor detour, a short trip down a dead-end path. Getting Lilah out of San Timoteo, back to her grandmother and her safe, privileged life was still his number one priority.

"Dominic?" Lilah's quiet voice curled over him.

He shifted his head and found her looking up at him, her gaze impossible to read in the shadowed light. "You're awake." It was an effort, but he deliberately relaxed his expression. Yeah, he needed to reestablish a little necessary distance between them, but he didn't want to hurt her.

She yawned and settled a little closer, sliding one hand up his chest to gently knead the point where his neck met his shoulder.

"I've been thinking. How *are* we getting off the island?" Rolling onto her side, she propped herself up on one elbow, the better to see him. Almost absently, the fingers of her free hand stroked the sensitive patch of skin behind his ear.

"Most likely someone will be coming to pick us up," he said, the ache of need he'd felt when she'd been sleeping throbbing annoyingly to life at her touch, "but I won't know for sure until we get to Santa Marita and I can check in with home."

"We're going to the capital?" Her dismay was obvious.

"Absolutely." He felt a spark of pleasure ignite as her hand wandered down his neck and trailed across his collarbone to tickle over the curve of his shoulder. "The safest place to hide is almost always in plain sight. Besides, it's the only location on the whole island where we're likely to find a boat fast enough, or better yet, a plane, to get us out of here, if that's what we have to do."

Her hand paused. "A plane?" she said dubiously. "What about a pilot?"

"You're looking at him." He jerked involuntarily as the warmth of her palm passed over his hip and her fingertips lightly brushed the aching length of him.

"You know how to fly?"

Her hand and the slender thigh she'd draped over his leg was making it harder to concentrate with every passing second. "SEAL stands for Sea, Air, Land. Part of the training is learning how to pilot anything that has an engine and moves."

"Seriously?" Her own voice was more than a little breathless now as, her gazed locked on his, she closed her hand around him, measuring his hard circumference.

"Oh, yeah." His brain had gone hazy, and his tongue suddenly felt thick, making it hard to talk. Still, for a moment he considered calling a halt, except that it was hours yet until dawn and this beat the hell out of being alone with his thoughts….

"Do you have other hidden talents?" she queried.

She gently tightened her grip and once again he felt the desire to be deep inside her. "Why don't you come here—" reaching across his body, he caught her by the hips and shifted her on top of him, gritting his teeth as he centered her and felt the slippery warmth of her settle against him "—and let me show you."

She laughed, low and throaty, a sound so innately sexy it made his skin prickle with need. "I don't think so. I think it's my turn to be…in charge."

Catching him off guard, she pushed herself up so she was straddling him, then rocked up on her knees. Before he could do more than swallow, she positioned him and rubbed slowly over the tip of him.

Then she wet her lips and came sliding down, her own breath catching as she took the full length and breadth of him. It was all he could do not to cry out as he felt the squeeze of her inner muscles tighten around him.

Oh, yeah. It's definitely going to be a heart attack that takes me out…just merciful heaven, don't let it happen now….

His mind went blank altogether as she reversed course, riding him up, paused again at the height of her stroke, then once again began to slowly, slowly lower herself.

"Li, you're killing me," he said in a guttural voice he barely recognized as his own.

"At least you won't die alone," she murmured, settling into an unhurried rhythm that threatened to turn him inside out. "And you have to admit, there are worse ways to go…."

Swallowing a groan, he squeezed his eyes shut and spent the next few minutes focused fiercely on holding back the tide already threatening to sweep him away.

Then her control faded, as well. "Dominic," she whispered urgently. "Oh, yes, there…right there, yes… Deeper. You feel so—*oh, sooo good—*"

The sound of her voice shattered his concentration. His eyes snapped open and locked on her. Bathed in moonlight, she looked stunning, her eyes rapturously closed, her pale hair tumbled around her like a golden cloak. A faint sheen of perspiration clung to her skin, making it glow as she began to pick up the pace, rocking up a little faster, sinking down a little harder—

Like a blind man caught in a whirlwind, he could feel himself spiraling out of control, tumbling toward the slippery edge of his own release. Needing an anchor, he slid his hands up her torso to cup her breasts, gently squeezing her nipples between his thumbs and forefingers.

Lilah's enthralled cry and the heart-stopping sensation of her clamping down and clenching around him shoved him over the brink.

In a sudden fever of need, he locked his hands around her slender waist, holding her in place as his hips slammed up, his back bowed. Nothing else mattered as he spilled himself into her, spinning away in a rush of pleasure greater than any he'd ever known.

Dom had just finished packing the last of their gear when he heard the distant whomp-whomp-whomp of the helicopter.

He scrambled to the clearing's edge. Scanning the sky as he stuffed his shirt tail into his pants, he narrowed his gaze against the rising sun and finally caught a flash of silver skimming the treetops. It was a whole lot closer than he'd expected, and all it took was a glance to identify it as a Bell Huey with the San Timotean flag painted boldly on its tail.

"Get back!" he ordered as he turned to find Lilah on her feet, coming his way. Charging toward her, he hauled her into the dense shadow behind the base of the largest tree.

No more than ten seconds later, the large metal bird passed directly overhead, making the trees shimmy violently in the rotor wash.

Ducking her head, Lilah burrowed against him and he instinctively wrapped his arms around her. "Do you think they're looking for us?" she asked the instant the chopper's deafening roar had subsided enough that she could be heard.

He let go of her and took a step back, starkly aware that if they'd broken camp even five minutes earlier the chopper would have caught them out in the open. "No. Most likely they're making a transport run. By the time we get something to eat and break camp, they should be long—"

He cut himself off as he heard the bird turn and head back.

What the *hell?* He knew damn well they couldn't have been spotted from the air. Even if the men aboard were equipped with high-powered binoculars, their incoming angle had been all wrong, and the trees were too dense, the shadows too deep, for him and Lilah to have been seen. He was equally certain that there was nobody on the ground close enough to have called in their location; he trusted his instincts and would've sensed their presence.

Which meant the chopper had to be flying a predetermined pattern.

Dom tried to tell himself he was wrong, but when the bird finished its current pass, moved roughly a quarter mile to the east, then turned yet again, his doubts vanished.

His mind churning, he turned to look at Lilah. "You want to tell me," he said, trying not to leap to conclusions even as he felt a tightness in his stomach that warned that somewhere along the way he'd dropped the ball, "what's going on?"

"What do you mean?"

Some of his tension eased at the look of genuine puzzlement on her face. Deciding she had no reason to lie, he glanced away long enough to finish securing the straps on the pack. "I wondered what the deal was when I heard that El Presidente kept raising the rent on you; it's not his usual pattern. And then I wondered again when I got here and found out that instead of being in Santa Marita, like every other person who's ever been detained, *you'd* been sent to *Las Rocas.*

"Now this. No way would Condesta send out what amounts to the entire San Timotean Air Force to look for you without a damn good reason. You want to tell me what it is? Does it have something to do with that guy you were with?"

Lilah's expression turned blank. "Guy?" she echoed. "Why would you think I was with a man?"

"Because your grandmother said so," he said flatly.

"She did?" And then her face cleared. "Oh! You must mean Diego."

"Yeah." His gaze held hers. "I guess I do."

A sudden flash of amusement lit her eyes. "Diego is irresistible—for a twelve-year-old!"

"He's a *kid?*"

"Yes. I was his family's guest at the Cinco de Mayo celebration at the town square. Things got out of hand, the *guarda* showed up, and somehow in the melee we got separated. The next thing I knew, a policeman had him. I tried to explain that he didn't have anything to do with the troublemakers, but the policeman wouldn't listen. He *struck* Diego—" a trace of remembered repulsion colored her voice "—I objected, and there was an altercation. Diego got away, and I got arrested."

Terrific. Diego was a victim, Lilah was a saint and he was an idiot. A *jealous* idiot. The discovery didn't do a thing to improve his mood. "And the chopper? You have any idea what that's all about?"

She pursed her lips a moment. "Did Gran explain why I came here?" she asked finally, falling in behind him as he hefted the backpack into place and they headed out.

He nodded, took a quick look around to get his bearings, then chose a path headed southwest. "Yeah. She said you'd come to see about providing money for what I assume is the kid's school."

Lilah was silent a moment, then made a soft sound that somehow conveyed both resignation and exasperation. "Apparently she didn't mention that I have an advanced degree in international finance. Or that for the past two years I've been *running* the Anson Foundation, which has a half-billion dollar endowment and now does educational outreach for children in thirty-seven countries. The school here is a good one, worthy of support, but obviously the situation is complicated by the government. The trick is figuring out a way to help without lining certain people's pockets. That's why I came myself. I'd just dealt with a similar problem in East Africa, so I thought I might be able to expedite matters here.

"The problem is, I couldn't. And when I told El Presidente there'd be no money, he was visibily angry." She fell silent as he helped her scale an enormous downed log. "Everything just happened so quickly," she went on as they resumed walking. "I went straight from the meeting with Condesta to meet Diego's family, and then I was arrested. I never even had time to call home and report I'd decided to pass on the money at this time."

It made perfect sense, Dom thought as he pressed ahead along the narrow track. Clearly Condesta intended to get his hands on the Anson money, no matter what it took.

"Any thoughts on why he's increased his demands the longer he's held you?"

"He has?" she said with surprise.

"Yes."

"I have no idea. Unless—"

He swiveled around to glance back at her. "Unless what?"

"Well…if I had to hazard a guess, it would be that he's still upset about his Mercedes."

"His Mercedes?"

She gave a faint, apologetic sigh. "Yes. I wrecked it. I'm afraid he didn't take it very well. The very next day I was shipped to *Las Rocas*."

"Lilah, what in the *hell* are you talking about?"

She tugged her hair away from a bush where it had caught. "When I was first being held, in Santa Marita, I tried to escape. Which must be why they upped the ransom demand," she added thoughtfully. "Anyway, Condesta is inordinately fond of the sound of his own voice, so after I got caught the second time—"

The *second* time?

"—he came to lecture me about the folly of my behavior. And since he fancies himself a ladies' man, and especially likes blondes, or so rumor has it, he delivered his message while trying to impress me with a tour of his new, private marina, built to house his yachts and speedboats and brand new seaplane. It didn't seem to occur to him that in a country where most of his people don't have enough to eat, I might find his conspicuous consumption less than laudatory."

She waved her hand as if that were beside the point. "Anyhow, when we finally got back to the part of the compound where I was being held, his driver assisted his excellency from the car—El Presidente doesn't walk anywhere he can drive, even on his own property—then came around to open my door. And that's when I realized the car was still idling and I just…I lost my head."

Dom quirked an eyebrow at her. "I'm afraid to ask."

"Well, it wasn't that big a deal, I simply climbed over the seat and put the car into gear and aimed it at the front gate. The Mercedes held up surprisingly well despite that barrier, and I still think I would have made the turn, except there was a woman on a bike and when I swerved to avoid her, I lost control and—" she drew a breath and gave a little shrug "—that was the end of the Mercedes."

Dominic just stared at her.

She flushed and looked away. "I know, it was a stupid thing to do. Except I thought… Condesta had told me Gran was refusing to pay. We'd disagreed about me making this trip, and I wasn't sure… Well, obviously I made a mistake. " She bit her bottom lip.

"You don't think maybe you should have mentioned this to me before now?"

Her head came up at that. "I did—or at least, I tried. It was back at *Las Rocas,* when you asked about the bruises. Remember? I started to tell you, but…."

But I cut you off. Their exchange was suddenly crystal clear in his memory. He remembered the tentative tone of her voice, the diffident way she'd said she'd been in a car accident. Not surprisingly, he'd been totally focused on making sure she wasn't trying to avoid telling him she'd been sexually abused.

Lilah laid a hand on his arm. "I'm sorry," she said quietly. "I honestly didn't think it was important. If I had, I would have insisted you listen, but the truth is, I was embarrassed. By then, I'd figured out that even if I'd been able to make good on my getaway, I didn't have any place to go, much less any way to get out of the country. Not to mention that my freedom probably wouldn't have lasted very long—" she gave a little gurgle of self-deprecating laughter, "—given the flags flying from the car's bumpers. Call it a hunch, but I think they would've made me pretty easy to spot."

Maybe it was that chuckle, but Dom suddenly realized he'd been deluding himself.

Okay, so he didn't foresee any long-term future for them. He simply wasn't the kind of guy to settle down. But by the same token, nobody was ever going to accuse him of being a boy scout. And when it came to Lilah, with her soft laugh and her silky skin and her unexpected little displays of bravery, the chances of him keeping his hands to himself between now and the time they got back to Denver were nil.

So he might as well quit second-guessing himself and simply enjoy whatever amount of time they had left together. After all, it wasn't as if he was going to give his heart to Lilah.

Hell, if everything went as planned, he'd have them out of San Timoteo as soon as tomorrow.

Nine

"I won't be long," Dominic said, gently cupping Lilah's shoulders in his powerful, long-fingered hands. "Just wait here, keep out of sight and I'll be back before you know it. All right?"

Lilah looked up into his compelling face. After walking for hours, they were standing on a slope above the narrow slash of the road, hidden from prying eyes by the combination of elevation and the thick foliage that continued to be both a blessing and a curse.

Half a mile back down the road, out of sight but the focus of their current conversation, lay a cluster of tin-roofed huts. The meager village was the first outpost of civilization they'd encountered since leaving *Las Rocas* and if Lilah had been allowed a vote, she would have chosen to give it a wide berth.

Dominic had a different plan, and it centered on securing them some sort of motorized transportation. "All right?" he repeated.

She shook her head, deciding she had nothing to lose by being honest. "No. It's not all right. What if something goes wrong?"

"Nothing is going to go wrong."

"But what if it *does?*" she persisted, not entirely sure herself of the cause of her misgivings. She ought to be thrilled at the prospect of getting off her feet and having a chance to rest. Because between that initial swim in the ocean, several days of hard walking, nearly drowning and two nights mostly spent making love instead of sleeping, she was down-to-the-bone tired.

And still she didn't want him to go. "You can't just steal a car and expect nobody to notice," she pointed out.

"I'm not going to steal anything," he said with remarkable patience. "I'm going to buy with good old American currency, at what will probably be several times more than the regular asking price. And that will not only make the seller exceedingly happy, but should also act as a deterrent to him sharing news of his good fortune with anyone—like the area police or one of Condesta's search parties. And even if another one of the villagers does talk, we should be long gone by then. Trust me. It'll be fine."

Knowing she wasn't being entirely reasonable but unable to stop herself, she shook her head. "But what if it *isn't?*"

He pursed his lips, then unexpectedly conceded. "All right. If I'm not back by noon, empty everything nonessential out of the pack, follow the road and head for Santa

Marita. We're only about thirty miles away. It's a hard thirty miles, but once you're there—"

"Dominic." Horrified, her voice rose. "Stop."

Maybe it was her obvious distress, but amazingly, he actually fell silent. "What?"

"Leaving without you isn't an option. So maybe you could give me an idea about the best way to help if there's a problem?"

He shifted back on his heels. "You'd do that? Come after me?"

How could he even ask? "Of course."

For an instant, his face softened, and then he seemed to catch himself. "Good thing you won't need to."

"Damn it, Dominic—"

He raised a hand to silence her. "Listen to me, Lilah. Could you take a knife and cut a stranger's throat? Or shoot to kill someone whose only mistake was that they were set to guard me?" Her sudden uncertainty must have shown on her face. "Yeah. That's what I thought. The point is, if something happens, either I'll be beyond rescuing—"

Lilah flinched; that possibility hadn't even occurred to her.

"—or you'll be giving El Presidente two hostages instead of one. The man's got a reputation for being vicious when he's crossed and if you think I'd just sit back and let him or anybody else hurt you…well, think again. So for both our sakes, if I'm not back by noon, get yourself to Santa Marita and call the number I gave you earlier. Whoever answers will get a message to Gabe, and he'll take care of everything. Okay?"

She nodded, not particularly concerned about her own potential safety, but not about to do anything that would put him at further risk. "Okay."

"Good girl."

A glimmer of approval warmed his face. It wasn't an emotion she'd seen much of in her life, and she savored it. With sudden insight, she realized the only gift she had to give back was peace of mind; he had enough to deal with without worrying about her. With an exaggerated toss of her hair, she gave him her best duchess-addressing-the-riffraff look. "What did you call me?"

His mouth tipped up. "Okay, I take that back. Pretend I called you a wise woman or an admirable adult or some other idiotic but politically correct thing."

She laughed, the sound soft but genuine. "An admirable adult? You can't be serious."

He hitched one shoulder, the smile suddenly dancing in his eyes. "Hey, you're the one with the problem." And forestalling further comment, he leaned down and kissed her.

The warm pressure of his mouth had the effect it always did, clouding her mind and stealing her breath. Lilah leaned against him, her hands spread flat on the hard planes of his chest, her palms absorbing the heavy thud of his heart.

She wished…what? That she could make this moment, this feeling, this connection, last forever? That she had the words—and the courage—to tell him how much he mattered to her?

As if sensing the tenderness threatening to overwhelm her, he slid his hands from her shoulders to her face, his warm fingers gently cupping her jaw, his thumbs resting lightly against her cheeks. Slanting his head, he unhurriedly kissed the corners of her mouth, the bow of her lips, before once more molding his mouth firmly to hers.

A sudden fierceness twisted through her. With absolute clarity, she knew in that moment that she could and would do whatever was necessary to keep him safe. He was her sun, her moon, her stars, her…heart. Without him, tomorrow would cease to matter. She loved him. With everything she was and would ever be.

She swayed, her hands bunching in his shirt as a mixture of certainty and wonder filled her. She leaned into him, wanting to feel the tall, warm, solid length of his body pressed against hers.

"Whoa." With a faint, rusty chuckle, he raised his head, then stroked his finger down her cheek before firmly setting her away from him. "I'd better go. While I still can." Before she could form a response, he stepped back and in less time than it took her to blink, her generous, demanding, heart-stealing lover was gone.

In his place was a warrior, his green eyes hooded, his sculpted mouth set, his expression resolute. "Be good, princess," he murmured, slipping into the trees. Before her very eyes, he appeared to simply vanish in the same unnerving way he had the night he'd ministered to her feet.

She stood motionless for a moment, overcome with a sense of loss and struggling with a selfish urge to call him back. Then the enormity of her feelings for him struck her anew and her heart seemed to stutter. She was abruptly glad to be alone, to have time to think.

I love him. With knees that were suddenly weak, she stumbled over to the nearest good-sized tree and sank to the ground, pressing her back against the trunk and linking her hands around her legs.

Merciful heaven. She loved Dominic. It was so obvious that it was almost funny that it had taken her until now to figure it out, she thought a little wildly. Her only excuse was that so much had happened in such a short time she'd been more than a little distracted.

But still… As if she'd been wearing a pair of blinders that had abruptly been torn away, she suddenly understood her reluctance to see him go into the village had as much to do with her selfishness as her worries for his safety.

Dominic himself had touched on it. Santa Marita was a mere thirty miles away. It would take them a few more days to get there on foot; it would take them mere hours to get there by car.

They could be out of the country, on their way home, as soon as tonight.

And then what? The question gnawed at her.

It hadn't escaped her notice that while Dom couldn't seem to get enough of her physically, he hadn't uttered a single word that might be mistaken as a declaration of love. Nor had he said anything that suggested he wanted a future with her.

And while she realized she hadn't made any declarations either, it wasn't the same thing. *Her* reluctance to address their future sprang from the fear that if she told Dominic that she wanted to be with him—not just now or back in Denver, but forever—he'd respond with the unwelcome news that he didn't feel the same way.

Oh, that's rich, Lilah. I thought you were done being

*a coward. And maybe I'm wrong, but wasn't it your fear
of being rejected that made you end things with him before? And haven't you regretted your behavior every
day since?*

She squeezed her eyes shut, finding it hard to breathe
as she remembered how she'd felt that long ago summer
evening when everything had gone so wrong.

It had been the day before Gran had been due back, less
than a week before Lilah had been scheduled to return to
school in California. She and Dominic had spent a heated
few hours at the estate pool, lazing in the hot afternoon
sun, sliding through the cool aqua water, kissing and
laughing and competing to see who could drive the other
past the point of restraint first.

Yet beneath Lilah's flirtatious smile was an escalating
sense of desperation. She'd never been in love before.
She'd never before let anyone get so close to her, physically or otherwise. She'd never wanted to be *wanted* the
way she did with Dominic, and the intensity of her feelings frightened her. She'd grown up being warned against
giving in to passion, and now she'd gone ahead and done
just that. Suddenly, disaster—in the form of Gran's expec-
tations and her own obligations—was about to strike. In
a frighteningly short time she was leaving Denver and either Dominic had forgotten—or he didn't care.

She tried several times over the course of the afternoon
to broach the subject, but he simply brushed away her at-
tempts, changing the subject with a joke or a kiss or a skin-
heating touch. By the time they finally succumbed to the
blaze they'd been feeding for hours and retreated into the

pool house, Lilah was feeling every bit as hurt and confused as she was frustrated.

They made love the first time with reckless urgency, so aroused they barely made it through the door before Dom was shoving down his swim trunks and snapping the ties holding her bikini bottom up, all without breaking the greedy fusion of their mouths. He lifted her blindly onto a bar stool, and Lilah feared she might pass out from the sheer pleasure of touching him, feeling all that sun-kissed skin and rock-hard muscle pressed up against her, warm beneath her fingertips. Her climax started to ripple through her with his very first thrust.

The next time took considerably longer. By then, they'd managed to get both naked and horizontal and spent a long time exploring each other—fingers reaching, mouths teasing and tasting. As if by tacit agreement, they didn't talk, just touched, slowly taking the embers of their mutual fire and building it relentlessly higher until it once again burned out of control and reduced them to ashes, leaving them both limp and breathless.

When Lilah finally had the presence of mind to notice, she was shocked to discover that the light was already fading outside, a reminder she didn't need that summer was giving way to fall.

"I leave Tuesday." She didn't plan to say it; the words simply seemed to slip out of her mouth without her making a conscious decision to utter them, prompted by her escalating need for him to tell her he cared about her and that her departure wouldn't change that.

Just for an instant, his arms seemed to tighten around her; then he rolled away and climbed to his feet. "Yeah, well, I have the feeling that with your grandma home, you won't need me to give you a ride to the airport," he drawled with a flippant smile.

The careless words were like a stake driven into her heart. And even so, she didn't have the sense to give up and just let it go. She scrambled onto her knees and reached for the oversize beach towel they'd tossed over a chaise longue pad to cushion the floor, wrapping it around herself. Lifting her chin, doing her best not to look as needy as she felt, she said, "I can come home at Thanksgiving, if you want."

He'd paused in pulling on his swim trunks and glanced over at her. "You don't have to do me any favors. And—" he shifted his attention back to tying the drawstring at his waistband and gave an indifferent shrug "—I don't even know if I'll be here."

"What?" Panic took a brutal grip on her. "But…where would you go?" Until that moment she hadn't realized how completely she'd been counting on him being here, waiting for her.

"I haven't decided. But tuition's going up at the community college and I got laid off from the garage last week, so…" He propped himself against the long counter of the wet bar. Folding his golden-skinned arms across the sleek, tanned expanse of his chest, he shrugged again. "I'm pretty much free to do whatever—or go wherever—I want."

The news that he'd lost the best-paying of his three jobs and hadn't bothered to tell her until now seemed to emphasize the suddenly yawning divide between them. Feeling frantic, Lilah spoke without thinking. "I have money," she blurted out. "I can pay your tuition. Better yet—" the idea popped into her head, prompted by his last words, and was so seductive it made her throat catch "—you could come to California and go to school. I don't think I can manage Stanford tuition, but there must be all kinds of first-rate community colleges. We could find you an apartment close to campus…" She trailed off, belatedly realizing from his rigid posture and the frigid look on his face that she'd made a serious misstep.

"And that'd be what, exactly?" he asked in a caustic tone she'd never heard from him before. "A loan? Something I'd repay by taking you to bed?"

Stunned that he'd suggest such a thing, for a second she couldn't seem to breathe. "No! Of course not—"

If anything, his expression grew even more remote. "So I guess that means I'd be your personal charity case, instead. And just think—not only would you have your own boy toy, but I bet you could write the whole damn thing off on your taxes."

This was all going so wrong, she thought wildly, even as she felt the first stirrings of temper. "Well, excuse me," she retorted, the coolness of her voice in inverse proportion to the sick sense of betrayal growing steadily inside her. She climbed to her feet and tugged the towel more securely into place before giving a dismissive shrug of her own. "Sorry if I offended you. I was simply trying to help."

"I don't need your help," he said flatly. "And I sure as hell don't want your money."

"Yes. You've made that perfectly clear."

And then, because he seemed so totally sure of himself while she was a mess of seething emotion, and because she wanted desperately to turn back the clock and return to the closeness they'd shared just ten minutes earlier, while he didn't look as if he gave a damn one way or another, she did what she'd been taught to do since she was a very small child. She deliberately pushed away the very thing she wanted most. "I think, under the circumstances, it would be best if you go."

He jerked as if she'd struck him, and for a second she thought that perhaps he wasn't as composed as he wanted her to believe. But then his face took on an expression of such utter indifference she knew she was only kidding herself. Drawing himself up, he gave one last, careless shrug. "It's your loss, princess." Clearly having said all he intended to, he strolled out of the pool house and out of her life.

And Lilah simply stood there and let him go.

The labored sputter of an approaching vehicle insinuated its way into her recollections. She sat frozen for a moment, welcoming the interruption even as she struggled to get a grip on her emotions.

God. She'd replayed that scene endlessly over the years, and even after all this time the memory of her own passivity made her cringe. Yet she'd also forgiven her and Dom's younger selves, having come to realize that, similar to her attempt to hijack Condesta's car, they'd been going full-out without a plan or a destination. Even if they'd managed to negotiate the obstacles in the road that would have cropped up over those next few months—her grandmother's certain opposition, their physical separation, the gaping disparity in their financial situations—the fact was they'd simply been too young.

Regaining a semblance of control, she pushed the thought aside and scrambled to her feet, pushing through the tangle of vegetation until she had a narrow view of the road below.

An ancient pickup trailing a noxious cloud of black exhaust hiccupped into sight, the body so rusted that it was impossible to tell the vehicle's original color. A tanned forearm rested atop the windowsill, only to be replaced by a gloriously familiar face as Dom stuck his head out and his gaze zeroed straight in on her hiding place. "Well?" He raised an inky eyebrow. "Are you coming or what?"

Relief flooded through her. *He was all right.* "I'll be there in just a minute," she called. With feet that felt suddenly light, she dashed back to retrieve their stuff.

She may have loved him as a teenager, she thought as she snatched up the backpack and slung it over her shoulder, but she'd been young and there'd been so much about herself that she hadn't understood. What she'd felt then didn't come close to the depth of her feelings for him now.

Fate or luck or life—whatever one wanted to call it— had given her a second chance. If things didn't work out this time, it wouldn't be because she hadn't opened her heart and shared what she really felt. When the time was right, when she was sure disclosing what was in her heart wouldn't serve as a distraction that could imperil their safety, she'd tell him the truth.

Until then… He was safe and they were still together.

And for now, it was enough.

Ten

The pastel stucco buildings of Santa Marita were fading to silver and the rich midnight-blue sky turning to black as they finally rolled into town that night.

Although "rolled" was a relative term when it came to describing the pickup's ride, Dom thought caustically. Limped was more like it. Or maybe lurched....

It had been a long thirty miles. The radiator had overheated, the choke on the carburetor had stuck, they'd had one flat tire, a near-flat spare and he'd had to rig a makeshift air filter out of the tail of Lilah's T-shirt.

Add to the mix a road so narrow that for most of its length meeting another vehicle meant somebody had to back up until there was room to pass, and his too-late discovery that tomorrow was Santa Marita market day, which had meant the closer they got to the San Timotean capital, the more up to the fenders they'd been in bleating, darting, unpredictable goats. It was a journey he had no interest in repeating. Ever.

About the only good thing, he thought, glancing down at the woman whose pale golden head was propped on his thigh, was that Lilah was finally getting some much-needed rest.

She deserved it. Without qualification, she'd turned out to be a real trooper, doing everything and anything he asked. She hadn't complained about their less-than-inspiring rations, or said a word about her mangled feet, or whined about being hot or dirty or tired, although she'd certainly experienced all three. She hadn't dissolved into hysterics yesterday when she'd answered the call of nature and a constrictor had dropped onto her out of the trees. Hell, she'd even been stoic about today's truck ride, not saying a single negative word, even though she'd been bounced and jounced and rattled around like dice in a gaming cup.

Unable to stop himself—hell, not even trying—he smoothed the back of his hand over the warm silky curve of her cheek. Murmuring drowsily, she surfaced just enough to clasp his hand and cradle it against the cotton-covered valley between her breasts.

A tired smile curved his mouth. Even dozing, she was luring him toward that coronary. It was just too bad for both of them that they were running out of time….

Smile fading, he reclaimed his hand, nudged the battered straw cowboy hat that had come with the truck a little lower on his forehead and told himself to knock it off.

Whether it was the hushed intimacy of the darkened truck cab or his lack of sleep finally catching up with him, he couldn't seem to rein in his brain. And though part of him was totally focused on keeping the shaky truck tracking straight down Santa Marita's traffic-clogged main street, while also keeping a watchful eye out for the *policia* as he considered the best route to the cantina he'd chosen as a fallback option before setting out for *Las Rocas*, part of him was fixed on Lilah…and him.

As galling as it was to admit it, a sort of melancholy had been niggling at him for the past several hours. And though he knew damn well it was just the normal letdown that usually accompanied the end of a job, he still couldn't seem to shake it.

Most likely, he told himself, that was because despite the usual stress and worry inherent to any hostage recovery, when you got right down to it, he was having a helluva good time.

Yeah. That's one way to put it. Or you could be honest with yourself and admit that not only is the sex a thousand times better than anything you've ever experienced in your life, but so is the company.

And he was about to bid adios to both.

He swore under his breath at the way his usually orderly brain kept circling back to dwell on that. Because, hell, it wasn't as if anything had changed. He and Lilah still came from different worlds. And though the divide between them may have narrowed over the years, he still wasn't a happily-ever-after kind of guy. Even if, for the first time in his life, the idea didn't seem completely outside the realm of some future, distant, maybe-when-I'm-older possibility.

But it wasn't going to happen any time soon. And definitely not now. Because if experience had taught him anything, it was that it was always a mistake to anticipate the end of an assignment. This was often the most dangerous time of all for various reasons. You were tired, the prospect of imminent success tended to tempt you to lower your guard, getting extracted usually required an increased level of exposure—the possibilities for mistakes were endless.

So until Lilah was safely beyond Condesta's reach, he needed to keep his mind on the job. There'd be plenty of time to get his head back on straight and his tangled feelings sorted out later. Over that ice-cold beer he kept promising himself he was going to have back in Denver.

Up ahead, a lighted sign running vertically down the corner of a building flashed on and off, advertising cold drinks and hot women. Saluting the landmark with a flick of his fingers, Dom drove past it and began counting off the following blocks. When he hit number five, he stuck his arm out the window to signal, since the truck's turn indicator didn't work, and wrestled the wheel to the right.

Blacktop quickly gave way to dirt, and without streetlights to keep it at bay, the darkness pressed in. Dom counted himself lucky that the pickup's headlights worked. God knew the dashlights didn't, but then, it didn't really matter. He didn't need an odometer to tell him how far he'd traveled; he was accustomed to navigating strictly by memory. And in fact, the more cloaked in darkness he and Lilah were, the better he liked it.

He took a left at a dilapidated warehouse, passed a crowded row of apartment buildings, took another right at a vacant lot. And there, dead ahead, was his objective: a long low stucco building with a broad, trellised patio strung with hundreds of gaily colored lights. A flotilla of old cars and trucks, most of them as decrepit as the one he was driving, packed an adjoining parking lot.

He could hear the noise—amplified guitars, the heavy beat of drums, singers pounding out something that was a rousing mix of country and Caribbean, an occasional shout or burst of laughter—half a block away. Slowing as he got closer, he drove into the parking area and headed for an empty space at the back, which happily happened to be sheltered by an enormous jacaranda tree. With an inexplicable twinge of regret and anticipation, he switched off the truck's engine. "Li. Wake up, baby. We're here."

For a moment she didn't respond. Then her eyelashes fluttered up. She lay still, clearly struggling to wake up.

"What time is it?"

"Going on eight."

"Umm. Feels later." Yawning, she sat up and stretched, rolling her shoulders. She looked around. "Where are we?"

"El Gordo Gato."

"Okay." She yawned again. "I'll bite. What does El Gordo Gato mean? And why are we here?"

"Back home we'd call it the Fat Cat Tavern. And we're here because it's got a big, diverse, constantly changing crowd and a pair of pay phones that are actually maintained. It's the perfect place to make a call and not get noticed."

"Oh." She shoved the hair off her face. "Okay. Just give me a minute to find my sandals and—"

"No."

She sat back from her search of the floor. "Excuse me?"

"Think about it. The way you look—you'd attract attention anywhere. And how many blue-eyed blondes do you think they get in here?"

She blinked. "If I can't go in, why did you wake me up?"

He shrugged. "The locks on this heap of junk are busted, like everything else. No way am I going to go off and leave you defenseless."

She considered that for a moment, then smiled. "All right, I agree that's a pretty good reason. Thanks."

Her smile went straight to his gut and the now familiar need for her twitched to life inside him. The one that should have been long past satisfied, given the level of sexual intimacy they'd already shared—but wasn't. "You can pay me back later," he replied, as serious as he'd ever been in his life.

Twisting sideways, he reached into the gap behind the seat and dropped his pack into the space between them. He retrieved the gun, racked a round into the chamber, double-checked the safety and handed it to her. "Keep that beside you. And cover your head." He removed his hat and thrust it at her. "Even in the dark, your hair stands out."

He watched as she bundled up her hair and settled the hat into place. It was too big and on anybody else it would've looked silly. On her, it looked good. But then, as he'd come to expect, she could wear a burlap sack—or nothing at all—and still somehow manage to look stylish.

Feeling oddly as if he were losing some sort of battle he didn't remember agreeing to fight, he dragged his gaze away from her and climbed out of the truck. Shoving the rusty door closed, he ducked down and leaned his head inside. "This shouldn't take more than ten minutes. If anybody who's not me comes close enough to touch the truck—shoot 'em."

Pushing away, he headed inside.

"This is…heaven," Lilah murmured, locking her fingers together over her head and stretching languidly atop the thin, blanket-covered mattress that took up most of the small, detached shed behind the cantina.

Dom glanced her way and shook his head. "You must have heatstroke. There's no bathroom, no box spring, no sheets, no electricity, for God's sake."

"True." She rolled on her side, propped her head on her hand and enjoyed the show as he stripped off his shirt and dropped it on the rickety chair in the corner. "I guess I've learned to appreciate the little things. Like being out of the truck, and getting to sleep on a level surface without bugs or rocks. Oh, and a hot meal. *That* was wonderful."

She didn't add that the very best thing of all was the gift of this night. Thanks to a storm that had apparently skipped past San Timoteo but was now blowing itself out to the north and east of them, they were on their own for at least the next twenty-four hours. And though that might change after Dom and his brother conferred again in the morning, for now it was just the two of them. Given the impending separation that she'd feared earlier in the day, that suited Lilah just fine.

"I'll give you the food, the truck and the rocks, but I wouldn't be so sure of the bugs," Dom said, recapturing her attention as he leaned over the basin of lukewarm water balanced atop a wooden shelf nailed to the wall. He splashed his face, and the muscles in his arms and shoulders, which were tanned bronze by a week in the sun, bunched and flexed like a living sculpture.

Except for the small, puckered scar just below his left armpit, which, after a lot of prodding, he'd reluctantly explained was the result of a "slight miscalculation" he'd made, his back was perfect, Lilah thought: broad across the shoulders, tapering to narrow hips and a tightly muscular backside an underwear model would covet. Cleaving the center, like an exclamation mark of perfection, was the long smooth valley of his spine.

Her breath caught with sudden longing—to touch him, to hold him, to never have to let him go. "It's also really nice," she said softly, "to have the candlelight so I can look at you."

He stopped drying his face on the threadbare cotton towel El Gordo Gato's owner had, for the right price, cheerfully supplied along with everything else, no questions asked.

Tossing the towel in the general direction of his shirt, he turned to look at her, his posture suddenly acquiring a sort of coiled watchfulness. "That sounded a lot like an invitation, princess." His gaze locked on her, he undid his pants and peeled them off, the washboard stretch of his abs hollowing as he flicked the garment toward the corner.

A little thrill of anticipation shivered through her. "You don't need one," she said honestly. "My door is always open to you."

He'd started toward her, but just for an instant, as her statement registered, he seemed to check himself in midstride, the strangest look flashing across his face. Then he sank down on his knees, and his gaze slicked over her like liquid heat. She was sure she must have imagined that look.

"Lucky me." His voice was hushed and as soft as cut velvet. "Now, what is it with you rich girls? Always over-dressed." He made a chiding sound and reached for her, wrestling her out of her T-shirt. "It's enough to make a guy—*aw, man.*"

She smiled at his reaction as she closed her hand around the thick, silky thrust of his erection at the same time she twined an arm around his neck and kissed him.

She flexed like a contented cat, exulting in the hard warmth of his chest against her breasts, the crisp tickle of the hair on his legs brushing her thighs, the rock-hard feel of his biceps as he braced himself above her.

Need tangled with all those delicious sensations, and it was way too much and not nearly enough all at the same time. The only thing she knew for certain was that she couldn't seem to get enough of him. Not of the taste of him on her tongue, not of the heated masculine weight of his arousal straining against her palm, not of the blatant, brash sugges-tion of what was to come as his tongue breached her lips.

Yet Dominic clearly had ideas of his own when it came to their upcoming schedule. "Slow down, Li," he rasped, lifting his head in the same instant that he captured her hands in his and stretched her arms over her head.

"But I want—I need—let go."

"I don't think so," he murmured. "I like looking at you, too, you know. Especially when you look the way you do right now, all flushed and ripe and…ready for me. And I like the way you feel. You're just so damn soft. All over…."

He shifted, his lips brushing unhurriedly over her temple and skating slowly, slowly down the side of her face. For all her impatience, there was something both electrifying and mesmerizing about what he was doing, and her eyes drifted shut as if weighted.

She savored the exquisite tenderness of his touch, her breath catching as he pressed butterfly kisses to her eyes, the curve of her cheek, the underside of her jaw, then shifted his attention to the silky stretch of skin behind her ear. She felt his mouth curve with satisfaction as she moaned, overcome by the contradictory sensations of his hands pressing her wrists into the mattress while his lips tied the rest of her in knots.

Once again he began a slow drift downward, honing in on the thudding pulse at the base of her throat, tasting it, testing it, stubbornly refusing to move on even as she began to twist restlessly beneath his touch. It seemed like a lifetime had passed before he finally painted a line of kisses down the midline of her chest, then blazed a trail up the soft inner curve of her breast.

Displaying a true talent for delectable torment, he slowly circled her nipple with the tip of his tongue. By then, she was strung tight and quivering, but still he refused to be hurried. With painstaking attention to detail, he repeated the action. Once. Twice. A third time.

Every nerve in her body screamed with expectation before he finally licked the sensitive tip of her breast, only to follow up with a soft stream of breath that sent her arching up off the mattress.

He laughed low in his throat, a purely male sound of satisfaction. "Aw, baby, you're so damn gorgeous," he told her.

His words soothed her only a fraction. Yet even as she blew out a breath of frustration, Lilah realized she wouldn't trade this pulse-pounding torture—or his obvious enjoyment of it—for the entire Anson fortune.

Still, she didn't want him to get too pleased with himself. "I see a pair of handcuffs in your future," she warned when she could finally form a sentence.

"Yeah?" He sounded anything but repulsed by the idea. "You better be careful what you say, princess. I might just hold you to it."

And just like that, she was twisting on the vision her own words conjured up. As if she were viewing a movie, she could see him lying on his back, tied to a massive bed, all that taut golden skin and sleek muscle on display, just waiting for her to explore.

There'd be candlelight, and she'd be dressed in something incredibly sheer and sexy. She pictured herself climbing up onto the mattress, straddling his narrow hips and giving him a taste of the same medicine he was giving her tonight. She'd string kisses along the achingly beautiful angles of his face. She'd feast on the hard curve of his mouth, lick an agonizingly slow path toward the shallow indent of his navel—

Without warning his mouth came down and settled squarely over her tightly beaded nipple. She cried out with delight, her fantasy melting away as he worried her with his lips. Her heels dug into the mattress and her hips once again lifted.

This time when she tried to get free, he obliged. But there was a reason for that, she quickly discovered. Raising his head, he rocked back on his knees and scooched lower. Before she had time to catch her breath—or divine his intent—he spread her thighs, propped them wide with the broad wedge of his chest and kissed her slippery center.

"Oh!" Her hands bunched in the blanket, jerking it loose from where it had been moored beneath the mattress.

"Oh *yeah*," he corrected her, rubbing his rough cheek against her hyper-sensitive flesh. The contrast with the cool silk of his hair brushing the inner curve of her thighs made her shiver.

But not as much as what he did next.

While she was still searching for breath, he raked the calloused pad of his thumb through her pale curls, then reversed direction, sliding the broad tip into her swollen wetness until it bumped up against her clitoris. Firmly, with a seemingly innate sense of exactly what she desired, what she craved, what she required, he pressed down. When her hips promptly jerked, he was ready, his tongue stabbing against her, rasping like a spear of silk against tender nerve endings.

Lilah's world exploded, her body bucking uncontrollably as her orgasm blasted through her like a lightning strike. Caught by surprise by the upheaval of her senses, all she could do was cry Dominic's name as she surrendered to a storm of sensation.

And then like a perfect dream, his body covered hers and he pushed deep inside, once again knowing what she wanted, what she needed, before she did.

He began to move, his body rocking against hers, his strokes slow, deep and unhurried, custom-designed to drive her crazy. Once again his hands sought hers, but this time it was to link their fingers together as if he felt the same insatiable need for closeness that she did.

Bending his head, he pressed an openmouthed kiss to the sensitive spot where her jaw met her neck. Her head fell back, granting him access, and he took full advantage, sliding his lips across her tender skin until he found the eager warmth of her mouth. She tasted herself on him as their tongues met, mated, twined.

Lilah was beyond thought, a vessel of pure sensation. Her thighs clamped on Dominic's hips, which moved faster now. She could hear herself panting, hear the equally harsh rasp of his breathing, feel the powerful expanse and contraction of his chest and arms, his stomach and thighs as he began to drive them toward completion.

Letting go of her hands, he caught her by the waist and shifted her beneath him with that effortless strength that was uncompromisingly masculine. The move steepened the angle of his penetration, opened her wider, allowed him to push even deeper, his pubic bone bumping against hers as he found a wildly sensitive spot deep inside her.

Once again, the sweet satisfaction started for her first. She felt her eyes glaze over and the breath leave her lungs and vaguely realized that the repetitive sobbing she heard was her. "Dominic. Dominic. *Dominic.*" She couldn't stop. She didn't want to. Skating closer and closer to the edge, she tightened her grip on him, crushing her breasts against his heaving chest as she clung to him with all her strength.

"Aw, no," he said between his teeth. "Not yet. Hang on, baby. I'm not ready. I don't want this to stop. Not yet—"

He might as well have tried to hold off an incoming tide. Her climax surged through her, catching him up, carrying him right along with her. Caught on the crest of something bigger than both of them, he drove even deeper, grinding against her as waves of pleasure crashed through him and his whole body jerked with the power of it.

"Aw, damn it to hell," he gritted out when he finally collapsed against her, a series of little aftershocks shuddering through him. "I'm sorry, princess. I meant for that to last a little longer."

"It's all right," she soothed, digging her hands into his trembling shoulder blades, massaging the rigid muscles of his back, still overcome with the need to touch him. "It was perfect just the way it was."

It took a while, but eventually he began to relax, the tension slowly leaking out of him until he was draped bonelessly against her.

By the time the candles finally flickered out, he'd fallen fast asleep. And still she cradled him against her, her fingers feathering through the cropped strands of his hair, her heart overcome with tenderness as she welcomed the solid press of his weight, not caring that she could barely breathe. She would have willingly given up breathing altogether if it meant she could go on holding him like this.

Because for this little while, he was all hers.

And she was all his.

Eleven

"**Y**ou can't be serious." Lilah swiveled sideways on the pickup's tattered seat. "We're going to the presidential compound so you can steal Condesta's plane? *That's* the plan?"

Dom felt her usually sunny blue eyes burning a hole in him and for a self-indulgent moment, allowed himself the luxury of glancing over and drinking in the sight of her in a temper. Then the sound of blaring horns refocused his attention on the morning rush hour traffic surrounding them and his mind settled solidly back on the business at hand. "You've got it."

"But that's crazy!"

He signalled, muscled the truck into a narrow opening in a stream of traffic in the far right lane and turned onto a cross street that would lead them past the government buildings and into the exclusive district that El Presidente called home. "Didn't we have this conversation, or a damn similar one, back at *Las Rocas?*"

Out of the corner of his eye, he saw her stiffen. "Maybe."

"And what did I say?"

For a second she didn't reply. Then she gave a faint sigh and her shoulders relaxed a notch. "To give you some credit. That you don't act impetuously."

"And?"

"Oh, all right! That you're a professional and know what you're doing."

"Yeah, and nothing's changed."

Now, there's a lie. Who are you kidding, Steele? Thanks to Lilah, nothing, including you, is what it was a week ago.

Annoyed, his voice came out flat and uncompromising. This was *not* the time to contemplate his personal life; hell, it wasn't the time to acknowledge he even *had* one. "This isn't open for debate, princess. Not after what happened earlier at the cantina."

Just thinking about it again further soured his mood.

After the soundest sleep he'd had in weeks, he'd awakened to find it was already going on nine o'clock. Chagrined by the lateness of the hour, he'd pulled on his clothes and, leaving Lilah still sleeping, had walked over to the tavern to get a cup of coffee and call Gabe.

The news from his brother hadn't been good. The seas in the friendly harbors closest to San Timoteo were still high, the weather improving but not yet stable, he'd reported. What's more, the storm causing the problem was running right up the island chain, inflicting just enough damage to keep every chopper for hundreds of miles occupied ferrying people and supplies.

Icing the cake, the buzz in the cantina last night had been all about how there were suddenly extra police blanketing the airport, stopping all incoming traffic, patrolling the hangars and runways, interviewing anyone entering the terminal.

"Isn't that special," he'd drawled, realizing that with boat and conventional air travel out, and no outside extraction for at least another day, he was probably going to have to go with Plan D. That is, if *it* was even feasible. "So, you get that other information I asked for?"

"She had it right," Gabe had replied, not wasting words. "It's a brand new de Havilland, top of the line. Our friend's only had it a month, which is probably why it didn't show up in the original information we received."

"Huh." New or not, when he got home there was going to be a meeting about the quality of the intel on this trip. They'd paid for quality information, and they sure as hell hadn't gotten it.

Yet that concern had vanished like smoke in the wind when a flash of movement outside the cantina had caught his eye. Shifting, he'd glanced across the room and out a fly-specked window. A newer model black sedan bearing the insignia of Condesta's special police on its door had been pulling into the parking lot.

"So, you going to do it?" Gabe had asked.

Adrenaline starting to pump, he'd watched as two uniformed men emerged from the car and headed for the steps leading up to the cantina's wide sunporch. "I'm seriously considering it."

"I think it's your best bet if the situation there deteriorates. Once you're in the air, it's a pretty quick run to Puerto Castillo. I'll book some rooms at the Royal Meridian, just in case."

"Do that." Outside the *policia* had reached the top of the stairs. "Look, I gotta go. Appears I've got unwanted company."

Gabe's reaction had been typical—he hadn't reacted at all, just responded in that same deliberate tone. "Okay. Call when you make your insertion point. And be careful."

"Will do."

They'd disconnected, and he'd had just enough time to assure the cantina's owner, who was alone in the bar with the exception of several snoring patrons sleeping off the previous night's libations, that he'd meant what he'd said earlier when he'd promised to pay double what he already had if the man would forget he'd ever seen Lilah.

Then, praying like hell that this was just a routine visit and that if it wasn't, that the owner's greed would prove to be greater than his fear of the police—and merciful God, that Lilah wouldn't show up looking for him—he'd splashed the front of his shirt with the stale bottle of beer somebody had conveniently left on top of the phone box, scrubbed his hands through his hair to give it that hard-day's-night look and slung himself into the nearest chair. He'd just managed to sprawl facedown across the table in imitation of the other overindulgers when he'd heard the screen door twang open.

His luck—*their* luck—had held. After an unhelpful chat with the cantina owner—*thank you, Jesus*—Condesta's men had tried rousing the two nearest drunks, had met with zero luck and, after a few choice words of disgust, had exited the building.

Still, Dom's jaw got tight every time he thought about

what could have happened. Because the men *had* asked, among other things, if the bar owner had seen or heard talk of *una gringa bonita rubia*—a pretty blond foreigner.

Dom had already been inclined toward taking matters into his own hands regarding their extraction, but that had cinched it. If Condesta's people were actively searching the city for Lilah, it was time to go. ASAP.

"Dominic." Lilah reached over and laid her hand on his arm. "I'm sorry. I don't mean it to sound as if I'm questioning your competence or your judgment. I'm not. I'd trust you—I *do* trust you—with my life. It's just…this seems so contradictory, like trying to avoid a tiger by walking into its cage."

He bit off a curse as a kid on a motorized scooter darted in front of him and he had to stand on the brakes to avoid hitting him. "Condesta's no tiger, Lilah. More like a snake. Or a toad. And not a real bright one at that. This is the very last thing he'll expect."

Her hands braced on the dashboard to stop her sudden slide forward, she reluctantly smiled. "I suppose you're right." Despite her brave face, he didn't miss the faint tremor in her voice.

Damn it. He hated that she was afraid. Hated the threat hanging over her, hated the man who was responsible. *All the more reason to end this thing.* "Look, I don't give a damn if he thinks he's king of the jungle. I can handle him and anything he throws at me. So quit worrying. It's not like I'm going to do something crazy like crash the truck through the main gate."

Sitting back, she again turned to stare at him, only this time without any heat. "That's not funny," she said.

"Yeah, actually it is." Or would be, once the idea of the risk she'd taken no longer made his gut clench. He reached over and gave her thigh a brief squeeze. "It was also incredibly brave. And if you even think about doing something that reckless again, I'll hunt you down and lock you up myself."

Apparently reassured by his easy manner as he'd hoped, a little more of the tension left her. "Thanks," she said dryly.

"You're welcome. Now sit back and listen and I'll tell you what we're going to do."

Just as Dominic predicted, getting onto the grounds of El Presidente's compound proved to be ridiculously easy.

Dressed like the rest of the help, in a loose black skirt and plain white blouse, with her hair hidden by a bandanna, Lilah concentrated on keeping her eyes downcast as she followed a small troop of cooks, maids, mechanics and gardeners toward the estate's wide-open service entrance.

Yet all she had to do was lift her gaze a fraction and she could see Dominic trooping along ahead of her with some other men. He, too, was dressed in the standard worker's uniform, in his case a cotton shirt, baggy trousers and sandals. In addition, his shoulders were hunched and his dark head bent in a servile manner that helped to disguise both his height and his strength.

Lilah found his presence beyond reassuring. She still couldn't quite believe the fearless way he'd slipped into the off-site dormitory where some of the senior staff lived, and coolly commandeered the clothing and the simple name tags that identified them as complex workers. He obviously hadn't been kidding when he'd claimed he'd put in some serious time studying the place both before and after he'd arrived in San Timoteo. Now, that homework was paying off.

She didn't have a doubt he could—he would—handle anything.

There was no need for heroics, however, as they walked through the gates and into Condesta's stronghold. Although they'd gotten some curious stares from the other workers, nobody seemed inclined to do anything that might call attention to themselves. While it seemed the lone pair of guards monitoring the entrance were far more interested in making sure none of the departing workers had stolen any of El Presidente's treasures than scrutinizing those people coming in to work.

That hurdle cleared, her little group proceeded along a gravel path bounded on either side by a tall, seemingly impenetrable hedge. No doubt to keep them from being seen and ruining El Presidente's view, Lilah thought tartly.

From what she'd seen during her brief contact with San Timoteo's self-appointed leader, the dictator preferred not to rub elbows with the common people. His style was purely rule from above. Way, way above.

After more than a month in the country, she was starkly aware of the contrast between the presidential compound and the rest of San Timoteo. Here, there were no unwashed, uneducated, barefoot children, no hungry young mothers begging on street corners, no unemployed men slumped in back alleys drinking away their despair.

Instead, she thought, as she emerged from the tunnel

of shrubs, Condesta's personal playground was all exquisitely maintained lawns and brilliant tropical flowers,
graceful Spanish colonial buildings and breathtaking
views of his own private section of Santa Marita Bay.

Yet it wasn't the spectacular scenery that made her give
in to temptation and flick her gaze to the right. There, a
mere football field length away, perfectly outlined against
the blue water and azure sky, was Condesta's yacht. And
rising up on the other side of the wide dock where the
spanking white pleasure craft was moored, was the huge
new boathouse that sheltered El Presidente's other toys.

Including the aircraft Dominic intended to steal.

Her heart thumped, and she jerked her gaze back toward
her feet, praying the guilty flush of fear she could feel
prickling through her wasn't visible to anyone else.

Ahead of her, the rest of the workers slowed as they entered a large courtyard that stretched behind the main residence. Most of the group headed inside, but a few,
Dominic and Lilah included, continued moving and soon
left the courtyard, passing beneath a broad archway.

Here, the single path split into several branches that led,
according to her fearless leader, to the laundry, the green-
house, the groundskeeper's facility—and the marina. Entering the welcome shade of an enormous sea grape tree,
Lilah slowed. Deliberately falling even farther behind the
others, she pretended to stumble and stopped, then leaned
down and made a show of rubbing her ankle and adjust-
ing her sandal. By the time she straightened, the others
were out of sight, Dominic included.

And then his voice sounded from behind her, making her
jump even though she'd expected it. "Nice job, princess."

She swung around, relieved as he emerged from behind the sea grape's thick trunk. "Thank God."

Taking her hand, he gave it a reassuring squeeze. "You're doing great. A little longer, and this will all be over."

She felt the now familiar clench of her heart, and told herself not to be ridiculous. Under these circumstances, his words were meant to comfort, not dismay. She forced herself to smile. "I know."

"Come on, then." Keeping his hold on her hand, he reassumed his hunched posture, only this time he kept his head bent toward hers, doing his best as they took the far right path to make it appear as if they were engaged in nothing more sinister than a lovers' tryst.

Just as he'd told her he would, when they did hear approaching footsteps, Dominic promptly pushed her back against the nearest vertical surface, which turned out to be a some sort of large flowering shrub, plastered himself against her and kissed her.

The intruder's footsteps stopped. "You there! Knock that off and get back to work!"

"Yes sir, sorry sir," Dom said immediately in the local dialect, jerking away. Head bent, he cupped Lilah's shoulder and ushered her back onto the path, neither of them saying a word until they rounded a sharp bend without further challenge.

"You okay?" he asked, his gaze flicking over her for one intense second as they reached the end of the path.

She scrubbed a knuckle over her pounding heart and told herself to focus. "Yes, of course I am."

"Good."

He turned his attention to the boathouse dominating the landscape straight ahead of them. Doing her best to emulate his composure, she, too, turned to study El Presidente's newest architectural extravagance.

The building was a large, long, rectangular structure with an impressively high roof. From their current vantage point, it appeared to be completely enclosed, but she knew from her previous visit that it was open to the water on its far side. Ramps at either end provided access to the long apron of awning-covered dock that paralleled the shore, with a double door in the middle big enough to accommodate El Presidente and his usual entourage, and a far less obtrusive service entrance at the extreme right corner.

The good news was that that particular door happened to be almost directly ahead of them. The not-so-good news was that in order to reach it, they needed to move out into the open and cross a paved parking area at least fifty feet long.

And while Dominic's presence might not be remarked on if they were seen, Lilah's most definitely would.

"Too bad Condesta was too cheap to buy a yacht with its own chopper and pad," Dominic commented caustically. His statement was accompanied by the now-familiar snick of sliding metal.

Lilah glanced over to see that the automatic, which just minutes ago had been secured under his shirt at the small of his back, was now out in the open, an extension of his hand.

"Okay, here we go." The hard look on his face lightened momentarily as he glanced at her. "You ready?"

She took a deep breath and turned back to face the building, doing her best to strip the wings off the butterflies dive-bombing her stomach. "Yes."

"Just take it nice and easy and act like you have every reason to be here."

"I will."

"Just one other thing, Li."

She could feel her patience fraying as her butterflies morphed into F-16s. She swiveled to look at him. *"What?"*

"Try not to look like your dog just died. It sort of ruins the illusion of our being trusty workers, you know?"

Lilah stared at him. For all that he was deadly serious about what he was doing, it was also equally obvious that on some level he was enjoying himself. And heaven help her, although it probably meant she was certifiable, she'd never been able to resist Dominic in a good mood.

Just looking at him, his big body vibrating with energy, his eyes holding just a hint of wicked humor, made her feel better. At least for the moment, her killer butterflies were gone. "You know you're a lunatic, right?"

A genuine grin flashed across his face. "Oh, yeah."

Tucking the gun to his side, where it was mostly obscured by the folds of his shirt flapping in the breeze, he gestured for her to precede him and they stepped out into the glaring sunlight. As uneventfully as if they were crossing Silver Street in downtown Denver, they walked across the pavement, went unhurriedly down the ramp and slipped into the boathouse's cool interior, stopping just inside the door to get their bearings.

The largest expanse of dock stretched along the long side of the building that was closest to shore. Two shorter but still substantial sections of walkway projected at right angles from each end. In between were eight individual slips, separated one from the other by even shorter, narrower sections of planking. Lined up like blooded horses, one to a stall, were three sleek speedboats, two tall sportfishing vessels and a single muscular Cigarette boat. One berth was empty and the other held the prize that they'd come for: El Presidente's shiny new float plane.

Its pristine white exterior gleamed like polished pearl in the dappled light reflecting off the gently lapping water. Drawn like a moth to a flame, Lilah automatically took a step toward it.

In the next instant, her ears were assaulted by a sudden shout of laughter accompanied by the din of at least three other loud male voices, all talking at once.

Before she could even figure out where the threat was coming from, a hard familiar hand closed over her mouth and Dominic yanked her off her feet, hauling her back behind a huge wooden crate she hadn't even noticed was there.

His warm breath suddenly tickled against her ear. "Shh," he whispered. "Be quiet and stay here." Then the grip on her waist eased, the hand on her mouth slid away and he stole soundlessly away.

She sagged back against the crate, which was easily twice as tall as she was, knees weak, pulse pounding. Wrapping her arms around herself, she ordered herself to calm down and stop shaking, only to find that her body didn't seem inclined to listen. Silently cursing herself, she squeezed her eyes shut in disgust.

"Li."

A warm hand touched her arm and she jerked her eyes open. Dominic was back, standing just inches away. Given his size, how on earth could he move so silently?

"No big deal," he reported, his voice a mere suggestion of sound. "It's just a bunch of dockhands down by the gas pumps playing cards, okay?"

She nodded, not trusting herself to speak.

"Wait here, then come when I give you the signal."

She bobbed her head again. Counting to ten as he moved away, she got a choke hold on her rioting nerves, then turned. Peeking around the corner of her sanctuary, she watched as the love of her life cat-footed it over to the plane, released it from its moorings, lifted himself up and carefully tried the door.

When it opened, he turned and hooked his finger at her.

Praying she wouldn't suddenly trip and fall on her face, Lilah took a fortifying breath, found a remnant of courage and tiptoed as fast as she could toward him. The second she was within reach, he leaned over, wrapped his hand around her forearm and lifted her up, effortlessly pulling her with him as he climbed into the cockpit and moved across to the pilot's seat.

He really was good at this.

"Get yourself strapped in," he said, stowing the gun out of his way as he examined what to her was a bewildering display of dials, gauges, knobs and switches.

Before she could even manage to find her harness buckle, he'd flipped several switches and made a series of quick adjustments to a variety of gauges and knobs. In the next instant, the engine caught and the propeller spun to life. As easy as that, the plane began to move, skating smoothly out of the boathouse and beyond the reach of the men she could hear shouting behind them. Slowly picking up speed, the aircraft readily responded as Dom adjusted the ailerons so that they were headed squarely into the wind blowing in from the mouth of the bay.

And then, just when it seemed that they'd made a perfect getaway, their luck ran out.

Sweeping majestically around the breakwater came a pricey-looking speedboat throwing up impressive jets of spray in its wake. The hull was a metallic gray in color, with the bow painted to resemble a shark's deadly mouth and a pair of San Timotean flags fluttering from the gunwales. Standing in the stern were a pair of brawny, hatchet-faced men dressed in black.

Seated at the wheel was none other than Manolo Condesta himself. And he was steering a course for home that had the boat barreling straight toward them.

"Ohmigod," Lilah gasped.

Dom uttered a single syllable that was considerably more profane. "I wondered about that empty berth," he said with unmistakable disgust. "What do you suppose the odds of *this* are?"

Her reply was automatic since her attention was focused on Condesta, whose face she could see making the transition from puzzlement to disbelief to dawning outrage. "I have no idea." She swallowed. "What are we going to do?"

"Pray like hell he slows down or turns away, because I'm sure as hell not about to."

She tore her gaze away from El Presidente to stare at the man beside her. She wasn't mistaken; except for a faint tension in the set of his shoulders, he was once more calm and utterly under control. "You're not?"

"Nope." He pushed the throttle more fully forward and

made another slight adjustment to the flaps. Skimming steadily over the water now, the plane seemed to skip from wave to wave as the wings caught the air.

"But…we're headed straight at them."

His shoulders hitched in a ghost of a shrug. "Can't help it. We have to take off into the wind and ole Manolo there just happens to be dead center in our path."

She thought for a moment. "But his bodyguards—don't they have guns?" Recalling every action-adventure film she'd ever seen where a boat and plane played chicken, she realized they always ended the same way, with the opposing parties blasting away at each other….

"Handguns," Dom specified. "Which aren't very effective under these conditions in the best of hands. And from what I've seen of Condesta's men, best anything doesn't describe them. They're big on brute strength, weak on finesse. Don't worry—" he took his eyes off the instrument panel for a moment to glance over and send her a look of reassurance "—everything's going to be fine. I'm not about to let anything happen to you."

Even if it means his life, she realized. It was a reality that had been there all along. Yet now it was suddenly in her face, impossible to ignore. If not for her, he wouldn't be here now, in this awful, no-options-left situation. He wouldn't be taking this chance, risking injury or mutilation or worse….

Her heart thudding, Lilah turned to face him, not sure where to start but knowing that she had to. "Dominic?"

"What?"

"Just in case this doesn't work out, I want you to know I wouldn't trade these last few days for anything. Or change anything that happened."

Gaze firmly locked on their flight path, he reached over and gave her thigh a comforting pat. "Come on now, princess, quit worrying. I mean it. We'll be in the air in just a minute."

"I'm sure you're right. But if something does go wrong, I want you to know—" she stopped to breathe, then slowly lifted her chin "—you're the finest man I've ever known. I love you. I love everything you are and everything about you, and I always will."

Except for the steady roar of the engine, the cockpit suddenly seemed very quiet as he glanced over at her, his hand on her leg now very still. For one endless second their gazes meshed. But before she could decide what was in his eyes—shock, dismay, joy?—a crosswind caught the plane, making it bounce sideways.

He jerked his attention back to the task at hand. "Like I said." He twisted the knob marked "Fuel Mix" a fraction. "Everything will work out. Trust me. Now give me a minute here to concentrate, okay?"

Was it just her imagination or was his voice just a fraction less warm than it had been moments earlier?

He made one last adjustment to the flaps, then squared his shoulders and pushed the throttle forward the last inch. Dead ahead, the boat continued to come, getting larger and larger the closer the two crafts got.

"I do trust you," she whispered. And unable to do anything else, Lilah closed her eyes and prayed.

Twelve

Lilah considered her reflection in the dressing room mirror.

Not great, she decided, frowning at the faint shadow of exhaustion smudging her eyes, the angry-looking scab running down the ball of her shoulder, the still visible bruises on her arms courtesy of the *Las Rocas* guards' rough handling.

Then again, she didn't look totally awful either. Her time in the sun had given her hair a streaky look that would cost a fortune to duplicate in a salon and enough of a tan that her eyes looked bluer than usual. What's more, all the walking and running had added a pleasing touch of definition to the sleek muscles of her arms and legs.

There was also nothing quite like a long bath, access to toiletries and makeup, plus ownership of a new dress worn over a red satin bra and matching thong panties, all hastily purchased at the hotel boutique, to give a girl a glow.

She'd do, she concluded. And that was saying a lot considering that eight hours earlier she hadn't been sure she'd live to see another day, much less ever again be in a position to worry about something as trivial as what shade of lipstick to wear....

She squeezed her eyes shut, the plush cocoon of the Royal Meridian's finest guest cottage fading away as she recalled that headlong charge across Santa Marita Bay, the sunlight flashing on the water, the float plane going faster and faster. And Dominic, with courage to burn, as solid and steady as a rock, refusing to flinch as El Presidente's speedboat filled more and more of the plane's windshield. His eyes had been steely with concentration as he repeatedly checked the airspeed, waiting, waiting, waiting before he finally eased back on the yoke.

Lilah's pulse fluttered at the remembered feel of the plane lifting out of the water into a steep climb that had pushed her back against her seat, leaving gravity and her stomach behind. Nor was she likely to ever forget how, once they were airborne, Dominic had made a lazy circle, bringing the plane back around so she could see for herself the great El Presidente, thrashing and bellowing in the water like a crazed crocodile as his bodyguards struggled to haul him back into the boat.

Dominic had then shared the news that when the dictator's nerve had finally broke and he'd frantically flung himself overboard—a sight she'd missed because she'd been too afraid to look—he'd executed a truly world-class belly flop.

Lilah's mouth quirked with residual glee at the thought. But when she considered the rest of their flight, her mirth quickly evaporated. Because, during those brief times when he hadn't been occupied on the radio talking to his brothers or the air traffic controllers or various Puerto Castillo authorities, Dominic had told her a few other things, as well.

He'd warned that due to certain circumstances—the plane being stolen, the identity of its rightful owner, the fact that Lilah had neither passport nor papers—their arrival was going to cause a flap.

He'd told her that upon touchdown, they'd most likely be detained, separated and interviewed, but he'd been confident it wouldn't take too long to sort things out. He'd explained that once they were released, he'd have some additional details he'd need to take care of, so she should go on to the hotel and he'd call her when he could.

Which he had, nearly an hour ago. He'd said he was on his way, claimed to be starved and asked if she was up for dinner.

The one thing he hadn't said—not then or on the plane or at any time in between—was that he loved her.

That was okay, Lilah quickly assured herself. She hadn't revealed her feelings to him because she expected a declaration in return. Not that she wouldn't relish having him take her in his arms and look at her with those Garden of Eden green eyes and declare that he loved her and couldn't live without her—

Stop it. Don't make yourself crazy about something you can't control.

Because when it came right down to it, she could live without hearing the words if she needed to. What she couldn't live without was Dominic—in her life, in her

arms, filling her heart with his presence. As long as they
were together, nothing else mattered. This time around,
she was determined not to rush things, to give their relationship the time—the chance—it deserved.

The soft peal of the door chime made her heart leap.
Dropping the lipstick wand onto the countertop, she
rubbed her lips together to distribute the clear coat of gloss
as she hurried eagerly into the other room. Her feet were
so light her high heels made only the faintest tapping
sound as she sailed across the tiled entry.

She opened the door. For a moment, she forgot to
breathe.

Freshly shaved and showered, dressed in fitted jeans, a
spotless white cotton shirt open at the collar and a beautifully tailored navy linen sport coat with the sleeves
shoved up his tanned forearms, Dominic looked superb.

"Wow," she said softly.

His eyes crinkled. "Wow, yourself." He spent a long
moment looking at her, his gaze sliding unhurriedly from
the top of her head down the length of her softly clinging
red halter dress to her bare legs and the strappy high-
heeled sandals that showed off her newly painted cherry-
red toenails. Finally, his gaze came back to her face. "You
look…incredible."

With a soft, giddy laugh that had nothing to do with the
compliment and everything to do with his presence, she
surrendered to impulse. Stepping across the threshold, she
went up on tiptoe and cupped his face in her hands. "I
missed you."

She kissed him then, her lips clinging to his as she
drank him in. "I needed that," she confessed when they fi-

nally came up for air. She realized then, as she leaned against him, soaking up his heat and scent and strength, that some part of her that had been strung tight during their brief separation had finally relaxed. "I needed you."

Taking his arm, she led him inside, and deliberately lightened her tone. "When did you shower? And where? You look fabulous, but I thought you'd come straight here to do that—"

"Whoa," he said with a laugh, reeling her in for another quick kiss. "Easy, baby. Slow down. One thing at a time. I stopped by my room—" he glanced around, his sharp eyes taking note of the opulent decor and the private pool beyond the veranda "—which is nice but doesn't come close to this."

His room? "But I thought—"

"What?"

She caught herself. She hadn't actually thought at all, she realized. She'd just assumed they'd be sharing a room. Yet she supposed there must be a reason, perhaps something to do with his business, why that wasn't a good idea. Even if she couldn't imagine what it might be....

It wasn't important, she admonished herself. He was here, now, and that was what mattered. She smiled. "It's nothing. I'm just glad to see you."

"Yeah. Me, too."

With a quick catch of concern, she realized that beneath his easy manner he seemed tense, although he was doing his best to hide it. "We could have dinner brought in if you like," she said, assuring herself he must be tired.

His eyes touched her again and for an instant that familiar heat flared in their green depths, crowding out any hint of darkness. Then his gaze hooded. "No. You look too damn good to keep hidden away. Plus it's a beautiful night, I hear the restaurant here has a five-star chef and a pretty good dance floor, and I'm looking forward to showing you off. I'll just leave this here—" he pulled a packet of papers out of his coat and set it on the breakfast bar "—and we're on our way. I'm pretty sure I hear a rack of lamb calling my name."

She obligingly picked up her evening bag. "What is that?" She nodded toward the packet.

"Stuff you can't live without." He ticked off the items as they ambled toward the front door. "Cash, new passport, first-class airline ticket, itinerary—"

"Itinerary for what?"

"Your trip home. I guess it's not news to you, but when your grandmother rattles cages, the fallout is impressive. A car will be here tomorrow at 9 a.m. sharp, complete with an escort from the U.S. consulate, to take you to the airport."

She jerked to a halt. "But—" oh, God, she had to remember to breathe or she was going to faint "—what about you?"

He shrugged. "I've got a little more diplomacy of my own to practice. Nobody likes Condesta, but the local government can't just ignore what happened. It wouldn't be good form."

"Surely they wouldn't send you back to San Timoteo!" Her voice trembled at the thought.

"No. Hell, no." He rubbed her arm, his fingers deliciously warm. "A few meetings, a lot of apologies, and everything will be fine."

Relief rolled through her. "Good. Then if that's all it is, I'll just stay here until you're free to go, too." She swiveled and started back toward the living room.

"Li—"

"Is there a phone number that I can call to cancel—"

"Lilah."

Just two syllables, but the way he said it... She stopped, knowing something was wrong and sensing that, unlike Condesta and his men, it wasn't something she could outrun. She turned to face him. "What is it, Dominic?"

He wasn't even pretending to smile now. "You and me...together... It's been great. But after tonight, we both need to get back to our real lives in the real world."

He was giving her the brush-off. It was her worst nightmare relived, her most shattering memory repeated, and she braced for a wave of loss and betrayal, as well as the pain that was sure to come when her heart shattered into a thousand pieces.

Except...the moment passed and her heart was still intact. Stunned, as much by her reaction as his words, she felt light-headed for a moment. Then that passed, too, and she realized he hadn't said the one thing she'd dreaded most—that he didn't love her. In point of fact, he didn't seem to be addressing *that* issue at all.

She also wasn't some powerless teenager anymore. She was a grown woman who could—and would—fight for what she wanted. She looked Dominic square in the face. "No," she said flatly.

For a second, he looked genuinely startled. "No, what?"

"No, I'm not going to just walk away and pretend that we never happened. I meant it when I told you I love you.

You're doing us both a disservice by implying that the past week has been some kind of frivolous game or fantasy. You know that's not true. What happened between us is very real."

A nerve twitched to life in his jaw. "All right, maybe I didn't say that right. But it still doesn't mean that this—the two of us together—will work. It won't."

It was a sweeping indictment. And she didn't believe it, not for a minute. "Why not?"

"Hell, there's my job, for one thing."

"What about it?"

He didn't bother to hide his impatience. "Jeez, let's see, Li. It's dangerous. It takes me away for weeks at a time. It puts me in risky situations."

She considered the closed, unyielding expression on his face. Why was he doing this? She knew he cared about her; it had been there in his every word, his every gesture, his every action the past few days. So why was he pushing her away now?

"My job requires me to travel, too," she informed him. "And you're certainly not the only man in the world with a dangerous profession. I'd never ask you to give that up, if that's what you're worried about."

He shook his head. "You may think you understand what it would be like, but you're wrong," he said stubbornly. "A few months, maybe a little more, and you'd get tired of my not always being around, of not having an escort to take you to the ballet or out to eat at your favorite French restaurant."

Now that made her angry. "Pay attention, Dominic. It's the twenty-first century. I can take myself anywhere I want to go. I don't have an exotic lifestyle, either. I live in a one-bedroom condo. The only concert tickets I have are for Tim McGraw and the only restaurant on my speed dial is Pelligrini's Pizza."

"Come on, Lilah. You're still an Anson."

"If this is about money, I'll sign over my trust fund to you first thing in the morning."

"Dammit!" he growled. "I don't want your money. I want you to realize that the only reason we're having this discussion is because we just spent some really intense time together, where you felt threatened and I was your protector. It's a classic case of—"

"Don't you dare say hero worship," she warned.

"—transference. And I *would* be doing you a disservice if I took advantage of the situation."

"You can't take advantage of someone by doing what they want," she said with implacable logic.

He went on as if he hadn't heard her. "You know what else? This is starting to feel a hell of a lot like ten years ago, when you tried to ride roughshod over my life. Well, I've got news, sweetheart. I didn't like it then and I like it even less now."

"Ride roughshod!" she repeated incredulously. "For heaven's sake, Dominic. I was nineteen years old and so in love with you I couldn't think straight! All I wanted was for us to be together, but I was afraid you didn't feel the same way. So instead of telling you how I felt, I let my pride get the upper hand."

"Oh, and I suppose it was your pride that told me to take a hike?" he said sarcastically.

She lifted her chin. "I messed up. And I'm sorry—

more than you'll ever know. But it's not like I was alone
in the pool house that day. You could've stayed, you could
have fought for me, for us. Instead, you charged out of
there so fast it was a miracle you didn't leave scorch marks
on the pool deck. And now you're doing it again."

"The hell I am. What I'm trying to do is make you see
reason, but you don't seem to have heard a word I said!"

"Oh, I've heard every word! But so far all you've done
is give me a laundry list of reasons why you're not right
for me, not one of which I care a flip about! But then, I'm
starting to think this really isn't about me at all. It's about
you. What is it you're so afraid of, Dominic?"

"Absolutely nothing," he shot back, "unless it's rich
girls who won't take no for an answer."

Lilah recoiled as if he'd struck her.

And before she could recover enough to think how to
answer, he turned on his heel and walked away.

Dom took a swig of the long-awaited beer he'd promised himself. The golden brew was just the way he liked
it: ice-cold and silky smooth.

So why did it taste like ditch water on his tongue?

He scowled at his image in the dimly lit mirror that
stretched behind the smallest of the Meridian's three bars.
It didn't take a genius to come up with an answer. He could
name that tune with a single word. *Lilah.*

Who would've guessed that in the blink of an eye the
sensible, agreeable woman he'd just spent some of the
most memorable days of his life with would become im-
pervious to reason?

Not him. But then, he hadn't expected himself to act

like the world's biggest jackass, either. Not that he'd been wrong to tell her what he had; he just hadn't expected to lose his temper, much less go stomping off like some damn fool kid.

For that, Lilah had to take some of the blame. Seeing her in that red dress had been like a direct attack on his better judgment. Then she'd complicated matters further by kissing him as if he were the only man in the world, triggering a voice in his head that had insisted he'd be crazy to give her up. Add in her unexpected declaration that she didn't intend to go home without him and he'd felt as if his back were to the wall. So instead of waiting until they were at dinner and letting her down easy the way he'd planned, he'd gone ahead and baldly told her they'd reached the end of the line.

He'd expected that once she thought it over she'd see their time together the same way he did: as a hell of an adventure that had been destined to be short-lived. He'd also supposed she'd concede that she wasn't cut out to be exposed to the ugly, life-and-death matters he regularly encountered.

After all, she was Lilah Anson Cantrell—wealthy, privileged and far too sheltered to deal with the gritty reality of his world.

Yeah, right. That would explain where she found the courage to jump off a cliff at midnight with nothing more than your word she'd be okay. That's why she had the starch to fight off drowning, then make love half a day and most of a night. That'd be why she gritted it out when it looked as if you were about to put the plane into Condesta's boat.

Ignoring the bitter taste in his mouth, he drained his beer in one long pull and signalled for another. Yet neither the slight kick of the alcohol or a brief exchange with the bartender put a halt to the inexorable march of his thoughts.

Yeah, that's Lilah, all right. She's nothing more than a spun glass angel meant to sit prettily on a shelf. And if you believe that, pal, you've got an upcoming date with a padded cell.

He stroked his thumb down the condensation filming the beer bottle. Okay, so he had ample reason to know she wasn't the fragile flower he'd painted her for years. And he'd done a really lousy job of making the case for them going their separate ways, just as he'd completely misjudged her probable reaction.

But then, he'd done a number of stupid things lately. Like breaking his own rule about getting involved. Like not letting her know up front that there was no chance of them living happily ever after. Like refusing her gift of love—

He hastily rejected that last thought. Yet the longer he considered, the more he had to concede that some of the things she'd said did have a little merit. There was that business about their long-ago breakup, for one. They *had* been young and her pride hadn't been the only one in play that day.

When it came to her preposterous charge that he'd fled as if his feet were on fire, however, that was a load of bull. He'd simply been cutting his losses, since he'd known all along their relationship would never last. She'd been rich; he hadn't. She'd been on track to get a first rate education;

he hadn't. She'd been envisioning a future together when he'd already learned that you couldn't trust people not to go off and leave you behind, not even your own mother—

Whoa. Wait one damn minute, Steele. That's not right.

He was the one who'd decided he wasn't interested in being committed to anyone. That had been his choice. It was a matter of being strong, self-reliant, of charting his own course. It wasn't because he was incapable of trust or afraid to risk his heart.

Was it?

The beer bottle slipped out of his hand, nearly hitting the counter. Catching it just in time, he ignored the foam fizzing over the top and spilling down his suddenly shaking fingers as he heard Lilah's voice in his head. *What are you so afraid of, Dominic?*

And Holy Merciful Mother, the answer—to a question he would have sworn ten minutes ago had nothing to do with him—surged fully formed into his mind.

I'm afraid that if I let myself love her and things don't work out, I'll never recover.

Thunderstruck, he waited for the denial that was sure to come—only to be met by a telling internal silence. And then the voice in his head, the one that rejoiced in playing devil's advocate, said, "So what are you going to do about it? Sit here for the rest of your life? Go on deluding yourself? Play it safe, refuse to take a chance, go back to Denver and pray you never see Lilah again? Dread the day that you do, only to discover she's moved on to somebody else?"

Hell, no. His negative reaction to that idea was so strong it propelled him off the bar stool and onto his feet. Tossing some bills onto the counter to cover his tab, he suddenly knew without a single doubt just what it was he had to do.

Because somewhere along the way, he'd already crossed the line. He loved Lilah. And the one thing that would be worse than losing her would be knowing that he was too cowardly to take a chance on happiness.

He also knew, with a certainty he didn't question, that if he couldn't make things right, he'd spend the rest of his life living with the very hole in his heart he'd been trying so hard to avoid.

The night was spectacular.

Too bad she barely saw it.

Lilah lay in the dark on a chaise by the pool and ignored the stars glittering overhead like a spill of diamonds against the ink-blue sky. She disregarded the ribbon of breeze that moved through the surrounding trees and plucked at the hem of the filmy sarong she'd thrown on over her bathing suit.

All she could think about was Dominic.

If she were a better, stronger, more disciplined person, she'd go swim laps the way she'd planned when she first came outside. She'd lose herself in the comforting silence of the water and the mind-numbing rhythm of propelling herself from one end of the pool to the other.

She wouldn't be lying here staring blindly into the dark endlessly replaying her conversation with him, belatedly thinking of all the things she should have said.

She wouldn't be second-guessing her decision to tell him she loved him.

She wouldn't be wondering what to do next.

Not that she really had a lot of choices. Because whether he believed her or not, whether she should have told him or not, she *did* love Dominic.

And she wasn't going to repeat the mistake she'd made before. She wasn't going to wrap herself in her wounded pride and walk away. She refused to spend another ten years wondering what might have been if only she'd had the courage to see it through.

So sometime tomorrow, she'd come up with a plan. She'd put away the hurt that splintered through her every time she thought about him walking away. She'd forget the angry words they'd exchanged. She'd put aside his lack of faith and conquer the despair that threatened to overwhelm her every time she started to wonder if she was deluding herself that maybe they still had a chance.

And maybe she should take that swim, she decided, as a fresh wave of uncertainty threatened to overwhelm her. She'd swim until she was too tired to think, and then maybe she'd be able to sleep, and when the sun came up tomorrow she'd know what to do.

Swallowing hard, she climbed to her feet and reached to untie the sarong, only to have a prickle of awareness skate down her spine. Tensing, she straightened and turned, then felt her heart go thump.

Dominic stood no more than five feet away, his hips propped against the rim of the wrought iron patio table, his arms crossed over his chest. He'd shed his sport coat, and his white shirt looked almost blue in the wash of the moonlight as the breeze molded the cloth to his muscled chest. His face was shadowed, however, and impossible to read.

Their gazes locked for what felt to Lilah like the longest moment of her life. She wanted in the worst way to fling herself into his arms, to burst into tears, to beg him to take away her hurt. Instead, she lifted her chin and said with all the dignity she could muster, "What are you doing here?"

"I'm thinking how beautiful you are. And what an idiot I am. And how you have to stop scaring the hell out of me or I really am going to have a heart attack."

She numbly responded to the least important of his three statements. "I scared you?" It was the only safe thing she could think to say.

"Yeah. Your front door is wide-open. When I couldn't find you, I thought that maybe Condesta had been stupid enough to send someone after you."

"Oh." She wet her lips, compelled to ask the next question even though she dreaded the answer. "And that would be a bad thing?"

"That would be beyond bad," he replied firmly. "That would be catastrophic." He pushed away from the table, eliminating the distance between them with just a trio of steps. And though it was the hardest thing she'd ever done, she held her ground, refusing to retreat even when he was so close she could feel the heat radiating off him.

She did her best to armor her heart as she waited for him to add that then he'd be forced to return to San Timoteo or—worse—that he'd be out his fee.

"Because—" he reached out and cupped her face in his hands "—I love you, Li. I think I always have and I know damn well I always will. And I hate the thought of anything hurting you. Even me. Especially me."

"Oh, Dominic…" She swallowed, overcome, and one of the tears she'd been holding back spilled over, tracking down her face.

"Oh God, princess, please don't cry." He swiped away the bead of liquid with his thumb, his voice suddenly agonized. "I'm sorry for those things I said. I didn't mean them. It's just taken my head a while to catch up with my heart. Say you'll marry me and I swear I'll spend the rest of our lives making it up to you."

"You want to get married?" She stared at him in surprise, the tears coming a little faster, afraid to believe she'd heard him right.

"Absolutely. You've been the only woman for me ever since I first saw you. Like I said, it just took me a while to figure it out. But now that I have, I'm not letting you go. That is, if you'll still have me."

"Yes. *Yes.*" Smiling through her tears, she threw herself into his arms.

They closed around her. "God. I can't believe I almost let you go," Dominic said in a raspy whisper.

And then he lowered his head and kissed her, and all was right in her world.

Epilogue

Denver, Colorado
Three weeks later

The massive arches of Denver's First Church Cathedral soared high above Lilah's head.

A sea of white flowers—lilies, sweet peas, hyacinths and roses—cascaded from the ends of the seemingly endless line of pews that stretched to the altar, where more white blooms were massed along the sides of the broad, shallow steps. Their sweet fragrance drifted on the early evening air, aided by the banks of snowy candles sharing those same steps, their flickering, golden light glowing in contrast to the vast church's shadowed interior.

"Nervous, darling?" Gran inquired, leaning slightly against her as they stood, arms entwined, just outside the inner entrance to the church proper, waiting at the top of the aisle for their cue to enter.

"No." Lilah's gaze was all for Dominic, who stood what seemed like half a mile away, staring back at her, flanked by his phalanx of tall, black-haired, Armani-clad brothers. "I've been waiting my whole life to be Dominic's wife."

"Oh, good grief, Delilah." Gran's tone made clear her opinion of that. "You've only been back from San Timoteo a few weeks. And given that your Mr. Steele insisted you move straight in with him, it's not as if the two of you have waited for much of *anything* that I can see."

"Yes, Gran." Lilah's serene smile didn't falter. She rather liked having Dominic referred to as *her* Mr. Steele, she decided.

As for the other… Well, except for admitting to a previous acquaintance, the two of them had agreed that the rest of their past wasn't any of Abigail's business. They knew the truth and that was what mattered.

"You must admit, there aren't many people who could have put something like this together in less than a month," Gran went on with an autocratic sniff.

"There certainly aren't." Lilah squeezed her hand. "You've been wonderful." There was no reason to reveal that Abigail cared far more than she did about the big church, the ocean of flowers, the crowd of people straining to get a glimpse of her. As Lilah had warned Dominic she would, her grandmother had pounced at the chance to plan their wedding, and Lilah, who finally no longer doubted that beneath her crusty exterior her grandmother loved her, had wanted her only relative to have her fun.

"Yes. I have been wonderful," Abigail agreed. She paused, then said as if she'd read her granddaughter's mind, "And so have you. You do realize that I'm proud of you, don't you, Delilah?"

"Yes, Gran."

"And that I've only ever wanted what's best for you."

"Yes."

"Are you positive this is the right man for you?"

"Absolutely." She smiled at Dominic, who was starting to look just the least bit impatient.

"Then you really do have my blessing. As long as—good heavens!" Abigail stiffened, staring at the big man who'd just emerged through the side door next to the altar and was joining the impressive line of assembled Steeles.

He was wearing the same severely simple, expensively cut suit as the others, one that had been ordered to his specific measurements. But somehow he still managed to look as if he ought to be decked out in camouflage gear and face paint while armed to the teeth. "Who on earth is that?" Gran demanded. "And what is he doing…*here?* In my wedding?"

"That's another one of Dominic's brothers," Lilah replied, completely understanding the older woman's reaction. "I met him last night." Although "met" was definitely too tame a word to describe her first encounter with John Taggart Steele.

She'd been standing in Dominic's darkened kitchen, enjoying a cup of tea while clad in nothing except her underwear and one of his T-shirts, when she'd glanced over to find a stranger standing a mere six feet away, silently scrutinizing her.

Once she'd decided she wasn't going to scream or faint—reasoning that if the stranger was a threat Dominic would have already been there instead of lingering in the shower—she'd realized who he was, since there was a strong family resemblance and he'd been the only brother to miss the rehearsal dinner earlier that night.

She'd been assured by every one of the tall, dark, ridiculously attractive men who claimed Dominic as a relative that though their second-oldest brother was currently immersed in a tricky fugitive recovery case—she wondered if she'd ever get accustomed to hearing real people talk that way—he would turn up.

And he had. Setting her cup down on the counter, she'd pulled herself together, did her best to pretend she was fully clothed and offered him her hand. "I'm Lilah. You must be Taggart."

He'd looked at her with that hard hard face, so much like Dominic's and yet so totally different. He was a little bigger, a little broader and a lot less...civilized-looking...than his younger brother, with the most shuttered eyes she'd ever seen.

And then the straight, sober line of his mouth had relaxed a fraction and a glint of approval had warmed the cool green depths of his eyes, and everything had changed.

"Dom said you'd remind me of a fairy-tale princess, pretty but brave," he said in a quiet, deliberate voice. "He was right. Welcome to the family, little sister." Reaching out, he'd taken her hand as if it was made of the finest crystal and given it a gentle squeeze.

"If he gives you any trouble—" well, actually, Taggart hadn't used the word *trouble,* but she wasn't so far gone to even think that other word while she was standing in a cathedral next to her grandmother "—let me know. I'll

knock some sense into him." With that astonishing declaration, he'd relinquished her hand and melted back into the
darkness as noiselessly as he'd arrived, leaving Lilah wondering if she'd imagined him.

When she told Dom about it, he'd just shook his head,
murmured darkly about ex-Army Rangers who ought to
know better than to break into other men's houses, scaring their women, and taken her back to bed to soothe her
nerves.

Not that her nerves had needed soothing. At least, not
at first....

"Good heaven's," Gran repeated, still staring at the
newcomer with a scowl. "I must say, he doesn't look completely civilized. But then, none of them do."

If only she knew, Lilah thought, fighting a smile. But
then, as she'd learned during her wild San Timotean adventure, sometimes civilization—and civility—were
highly overrated.

"I must admit, however—" Gran gave an unexpected
sigh that made Lilah turn to look at her "—I might be
tempted to take one of them on if I were fifty years
younger."

"Gran!" She bit back a startled gurgle of laughter.

"You really must learn to loosen up, darling," the old
lady said with a sudden twinkle in her eyes. "It's about
time you realize that if I didn't appreciate fine-looking
men, I certainly never would have married five times."

Lilah just stared at her, saved from having to reply by
the onset of the processional signaling that it was finally
time to commence the Wedding March.

"All right, now. Chin up, spine straight. It's time to go."

Lilah didn't need urging. With a steadying grip on her grandmother's arm, she started eagerly down the aisle toward her love, her life, her man.

Dom watched her come, feeling his heart squeeze in his chest at the radiant look on her face. She seemed to float toward him in her billowing satin-and-lace gown, the picture of perfection with her pale hair and flawless skin.

And then she was there, and he was reaching for her hand and drinking in the delicious fragrance of her skin. Not giving a damn if he scandalized the whole of Denver society, he leaned in and pressed a lingering kiss to the porcelain softness of her cheek. "Okay?" he asked quietly.

She looked at him, all the love she felt for him blazing without reservation in her summer-sky eyes. "Perfect," she whispered. "What about you? Any second thoughts?"

"No." He shook his head. "Trust me, princess. I've never been more sure of anything in my life."

And drawing her close, he walked with her to the altar, knowing she was about to make him the happiest man alive.

* * * * *

SILHOUETTE®

Desire™

Dynasties:
THE ELLIOTTS
Mixing business with pleasure

January 2007
BILLIONAIRE PROPOSITION *Leanne Banks*
TAKING CARE OF BUSINESS *Brenda Jackson*

March 2007
CAUSE FOR SCANDAL *Anna DePalo*
THE FORBIDDEN TWIN *Susan Crosby*

May 2007
MR AND MISTRESS *Heidi Betts*
HEIRESS BEWARE *Charlene Sands*

July 2007
UNDER DEEPEST COVER *Kara Lennox*
MARRIAGE TERMS *Barbara Dunlop*

September 2007
THE INTERN AFFAIR *Roxanne St Claire*
FORBIDDEN MERGER *Emilie Rose*

November 2007
THE EXPECTANT EXECUTIVE *Kathie DeNosky*
BEYOND THE BOARDROOM *Maureen Child*

0107/SH/LC157

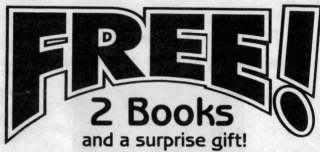

FREE!
2 Books
and a surprise gift!

We would like to take this opportunity to thank you for reading this Silhouette® book by offering you the chance to take TWO more specially selected titles from the Desire™ series absolutely FREE! We're also making this offer to introduce you to the benefits of the Mills & Boon® Reader Service™—

- ★ FREE home delivery
- ★ FREE gifts and competitions
- ★ FREE monthly Newsletter
- ★ Exclusive Reader Service offers
- ★ Books available before they're in the shops

Accepting these FREE books and gift places you under no obligation to buy. you may cancel at any time, even after receiving your free shipment. Simply complete your details below and return the entire page to the address below. You don't even need a stamp!

YES! Please send me 2 free Desire books and a surprise gift. I understand that unless you hear from me. I will receive 3 superb new titles every month for just £4.99 each, postage and packing free. I am under no obligation to purchase any books and may cancel my subscription at any time. The free books and gift will be mine to keep in any case.

D6ZEF

Ms/Mrs/Miss/Mr ....Initials...................

BLOCK CAPITALS PLEASE

Surname ....

Address...

....

....Postcode.........................

Send this whole page to:
UK: FREEPOST CN81, Croydon, CR9 3WZ